Between You & Me

Between You & Me

JOANNA HORTON

ultimo
press

Published in 2023 by Ultimo Press,
an imprint of Hardie Grant Publishing

Ultimo Press   Ultimo Press (London)
Gadigal Country   5th & 6th Floors
7, 45 Jones Street   52–54 Southwark Street
Ultimo, NSW 2007   London SE1 1UN
ultimopress.com.au

    ultimopress

 A catalogue record for this
book is available from the
National Library of Australia

Between You and Me
ISBN 978 1 76115 081 4 (paperback)

Cover design Alissa Dinallo
Cover images Girl with hand up by Rizky Sabriansyah / Unsplash; Couple laying together
by Matt and Tish / Stocksy
Text design Simon Paterson, Bookhouse
Typesetting Bookhouse, Sydney | 12/18.2 pt Baskerville MT Pro
Copyeditor Simone Ford
Proofreader Alan Vaarwerk

10 9 8 7 6 5 4 3 2 1

Printed in Australia by Griffin Press, an Accredited ISO AS/NZS 14001 Environmental
Management System printer.

 The paper this book is printed on is certified against the
Forest Stewardship Council® Standards. Griffin Press holds
chain of custody certification SCS-COC-001185. FSC®
promotes environmentally responsible, socially beneficial
and economically viable management of the world's forests.

Ultimo Press acknowledges the Traditional Owners of the Country on which we work,
the Gadigal People of the Eora Nation and the Wurundjeri People of the Kulin Nation,
and recognises their continuing connection to the land, waters and culture. We pay our
respects to their Elders past and present.

PART I

PART I

1

THE NIGHT WE met Jack, I was wearing a yellow dress, and I remember wishing I'd worn something else. All the other people in the reception hall were dressed in black and white, and as soon as I arrived I felt conspicuous and slightly garish, a canary among penguins. In those days I had a complicated relationship to feeling conspicuous: I liked the idea of being the kind of person everyone would look at and wonder about, but I didn't want anyone to actually look at me or wonder about me. I glanced around for Mari, who I assumed had been funnelled into the reception area through a different door, but I couldn't see her. She had a talent for being late.

Eventually I saw her head bobbing through the crowd, and slowly little bits of her emerged from the crush of other people: her tall body in a neat black dress, long fingers tucking her hair behind one ear. Her liquid eyes and thick brows. Mari wasn't exactly pretty, but she was striking in a way that made everyone else look washed-out and forgettable. When she reached me she pulled an exaggeratedly ironic face of excitement, which made me feel a little defensive about my own sense of anticlimax, the flatness I'd felt ever since I'd crossed the stage and become someone with a master's degree.

'Congratulations,' she said. 'I couldn't spot you at first. I thought you'd be in your cap and gown.'

'Oh, I returned them. They made me feel stupid.'

'No, that's the whole point, you're smart now. You should be putting yourself out there. Trying to find people to connect with on LinkedIn.'

I made a noise of disgust, and she laughed. We leaned against the wall beside the drinks table and gossiped, without any real malice, about the other people at the function. We knew most of them from our time as undergraduates (I'd studied philosophy and Mari anthropology – our degrees were, as she liked to say, aggressively useless) and we waved hello and smiled at them when they looked at us. We discussed the concept of networking and decided we hated it.

'Should we go?' Mari asked. 'Unless you want to talk to people.'

'No, I don't want to talk to people.'

'You never know. You could be missing out on some exciting career opportunities.'

'I don't think that's very likely with a master's in philosophy.'

Someone beside us laughed then, and we both turned our heads. It was a tall, lean man who looked to be in his forties, wearing a white linen shirt and reaching across the table for a glass of champagne. We looked at him; he caught my eye, or maybe it was Mari's eye, and he said, 'Sorry, I didn't mean to eavesdrop. That was a bit brutal, though.' It was Jack, of course: that was how we met him.

•

IF IT HAD been up to Mari, they never would have spoken to him. Generally she didn't enjoy talking to strangers, especially strangers who made conversation, and this particular stranger was getting in the way of the cigarette she wanted to smoke. She smiled half-heartedly at him and began turning away, but it was too late: Elisabeth was making eye contact, wearing a polite smile. 'Well, I'm only being brutal to myself,' she said. 'I work in a café, I don't think that's about to change.'

The stranger smiled back at her. His face was open and relaxed, and he stood with the slightly lolling posture of tall men. 'I see,' he said. 'Well, I don't condone being brutal to yourself either. But I take your point.'

He introduced himself and shook their hands. He had a very firm handshake, which Mari registered with surprise and a flicker of appreciation; shaking hands with men her own age was usually a limp, dead-fish experience. Elisabeth asked Jack if he was an academic, and he made a wry expression with his mouth and said, 'For my sins.'

'Which department?'

'History, actually. I supervised a few people graduating tonight, so . . . Sorry, this isn't very interesting, is it? I suppose historians have a reputation for being boring.'

'Oh no,' said Elisabeth. She was using what Mari recognised as her social voice, the voice she used to flatter people and draw them in. 'History's fascinating. Not enough people care about history, don't you think?'

Jack looked pleased – clearly, that was exactly what he thought. Mari picked up a glass of champagne and let her gaze drift away, over the crowd of ironed shirts and silk blouses. Polite smiles, no teeth. Her dress felt scratchy against her skin. She could tell that

Jack was making an effort to include her in the conversation, and she answered his questions dutifully: yes, she was here for Elisabeth's graduation, no, not her own. She had a degree in anthropology and was putting it to good use by working part-time in admin. 'Pretty unimpressive,' she said, using the light tone she'd developed for conversations about her future. 'At least Elisabeth has her master's, I don't know what my excuse is.'

'I wouldn't put it that way,' Jack said mildly. 'Seems perfectly normal for someone your age.'

Mari tried not to show her surprise. Usually, if she mentioned her lack of career prospects to an adult, they took it as an opportunity to dispense unsolicited and often terrible advice. (Elisabeth's parents had suggested that she simply call the museum, explain her qualifications, and ask for a job.) She sipped her champagne and met Jack's eye. He wasn't smiling, but his lips looked loose and ready to smile. 'That's nice of you,' she said. 'I do aspire to be perfectly normal.'

He did smile then. He had a nice face, Mari thought, although he was wearing the kind of squarish black-framed glasses that older men wore in an effort to look young. 'Well, anyway,' he said. 'When you're in the death grip of a so-called real job, you'll wonder what all the fuss was about. Take it from me.'

'Do you fantasise about long-term unemployment?'

He laughed, and Mari saw the phantom flash of a gold tooth in the back of his mouth. 'More often than I'd like to admit.'

Elisabeth said that she didn't mind working and there would always be a need for people to make coffee, but they should be paid as much as academics, or maybe the other way around. 'It's the emotional part that's difficult,' she said. 'Having to put on a different personality at work. People expect you to be servile.'

'Plenty of that in academia too,' Jack said. 'Anyway, I think we all put on different personalities at work. It's part of what makes wage labour alienating.'

Elisabeth just smiled; as a rule, Mari knew, she refused to be impressed by jargon. The conversation moved on to the general encroachment of neoliberalism into higher education, a topic that Mari had read about online but never considered in any depth. Elisabeth probably had real opinions on it, but she stayed quiet while Mari talked. Jack nodded at everything she said. History was out of fashion in universities, he told them, especially his kind of history. He said it like that, as though he owned the history of communist thought in Italy during the early twentieth century.

'That's broadly speaking, of course,' he said, with the air of someone getting into his stride. 'More specifically, I've spent most of my working life writing about a heterodox Italian Marxist called Antonio Gramsci. He –'

'Pessimism of the intellect, optimism of the will,' Mari said. She didn't know what made her say it – she'd never read Gramsci, had just seen the quote on the internet. Jack looked at her curiously, and she felt a lift of pleasure. She wasn't quite sure what she would say if he asked her any questions about Gramsci's work.

He didn't. Instead he smiled, turned to Elisabeth and said, 'Well, speaking of optimism – listen, Elisabeth, here's my card. Give me a call if you ever want to discuss history. Or philosophy, the life of the mind, anything, really. I'm always up for learning something new.' He handed her a business card and nodded to them. 'It was nice to meet you both. Enjoy the rest of your evening.'

When he'd gone, Mari looked at Elisabeth and rolled her eyes. She didn't know exactly what she was rolling her eyes about, and Elisabeth didn't roll her eyes back, which left Mari feeling wrongfooted and slightly juvenile.

Elisabeth put the card in her bag and smoothed down her hair. 'How did you know to wear black?' she asked. 'I'm the only person here wearing colour.'

Mari hadn't noticed this. In any case, she thought the yellow dress suited Elisabeth, who had an elfin prettiness about her – silky fawn-coloured curls surrounding a delicate face. 'Don't worry about it,' she said. 'You look nice, your boyfriend there certainly thought so. Can we go now?'

Outside in the thick warm darkness, they leaned against the building while Mari lit a cigarette. 'You should quit,' Elisabeth said. 'Make it your New Year's resolution.'

'I think you might have suggested that once or twice before.'

'You'll get cancer and die.'

Mari blew smoke over her shoulder. 'Well, at least when I'm dead you won't be able to lecture me about quitting.'

Elisabeth didn't reply. Behind them, the doors of the reception hall opened to a burst of noise, closed again. 'He was nice,' Elisabeth said, leaning her hands flat against the building. 'Don't you think?'

Mari drew on her cigarette. She didn't know why Elisabeth was asking her opinion – she would have formed her own already, and soon she would present it for both of them to adopt. 'Well, he's like sixty years old,' she said. 'And he used the phrase "life of the mind" unironically.'

'I thought he was being a bit ironic.'

'Well, whatever. Good firm handshake, though.'

'I noticed that too. He seems like a classic firm-handshake person, don't you think?'

Mari exhaled slowly, watching the smoke float in the air. Elisabeth was in the habit of establishing typologies that seemed random and meaningless but turned out to be surprisingly accurate: Mari would find herself realising that some people could, for example, be summed up by the term 'classic firm-handshake person'. 'Right,' she said. 'I guess so.'

'Well, I liked him. You know, most academics just think everyone younger than them is basically their student, but he talked to us like we were adults.'

'I know.' Mari dropped her cigarette and twisted her heel over it. 'That was weird.'

They took the ferry back across the river, dark water rushing under the boat. Elisabeth didn't mention Jack again as they walked home, although Mari didn't know if that was because she didn't want to talk about him or because she wanted to make a point of not talking about him. They reached Paris Street, the weatherboard cottage where Mari lived with their friend Heidi.

'See you tomorrow?' Elisabeth said.

'Yeah, see you then.' Mari shoved the gate open with her hip. She felt like teasing Elisabeth a little, just to prove she could. 'By the way, you know he doesn't actually want to talk to you about history.'

Elisabeth was turning away, but she gave Mari the finger over her shoulder. Mari laughed. She went inside already planning how she'd tell Heidi about Jack, how she'd make it into a funny story, but the house was dark and quiet. There was no sign of Heidi except for a damp pink towel hanging over the back of a chair.

On the kitchen bench was a half-empty bottle of cheap red wine, left over from the night before. Mari took a glass out to the back deck and, in the warm jasmine-scented darkness, tried to replay the evening from a distance. The overall impression was of herself talking mindlessly and making stupid jokes. She couldn't get a clear picture of Elisabeth, but it seemed likely that she'd been poised and polite, saying all the right things. Elisabeth seemed to have access to many different versions of herself that could be brought out and used as the situation required, like trying on clothes. Mari had only one version of herself, and she was stuck with it. She thought of Jack pretending to listen to her, the way he'd nodded politely as she spoke, and her face felt blank and hot.

•

IN THE MORNING I woke early and lay in bed looking at the card Jack had given me. I studied it in the clean pale light: the university crest, the simple black serif font. Jack Bloom, senior lecturer. I put the card on my chest and let it lie there, rising and falling with my breath. It was early December, the edge of summer, and I was wearing a thin cotton nightgown.

I didn't know exactly what a senior lecturer was, or how old they usually were. Jack had looked the way I imagined someone in their mid-forties to look, but all older people seemed broadly similar to me. At the time I had just turned twenty-five, and no one over thirty had ever taken me seriously. But I could hardly blame them – I lived in a share house and my parents still paid for my car registration. I was trapped in an endless cycle of downloading, deleting, and re-downloading dating apps, despite the fact that even a minute of swiping made me feel clinically depressed. Mari was the same. Once, listening to her complain about the lack of options, Heidi had asked why she didn't just date girls.

'Too much drama,' Mari said, not looking up from her phone.

'What, as opposed to men? Just try turning the filter on, you might be surprised. Right, Elisabeth?'

I shrugged. Heidi believed in queerness as the solution to most, if not all, of the world's problems, but I didn't necessarily agree. 'There are lots of mediocre women out there,' I said. 'At least men are easy to understand.'

Heidi raised her eyebrows. 'You understand Mari,' she said. 'Why don't you just date her?'

'Ha ha,' Mari said. I didn't say anything.

Later that morning I looked at Jack's staff profile on the university website. His publications were listed at the bottom, and I found one article on an open-access website and read it all the way through. It was mildly interesting. The profile included a picture of him standing in front of a sandstone building and giving the camera a half-smile. I kept looking at it on and off, in between doing my laundry and listening to a podcast about the Iraq War.

In the afternoon, Mari came over with our friend Alex, and we lay on picnic rugs in the garden and played gin rummy. A breeze had started up, and shadows skittered and danced on the grass. Alex and I drank beers. Mari said she wasn't going to drink one, but then she did. We talked about Alex's housemate Jen, who had a long-running feud with Mari and had recently accused her of having 'bad politics'.

'I asked her what she meant by that and she couldn't tell me,' Mari said. 'Anyway, having so-called good politics isn't a substitute for having a personality.'

Alex whistled through his teeth. 'Are you filming this, Elisabeth? I think you should be filming this.'

At the time I was experimenting with a project that involved me filming my friends in the course of their ordinary lives. I hadn't really committed to the execution, and so far I had several hours of wobbly drunken footage interspersed with crushingly boring scenes of Heidi washing dishes, or our friend Paul explaining his comic book collection. Whenever I told anyone about the project they always said, 'Oh, like *Reality Bites*,' and I was forced to admit that yes, it was like *Reality Bites*. My friends had mixed feelings about being filmed – Paul loved it, but he always hammed it up so much that the footage of him was basically unusable; Mari hated it and often refused to speak when I held up my phone.

'If you start filming, I'll leave,' she told me.

'Okay, okay. No filming.'

'Sorry I brought it up,' Alex said. 'Oh, how was last night? The graduation thing.'

'Unbelievably boring,' Mari said. 'Went for hours.'

'That's one good thing about medicine,' said Alex. 'Everyone's too busy saving lives to bother with long events. You know, actually making a difference in the world. Wouldn't expect you to understand.'

'Well, at least we've got our degrees,' Mari said. 'What is this, your fifth year of studying? Maybe one day you'll graduate yourself, then you can see how boring it is.'

He gave her the finger. I thought the conversation would move on, but Mari darted a glance at me and said, 'One interesting thing did happen.'

'Oh yeah?'

'Elisabeth attracted the attention of an older gentleman. A historian, I believe. He gave her his card – where's that card, Elisabeth?'

'I don't know.' It was on my desk, propped against the mug where I kept my pens.

'Well, anyway. He said she should call him, he offered to teach her about history.'

'Hot,' said Alex. 'I always wondered what it'd be like to sleep with a lecturer.'

'Probably just like sleeping with anyone else,' I said. 'Anyway, I doubt he meant anything by it. Mari's exaggerating, as usual.'

'No, I'm not,' Mari said. She was eating a peach, the juice dripping down her chin. 'So is he about your dad's age, or what? Just wondering.'

I rolled my eyes. 'No, he's not my dad's age.'

'Mmm. As I think Freud once said, close enough.'

'Okay, you've made your point. Anyway, it's not against the law, is it? We're two consenting adults.'

She laughed, a bit hollowly. 'Plenty of bad things can still happen between two consenting adults.'

Sometimes she adopted this world-weary air with me, as if to emphasise how naïve I was compared to her, and I always found it irritating. I laid my cards down. 'Gin.'

She gave me a look, but she was wearing sunglasses and it was easy not to meet her eye. 'Trying to change the subject?'

'No. I don't know what you want me to say, though. Look, gin.'

After they'd gone home, I went to the School of History website and clicked on the 'Upcoming Events' tab. It appeared that the School hosted a seminar every Thursday evening, and the next one was on 'The 1944 Referendum on Reconstruction'. I wrote down the time and room number on a green sticky note, and I stuck it to the wall above my desk.

2

AFTER WORK THE following Tuesday afternoon, I walked over to Mari and Heidi's house and let myself in through the back door. At the time, Mari was working three days a week as an admin officer in the public service, and Tuesday happened to be one of her workdays. It didn't take me long to find her navy dress in a pile of mostly clean laundry. She would never notice it was gone; she was careless about her possessions and had twice lost things I'd given her for her birthday, which was a source of ongoing conflict between us.

I tried on the dress when I got home. Mari was taller than me: the hem hit her thigh, but on me it was knee-length. That was okay, though. Now I had taken it, I felt like I had to go through with everything else, or else be left with an embarrassing memento of my own cowardice. On Thursday evening I put it on and took the ferry to campus. I sat on the front deck so I could watch the last of the day's light bleeding pink and purple into the horizon, and the dark shapes of bats scattering silently across the sky.

I'd timed it so that I would arrive just before the seminar started, and when I slipped into the room, the lights were already dimmed and people were in their seats. I sat at the back and scanned a row. Two rows. Three rows. There was one dark-haired man of about Jack's age, and when my eyes passed over him I felt a little jolt, but I knew it wasn't really him. Then, in the fourth row, I saw him.

He was sitting with a group of women, two on his left side and one on his right. The one on his right was saying something to him, and he was smiling at her with his mouth a little open, like he was about to reply. As I watched, he touched her gently on the upper arm – he was the kind of man, I could tell, who touched women easily and unselfconsciously – and I looked quickly towards the front of the room. A sandy-haired man was making his way to the lectern.

There was a hiss and screech from the microphone, and then he thanked us all for coming and introduced the speaker, a woman in a green dress. Everyone clapped politely. The green-dress woman began to talk, and intermittently I tried to pay attention so that I could form an original and intelligent opinion of what she was saying, but it was incredibly boring and my attention kept wandering. It seemed unbelievable that Jack could listen so attentively, never even looking my way. He was wearing a dark blue shirt, and I thought the buttons were tortoiseshell, but I was too far away to know for sure.

After the presentation I went out to the reception area and poured myself a glass of white wine. It tasted like a hangover, but I kept drinking it for something to do. People were milling around, making conversation, and I could see Jack across the room talking to two women and a man. He didn't seem especially enthralled by the conversation: even as he talked, his gaze roamed the room absently, as if he were half-looking for something better. It didn't take long before he saw me.

I let myself meet his eye for a second, and then I turned away and pretended to be absorbed in a poster about the requirements for completing an undergraduate history major. In my peripheral vision, I saw him cross the room.

'Hello,' he said when he reached me. 'I think we've met before.'

I just nodded. The sleeves of his shirt were rolled up and I found myself noticing his forearms, which were tanned and had prominent veins running through them. I could imagine him tinkering with small appliances around the house, opening them up and using a range of different screwdrivers to fix whatever was wrong with them. He would know how to do this; he wouldn't have to watch instructional videos on YouTube to find out.

'No Mari tonight?' he asked. 'It was Mari, wasn't it? Your friend, from the other night.'

'Yeah. I mean, no. She's not here.'

'Right.' He sipped his wine. If he was disappointed not to see Mari, he didn't show it. 'Well, it's very nice to see you again. What did you think of the talk?'

My cheeks felt warm. I couldn't remember a single thing about the talk except that the presenter had been wearing a green dress, and that it had been boring. 'Well, you can't go wrong with the 1944 referendum,' I said lightly. 'In fact, it's probably my favourite referendum. If I had to choose.'

He smiled. 'I had some fairly major problems with it myself, but I didn't want to be that person. You know, the one who stands up during the Q&A and gives a ten-minute diatribe thinly disguised as a question. By that point everyone just wants to get out and start drinking the free booze.'

'Actually, this wine is pretty horrible.'

'It is, isn't it?'

'Yeah.' The room seemed hot, a little airless. Out of my mouth came the words: 'You could take me out for a proper drink.'

For a second he looked taken aback. Then he smiled at me, raising his eyebrows. 'Could I?'

'Yeah. Theoretically, you could.'

'Theoretically, I see. And what about actually?'

'Actually too.'

'All right,' he said easily. 'You always have to check these things, with philosophy graduates.'

He told me he had to say hello to a few people before he left, and I walked down to the ferry stop to wait for him. I sat on a hard metal bench and let it dig grooves into my hands. The river was black and glassy, and occasionally I heard the neat splash of a fish jumping. No one else was waiting. I thought: If the ferry comes, I just have to get on it. After about fifteen minutes I heard footsteps echoing down the ramp, and I forced myself not to turn around. Jack sat down beside me and said, 'Sorry. That took a bit longer than I thought it would.'

'That's okay.' In the distance, I could hear the ferry chugging towards us. I tried not to let him see how happy I was. 'Just in time.'

When we got on, Jack touched his card to the fare reader, but I didn't. Fare evading was just something my friends and I did, one of the things that we felt vaguely constituted our politics, along with shoplifting from the supermarket and hating our landlords on principle. If Jack noticed, he didn't say anything. We sat in silence on the front deck, and I began to feel awkward and childish, like I'd started something I couldn't finish. When we got off, he said, 'I'm parked along here, so I can drive if you like. Quicker than taking the bus.'

His car was a black Honda, very clean inside. I asked if it was new and he gave me a funny look and said, 'No, I've had it about five years, I think.'

'Oh. It's so clean, that's all. Mine's like an archaeological dig, layers and layers of crap.' It wasn't actually that bad, but for some reason I felt the need to exaggerate, as if to point out how carefree and happy-go-lucky I was in comparison to him.

'Oh well,' he said. 'You're young.' I couldn't see how that was relevant, but I didn't press him.

He drove through the dark streets. It had started to rain lightly, and the wipers juddered across the windscreen. I'd always liked watching men drive, and when I mentioned this to Jack, he said, 'Well, you're easy to please.'

'I'm not, actually. Not at all.'

Saying it felt daring and precise, like lobbing a tennis ball over a net. Jack shot me a quick look and turned his eyes back to the road. He was smiling. 'Okay,' he said. 'Forewarned is forearmed.'

He parked around the corner from a bar where my friends and I often went. I was surprised but not opposed, although I wasn't quite sure what I would say if we ran into anyone I knew. Inside it was full of buttery light and they were playing a Caribou song, one of Mari's favourites. Rain dripped down the leaded-glass windows. Jack asked me what I wanted, and I said a gin and tonic.

He came back to the table holding two glasses and handed one to me. 'Better than anything the history department has to offer,' he said. 'Mind you, there's so little funding for history these days, I'm surprised they can afford to put on any booze at all.'

'I didn't realise it was so bad,' I said. 'Are you going to lose your job?'

'No, I'm tenured, thankfully, but plenty of my colleagues are staring down that particular barrel. I suppose it's the logic of ideology – radical histories pose a threat, and you can't have history being contested. That's what I like to tell myself, anyway. Maybe I'm just making excuses for spending my life in the ivory tower.'

'Well, what's the alternative? Selling socialist newspapers on the street?'

'Yeah, nice of you to let me off the hook. I suppose the real alternative would be to take up some kind of proletarian occupation, quote unquote – working in a factory or something like that. These days it'd probably be packing boxes in an Amazon warehouse.'

'Most Amazon workers would kill for a tenured position in a university history department.'

He gave me a half-smile; I recognised it from his picture online. 'You're right,' he said. 'It's self-indulgent, feeling guilty about these things. What about you, though? What's it like to be a barista?'

I told him about the café I worked at, where the employee dress code specified all-black clothing and encouraged us to display our tattoos, if we had any. There were vicious arguments among the staff over the music we played, which had only last week resulted in one of my co-workers accusing another of being a Stalinist.

'I didn't know Stalin had strong opinions about synth pop,' Jack said.

'Oh yeah, he was a real purist. I'm surprised you didn't know that, being a historian. Although I guess you don't have much to do with Stalin in your field.'

'No, not much. Although I'd probably have a far more successful career if I'd specialised in him, instead of poor old Gramsci. It'll shock you to hear that no one cares very much about an obscure Italian Marxist who died in prison in 1937.'

'That does shock me.'

'Really? I was beginning to think nothing had the power to shock you.'

I kept my face steady. 'What do you mean by that?'

'Oh, nothing. But you seem – well, okay, I should just ask. How old are you?'

I twisted my ankles around each other. It seemed important that I not answer the question directly. 'How old do you think I am?'

'Well, from certain angles you look about nineteen. You're not nineteen, are you?'

'No, I'm not nineteen. I'm twenty-five.'

I was looking away from him as I said it. When I looked back, he was rubbing his face with one hand. 'Fuck,' he said mildly.

I felt a jab of panic, and vague shame. 'I mean, you gave me your card,' I said. 'At the graduation thing. How old did you think I was?'

'No, you're right. I knew you were younger, obviously, I just didn't put it together. My fault.' He sipped his drink. 'You know I'm forty-four.'

'Okay.'

'Is that – I mean, does that surprise you?'

I shook my head. Now that the initial awkwardness had passed, I was enjoying his discomfort: it seemed to give me an advantage, as if I had a script for the conversation and he didn't. 'I was prepared for you to be forty-eight,' I said. 'Forty-eight is probably my limit.'

He laughed. 'I don't know if that's a compliment or an insult. But no, I've got a few more years before forty-eight, thank God.

I feel like I've only just made peace with turning forty.' He took his glasses off and rubbed the bridge of his nose.

'So you don't do this kind of thing often?' I asked.

'What, bore young people with my anxieties about the aging process? I try not to.'

'No, I meant picking up women twenty years younger than you.'

There was a small silence, during which I replayed the exchange in my head with a mounting sense of unease. I'd intended it as the kind of knowing joke that adults made with one another, but it had come out sounding like an accusation. Jack looked down at his drink and laughed a little. I could tell he was shocked.

'Jesus,' he said. 'Is that what I'm doing? Picking you up?'

I sipped my drink and tried to look unconcerned. Other than admitting defeat and pretending that I'd asked him to take me for a drink on purely platonic grounds, there was only one way to go. 'I guess that's up to you,' I said. 'I wouldn't necessarily complain, though. If you did.'

He kept looking at his drink. A woman at the next table was showing her friends pictures of either a puppy or a baby, I didn't know which, but there was a lot of cooing and exclaiming. I fantasised about being part of that conversation rather than the one I was actually having, which was clearly about to end in a humiliatingly kind rejection. I opened my mouth, deciding to get in first by claiming I'd been joking, but then Jack looked up and met my eye.

'All right,' he said quietly. 'Well, I'm glad to hear that.'

When he said that I felt a rush of triumph and pleasure, like I'd pulled off some technically difficult manoeuvre in a challenging sport. Rock climbing, possibly. He asked if I wanted another drink, and while he was getting it I tried to remember every detail of the exchange so I could recount it to Mari later. (My recounting, admittedly, would play up Jack's embarrassment and erase my own.) I thought about drafting it in my Notes app, but I decided that would be weird, and very difficult to explain if Jack happened to catch sight of it.

We had another gin and tonic, and another one after that. Jack told me funny stories about his students, the things they said in class and wrote in their essays. He spoke about them affectionately, like he was on their side, and I thought a good chunk of them were probably in love with him. I asked him about this and he said, 'My God, I hope not. Although maybe if they were in love with me they'd be better about doing the reading.'

'Young people today are so lazy,' I said. 'I did the reading every week when I was a student.'

'Oh, that doesn't surprise me.'

'No?'

'No, not at all. You strike me as everyone's ideal student – you know, intelligent, engaged, actually does the fucking reading for a change. On the other hand, you were probably cleverer than most of your lecturers, so I imagine that was a bit awkward for them.'

I tried to think of an ironic response and couldn't, I was too pleased. Finally I said, 'Very flattering.'

'No, well, it's true.' He leaned back in his chair and gave me his half-smile again. 'Luckily we're in different fields, so I don't have to suffer a crushing intellectual defeat at your hands.'

'Oh, that's what you think.'

He looked like he was about to reply, but the bartender came over and told us the bar was closing. I felt vaguely furious about this, but there was nothing I could do. Jack said he was going to come back for his car the next day – he lived on Baynes Street, he told me. 'Huh,' I said. 'That's so close to my house. I'm on Spring Street.'

'Oh, that is close. Do you live with Mari?'

I shook my head. In truth, although I'd suggested it a few times, Mari didn't want us to live together. She always said that I'd end up hating her, and I always pointed out that Heidi didn't hate her, to which she shrugged and said: Heidi has the patience of a saint.

'No,' I said, 'just in a share house. I have three housemates and I'm still paying one-eighty a week for my room. It's pretty obscene.'

'West End real estate, hey. It's getting unliveable.'

I considered asking whether he really found it unliveable on his salary, but it seemed safer not to. We walked up Boundary Street together. The rain had stopped, but there was hardly anyone else out, and the street looked empty and shrunken. I made some comment about how early everything closed in Brisbane, and Jack said, 'Yeah, in Italy they'd just be getting started.' He shook his head. 'Sorry, I can't stand people like that.'

'People like what?'

'You know. Australians who are so keen to tell you that they've been to Europe and everything is better over there.'

I laughed. 'It's okay, I've been to Europe too.'

Out of the corner of my eye, I saw him glance at me. 'Nothing gets past you, does it?' he said.

I looked away, trying to hide the smile on my face. I put my hands in the pockets of Mari's dress and my fingers found an old tissue in the left pocket, shedding tiny scraps. Mari was not the kind of person who checked her pockets before she did laundry. We reached the corner of Spring Street and Jack said, 'Okay, well.'

'Okay.'

I was the one who kissed him, I still remember that. And I remember the clean soapy scent of his skin flooding over me, and the way my body hummed when he put his hands on my waist. I couldn't have said how long it went on for. When we broke apart I said softly, 'You know, I'm not actually interested in the 1944 referendum on reconstruction.'

He smiled; I saw the slick white shape of his teeth in the dark. 'No way,' he said. 'How could anyone not be interested in that?'

I leaned against the brick wall behind me. It was still warm from the heat of the day. 'I know,' I said. 'I'm a philistine.'

We kissed some more. His tongue in my mouth, the unfamiliar weight of his body pressing me against the wall. My mind seemed to have disappeared, or at least become temporarily inaccessible to me. With his face close to mine, he said, 'Honestly, this isn't how I thought tonight would end up.'

'No? You don't regularly kiss twenty-five-year-olds in the street?'

'Not that regularly, no.' He leaned against the wall beside me. Ask me to go home with you, I thought. Ask me. Instead he said, 'Look, not to be too ceremonial about this, but will you have dinner with me?'

'It's like eleven o'clock at night.'

He laughed. 'Not now. Another time.'

'Oh.' I tried not to show my disappointment. 'Yeah, if you like.'

He looked at me curiously. 'Well, I would like it, but of course you don't have to.'

'No, no.' My elbow had been touching his, just barely, but I moved it away. Everything between us suddenly felt slightly formal. 'I mean, yes. I'd like to.'

'All right,' he said. 'If you give me your number, I'll call you. Sorry, that's probably quite retrograde of me, isn't it? People of your generation all seem to have a pathological fear of talking on the phone.'

'Actually, I like talking on the phone. Mari says I'm a Luddite.'

I typed my number into his phone and waited for him to kiss me again, but he just rocked back on his heels and said, 'Okay. Goodnight, then.'

'Goodnight.'

I turned and walked towards my house. The rain had cut briefly through the warmth, but now humidity was steaming up from the street again, and the night smelled of jasmine and damp concrete. Possums screeched and rattled in the mango trees. When I got home my housemates were all asleep, and I shut myself in the bathroom and looked in the mirror. The person who looked back had flushed cheeks, a soft mouth. I turned from side to side. I touched my lips, my hair. I remember thinking that I looked younger than I would have liked.

3

ELISABETH HAD DINNER with Jack the following Saturday, and Mari found herself, through no particular premeditation, at Elisabeth's house in the afternoon and enlisted to give opinions on several possible outfits. It wasn't like Elisabeth to be preoccupied with clothes, and Mari found it a little off-putting; she had never thought of Elisabeth as someone who cared at all about how other people saw her. 'Why are you getting so worked up, anyway?' she asked, half-scrolling on her phone.

'I'm not getting worked up.'

'Yes, you are. Honestly, I'm surprised you're even seeing him again, he's so old.'

In truth, Mari wasn't really surprised – she could see that a twenty-year age gap was exactly the kind of boundary that Elisabeth would enjoy pushing. The fact that it made other people uncomfortable would only heighten the appeal.

'Don't be a puritan,' Elisabeth said, smoothing down the skirt of a red linen shift dress. 'Does this make me look like a wine mum?'

'Yes.'

Elisabeth made an exasperated noise and began unbuttoning the dress. 'No, no,' Mari said, foreseeing another forty-five minutes of outfit changes. 'I'm joking.'

'Are you?'

'Listen, I guarantee he's not interested in you for your fashion sense. Anyway, it's a compliment. You're looking the part.'

Elisabeth paused. The half-buttoned dress gaped down the middle, and Mari could see the tender flesh of Elisabeth's stomach, the dark twist of her navel. 'What part is that?'

'You know, ready for your new life as an academic's wife. Or mistress. He's not already married, is he?'

Elisabeth looked at her with a funny expression, as though part of her wanted to smile and the other part wanted to suppress the smile. 'I don't think so,' she said, rebuttoning the dress. 'But if he wants to cheat on his wife, that's his decision, not mine.'

Mari gave a half-amused laugh, although she knew Elisabeth was serious. She wouldn't be put off by Jack being married – in fact, she'd probably relish it. She would see it as an invitation to play a complex and intellectually challenging game, a game she knew she could win. But all women thought that at the beginning, didn't they? Mari remembered Jack's firm handshake, his easy smile. He seemed like the kind of man who could arrange everything the way he wanted it.

Out loud, she said, 'Right. Well, I should go – Heidi wants me to clean the bathroom before people start coming over.' She and Heidi were throwing a party that night, which Mari usually would have been looking forward to, but now it seemed boring and possibly a little juvenile. She got up from the bed. 'I take it you'll call me tomorrow with the full report?'

Elisabeth was looking in the mirror, blending some kind of tinted cream into her face, and she kept her eyes on her reflection. 'Actually,' she said, 'I was thinking I might bring him to your place after dinner. If you don't mind.'

Mari raised her eyebrows. 'I'm not sure. Let me ask Heidi, there might be a maximum age limit.'

'Mmm. Very funny.'

'Anyway, do you think he'll want to come? Surely he'll want to take you somewhere more sophisticated – a jazz club, maybe, or a whiskey bar. Or you could just go back to his place and fuck, if his wife isn't there.'

She said it deliberately, hoping to get underneath Elisabeth's cool poise, but Elisabeth just smiled. 'Don't be crude,' she said. 'Anyway, I don't want to go to a boring whiskey bar, so – oh, before you go –' She reached into a drawer and pulled out a handful of fabric, which Mari gradually recognised as her own navy dress. 'I borrowed this the other day, to wear to the seminar thing.'

'Oh, right.'

Elisabeth gave her a quizzical look. With makeup, her face looked smooth and ripe, almost imperceptibly older. 'I thought you wouldn't mind,' she said.

'No, no. I don't mind.'

The evening air was thick and humid, and by the time Mari climbed the steps to her house, she could feel sweat dripping down her back. Heidi was pacing in the living room, phone to her ear. Mari could tell from her distracted frown that she was talking to Verity, with whom she broke up and reunited on a roughly fortnightly basis. 'Bathroom,' she mouthed to Mari, cocking her head in its direction, and Mari nodded. When Heidi turned away, she went to her room, stripped off her sweaty clothes, and opened her laptop.

She had looked at Jack's staff profile a number of times already, so when she began typing his name into the search bar, the URL autofilled. She hit enter. There he was: the sandstone background, his little half-smile. She scrolled down the page, which informed her that 'Dr Bloom' had 'published widely' on Gramsci, Marxist theory, and Italian intellectual history in the early to mid-twentieth century. Mari imagined that Elisabeth had already learned about these topics and developed sophisticated opinions on them. Closing the laptop, she turned on her back, and the drift of the ceiling fan cooled the small pockets of sweat under her breasts.

Outside her window, the deep blue air of twilight had darkened into night. Tree frogs croaked steadily. Mari ran her hands over her body: the jut of her hipbones, the ladder of her ribs. She was so bony, like an underfed farm animal. She dug her fingers between her ribs until it hurt and then, silently and without thinking about it, she made herself come. Afterwards she lay blank and relieved, an empty vessel. In the living room, she could hear Heidi saying: Yes, I know that's the narrative you like to tell yourself, but that doesn't necessarily make it true.

•

THE RESTAURANT WHERE I met Jack was tucked away in a side street. The facade was dark, the name written in small letters, and I had to look twice to make sure it was the right place. I knew I was nervous, but I had already decided to ignore that. Inside it was full of small knobbly tables and soft sepia light, and I could see Jack sitting in a corner with a glass of red wine. When he saw me, he smiled.

'Hello,' he said, as I sat down. 'You look very nice.'

I couldn't think of anything to say except, 'You too.'

'I hope this is okay,' he said easily. 'The place, I mean. I thought it was a good idea, and then I got here and realised I was showing my age a bit. I've been sitting here thinking I could hardly have chosen a more geriatric venue.'

I tried to smile, but my face felt hot and stiff. Up until then, I'd been secure in the version of myself for whom having dinner with a much older man was no big deal, even if said dinner came with a non-zero chance that we might sleep together afterwards. But now that it was actually happening I felt totally unable to navigate the situation. I tried to relax my cheek muscles by rubbing them with my fingertips, which only made things worse.

Jack pretended not to notice and poured me a glass of wine from the bottle on the table. I'd never been to a restaurant with anyone who ordered wine by the bottle and I was impressed, but also faintly annoyed with myself for being impressed. 'Thank you,' I said.

'You're welcome.' He glanced at me, smiling a little. 'I feel like I'm always plying you with alcohol.'

'That's hardly fair. I kind of forced you to take me out for a drink last time.'

'You didn't force me. Far from it.' He was looking at his menu. I waited for him to say something about how much he'd enjoyed it, but he didn't, so I looked at my own menu. There were a lot of Italian words and I didn't know what most of them meant.

After we ordered I asked him, in slight desperation, how Gramsci was.

'Oh, Gramsci,' he said. 'Well, I haven't been able to do much with him lately – end of semester, you know – but I should be able to spend more time with him over the summer.'

'Have you devoted your entire life to him?'

He smiled. 'Not my entire life, no. I have to teach a fairly wide range of modern history subjects too, and I'm supervising five PhD students at the moment. And then there's endless admin work, conferences, grant applications . . . It's mostly pointless, but it does suck up time. Actually, Gramsci's lucky to get a look in.'

'And outside of work?' I cleared my throat. Jack was looking at me curiously. 'Okay,' I said, 'to be honest, Mari told me to make sure you weren't married.'

He laughed. 'She's looking out for your best interests, then. That's good.'

'So you're not?'

'No, no. I'm not married, never have been. Tell Mari I'd be happy to sign a statutory declaration to that effect.'

'All right.' I had not actually believed that Jack was married, but I was still looking forward to telling Mari that she'd been wrong; briefly, I considered going to the bathroom to text her. 'I thought you probably weren't. You don't strike me as the marrying type.'

He smiled at me. 'You're quite an observant person, aren't you? That's how you strike me, anyway.'

I felt a burst of pleasure. I knew he was charming me, and as a rule I resented being charmed, but the rule no longer seemed to apply. If I knew it was happening, I reasoned, then I wasn't actually vulnerable to it. This seemed like watertight logic at the time.

Our food came. I had some kind of pasta; I barely registered its taste. Jack asked me where I'd grown up and I told him about my parents' property on the Sunshine Coast. 'It's just a small one,' I said. 'In the hinterland.'

'Oh, you're part of the property-owning class, then.'

'Well, not me, I'll probably never own property in my life. Anyway, Mum and Dad just bought the land when it was cheap. They're both high school English teachers, it's not like I grew up wealthy.'

'No, I'm just teasing you. I actually grew up on a property too, on the Darling Downs. But English teachers, that's nice. You must have had a lot of books in the house.'

'Oh yeah. My sister and I weren't even allowed to watch TV.' I paused. 'Sorry, I know that's kind of pretentious.'

'Is it?'

'Well, not that my parents are pretentious, but their lifestyle . . .' I stopped, feeling inarticulate. 'I don't know. They vote Greens, they read the *Guardian* and everything, but their lives are so comfortable. The way things are, capitalism or whatever, it suits them. That's probably really ungrateful of me, isn't it?'

'Oh well,' he said. 'I think we all have the right to be ungrateful to our parents. And it's not a crime, you know, to grow up in a middle-class family. Lots of people do.'

'Mari didn't.'

'Oh?'

'Yeah, she had a single mum and they lived all over the place. Her mum was in a lot of different bands in the nineties, or else she was sleeping with people in bands, it's not that clear. Anyway, that wasn't middle-class.'

'No,' he said. 'But probably not much fun for Mari, either. I'm sure she'd choose your nice Greens-voting parents if she could.'

I knew he was wrong about that. To Mari, our different upbringings had come to stand for a fundamental divergence in our characters, and she was a little derisive of my family background. (She had once told me that anyone our age whose parents were still together didn't understand hardship.) Really, we both knew that she was a freer person than me, maybe because she'd grown up differently; she found it easier to relax, to just enjoy things. She never thought much about the future, or about the past.

But to Jack I just said something noncommittal, and we talked about other things. I told him about my film project, which he said sounded 'full of potential', and he didn't even mention *Reality Bites*. As I drank more of the wine I started to worry less about coming up with intelligent things to say. After our plates had been cleared away, I asked him if he ever went to student parties.

'Oh, I've been known to,' he said, 'but not recently. I think the code of conduct is getting stricter and stricter on that sort of thing.'

'Well, my friend Heidi is having a party tonight. It's not actually a student party, we're not students anymore, so you don't have to worry about the code of conduct. Mari will be there – she lives there, actually, with Heidi.'

'I see.' He surveyed me over the top of his wineglass. 'Okay. It sounds fun.'

'Not geriatric, at least.'

'No, definitely not that.'

We left the restaurant and got in a taxi, stopping at a bottle shop so that Jack could buy a bottle of gin. 'We can't arrive empty-handed,' he said. When the taxi pulled up on Paris Street, there was a lot of noise coming from the house, and a girl on the front steps was crying into her phone. It occurred to me that everyone would be hopelessly drunk, and that Jack was possibly unprepared for this, but he just raised his eyebrows at me and said, 'Shall we go in?'

Inside they were playing Kendrick Lamar very loudly and dancing in the living room, with all the furniture pushed up against the walls. It was too noisy to talk properly, and we stood awkwardly on the threshold while I tried to remember what people usually did with their hands and faces. Bringing Jack seemed like an awful, humiliating mistake; I was sure he would make his excuses and leave soon, and maybe that would be for the best.

Across the room, Mari was dancing, her body making fluid shapes in the heaving crowd. She was wearing a skimpy black top and shorts, and her face was pink and gleaming with sweat. I felt too self-conscious to wave at her, but after a moment she spotted us, grinned, and pushed her way over.

'Hello, Mum and Dad,' she said, shouting over the music. 'Did you have a nice dinner?'

Stiffly, I said, 'Mari, you remember Jack.'

She shook her head at me, laughing. 'Oh yeah, I think I remember him.' To Jack, she said, 'I'm surprised you came. I suggested you might take Elisabeth to a nice whiskey bar after dinner, but she said – I think the word she used was "boring".'

He laughed. 'How right she was. No, this is great, I'm glad she invited me. And you live here? This is your house?'

Mari nodded. She opened her mouth to say something else, but the music stopped abruptly and someone – I suspected Paul – put on that Carly Simon song 'Coming Around Again'. There was a general howl of protest and most people left the room.

'Shocking,' Mari said. 'Let's go to the kitchen. Oh, is that gin? Can I have some?'

'Of course you can,' Jack said. 'That's why we brought it.'

She took the bottle out of his hands and examined it. 'Wow, this is expensive stuff. Well done, Elisabeth.' She gave me a little smile. 'You've found yourself a wealthy benefactor at last.'

I was worried Jack would be offended by this but he didn't seem to take it seriously; in fact, he laughed. I gave Mari the finger, and she blew me a kiss.

•

IN THE KITCHEN, Jack and Elisabeth sat at the table while Mari looked in the cupboard for glasses. She hadn't really expected Jack to come, and now that he was here she found herself feeling self-conscious about the house, a crumbling old Queenslander with high ceilings and decorative arches carved over the doorways. The paint was peeling, the gutters clogged every time it rained, and there was a rotting floorboard situation in the bathroom that neither Mari nor Heidi wanted to investigate further. She knew Jack probably found it squalid, and she had a perverse desire to make him admit this, so she could accuse him of being a snob. 'What do you think of the place?' she asked. 'Is it like the share houses of your youth?'

'Oh, much nicer,' he said. 'When I was an undergrad I lived in a house where the ceiling leaked, and by the end of summer there was black mould growing everywhere. It's a miracle we all survived with our lungs mostly intact.'

Mari reached up to the top cupboard to get a bottle of tonic water. She was aware, as she did this, that the hem of her top was skimming over her stomach. 'Well, we don't have black mould, but we do have that panel in the wall – see that one there? It's exposed asbestos. The real estate agent says it'll be fine as long as no one knocks it.'

Jack laughed. 'Well, at least real estate agents haven't changed since I was young. I always thought they'd be the shock troops for fascism.' He was opening the gin, glancing at her as he twisted the cap. 'Do you have ice?'

'Sure.'

Jack's movements as he poured the gin and tonics were confident, assured, as if he were in his own kitchen making drinks for his guests. Mari watched him sipping from his glass, looking around the kitchen: its grease-spotted walls, shelves crowded haphazardly with packets and bottles.

'Yeah, this is nice,' he said. 'Your place, I mean.'

There was an empty chair at the table, but Mari hopped onto the kitchen counter and swung her legs, banging her heels against the cabinets. 'It's kind of shitty,' she said. 'You should see Elisabeth's place – that's nice. Her room is, anyway. She's got good taste.'

'It's not that nice,' Elisabeth said.

Mari smiled and said nothing. She knew Elisabeth was embarrassed by the implication of Jack seeing her room. Elisabeth was always poised, she had a forthright intelligence that she used to direct conversations exactly where she wanted them to go, but she could be reticent about sex. Mari attributed this to her conventional upbringing, or else her tendency to intellectualise everything to the point of coldness. She tipped an ice cube into her mouth and cracked it between her teeth. With her mouth full, she said, 'This gin is really good.'

Jack spread his hands in front of him. 'I thought I'd better come bearing gifts,' he said. 'Ingratiate myself with your friends, and so on. Speaking of, are you going to introduce me to anyone, or do I have to stay sequestered in the kitchen all night?'

'We'll introduce you,' Mari said. 'We're just preparing the ground. We thought we'd let them get a brief glimpse of you, build up their curiosity, and then we'll take you out and display you.'

'All right. Good to know I'm not embarrassing you.'

'Well, I never said you weren't embarrassing us.'

Mari noticed that Elisabeth was filming them, and she made a face at the camera. 'This is Elisabeth's surveillance camera,' she said to Jack. 'I'm sure she told you about it. I hate it.'

'Well, you ruin it when you break the fourth wall like that,' said Elisabeth. She passed her phone to Mari. 'Here, you film for a bit.'

Mari pointed it at Jack. Outside, she could hear Heidi laughing at something. Jack was leaning back in his chair, and he looked into the camera lens with a slight smile.

'Hello,' he said.

Mari held the phone steady. 'Hey.'

'My cinematic debut. What should I say?'

'Doesn't matter. Say anything that comes to mind.'

She dared herself to look straight at him, meeting his eyes over the top of the phone. Something tugged inside her, a snaking tendril in her stomach. From offscreen, Elisabeth said, 'You should educate us. Teach us about history.'

'No, history's boring,' Mari said. 'Teach us something else.'

He smiled at her. Not at the camera, but at her. 'I don't think there's anything else I'm qualified to teach you,' he said.

A rush of heat went through Mari's body and she dropped her gaze, her fingers slick and clumsy on the phone screen. 'There,' she said, handing it back to Elisabeth. 'Scene. Or cut, or whatever. The end.'

Jack refilled their glasses, and they talked for a while about Christmas plans. He was the much younger brother to two sisters, he explained, one of whom hosted Christmas every year. 'Our parents died a few years ago, which I think was a relief all around, but of course they've got their own families now. It's funny, when I was little, they spoiled me rotten. We never fought, we were never jealous of each other . . . Not really a typical sibling situation.'

Mari wasn't surprised by this. Jack had the self-possessed manner of someone who had grown up with the security of being adored, a security so complete he didn't even know it existed. Elisabeth was the same. 'Are you still close with them?' she asked.

'Not really. They both moved out of home when I was quite young, and then I grew up and went to university and now we hardly see each other. I think they're waiting for me to get married, have a family, that sort of thing. Of course, I've explained that marriage is a patriarchal institution, but I don't know if it's getting through.'

'So you're not married,' said Mari. 'No Mrs Rochester up in the attic.'

'For the last time, no. Mari, you seem to have a very low opinion of me.'

She laughed, drawing one knee up to rest her chin on. The gin and tonic he'd made was pleasantly bitter on her tongue. 'Don't worry,' she said. 'I have a low opinion of everyone. So does Elisabeth, that's why we're such good friends.'

It wasn't quite true. In fact, before she'd met Elisabeth, Mari hadn't thought of herself as having any opinions at all. Elisabeth was the first intelligent person Mari had ever met who wasn't a dominating conversationalist or an egomaniac. She was the first person to make Mari feel intelligent too, to ask about her opinions as if they mattered. Sometimes Mari tried to imagine her life without Elisabeth, and what came to her was a disturbing sense of formlessness and lack, random elements that added up to nothing. She had never tried to put this feeling into words, partly because she knew that Elisabeth didn't feel the same way.

Jack asked how they'd met, and Elisabeth explained about the boarding house they'd both lived in during their first semester of university. 'I'd just moved down here and I didn't know anyone,' she said. 'At home I was kind of a big fish in a small pond, so it was a shock to find out that nobody in Brisbane cared about me being dux of my school or whatever.'

Mari saw Jack smile into his drink. 'Of course you were dux of your school,' he said.

'What's that supposed to mean?'

'No, it's a compliment. And what about Mari, was she dux too?'

'No,' said Elisabeth. 'She was –' She broke off, met Mari's eye.

'Go on,' said Mari. She felt rash, on the edge of something. 'Tell him.'

'Tell me what?'

'You tell him.'

'Okay,' said Mari. 'In high school I had a relationship with one of my teachers.' She paused. 'A sexual relationship.'

Jack raised his eyebrows. Mari took a careful sip of her drink. 'Really,' he said.

'Yeah, my English teacher. No one ever found out – well, not at the time. Elisabeth was actually the first person I ever told.'

'How did it happen?'

Mari raised her glass, heavy and slippery, to her lips. 'How does anything happen?' she said. 'I didn't know any better, he didn't know any better. That was it, really.'

'You were young,' Elisabeth said softly.

Jack glanced at her, then at Mari. He was frowning a little. 'I'm sure he did know better. How old were you?'

'Oh, I wasn't underage – I was sixteen when it started. He was thirty-one, thirty-two. It wasn't ideal, from an ethical standpoint, but I did consent. For what that's worth.'

'Yeah,' said Jack. 'Honestly, I don't know how much it's worth.'

Mari felt the bottom drop out of her stomach. She'd thought the story would make her seem sophisticated, grown-up, but it had disgusted him. Of course it had. She got up to refill her drink, face burning, and in a dim corner of her brain she heard Elisabeth change the subject. Elisabeth could always tell when Mari was upset or uncomfortable, and she would often execute quietly diplomatic gestures to move the conversation onto a different track. It was thoughtful of her, but sometimes Mari herself found it disorienting to realise how keenly attuned Elisabeth was to her temperament, how closely she must have been watching Mari as she spoke.

•

AT AROUND ONE o'clock, after the neighbours started making a fuss about the noise, Jack and I walked back to his house. Once it had been a mansion, but now it was subdivided into four flats. His was on the second floor. We climbed a flight of rickety stairs at the side of the building, and as he unlocked the door, I turned to look at the city skyline: the apartments and office buildings peppered with tiny squares of light, and the jagged shard of the government building. A cool night breeze drifted over my face.

When we went inside and Jack switched the lights on, I saw that the place was nicer than I'd expected. A thick red Turkish rug lay on the polished wooden floor, a potted palm waved its delicate fronds by the window, and the tall bookshelves were jammed with books in English and Italian. Framed art hung on the walls: a series of abstract black-and-white line drawings, and a large painted poster of two women in red dresses against a green background. Underneath was a row of thick block letters spelling out something in Vietnamese.

Jack saw me looking at the poster. 'I got that in Hanoi a few years ago. One of the posters from revolutionary Vietnam. I think the slogan says something insurrectional like, "Produce more coffee for export!"'

'It's beautiful,' I said, stepping back. 'Your house is beautiful.'

'Thank you. Coming from someone with renowned good taste, too. Would you like a drink?'

'Okay.' I sat on the couch and waited for him to bring me a large stemless glass of red wine. I cradled it in one hand and tilted it from side to side, watching the dark liquid slosh cleanly against the glass.

Jack sat beside me with his own drink. 'What are you thinking about?'

'Well, I want to ask you something.'

He laughed. 'Shit. Okay, go ahead.'

I took a sip of wine. Usually red wine left the taste of charcoal in my mouth, but this went down smoothly. 'That night at the graduation thing,' I said. 'When we first met. Why did you give your card to me and not Mari?'

He looked at me with his mouth a little open. 'What do you mean?'

'Well, she's more . . . I don't know, sometimes people find me kind of uptight compared to her. Or, like, not very much fun. And you seemed to enjoy talking to her, so when you gave me your card . . . I was surprised, that's all. I just wanted to know why.'

'Oh.' He leaned back, looking into the middle distance. 'Well, I don't know. I mean, I do know, but it's kind of a cliché.'

'That's all right. I'll let you get away with a cliché this time.'

'Very generous of you. Okay, well – when I first saw you, I just thought you were really beautiful.' He glanced at me. 'You were wearing that yellow dress, and everyone else was wearing black, and you were standing there with this slightly pissed-off expression, and – what can I say? I was actually going to talk to you then, but Mari arrived.'

I exhaled slowly. 'Oh.'

'Then when we did meet, you seemed very – I don't know, very astute, very switched-on. You're right, Mari did most of the talking, but that doesn't necessarily mean anything. Lots of my students talk without having much to say. Not that I thought she had nothing to say, but you . . . I just noticed that watchful face of yours, looking back and forth between us, and I thought, she seems like an interesting person. And I was right, as it turned out.'

I smoothed my dress down, looking at my knees. I could feel a smile squirming across my face. 'That's nice of you to say.'

'I'm not just saying it, it's true.' He paused. 'Honestly, when you came into the restaurant tonight, I was so happy to see you. I'd been sitting there thinking you probably wouldn't turn up.'

'What? Why wouldn't I turn up?'

'Well, you seemed kind of unexcited by the prospect of having dinner with me, when I asked. I thought you probably had better things to do.'

I drank my wine and let the pleasure of that statement sink in. A moth fluttered through the open window, heading straight for the light. 'Well, I actually did have better things to do,' I said. 'But I decided to give you a chance, see how it worked out.'

'Oh, thanks. And how did it work out?'

I put my glass down on the floor, took his hand and held it to my lips. The smell and feel of his skin was so immediate. 'Pretty good,' I said. 'So far.'

His bedroom was a big white room with bookshelves along one wall. An abstract painting in red and blue; a pendant globe light with a rice-paper shade. We lay on the bed and he touched my cheek gently.

'This is only if you want to, you know,' he said softly.

'I know.' His face had a new, serious expression, and it occurred to me that he might think I was inexperienced. I wanted to reassure him that I wasn't, but it seemed impolite to bring up all the other people I'd had sex with, so I just unbuttoned my dress. We stopped talking then. When he touched me I felt that I was losing my grip on my body, melting into something else entirely: a hot throbbing ache, a guitar waiting to be played.

He leaned over to the drawer beside the bed, and I heard the adult rustle of condoms. He said, 'Okay?' and I said, 'Yes, you don't have to keep asking.' He laughed then, a quick little exhale of a laugh. I thought about telling him how much I wanted him, but it felt better to let him be the one who wanted me, so I knelt above him with the tips of my hair brushing his chest. His lips were parted, and the inside of his mouth looked dark.

'Is that okay?' I asked. 'I can stop anytime you want.'

He let out his breath. 'No,' he said quietly. 'Don't stop.'

I liked hearing him say that. 'All right.' His hands were gripping my hips, and his expression was a little pensive, as if he were seeing something else when he looked at me. I closed my eyes. This was how sex worked best for me: when I could concentrate on physical sensation and almost forget the other person was there. When he put his mouth between my legs, I couldn't think about anything. Violet and red streaked behind my eyes, and the hot electrical aching gathered and gathered to a peak, a peak, a plateau.

Afterwards, we were both quiet. I felt relieved, as if a hurdle had been gotten over, although I didn't know why that would be. Jack was playing gently with a strand of my hair. After a while he said, 'Okay?'

Now that it was over, I felt able to be ironic again. 'Not bad,' I said. 'Five out of ten.'

'Oh.' His hand stilled. 'Right. Well –'

'No, that was a joke. I'm joking.'

'Oh.' He laughed, and I laughed too, mostly at the relief on his face. 'Thank God for that. If I'd only managed five out of ten, I think I'd have to die of shame.'

'Well, you don't have to die of shame. Not because of that, anyway.'

'No, not because of that.'

He was stroking my cheek with his thumb, sort of absentmindedly. It was hard to believe that only a few hours ago I'd been in my room, trying to decide what to wear. I thought about Mari saying: I guarantee he's not interested in you for your fashion sense, and that made me smile. Jack asked what I was smiling about, but it seemed too convoluted a story, so I said, 'Nothing, really.'

'You're happy?'

'Yeah, I'm happy.'

He seemed satisfied with that. We went to sleep soon afterwards, and I slept well. His bed was much more comfortable than mine, and I loved his off-white linen sheets: how cool and expensive they felt against my skin.

•

THE NEXT DAY happened to be the day I'd agreed to drive to my parents' house for Christmas, and in the morning I announced this to Jack. I thought he'd be disappointed, but he only glanced up from the coffee he was making and said, 'Oh, okay. You certainly take your filial responsibilities seriously.'

I was sitting at his kitchen counter eating an apple, a pose that suddenly seemed childish. 'You know, it's Christmas,' I said. 'It's a big deal to them.'

'Of course.' He handed me a mug of coffee. 'Well, tell them I said hello. Or don't, actually. I'm not sure they'd be thrilled to learn of my existence, would they?'

I considered telling him that my parents' greatest wish was probably for me to settle down with a tenured academic, but I knew that would sound way over the top, like I expected us to get married. So I just smiled and drank my coffee. Jack asked if I wanted some toast and I said no.

He came around the kitchen counter and sat next to me. 'So, how long will you be away?'

'Two weeks. I'll be back on the second.'

'Right.' He sipped his coffee, and I studied the copper pots hanging from a rack above his stove. I had finished my apple but didn't know where to put the core, so I held it awkwardly with sticky fingers. After a minute he said, 'I had a good time last night.'

I had no idea what he meant. Possibly he was implying that he wanted to see me again, but on the other hand it also had the tone of polite conclusion – a way of saying, thanks for the sex, now please leave. I said I was glad he'd had fun, a statement which came out sounding both too suggestive and too formal.

'I did,' he said. 'Not only – well, I mean, I enjoyed spending time with you. And your friends, they all seemed like cool people. Not as cool as you, but I suppose very few people are.'

I looked into my coffee and tried not to smile. 'I know what you're doing,' I said.

'What am I doing?'

'You're charming me.'

When I looked up, he was laughing, in a way that suggested he didn't exactly want to laugh but couldn't help it. 'Well,' he said. 'I'm certainly trying my best.'

I slid off my stool, he put his hands on my waist, and we kissed. He was wearing a soft blue cotton T-shirt, and his skin was warm. Knowing I wouldn't kiss him again for two weeks made it more pleasurable, but also bittersweet, the way I imagined lovers felt before one of them went off to war. I knew this comparison was objectively idiotic. After a while I pulled away and said, 'I should go.'

'Mmm. Oh. Are you sure?'

'Yeah, there's probably traffic on the highway already.' I paused. 'Actually, before I go . . . Could I ask you a favour?'

'Of course.'

'Well, if you're around . . . You might think about going to see Mari once or twice while I'm away. She'll be on her own for most of the break. Heidi goes back to her mum's place in Grafton.'

He raised his eyebrows. 'Oh. Okay.'

'It's just that I worry about her, staying there by herself. But you don't have to, of course.'

'No, no. If you want me to, I will.'

I touched his face. 'Thanks.' He said I was welcome.

4

ELISABETH WAS THE first to go, but over the next week, everyone drifted home for Christmas. Her friends' absences left Mari feeling bereft, as though large holes suddenly gaped through the fabric of her life. She couldn't summon the will to do much – three days after Heidi left, the kitchen was full of dirty dishes and Mari was lying on the battered old couch on the back deck, half-reading with heavy eyelids. It was a hot day, the sun burning white in a deep blue sky, and a mosquito was biting her calf. She swatted at it and missed, watched its bloated body float lazily away.

She was thinking about getting up to find some insect repellent when she heard footsteps in the house – heavy footsteps, with a measured rhythm to them. Mari stumbled to her feet, fear clutching her chest. She was looking around for a defensive weapon when Jack put his head around the door and said, 'Hi, Mari.'

She sank back onto the couch, knees shaking. 'Jesus Christ.'

'Did I give you a fright? I'm sorry.'

'I thought you were a murderer.' She found her cigarettes and lit one with trembling hands. 'Haven't you ever heard of knocking?'

'Oh, I did knock, but you must not have heard . . . I'm sorry, it was Elisabeth's idea. She just asked me to stop by and make sure you were all right.'

Mari drew on her cigarette. Now that the initial shock had passed, she felt a little caught out, and conscious of the fact that she was wearing only an oversized Spinal Tap T-shirt and her least presentable underwear. She tried to think of something arch and ironic to say. 'Good thing she did,' she said. 'I was just about to call the suicide hotline. Anyway, did you have a good time the other night?'

Jack sat in a chair opposite her, his sunglasses hooked over the neck of his crisp white shirt. He looked out of place on their deck, among the straggly plants and Tibetan prayer flags, but he didn't seem to mind. 'I did, yeah,' he said. 'It's been ages since I went to a party that ended with the neighbours coming out to yell about the music.'

'What kind of parties do you normally go to? Terribly sophisticated dinner parties?'

'Well, I used to go to dinner parties, although I don't know if they were all that sophisticated. But now everyone has kids, so these days it's mostly afternoon barbecues. Children screaming and warm beers in the sun. Very grim.'

'Is that why you're adopting us? To improve your social life?'

He smiled. 'I thought you were adopting me.'

Mari blew smoke at him, trying not to smile back. 'We're considering your application,' she said. 'Anyway, do you want a drink? I've still got some of that gin you brought.'

'Thank God. I can imagine the cheap stuff you drink when you're left to your own devices. That's one part of my youth I'm not keen to relive.'

Inside, Mari brushed her hair and put on a semi-clean pair of shorts. The dirty dishes in the kitchen brought a small pulse of shame, but she concentrated on pouring the drinks with a steady hand. When she came out Jack was examining her cigarette packet, which showed a close-up of a diseased lung below the words SMOKING CAUSES CANCER.

'These'll kill you, you know,' he said mildly.

'Oh, not you too. It's bad enough getting that from Elisabeth.'

'All right.' He tucked the cigarettes into his pocket. 'I won't say anything else but I'll keep these here, so you can't do yourself any more damage. Anyway, Mari. How are you enjoying your holiday?'

'Oh, it's . . .' She lay on the couch and waved her glass vaguely in the air. 'I don't know. Fine. I'm getting a lot of reading done.'

'What are you reading?' She held up her dog-eared copy of *The Mandarins*, and Jack smiled. 'Good to see Simone de Beauvoir hasn't gone out of style.'

'She might have, I don't know. I don't read modern books. Literature went downhill after 1970.'

It was one of the things Elisabeth had noticed about her, back when they first met. Up until then, Mari hadn't given much thought to her own reading habits, but one day they'd been talking about what they were reading and Elisabeth had said: Oh, but you don't like modern books, do you? It was clear that she took this preference as a sign of intellect. Mari could still remember how pleased she'd felt, and ever since then – even when a new novel came out that did sound interesting – she'd taken care not to break the habit.

'Well, you might be onto something there,' Jack said. 'What are you doing for Christmas, though? You won't be here reading all alone, will you?'

She looked at him quickly, trying to detect if he was teasing her, but his face was open and sincere. 'No,' she said. 'I'm going to Lismore to see my mother. But how's your holiday? Escape from the ivory tower, hey? Must be a relief to have a break from doing nothing.'

He laughed. In the neighbour's garden, a lawnmower sputtered into a crackling roar, and the fresh scent of cut grass drifted through the air. 'All right, all right,' he said. 'It might surprise you to learn that academia does involve a fair amount of work, even though it's mostly make-work. Teaching, grants, all the rest of it. We're slaves to the H-index.'

'I always think it's funny,' Mari said, drawing circles in the condensation on her glass, 'how upset academics get about the H-index. I mean, all it's doing is bringing academia into line with the rest of neoliberalism. You know literally every other workplace has KPIs, right? Why should you be any different?'

'Don't you think we should resist neoliberalism everywhere we can?'

'Sure, but you all seem to think the revolution should start with the H-index and not, for example, in the factories and slums and McDonald's of the world. Kind of hypocritical if you ask me.'

She expected him to be offended, but he looked interested, almost pleased. 'Well, I appreciate the moral lesson,' he said. 'Is this what people mean when they talk about call-out culture?'

Mari laughed. It was gratifyingly easy to make fun of him, even though she had the sense that he was mostly letting her do it, and that he could have very deftly swung the conversation around if he'd chosen to. 'That's a completely different thing,' she said. 'Don't you read the internet?'

'No, never. I can't keep up with your generation. Anyway, hypocrisy aside, what's your critique? I'm interested to hear.'

Mari pressed the soles of her feet together, letting her knees splay sideways. It occurred to her that this was exactly the sort of conversation Elisabeth would have wanted to film, and she took some pleasure in the fact that she was missing out. 'Well, it's kind of a bubble, isn't it?' she said. 'Everyone rushes around taking themselves so seriously, but they're totally disconnected from reality. I mean, I hate to break it to you, but your latest journal article on Gramsci is going to have precisely zero impact on the global class struggle.'

'Actually, it might interest you to know that Gramsci himself has a lot to say on this topic. The role of intellectuals in society, and so on.'

'That doesn't really interest me.'

He put his hands over his face in mock despair, but she could tell he was smiling. 'All right,' he said, dropping his hands. 'I take your point overall, but you were in anthropology, weren't you? Surely anthropologists can't be accused of staying inside their bubble, whatever else they might be accused of.'

'Ah, see, that's an interesting point, and I've thought about it a lot. But actually, anthropologists are the worst offenders.'

'Oh, really?'

'Think about it.' Mari took a drink, the ice cubes clinking in her glass. 'It's actually much easier, in terms of praxis or whatever, to do a stint of fieldwork in rural Cambodia than it is to get out to Darra or Logan. You're examining another society to avoid examining your own, and especially to avoid examining your class position. And meanwhile, the so-called exoticism of ethnographic fieldwork makes it impossible for anyone to accuse you of not leaving your bubble. Never mind that when you're at home you don't dream of going further south than Annerley.'

'Hmm,' said Jack. A smile was playing around the corners of his mouth. 'And what about you, do you get out to Darra to mingle with the masses on a regular basis? I can't really imagine you outside of West End.'

'I'm not a snob. I just like it here.'

'Well, they should put that on a bumper sticker. Listen, Mari, ideological objections aside, I think you'd be a great addition to any department. You're obviously very bright, and you strike me as someone with a lot of creative energy. That's all I wanted to say. Don't hold it against me.'

Mari was so pleased that for a few seconds she couldn't speak or look at him. 'Very bright' was the kind of thing people were always saying about Elisabeth, not about her. 'Well, okay,' she said. 'Thanks.'

Jack swallowed the last of his drink and stood up. 'All right, I'd better go.'

'What, now? Why?'

'Things to do, people to see.' He smiled down at her. 'No, I've got to get some presents for my sisters and their kids. And my sisters' kids' kids. Families start ballooning when you get to my age, it's a real hassle.' He paused. 'I'll come and see you tomorrow?'

Mari traced another circle, her thumb squeaking on the wet glass. She liked the feeling of lying there on the couch, one foot resting on her bare knee, while he stood over her. 'Yeah,' she said, without looking up. 'I'll be here.'

•

AFTER THAT, JACK came to spend almost every afternoon with her. It was always hot, and they sat on the back deck drinking gin and tonics and smoking Mari's cigarettes.

'Just one,' Jack would say, his voice muffled around the cigarette clamped between his lips. 'One won't hurt.'

'I should charge you by the cigarette,' Mari said. 'They're not cheap, you know.'

'Are you short of money, Mari? I'd be happy to contribute. A fund, maybe, a grant for starving artists. Only you're not starving. Or an artist, come to think of it.'

'You should fund Elisabeth, she's the artist. Well, the filmmaker.'

She watched him carefully to see how he'd react to Elisabeth's name, but his expression didn't change. 'Right,' he said. 'Only Elisabeth wouldn't take my money.'

'And you think I would?'

He took a drag on his cigarette and leaned back in his chair. On the exhale, he said, 'I know you would.'

She didn't mention Elisabeth again, and neither did he. They talked about other things: Jack told her about his childhood on a Darling Downs cattle station, the dry yellow grass and the summer air thick with flies. Mari asked why he hadn't become a farmer himself and he said he'd never been interested, and anyway, he hated seeing the animals sent off to slaughter. Farm kids were supposed to be pragmatic about it, but it had upset him when he was small and it had carried on upsetting him even when he was a teenager – it still upset him now, when he thought about it, which admittedly wasn't very often.

'So you're a vegetarian?' Mari asked.

He looked taken aback. 'Oh. No. I suppose I should be, I did consider it once . . . But no, I'm not.'

'It's all right. I'm not either.'

He asked where she'd grown up and she said, 'Oh, here and there . . .' She saw herself as a little girl, pale face and straggly hair, trailing behind her mother. They'd drifted all around Sydney before they came to Brisbane and lived in a share house in Paddington, where Mari sometimes wandered into the living room to find her mother's friends slumped on the couch, belts or shoelaces loosened around the crooks of their arms.

'It's a drug,' her mother had said matter-of-factly when Mari thought to ask. 'It's called heroin.'

'Oh,' said Mari.

She told Jack about that, making it sound funny and bohemian. But she didn't tell him about the weeks spent with people she didn't know, never sure whether her mother was going to come back for her. She didn't tell him about being the dirty kid at school, the one who everyone said had nits. Maybe she had been dirty. She remembered once being called in for a bath by her mother, who was tense and frustrated – as Mari remembered it, they'd been running late for something. They were walking into the house when her mother said, 'Oh my God. You've got ringworm on your neck.'

Mari stopped, gripped by cold dread. 'A worm on my neck?'

'Ringworm,' her mother said, leaning over her. Mari could remember the freckles on her chest and the way she smelled: cigarette smoke mingled with a spicy perfume. 'It's a disgusting fungus that grows on you and eats your skin.'

Mari was silent. She could feel the blood pounding in her face.

'You need to wash yourself better,' her mother said, her voice barbed with cruelty. 'You need to take better care of yourself.'

Mari swallowed hard and didn't reply. In the bath, she scrubbed her neck until blood beaded on the flushed pink skin.

In high school, she wasn't teased for being dirty anymore. They moved across the city and Mari went to a new school, where she put a lot of effort into playing the role of a normal teenager. She had friends, or people she would have described that way if asked – she felt no real closeness to them, but they filled out her life. She smoked with them behind the toilet block at lunch, roamed the city with them on idle afternoons. She safety-pinned her skirt above her knees and learned to shoplift. Her school reports all said the same thing: Mari needs to make more of an effort.

Making an effort was the last thing Mari felt like doing. She spent most of her classes thinking about other things, except in English, where lessons often took the form of an hour-long discussion between her and the teacher. The teacher should have put a stop to this, but he didn't. He began lending Mari books, finding excuses to keep her back after class. One afternoon in an empty classroom, he touched her hair and said he thought she'd be a writer one day. Mari stood very still and felt all the air go out of her lungs. As it happened, she'd never had any ambition to be a writer, but she didn't remember that until later.

High school came to its eventual end, and her teacher's fiancée returned from a year-long placement in central Queensland. The following week Mari went to schoolies with her so-called friends and blacked out from drinking, waking up alone on the beach with mysterious bruises all over her legs. Her grades were mostly mediocre, but it didn't matter because she was only doing an arts degree. She chose an anthropology major because it was the first one she saw, and she had no intention of ever studying English again.

Once she got the acceptance email from the university, her mother decided there was no reason for her to stay in Brisbane. 'Mari has no use for a mother anymore,' she said pointedly to a friend, while Mari was in the room. Through a friend of a friend of an ex-boyfriend she was offered a job in a café in Lismore, and decided to take it. Mari found a room in a boarding house on Vulture Street, which was full of international students and had laminated notices in the hallway about not making noise at night.

'You've got your own life now,' her mother said solemnly, the day they moved Mari's boxes into the Vulture Street house.

'Didn't I always?' Mari said.

She told Jack about this exchange and he laughed. 'Your poor mother,' he said. 'I can only imagine.'

'Oh, my poor mother. Poor me. You should meet her one day, then you'll see what I had to put up with. Actually, the two of you might get along, she's about your age.'

'Hey, if you're going to be cruel about my age, I'll leave.' He was smiling at her. 'I didn't come over here to be made fun of.'

'Oh? Why did you come?'

He glanced at her and didn't answer. It had been sunny when he arrived, but the sky had clouded over, and the air was heavy and fragrant with the promise of rain. Putting his drink down, he said, 'As you know, Elisabeth asked me to.'

Mari looked away, scratching a mosquito bite on her ankle. The inside of her mouth felt thick and sour. 'Right,' she said. 'Well, you've done your duty.'

'She's coming back today, actually. So it's probably – I mean, I should go.'

'Sure. Have fun.'

He stood, but didn't move towards the door. When Mari looked up at him, his face was pained and uncertain. 'Was there something else you wanted?' she asked.

'No, no.' He rubbed the back of his neck. 'Bye, Mari. I'm sure I'll see you soon.'

She didn't reply. He went into the house and she heard his footsteps going down the hallway, out the front door. When he had gone she drank the rest of her gin and tonic, almost the whole glass, in one go. It felt easy, nourishing even, like drinking water.

•

I CAME BACK to Brisbane on a Sunday, the second day of the new year. The traffic on the highway was even worse than when I'd driven out, and it was more than three hours before my exit came up. I drove through the flat sprawl of the suburbs, the leafy hills of the inner north, and then through the loop and snarl of city roads and over the bridge. The river glittered calmly in the afternoon sunlight. When I got home, I sent Jack a message and took a shower. As I was wrapping myself in a towel, he knocked on the door.

I ran to answer it before any of my housemates got there. During the two weeks I'd been away, I'd suffered a bit of uncertainty about him. Forty-four seemed old in a way it hadn't before, and I could no longer remember whether his face in person looked anything like his staff profile. I'd begun to worry that I'd accidentally fucked an unattractive middle-aged man. It was a relief to see, when I opened the door, that he looked normal. Good, even. I worked hard to keep my face still. 'Hello,' I said.

'Hi.'

I cleared my throat, wishing I'd put some clothes on. Answering the door in a towel seemed ridiculously provocative. 'Come in,' I said stiffly.

He followed me into my bedroom and looked around alertly, taking in the drawings tacked to the wall, the overburdened clothes rack, the plants in ceramic pots on my desk. 'Mari was right,' he said. 'About you having good taste, I mean. Your room is nice.'

'Thanks.' I was actually wishing I'd had the chance to tidy, or at least prominently display some of the non-fiction books I'd bought in Verso sales. Jack went over to my desk and picked up a necklace I'd made out of polymer clay, examined it and put it down.

I sat on the edge of the bed, and he sat in my desk chair and looked at me. 'It's really nice to see you,' he said quietly. 'I've been thinking about you a lot.'

A light shiver of happiness went through me, and I looked away, couldn't meet his eye. I said the first flippant thing that came into my head: 'What was the nature of these thoughts?'

'Oh, just thinking about how much I was looking forward to discussing current events with you, that kind of thing. You seem like you'd have some worthwhile opinions about Syria.'

I bit the smile off my lips. My shoulders were still damp from the shower, and the breeze from the ceiling fan cooled my skin. 'Well, how did you keep yourself busy while I was gone?' I asked. 'Apart from current events fantasies, I mean.'

'Ah, nothing very exciting. Christmas at my sister's place wasn't anything to write home about, but at least I managed to leave the next day. And I went to see Mari a few times, like you asked me to.'

'Oh, right, she mentioned that.'

'Did she?'

She had, although I hadn't been entirely sure how to interpret it. Her message said that Jack was 'making himself useful' by visiting 'vulnerable community members', which could have meant that she was either pleased or annoyed by his presence. When I asked what they'd talked about, she only said that the conversation was 'intellectually stimulating'.

'Yeah,' I said. 'We stayed in touch.'

He raised his eyebrows, but he was smiling, and I had the sense that he didn't mind the idea of Mari and me discussing him behind his back. I pulled the towel tighter around my body. 'Anyway, thanks for doing that,' I said. 'I appreciate it.'

'No, it's fine. I enjoyed talking to her – she's sweet, really.' This struck me as strange: I was fairly sure that no one had ever described Mari as 'sweet' before. 'In some ways she seems younger than you.'

'Really?'

'I just get the sense she's not completely sure of herself, even though she blusters around a bit. You're more – I don't know.'

'What?'

'Well, you've got this quiet confidence about you. It's kind of scary, actually.' He picked up the necklace again and slid the beads back and forth along the string. On the roof, I heard the hollow tap of rain. 'You seem like the kind of person who always gets what she wants.'

We looked at each other and the silence between us felt thick. I could feel my cheeks prickling, and I was very aware of the existence of my lips. Jack put the necklace down and came to sit beside me on the bed.

'I think I might have mentioned this before,' he said, 'but it's really good to see you again.'

'Did you miss me?'

'Yeah. I did.'

'Aren't you going to ask me my opinions about Syria?'

'Maybe later.'

When he touched my cheek, I let my breath out in a sigh. I couldn't help it. I'd been worried that kissing him again would be strange, but the scent of his skin turned my brain woolly and unfocused, and when he asked me if I'd missed him, I heard myself say yes. In bed he was slower and more tender than before; he touched my face and said my name a lot, and my body felt small and open, like a flower, under his touch.

5

I'M SURE I'LL see you soon, he'd said, and he'd been right. In the first few weeks of the new year, Mari saw Jack often – Elisabeth seemed to bring him everywhere, to all their parties and dinners and drinks. He charmed all their friends, except Heidi, who told Mari that she considered the age gap between him and Elisabeth to be 'pretty sus'.

Mari rolled her eyes, irritated in a way she couldn't quite identify. 'You're being a puritan, Heids,' she said. 'It's not the 1950s.'

'Actually, that kind of thing was common in the 1950s. It's the mark of a patriarchal society, you know – older men with younger women, taking advantage. We're supposed to have moved past that by now.'

'Do you think that's what he's doing? Taking advantage?'

'Maybe he doesn't mean to, but you can't narrow these things down to individual intent, can you?'

'I think you're being silly,' Mari said shortly. 'Elisabeth can look after herself, she's not an idiot.'

'I never said she was an idiot. I just wonder if she's in over her head.'

Mari found it hard to imagine Elisabeth being in over her head. Historically, Elisabeth's problem with romantic relationships – as she'd explained to Mari several times – was that she couldn't be with someone she didn't respect, and she couldn't respect someone who wasn't intelligent, and most people weren't intelligent. Mari also suspected that the things she liked most about Elisabeth – her intellect, her sharp sense of humour, the way she always knew what she thought about everything – were the things that sometimes turned other people off. Once, at the pub, a friend of Heidi's had referred to Elisabeth as a 'stuck-up bitch'. Elisabeth hadn't been there to hear the remark, and no one had ever told her about it, but it had upset Mari so badly that she'd cried furious tears on the way home. The worst part was that she hadn't had the courage to defend Elisabeth, the way she knew Elisabeth would have defended her.

Elisabeth was staying at Jack's house three or four nights a week, she told Mari. He made dinner for her, and breakfast before she left the next morning. 'He's actually a good cook,' she said. 'I thought he'd be like you, toast for dinner and that kind of thing, but he really cares about food. He made me dumplings the other day from scratch.'

Mari didn't find this surprising at all. She could picture Jack being fastidious about cooking, buying expensive ingredients and measuring the exact amounts of everything. The fact that Elisabeth hadn't immediately seen this aspect of his character made Mari feel like she'd won a small, anonymous victory. 'House-trained and everything,' she said. 'Does he do the washing up too?'

Elisabeth smiled and tucked a strand of wet hair behind her ear. They were at the reservoir, bobbing side by side in the water. 'I tried to do it once and he wouldn't let me,' she said. 'He just puts everything in the dishwasher.'

'Oh well, he's an academic. I guess he's not familiar with the concept of hard work.'

'He'd probably say the same thing about us.'

'Well, we aren't paid as much as him.'

'Yeah, but shouldn't the goal be to get paid as much as possible for doing as little as possible? It's not, like, a sign of political virtue to be broke.'

Mari decided to let it go. Elisabeth said she was going for a swim, and she kicked off from the floating barrier and breaststroked out into the middle of the reservoir. Mari watched her body move steadily through the water, the sky stretched taut overhead like a piece of blue silk. A few times, when Mari and Jack had run into each other at some social occasion, she'd seen him looking at her with a hint of wry humour on his face; the same look he'd had when he found her on the back deck wearing only a T-shirt and underwear. She'd let herself feel the pleasure of that look, just for a few seconds, before turning away to strike up a conversation with someone else. Afterwards, standing under the spray of the shower at home, she would have the sudden, blank thought: Stupid girl. It was as if a loudspeaker were playing in her head: Stupid, stupid. The sentiment held some degree of confused pleasure, and the pleasure made her feel worse.

Elisabeth swam back and grabbed onto the barrier, only a little out of breath. 'You should come for dinner one night,' she said.

'What?'

'With me and Jack. It'll be fun.'

Mari kicked her legs thickly under the water. 'Tempting,' she said. 'But I think I'm washing my hair that night. I don't really want to be your third wheel.'

Elisabeth rolled her eyes. Mari saw that it had been the wrong thing to say: the concept of a third wheel was too conventional for Elisabeth. 'It's not like that,' she said.

'Well, what's it like? I mean, not to embrace heteronormative labels or anything, but isn't he your boyfriend these days?'

Elisabeth trailed her fingers through the water. Mari let the silence draw out – it was unusual, and a little enjoyable, to watch Elisabeth struggle for an answer. Eventually Elisabeth said, 'I don't know. I feel like he's probably too old for the title of boyfriend.'

Mari laughed. 'Don't tell him that, it'd kill him.'

'No, I won't.' Elisabeth dived under the water briefly and surfaced, her face pearled with shimmering droplets. 'Actually, I usually forget how old he is. Just sometimes he'll do something middle-aged.'

'Like what?'

'Like, I asked him if he was on the apps, you know, before we met? And he said he found all those things appalling.'

'Well. He's not wrong.'

'No, but he had a whole ideological objection. Something something commodification of human emotions, something something quantifying sexual desire and turning it into data to extract profit, something something.' They both laughed. 'Anyway, so there's that. And sometimes he says his back hurts.'

'Well, everyone's back hurts.'

'True.'

Mari skimmed her hand across the surface of the glassy brown water. 'Heidi thinks he's taking advantage of you,' she said. 'Because he's so much older.'

Elisabeth smiled, as if Heidi's opinions were amusing in how simplistic and wrong they were. 'Is that what you think?'

'No.'

'Good.'

She said it lightly, resting her arms on the barrier, and Mari felt a small pulse of pleasure at her approval. A coot glided past, trailing a faint line of ripples. 'Okay,' Mari said. 'I'll come for dinner, why not.'

'Cool. He'll like cooking for you, I bet.'

Mari thought that was probably right: Jack struck her as the type of person who enjoyed himself most when he had an audience, especially an audience of women. It was pleasurable, if a little strange, to think of him performing for her. She let go of her pool noodle and felt herself sink under the water slowly, almost lazily. Her hair floated out; her feet drifted into a current of cold. The water in the reservoir was too deep to ever touch the bottom. When she kicked herself to the surface, Elisabeth was swimming out to the middle again.

•

THAT FRIDAY EVENING, Mari walked to Jack's flat wearing a black dress and red sandals. The sun was setting, turning the sky lush and heavy with colour, and she could smell damp earth and roasting meat. Before she left she'd spent a long time looking in the mirror, noticing the things that were wrong with her face and wishing she knew how to use makeup. She climbed the stairs to Jack's flat and banged on the door.

When Jack opened it he was saying something over his shoulder to Elisabeth, Mari couldn't quite hear what. He turned to face her, smiling, and her stomach dipped. 'Hello,' he said. 'You came.'

She swallowed. 'As instructed.'

'Well, come in. Elisabeth's in the kitchen.'

She followed him down a hallway to the living room, which opened onto the kitchen. Elisabeth was standing at the kitchen counter slicing onions, and when they came in she looked up and smiled. Her eyes were streaming, but she looked pretty in her loose striped T-shirt and high-waisted denim shorts, a gold triangular pendant on a delicate chain around her neck. In comparison, Mari felt overdressed and hulkingly tall. She wondered what would happen if she took off all her clothes or threw a plate against the wall.

'Hi,' Elisabeth said, wiping her eyes with her forearm. 'Sorry, these onions are making me cry.'

'Poor thing.' Jack tore a paper towel from a roll and dabbed at Elisabeth's eyes, holding her elbow gently with his other hand. 'Go and pour Mari a drink, you're released from further duties.'

Elisabeth fetched a glass from a cupboard and filled it with straw-coloured wine. Her movements were sure and precise: clearly, she was familiar with the kitchen's small universe. Mari sat on a stool at the counter and watched Jack roll pasta dough, a tea towel over one shoulder. The tea towel made him look domestic and a little vulnerable. Music was playing softly from a record player in the living room – Mari recognised *Moon Safari*. It would have been Jack's choice, not Elisabeth's. Elisabeth didn't care about music.

Mari twisted her legs around the stool. On her own back deck, smoking her cigarettes, it had been easy enough to handle Jack just by being ironic. But in his flat, drinking unpronounceable wine from a bottle with a stylishly understated label, she felt a little shy. 'Your place is nice,' she said.

'Thank you.'

'Do you rent it? Or own?'

'Oh, well, I got lucky – I bought it about ten years ago, before real estate prices started really taking off. I'm sure I wouldn't be able to afford it these days.'

Mari sipped her wine. She had the sense – familiar from their other conversations – that he'd made the comment as an invitation to tease him, and there was a certain pleasure in picking up the rope he'd thrown to her. 'You know, anyone can look up academic salaries on the university website,' she said.

'Well, a lot of that goes to tax.'

'Right, very convenient.' She turned to Elisabeth. 'How much did this wine cost?'

Elisabeth smiled, leaning back against the kitchen counter with her wineglass cupped lightly in one hand. 'You know it's gauche to talk about how much things cost,' she said. 'But I think about a quarter of my weekly rent.'

'All right, calm down,' Jack said. He was smiling, cutting the long roll of dough into small delicate shapes. 'The wine cost somewhere between twenty and forty dollars, there's no need to go into specifics. Mari, tell us about work. What were my substantial tax dollars spent on today?'

'Oh no. Don't make me talk about that place, it's bad enough having to go there. I'm considered the office radical because I live in West End and ride a bike.'

'Mari has a healthy contempt for her colleagues,' Elisabeth told Jack.

'Yes, I can tell. Mari, haven't you ever heard of making common cause with your fellow workers? Comrades in struggle and all that?'

'I don't want to be comrades in struggle with those people.'

He laughed, as she'd hoped he would. 'So what's your plan, then? Long term, I mean. Is there a job out there that wouldn't earn your total disdain?'

'Probably not.' He was looking down at the bench when she said this, but she saw his mouth move into a little smile. It was gratifying to know that she made him smile privately to himself. 'Anyway, didn't you tell me that it's fine to work a dead-end job? Normal for someone my age?'

'That's right, I did. Good memory.'

Mari's cheeks warmed. It wasn't really a compliment, and probably he didn't even mean it, but she still felt wrong-footed and a little exposed. She reached for her wine. The conversation moved onto a more general discussion of the job market, and Jack told them that he had seen a posting earlier that day for a lecturer in the School of Philosophy. 'I thought of you,' he said to Elisabeth. 'That's one job going in philosophy, at least.'

'Should I apply?'

'Well, you're not entirely qualified. But I'm sure you'd be a better candidate than most of the applicants.'

Mari watched pleasure move over Elisabeth's face, even as she tried to hide it. 'Flattery will get you everywhere,' she said lightly.

It occurred to Mari that it had already got Jack quite far, but she decided not to say this out loud. 'I can see you as a philosophy lecturer,' she said to Elisabeth. 'Dressed all in black, talking about the impossibility of knowledge or whatever. You should go for it.'

'Is that a compliment?'

'I'm just saying it would suit you. You'll become wildly successful, and I'll still be living in a share house and smoking weed when I'm thirty-five.' Mari poured a little more wine into her glass. 'I should probably move to Melbourne just for something to do.'

Jack smiled. 'Living in a share house and smoking weed isn't too bad, surely.'

'You say that, but you haven't had to listen to one of Heidi's vacuuming lectures recently. Anyway, you're rich, you can afford to romanticise it.'

'I'm not rich. And I don't think I romanticise it.'

Mari knew this wasn't true. Whenever he came to one of their houses, she saw him looking at everything – the worn furniture, the cleaning rosters on the fridge, the Stop Adani signs on the fence – with something like longing on his face. A complicated longing, because at bottom she suspected he didn't want to give up his air conditioning or his dishwasher. Yet he envied them. She didn't quite understand this, or know how to put it into words, so instead she said, 'Stop lying about being rich.'

He laughed. 'All right, I'm well paid, but I still have to sell my labour time. Listen, Mari, don't move to Melbourne. It's cold and expensive down there, you wouldn't like it. Stay here in the nouveau subtropics.'

'Oh, the nouveau subtropics, how romantic. More like, Brisbane – it's not Sydney, it's not Melbourne, it's the other one.'

'The liminal space of your dreams,' said Elisabeth. 'The world's best in-between city.'

'That does sound romantic,' said Jack. 'In its own way.'

They ate dinner in the small dining nook off the kitchen. Mari was onto her third glass of wine by the time they sat down, and she felt happy and light-headed. She could tell that Elisabeth was also in a good mood: she let Mari do most of the talking, but she chimed in at crucial points with observations that were always clever and astute, bringing the conversation into a new light. Being around Elisabeth, with her assured brilliance – which people always recognised, even if they didn't like it – made Mari feel a tiny bit assured and brilliant by association. Whenever Elisabeth laughed at her jokes, Mari felt as though she'd won a prize.

It was almost ten by the time they moved to the living room. Jack sat in a chair and Elisabeth lay on the couch, the curve of her neck like a carved piece of marble against her curls. Mari sprawled on the rug. The ceiling fan was spinning lazily, stirring the fronds of Jack's potted palm, but the air was damp and sticky. Mari fanned herself with one hand.

'Do you want me to turn on the air conditioning?' Jack asked.

She shook her head. In fact, she didn't mind the humidity of a Brisbane summer night; there was an enjoyable sensuality in the way it reduced everyone into their bodies. 'No, that's okay,' she said. 'Very chivalrous of you, though.'

He laughed. 'I thought chivalry was dead for your generation.'

'It's not dead, it just means different things. Like, men our age think it's chivalrous to go down on you for longer than two minutes. But I'm sure you're very good in that department too.'

He got up to refill his drink, but Mari could see that he was pressing his lips together, trying not to laugh. Elisabeth gave Mari a look of mild reprimand. 'Anyway,' Mari said, as Jack came back in with another bottle of wine. 'Chivalrous or not, I suppose I should ask you what your intentions are with Elisabeth.'

'Oh really? I think you should ask what her intentions are with me.'

Elisabeth laughed. Mari saw that it had been exactly the right thing to say, and Jack looked pleased as he sat down.

'I'm actually mostly in it for the apartment,' Elisabeth said, glancing at him and then back at Mari. 'It's such good real estate.'

'If you play your cards right, you could inherit,' Mari said. 'Probably won't have too long to wait.'

'That's what I thought too.'

They caught each other's smiles. Mari reached for the wine bottle and refilled her own glass, leaning back against the couch so that her head touched Elisabeth's leg. She was drunk in a pleasant, floating way. It occurred to her that Elisabeth hadn't tried to film them all evening, which seemed like a positive sign; maybe, with Jack, her personality could unwind itself a little. He did seem to have a talent for bringing out the best in people. Even when he'd come to see Mari over the Christmas break, he'd made her feel – she could admit it now, with the alcohol blurring her mind – as if he found her particularly amusing or interesting, as if she had something to offer him. It was strange.

It was late by the time she got up to leave. Standing up required more effort than she'd anticipated, and for a moment the room spun and rocked around her. She couldn't remember how many glasses of wine she'd had, but it now seemed like categorically too many.

'Are you okay to get home?' Jack asked. 'I can give you a lift, if you want.'

'Oh, thanks, I'll be fine. It's only a few blocks.'

'If you're sure.'

His voice was polite but mild, as if he were detaching himself from the whole problem of her existence. It reminded Mari of the afternoon when he'd sat on her back deck and said: As you know, Elisabeth asked me to. She watched Elisabeth collecting their empty wineglasses from the floor, hooking her fingers lightly between their rims. Something about the proprietary nature of the gesture irritated Mari, although she wasn't quite sure why. She wanted to say: You know you don't actually own this place.

They went down the hallway towards the front door. Jack had left it open, and Mari could feel the cool air coming through, wafting against her face and chest. When Elisabeth moved to hug her goodbye, Mari decided all at once to kiss her on the mouth. It was a gentle little kiss, it didn't last more than a few seconds, but when they broke apart Elisabeth's cheeks were pink. Mari felt a stab of pleasure and triumph. 'Goodnight,' she said.

She was aware that Jack was looking at them, but she didn't look his way. Elisabeth smiled and said, 'Goodnight,' in a small voice. Mari walked down the hallway and let herself out. She wanted to laugh.

When she got home, Heidi asked how it was. 'Oh, fine,' Mari said.

'Just fine?'

Mari shrugged. She had sobered up a little on the walk home, and now she had the feeling of holding the evening secretly within herself, letting it crystallise and take shape. Later on she would find out what it looked like. 'It was a nice dinner,' she said. 'Homemade pasta. They're playing house over there, it's all very sweet.'

•

AFTER MARI LEFT we cleaned up the kitchen, not saying much. I liked doing household chores with Jack, it made me feel like we lived together, although I never would have told him that. As we were getting ready for bed, he said, 'Are you sure Mari would have been all right getting home? I thought maybe I should've insisted on driving her.'

'She'll be fine. She walks home at night all the time.'

He was in the bathroom brushing his teeth. I heard him spit and run the tap, and then he came wandering into the bedroom.

'All right,' he said. 'I just noticed the class warfare about the price of wine didn't stop her from drinking most of the bottle.'

He said it mildly, as if he found it more amusing than anything else. I thought of Mari calling him a wealthy benefactor. I knew that really he enjoyed paying for things, it wasn't just because he had money. 'Well, it was nice wine,' I said. 'Anyway, I think she enjoyed herself.'

'Were you worried that she wouldn't?'

'No, not worried. I knew you'd have a talent for hosting.'

He smiled at that. He was sitting on the end of the bed, leaning back on his hands. 'What's her romantic history, out of interest?' he asked. 'Has she ever had a serious partner?'

I was changing into the nightgown I kept at his flat, and I pulled it over my head before answering. In truth, Mari had a habit of falling into brief and intense entanglements with men who treated her poorly, usually insofar as they were using her to either end or get over a more serious relationship with someone else. She always became very depressed when these flings disintegrated, but she never showed any sign of trying to break the habit in future.

'Not really, no,' I said. 'Why do you ask?'

'Oh, I was just wondering. I mean, she's funny and everything, but she's a bit of an unstable person, isn't she? Not like you.'

I felt a prickle of unease: it was the first unkind sentiment I'd ever heard him express. 'Don't say that about her,' I said.

'All right, sorry.'

'She's really smart, you know. She reads more than I do. Anyway, it's not her fault if she's a bit . . .' I paused. 'She had a hard time when she was younger. Her mum's not the easiest person in the world.'

'That's right, she told me about all that.'

'She told you? When?'

'Oh, just when I went to visit her over the Christmas break – we talked a bit about her childhood, school, that kind of thing. You're right, the mother does sound like a difficult character.'

I got into bed and pulled the sheet carefully over my body. Among our friends, I was the only one who knew the full story of Mari's background. It was a little hurtful to hear that she'd told Jack, especially when she hardly knew him. But of course, he was so personable, so understanding; I could see why women loved to tell him things. 'Okay,' I said. 'Well, you should cut her some slack.'

'No, you're right. I'm sorry.' He got into bed and handed me the air-conditioning remote so I could set the temperature how I liked it. 'Hey, that was an affectionate little farewell, though. Is that how the two of you usually say goodnight?'

I concentrated on pressing the buttons on the remote. Truthfully, Mari had never kissed me that way before, and I had no idea what it meant. 'No,' I said. 'Not usually.'

'So I shouldn't be jealous?'

'I didn't think you were the jealous type.'

He put his arm around me and kissed the side of my head, and I let myself relax against him. 'I'm not,' he said gently. 'Anyway, it was nice, having her over. We should do it again before semester starts, while I have a bit more time.'

'What, you won't have time to see us after semester starts?'

'Not as much time. Evenings and weekends, really, I'll be working during the day.'

'Well, I could come and meet you for lunch on campus. I've always wondered what the staff club was like.'

I felt him tense. 'What?' I said.

'What? Oh, nothing. The staff club's not very good, darling.'

I had noticed that he called me 'darling' whenever he wanted to affect a kind of ironic distance between us, often as a way of papering over an awkward moment. ('I'm paying, darling,' he'd say when the bill came at a restaurant.) It was never a mark of particular sincerity.

'Okay,' I said. 'We could go somewhere else, then. You pick.'

'Mmm. Yeah, maybe.'

'What's the matter?' I said lightly. 'Don't want to be seen with me in public?'

'I'm seen with you in public all the time.'

'But on campus is a different story.'

He sighed, rubbing one hand over his face. 'Well, you have to admit that if people saw us together on campus, they'd probably assume you were my student.'

'But I'm not.'

He didn't reply.

'Look,' I said. 'This seems a bit uneven, that's all. We have Mari over for dinner. You come with me to parties and things like that, with my friends. But you won't let anyone you know catch sight of me. It's not illegal, you know – I'm twenty-five, not fifteen.'

He laughed under his breath. 'Yes, practically ancient.'

'But you see what I'm saying.'

'Yes. No, I do.'

'Okay. So have you ever thought about introducing me to anyone you know? Your friends, your family?'

'Mmm.' He was looking at the ceiling. 'Well, to be honest, no.'

'You haven't even thought about it.'

'Oh, look, it's not that I'm embarrassed by you, don't get that idea. It's more that I'm embarrassed by them. And myself, a little bit. Nothing to do with you.'

I was quiet. On the wall opposite, cold air churned and rushed out of the air conditioner. 'Are you feeding me a line?' I asked.

'Am I what? Am I feeding you a line?'

'*It's not you, it's me.* I'm not an idiot, you know. I might not have a PhD but I'm not an idiot.'

'Elisabeth –'

'I know you smoke, for example.' When I was in a mood like this, I felt like a snake stalking some small prey through the grass, striking again and again until the prey was dead. 'You pretend you don't because I don't, and because I tell Mari not to, but I've seen your cigarettes hidden at the back of the bookshelf. It's not the most inventive hiding place, you know.'

'Jesus. Okay. Sometimes when you're not here I have one or two after dinner, is that all right? I'm an adult, you know, I can decide these things for myself.'

'Oh, I know, you're such an adult. What are you even doing with a child like me?'

He shook his head. I curled away from him, misery settling over me like a heavy coat.

'Elisabeth,' he said after a minute. 'Listen. Of course I don't think you're a child.'

I didn't reply.

'That would be fairly problematic for lots of reasons. Actually, I find you very . . . Oh, I don't know.'

I stared at the corner of the pillowcase. In a small voice, I said, 'You can't start that sentence and not finish it.'

He laughed quietly. 'All right. Well, I think you're extremely intelligent, as I've said. And obviously I find you very attractive, that goes without saying.'

I turned slowly back towards him. 'You can still say it.'

'Okay.' He held my face between his hands. 'I find you very attractive. Is that better?'

'A bit better.'

'A bit, okay. But it's not just that – you're so switched-on, you always have something funny and interesting to say. Honestly, that's what I was trying to get at before – all my friends seem old and dull compared to you. But then, I suppose they are. I suppose I am too.'

'I don't think you're dull,' I said. 'Old maybe, but not dull.'

It was a barbed little joke, the kind Mari and I made all the time. I didn't think Jack would mind, but I saw him flinch. 'Sorry,' I said quickly. 'That was just a joke.'

'Well, no, there's no point denying it. I'm twenty years older than you. Technically I'm old enough to be your father, as much as I hate to say it.'

'So?'

'Well, don't you ever think about that?'

'Not really. I mean, you're not my father, so there's that.'

'Oh, thanks. That's very comforting, I think Freud would be convinced by that argument.'

'Well, what I mean is, I know you're a lot older than me and obviously that shapes the dynamic between us; it's not the same as if you were my age. But I don't really think about it consciously, it's just who you are.'

'Yeah,' he said quietly. 'I guess that is who I am.'

I hated seeing him so sad. I pressed my face into his neck and he put his arms around me, a bit absent-mindedly. I thought about saying: I love you, but instead I said, 'You make me really happy.'

He tightened his grip a little. 'Do I?'

'Yeah. Really, really happy.'

'Good. You make me really happy too. Probably more than you know.'

I lifted my face, and our eyes met. He ran his finger across my cheek and onto my lips. He rested it there, still looking at me, and again I thought: I love you. The thought was clear and definite, like a stone dropping into a pond. I kissed his finger, and then I took it into my mouth, holding his gaze. He sucked his breath in and said my name, softly, as if he were saying it to himself.

I took his finger out of my mouth and trailed it down my throat, between my breasts. He stayed still, waiting for me to do the next thing. I took my nightgown off. In the moment I lifted it over my head, it was Mari I thought about: her soft little mouth, tasting of cigarettes. Then the thought was gone. Jack looked at me, his pupils big and black. I brushed my fingers against his cheek and he let his breath out in a long exhale. We looked at each other quietly, and when he reached for a condom I almost said: No, don't worry about it.

The moment the thought crossed my mind I felt terrified, like I was driving a car and couldn't reach the brakes. I tried to forget it. He kissed my neck, and in my ear he said how good it felt, how good I felt to him. Afterwards I found I had tears on my cheeks. I brushed them away quickly, hoping he hadn't noticed.

I turned on my side, he rested his hand on my hip, and I let my eyes close. The room was cool by then. I was beginning to feel heavy and swim-headed when he said, 'Listen, you're right, of course. It's not fair to keep you separate from the rest of my life.'

I rolled over to look at him. 'So . . .'

'So, yeah. I'll try to figure something out. Leave it with me, all right?'

'All right.' He turned out the light, I heard him sigh, and I took his hand and held it in mine.

6

MARI DID COME for dinner again, and then she came a third time. It was around then that we began spending a lot of time together: me, Mari, and Jack. The dynamic between the three of us wasn't exactly clear, but in those days I didn't feel any particular need to define it. It was enough to be happy, to do happy things together – to take a picnic and go swimming at the reservoir; to drive to the Byron Bay hinterland and have lunch at a Japanese restaurant. (We went to a lot of restaurants, because Jack paid for everything.) On the way back we stopped to swim at a deserted little beach, and Mari lay on the sand and took her bikini top off. 'Like the Europeans,' she said. I told her she was going to get sunburned.

She just laughed. She and I were getting along well that summer – we didn't get on each other's nerves, or have stupid arguments. I was rostered on morning shifts and she was still working three days a week, so we had a lot of free time and we spent it mostly together. She never mentioned kissing me that night in Jack's hallway. I still didn't know why she'd done it, and for a while I rehearsed different ways to ask her, but I didn't want to make a big deal out of something she considered insignificant. It was true that she'd drunk a lot of wine that night, so it was entirely possible that she didn't even remember.

Jack had to work more often than we did. Sometimes we met up with him in the evenings, but we spent the days without him doing things that we instinctively agreed – although we never discussed it – were too juvenile for him to enjoy. We shoplifted expensive cheese from the supermarket and had a picnic in the park. (We realised once we got there that we'd forgotten to get crackers, so we ate it with our fingers.) We found apartment complexes with unlocked pools to swim in. Once we got very high and wandered around the art gallery, whispering to each other about the paintings until we cried with laughter and they asked us to leave. We knew that if we hadn't been white the encounter would have gone differently, and we had a slightly stilted discussion about this on the bus home. But when we told Jack, he just said, 'Ah, the youth of today have it so easy. In my day they would've called the cops on you. No law and order in this country anymore.'

'Oh, let's not get into memories of Joh Bjelke-Petersen,' Mari said. 'It's so boring.'

'Joh Bjelke-Petersen?' said Jack, laughing. 'Mari, how old do you think I am?'

Jack talked about himself sometimes, but he was mostly interested in us. When we were alone together, he asked me about everything: my childhood, my feelings about my family, my plans for the future. If we went to the cinema, we'd walk home discussing what I thought of the movie, and he'd only offer his opinion if I prodded him. Once he saw me looking at the painting on his bedroom wall, a canvas painted half red and half blue. 'Which one are you?' he asked, pointing at it. 'Red or blue?'

'Blue,' I said. 'We're both blue.' It was true – I saw in him my own mild temper, my occasional coolness. Heidi, who believed in astrology, would have said it was because we were both water signs. Mari was a fire sign, the red half of the canvas.

When she was around, he liked to hear about the small dramas of our friends, their couplings and partings. (He was a bit awed by the wide array of these – once he asked, 'Aren't any of your friends just heterosexual?' 'What's that?' Mari said.) He wanted to know what we read and watched and listened to – sometimes his interest struck me as almost academic, an effort to construct an understanding through primary sources.

Mari just said it was because he was so old. She liked to tease him about his age: she'd tell him, during one of their long conversations about music, that he had good taste for a middle-aged man. She gave him the names of bands he should listen to, and when he asked if she'd make him a CD, she laughed and said, 'Oh my God, haven't you heard of Spotify? Do you want me to download it for you?'

'No, all right, I have heard of it. I'll download it myself, thanks.'

'You do know what an app is, right? You're familiar with the basic concept?'

He rolled his eyes, but the following week I noticed that he'd downloaded Spotify and was listening to some of the music she liked. She was a purist about classic literature, but Jack began looking through my bookshelf, borrowing Rebecca Solnit and Miranda July. For his birthday in February I gave him a copy of *I Love Dick*, and when he unwrapped it, he laughed a lot.

'Subtle,' said Mari. She was sitting across from us, drinking champagne. The table was cluttered with plates and glasses – Jack had cooked for us; he said he preferred that to going out. Earlier that evening we'd talked him into giving us his credit card so we could buy some champagne, and we'd chosen the most expensive bottle we could find. When we got back and told him the price, he'd looked a bit pale, but hadn't objected.

'Mind in the gutter,' I said to Mari. 'It's a good book.'

'No, I look forward to reading this,' said Jack. 'Especially in public. On the ferry, maybe, or before a committee meeting.' He leaned his head back, looking at the ceiling. 'Forty-five, Jesus. I can't believe it.'

'Old as the hills,' Mari said.

'Feels that way. Forty-four was bearable – you know, still technically early forties, not too far off late thirties. But forty-five, that's too old. That's objectively too old.'

'Are you having a midlife crisis?'

'I do seem to have acquired a much younger girlfriend. Cause for concern, isn't it?'

I pushed my finger through the sauce on my plate. It was the first time he'd called me his girlfriend, but given the context, it didn't seem like a particular compliment. Mari caught my eye and grinned, and I looked away.

'Anyway,' Jack said. 'What about you, Mari? Surely you didn't come empty-handed.'

'No, don't worry your greedy little heart.' From her bag she took a small squarish package wrapped in pink paper and threw it across the table to him. 'There you go. Happy birthday.'

Jack unwrapped it. It was a pack of cigarettes. He was laughing; Mari was too. 'To hasten your demise,' she said. 'Now you're forty-five you're nearly at the end anyway, so one pack shouldn't hurt.'

'Brutal,' he said. 'Okay, well, thank you. Seeing as it's my birthday, I think I should be allowed to smoke one or two.'

He passed the pack around and we all took one; even I did. Neither of them commented on this. We smoked in peaceful silence, all of us a little drunk. I sat with my legs across Jack's lap and thought about how sophisticated the scene would look: the champagne drifting bubbles in long flutes, the cigarettes trailing delicate plumes of smoke. From across the table Mari was watching me with an amused look, like she knew what I was thinking.

•

'SO TELL ME, are you fucking both of them?' Paul asked. It was Saturday evening, and he and Heidi were making mojitos. Mari was sitting at the table, eating a piece of toast. 'I mean, is it a threesome kind of situation? I'm not judging, I just want to know.'

Mari bit a neat semicircle from her toast. 'You think everything is about sex.'

'That doesn't answer my question.'

She rolled her eyes. 'No, I'm not fucking both of them. If you must know, I'm not even fucking one of them. Happy?'

'Well, like I said, I wouldn't judge. If anything, it's the cradle-robbing aspect I object to, rather than the ménage à trois aspect.'

'There is no ménage à trois aspect, I already told you. We're just friends.'

'Right, just friends, I see. Say no more.'

'Okay,' said Mari, irritated. 'I won't.'

From the other side of the kitchen, Heidi said, 'Leave her alone, Paul, you're meant to be slicing those limes. Mari, are you coming to Verity's later?'

'Oh, yeah. Maybe.'

While Heidi and Paul were occupied with an argument about sugar-to-rum ratios, Mari slipped out the front door and walked to the bar around the corner. The air was warm and thick, frangipani blossoms scattering the footpath, and fruit bats were screeching in the trees. She skipped and trailed her fingers along paling fences. Her friends were always talking about leaving Brisbane, everyone had it in the back of their minds that one day they'd leave, but on nights like these the idea seemed patently ridiculous. She thought of Elisabeth saying: The liminal space of your dreams. It was the kind of thing that would have sounded pretentious coming from anyone else.

When she arrived at the bar she found Jack and Elisabeth at a table near the back, a third drink sitting between them and dripping condensation on a coaster. Mari sat down and drained half of it in one swallow. She felt high, full of pleasure at seeing them and at escaping the boring prospect of Verity's party. 'Should we dance?' she asked Elisabeth. 'Let's dance.'

Elisabeth made a face. 'No, you know how bad I am. Dance with Jack.'

Mari flicked Jack's shoulder with her fingernails. 'I don't know,' he said. 'It's a bit early, isn't it?'

'Oh, come on. Or is dancing off the agenda at your age?'

He rolled his eyes, but she knew he wasn't really annoyed. He never responded to her mocking with anything other than cheerful equanimity. At these moments Mari often found herself feeling a little disappointed, as if a part of her wanted to be able to hurt him.

'All right,' he said, getting to his feet and holding his hand out to her. 'Come on, then.'

Mari took his hand. She expected him to drop it once she was standing up, but he kept holding it as they walked towards the dance floor, in a firm but relaxed grip. She remembered Elisabeth saying that he was a classic firm-handshake person. She'd been right, of course.

They danced together for one song, not touching very much, which Mari was thankful for. Just holding his hand had made her body feel lightweight and out of her control, as if it were a kite that might fly away at any moment. Jack was a good dancer, and she leaned closer to tell him that, shouting over the music, 'You're a good dancer!'

'So are you. Dancing is like fucking, don't you think?'

'How's that?'

'If you think too much, it doesn't work.'

She laughed. When the song finished she told him she was going to buy another round of drinks, and he took out his wallet and said, 'Here, take my card.'

'That's okay, I can afford it.'

'I know you can, but take the card anyway.'

'Jack, it's fine. It's government money, I should spread it around.'

'So's mine, I just happen to get a lot more of it than you.'

'Ah, but your work is much more important than mine. Shaping young minds, educating the future thought leaders of tomorrow . . .' She had only had one drink, but she felt quite drunk. It was surprising.

He was laughing. 'Mari, stop messing around. Take the card.'

She took it. Waiting at the bar, she ran her thumb over the raised letters that spelled out Jack's name.

When she got back to the table, Elisabeth looked up and smiled. 'How was the dancing?' she asked. 'Can Jack dance?'

Mari could feel Jack looking at her, but she kept her eyes on Elisabeth's face. 'He didn't totally embarrass me,' she said. 'Only about thirty per cent.'

'Thirty per cent isn't bad,' Jack said. 'I remember when I got to university there were parties every weekend, and it was the first time I'd ever seen people dancing. Apart from at weddings, I mean, and it was a bit different from your average country wedding. And all the girls seemed so grown-up, and they knew how to dance, and they were so beautiful . . . It was pretty thrilling, really, in the way that being hugely intimidated can be thrilling.'

Mari was taken aback; she couldn't imagine Jack being anything other than completely at ease with women. 'But you must have had girlfriends before then,' she said. 'In high school, I mean.'

'No. Actually, I was a virgin until about halfway through my first year of university.'

Mari sipped her drink, trying not to show her surprise. 'Interesting,' she said. 'But I guess things were different back then. In – when was this again? The 1940s?'

'Oh, very droll. No, it was the 1990s, and if anything, sexual mores were more permissive than they are now. People didn't worry so much about power dynamics and so on.' He smiled. 'That makes me sound antiquated, doesn't it?'

'A bit,' Elisabeth said affectionately.

'Ah well. But anyway, I was quite shy as a teenager, and I went to an all-boys high school, so there weren't many opportunities for anything. Actually, if there was a power dynamic between me and the girls I did come across, I think I was very much on the wrong end of it. Or that's how it felt, anyway. I'm sure it was more complicated than that.' He shrugged. 'In any case, when I finally got the chance to sleep with a woman, I couldn't quite believe it, I kept waiting for her to change her mind. But it was her first time too, so I think she was almost as keen to get it over with as I was.'

'What was it like?' Mari asked. 'Were you scared?'

'Yeah, in a way. I was scared I wouldn't be any good, and I only had the vaguest idea of what "good" even meant for a girl. And I was scared of hurting her, but I knew I'd have to, and I hated that idea, but on the other hand, you know . . . Anyway, I managed to stop overthinking it for long enough to do the deed. I can't imagine she got much pleasure out of it, but neither did I – I remember feeling so self-conscious and apologetic.' He smiled. 'Not the most impressive debut.'

Mari felt a rush of affection for him – for the fumbling, well-meaning boy he must have been. A boy who was afraid of hurting girls. 'Well, neither was mine,' she said. 'But you already know about that.'

'Do I?'

'My English teacher. I told you, remember? That night you came to our party.'

'Oh, yes.' She saw his mouth tighten. 'I remember.'

Mari stirred her drink and looked away. Part of her wanted to push the conversation further – maybe by telling Jack all the graphic details that he didn't want to hear, that no one wanted to hear – but she stopped herself. 'Elisabeth should tell us hers,' she said.

Elisabeth looked up. 'What?'

'Your first time. Or have you already told him?'

'Oh, no. There isn't much to tell.'

Mari settled back in her seat. It was satisfying to hear that Jack didn't know this particular story, and as Elisabeth recounted it – her school friend Amelia, her bedroom after school, telling no one even when Amelia suddenly and cruelly broke it off – Mari chimed in with pertinent details. It was one of her favourite stories about Elisabeth because it showed her in a rare moment of vulnerability, crying every night for a week after Amelia had told her, via instant messenger, that she didn't want to 'hang out' anymore. A part of Mari wished she could go back in time and comfort that younger version of Elisabeth. But really she knew that Elisabeth hadn't needed comforting: once the crying was over, she'd torn out all the pages in her journal that mentioned Amelia's name, and had never spoken to her again.

'Jesus,' Jack said, once she had finished. 'That sounds intense.'

'Oh, it was just high school. Everything was intense. Besides, relationships between women are more . . .' She shrugged. 'I don't know. Everything runs at a higher frequency.'

'No offence,' Mari said to Jack.

He laughed. 'No, none taken.' He stood up to get another round of drinks, collecting their empty glasses from the table. He often made these kinds of quietly solicitous gestures: it was clear, Mari thought, that he enjoyed tending to women and was good at it. It occurred to her that his first time had probably been nowhere near as inept as he'd described.

She watched him walk up towards the bar. Halfway there he turned and came back to the table, holding out his hand to Mari. 'My card?' he said.

'What?'

'My credit card. Can I have it back?'

Mari glanced at Elisabeth and smiled. 'Oh, that,' she said. 'I thought I could keep it. Seeing as you're so keen on wealth redistribution.'

'Yes, hilarious.' To Elisabeth he said, 'I gave Mari my card to buy some drinks and now she's trying to exploit my socialist principles.'

'That'll teach you,' Elisabeth said. 'Never have principles.'

'Yeah,' said Jack. 'I'm beginning to think that's the way forward in life.' He shot Mari a brief glance as he said this. She slid the card across the table.

•

SEMESTER BEGAN AT the end of February, and Jack went back to work. I liked seeing him in his work clothes: narrow-legged chinos, polished shoes, a crisp ironed shirt. By evening the shirt was always slightly crumpled, and his eyes, behind his glasses, were a little tired. I found the overall effect extremely attractive, for reasons I neither understood nor particularly wanted to interrogate. Sometimes I almost said: You're so good-looking, but I knew he'd probably had a lifetime of women telling him that. He was the only person who had ever told me I was beautiful.

He spent most of his free time with me, and Mari was around a lot, too. On Fridays they'd both be in good moods, and we'd have dinner and stay up late talking. If it got very late, Mari stayed over on the couch. (She insisted she could walk home, but Jack said he'd never forgive himself if anything happened to her. She said he wasn't her father, and he said he thanked God for that every day, but would she just sleep on the couch?) Once when I got up early for a glass of water, I saw her asleep there, curled on her side with her hair brushing dark against her pale cheek. All at once I had the strange, exciting feeling that I was seeing into her secret life: the person she became when I wasn't around. If I could have woken her then and asked her why she'd kissed me, that night in Jack's hallway, I knew she would have told me. But as it was, she woke up and asked me if it was possible to die from a hangover.

One Friday in March, she didn't come to dinner because she'd agreed to go with Heidi to the opening night of Verity's play. Jack and I went out to a Mexican restaurant where the vegetarian tacos came topped with sliced radishes, delicate white circles blushing pink at their edges. The waitress was enthusiastic about everything we asked for. Later, I knew, she would hand the bill to Jack without even glancing at me. Probably I would never find out how much the meal cost.

The question of money had been on my mind recently, as things between me and Jack had settled into a routine. At first it had been fun to let him take me to places I couldn't afford, but I was increasingly conscious of myself as the beneficiary of his largesse. My life seemed a little pathetic compared to his. In small, secret moments, I liked to imagine that I lived in his flat, and that all his things – the Turkish rug, the heavy copper pans, the delicate stemless wineglasses – belonged to me. It was never entirely clear how Jack himself fit into this fantasy; I liked the idea of having his life, but I didn't like to imagine him not being there. I hadn't mentioned any of this to Mari. I knew she would have said that I was overthinking it.

I leaned my elbows on the table and picked out a cube of charred eggplant from my taco. 'Does it bother you to pay for everything?' I asked.

Jack glanced up at me. 'Does it bother me? No, why would it?'

'It doesn't seem fair, that's all. We go out to dinner all the time and you always pay. With Mari, too.'

'Well, Mari thinks I'm overpaid anyway. Look, honestly, it doesn't bother me – if anything, you're doing me a favour. The more money I spend on other people, the less guilty I feel about everything else.'

'Everything else?'

'Well, you know, the whole business of earning a six-figure salary in a world where sweatshops and slums exist.' He wiped his hands on a paper napkin. 'And for what, delivering a few lectures and writing about a dead Marxist? I don't know, sometimes I think Mari's got it right about academia.'

'Oh, you still fantasise about working in an Amazon warehouse?'

He looked at me blankly for a second, and then he laughed. 'Right, I'd forgotten about that.' We were sitting beside each other at a long table, and even though we were surrounded by people and he usually wasn't affectionate with me in public, he touched the nape of my neck. 'I was so surprised to see you that night,' he said softly. 'When you turned up at the seminar.'

'Were you?'

'Yeah, and you were really cool about it, like you did that kind of thing all the time. I felt so, I don't know, caught off guard. But in a good way. And I still remember that dress you were wearing, that blue one, it was very . . .' He smiled and broke off, lifting his fingers from my neck.

'Oh, I see,' I said. 'Were you objectifying me?'

'Yeah, probably. Sorry about that.'

He sounded embarrassed, and I laughed. I loved conversations like these, when he let me push him in whichever direction I wanted. 'Were you surprised when I kissed you?' I asked.

'Oh, very. Again, in a good way. But, as I think I said at the time, I didn't expect a work seminar on the 1944 referendum to take such an erotic turn.'

'Erotic, I love that.'

'What, you didn't think so?'

'No, I just meant – you have such an academic way of talking. You know, most people would say it was hot. But you go with *erotic*, like it's a piece of art or something.'

He laughed. 'Okay. Well, erotic, hot, whatever, it was pretty –' He stopped suddenly, glass halfway to his lips.

'What?'

He didn't reply. He wasn't looking at me. His eyes were fixed on a point behind me, and his face was arranged in an expression of polite acknowledgment, mouth curved in a smile. I started to turn, and he said quietly, 'Don't.'

I stayed still and watched him nod, raise his glass briefly in greeting. I had to admire the way he did it: polite but final, making it graciously clear that no further interaction was welcome. When he turned back to me, his face looked slack and tired, and he closed his eyes for a long moment before he said, 'Sorry.'

'Who was that?'

'A colleague.' He drained the rest of his drink in one swallow. 'He and his wife were just on their way out. I didn't see them when we came in. Sorry, Elisabeth, I just –'

'I asked you about that,' I said. My voice was small and tight, folded up like a piece of paper. 'You agreed.'

'No, I know. I'm sorry.' His tone sounded harried and somehow more adult, like I was a colleague asking him for a piece of work he hadn't done and privately didn't think was very important anyway.

I angled my body away from him, concentrating on breaking a tortilla chip into smaller and smaller pieces. I didn't feel like eating anymore.

After a while he said, 'Look, I just panicked when I saw them, I didn't have time to think. You have to understand, it's a bit difficult.'

'Difficult how?'

'Well, I'm not sure if you've noticed, but I'm a lot older than you. I'm forty-four – Jesus, no, I'm forty-five now. Weird, isn't it?'

'I don't think it's weird.'

'Well, if only everyone thought like you.' He took his glasses off and rubbed the bridge of his nose. 'I mean, on a more serious note, I do sometimes wonder about myself. I've got a fairly successful career, tenure and everything . . . I even published a book with Cambridge University Press a few years ago, I can't remember if I told you about that. But I spend most of my time with a twenty-five-year-old – two twenty-five-year-olds, when Mari's around.'

'Right.' I could feel my face hardening. 'Dumb girls. I doubt they've even heard of Cambridge University Press.'

'Oh no, I didn't mean it like that. It's just – well, it's so unusual, the whole thing. You'd have to wonder what my motivations are.'

'Sex,' I said coldly.

He shot me a careful look. 'I don't think it's just sex, no. Although obviously there's an element of that, and it's certainly what most people would zero in on. I don't know, what do you think? Am I just a walking cliché, trying to live out my youth again through you?'

He said it wryly, with the hint of a smile, but I didn't smile back. I had my snake-in-the-grass feeling again. 'Maybe,' I said. 'You should've just spent too much money on a sports car, saved yourself the embarrassment.'

I could tell this hurt him. He finished his food without looking at me, and I kept my body very still and listened to the blur of talk and laughter around us. After a minute, he said, 'Are you going to be cruel to me every time I don't do exactly what you want?'

'I'm not asking you to do exactly what I want. I asked you for one thing, which you did agree to. If you're going to go back on it, you should just say so.'

'No, no, I'm not going back on it.'

'Well, what are you doing? It's not very clear to me, that's all.'

'Yeah. No, it's not clear to me either. I'm sorry.' He rubbed his face. I knew he really was sorry, and I hated being the object of his sorriness; I wanted to be the only one who did things that I had to feel sorry about. 'I'm being a coward about this, I know.'

I hated hearing him say that, because I knew it was true. A miserable silence settled in. Finally he said tiredly, 'Fuck, Elisabeth, I hate this. Let's not argue, okay?'

I took a long time to swallow a sour mouthful of margarita, the salt stinging my lips. The humiliating truth was that I had often imagined Jack taking me to parties and dinners, introducing me to the people who shared his world – academics with money and sophisticated opinions, who would find me interesting and be impressed by my intellect. But clearly this had been a delusional fantasy. I would never fit in with his friends; he'd said himself that I looked like a student. 'Okay,' I said. 'Argument over.'

'Good.' He stood up, offering me his hand. I took it.

When we got back to his flat, he pushed me against the wall in the hallway, and I unzipped my skirt and let it fall around my ankles. All summer we'd been having increasingly intense sex, the kind where we lay in slightly anguished silence for minutes after it finished. I hadn't cried again, which I was thankful for, but sometimes I found myself doing or saying things I hadn't anticipated. Those moments brought a thrill with an edge of pure horror. I knew I was in love with him, of course, but I wasn't going to tell him that.

That night was similar. When it was over I lay curled on my side, facing him. My face felt hot and damp, and there was a breeze coming through the window.

Jack smoothed the hair off my forehead. 'You know you're the best part of my life,' he said.

'Am I? That's nice.'

'Yeah, even when you're being a little bit petulant. Like now, for example.' He touched the tip of my nose with his finger.

I liked him touching me that way. 'So are you saying you have a thing for me?'

'Yeah. Actually, I have a pretty serious thing for you.'

'God, that's so embarrassing. I can't believe you told me that.'

'Oh well. I'm sure I already embarrass myself around you all the time.' He stroked my hair. 'But you wouldn't call me the best part of your life, would you? That honour would go to Mari.'

I didn't reply. I knew he was looking for my reassurance, and a part of me wanted to give it to him, but another part of me relished holding it back. I thought of him raising his glass in the restaurant, smiling somewhere beyond my face. Lightly, I said, 'You shouldn't fish for compliments.'

There was a little silence. 'Sorry,' he said. 'You're right. I'll stop pushing my luck.'

He said it in a way that was mostly joking, but there was an edge of hurt underneath. I felt bad then, but there was a certain reassurance in feeling bad, in knowing that I'd hurt him and now I had the power to comfort him. I took his hand and kissed it, and then I kissed his mouth; it tasted clean and sweet. 'Hey,' I said softly, resting my forehead against his. 'Will you read something to me?'

'Read something to you?'

'Read something to me in Italian. I want to hear what it sounds like.'

He looked surprised, but he said, 'Okay, if you like. What should I read?'

'Doesn't matter. You could read the most boring political economy book you own, I wouldn't understand a word.'

'Well, I wouldn't subject you to that. Not even in a foreign language.' He got up and looked through the shelves, and when he came back he was holding a slim book with a red-and-white cover. 'This is a novel, actually. *Vogliamo Tutto* – the title in English is *We Want Everything*. It's about a strike. You'd like it – so would Mari, now I think about it. I'll find you the English copy tomorrow if you want.'

'Okay.'

He held the book in one hand, and with the other hand he played gently with my hair. I felt very sleepy and warm inside. He began to read, and I let the unfamiliar words wash over me in their strange staccato rhythm. It occurred to me that this could well be it, the high point of my life so far, and the only thing marring my happiness was a strange, half-formed wish for Mari to be there too. Of course I would tell her about it later, but I wished she could be there with me, in the softly lit room with the breeze coming through the window, listening to Jack's familiar voice form the sounds of a new language.

7

WHEN I WOKE up the next morning, Jack was in the kitchen, drinking coffee and reading the *Saturday Paper*. (Mari teased him mercilessly about his subscription – she called it the inner-city liberal guilt weekly.) Later Mari came over and told us about the play, and then she and I made up a game where we pulled a book off Jack's shelves at random and quizzed him on its contents. The objective of the game was to see whether Jack had actually read all his books, and I sensed that Mari was a little disappointed when it turned out that he mostly had. We went home in the afternoon, and Jack gave me the English copy of his Italian novel and kissed me goodbye at the door. After that, I stopped hearing from him.

Usually he sent me messages or emails every day, little things that I didn't always reply to, or he'd call me as he was walking home from work. But Sunday went past with nothing, and then Monday and Tuesday went past with more nothing. I didn't usually initiate contact with him, and I knew that doing so now, especially after our conversation on Friday, would cement my status as needy and slightly desperate. That was fine, though. I could let him figure out that I wasn't. It was actually a good opportunity to do some of the chores I'd been putting off, like sorting through clothes to donate to the op shop. Mari, when she came over on Wednesday evening to return a book, saw the pile on my bed and made an excited noise.

'Are you getting rid of that green top?' she asked.

'I never wear it anymore. You can have it, if you like.'

She took off her own blouse and pulled the green one over her head. It looked wrinkled and baggy on her, but in a vaguely chic way. 'I don't know,' she said, staring at her reflection in the mirror. 'Is it a bit too . . .'

'A bit too what?'

'I'm just saying, I might not look out of place at a suburban P&C. That's all.' She took it off and tossed it aside. Her small breasts were round dabs of white flesh, the nipples rising to dark pink peaks. 'Can you pass me that dress? The pink one?'

I threw it to her and she wriggled her long, pale body into it. 'Actually, I don't mind this.' She squinted at her reflection, turning side to side. 'Twee as fuck, but maybe in a good way? What do you think?'

It was a pink cotton dress with cap sleeves and white buttons down the front. On me it had looked childish, but it suited Mari, even though it wasn't the kind of thing she usually wore. 'Yeah,' I said. 'It looks good.'

She tilted her head to one side. 'What's up with you?'

'What?'

'You're all quiet. And checking your phone every five seconds. What's the matter, trouble in paradise?'

I told her about my argument with Jack. I did it in a lighthearted way, framing the incident in terms of his character flaws and avoiding any mention of my own emotional reaction, except to say at the end that I found the whole thing a little humiliating.

Mari frowned. 'Why humiliating?'

I brushed a piece of lint off my doona. 'Just the stuff he said about you and me. About how weird and embarrassing it is for him to hang out with us, seeing as he makes so much money and has such a great career.'

She unbuttoned the dress, and when she bent to pick up her blouse from the floor, I could see the pale knobs of her vertebrae. 'I'm sure he didn't mean it that way,' she said.

'I don't know how he meant it, I'm just telling you what he said. It's such a cliché, you know – he liked the idea of having a young girlfriend, it was fun to begin with, but as soon as I make any kind of emotional *demand* on him, he backs off. Like I'm getting too attached or something. Fuck that.'

She turned back towards me. The lamp on my desk illuminated her face, her eyelashes casting fringed shadows on her cheeks. 'Did he actually use those words?'

'He hasn't used any words, that's the point. I mean, maybe I misjudged it. Maybe to him it was just some kind of midlife crisis sex thing.' I didn't really think this was possible, but it felt masochistically good to say it, like picking at a scab. 'That's what men are like, right?'

Usually, when I raised this kind of moral condemnation, Mari was happy to go along with it. But now she just said, 'Maybe. I don't think he's like that, though.'

'He's not a saint, you know. He just wants everyone to approve of him all the time. It's actually kind of a weak personality trait.'

She poked my shoulder, and I shifted over on the bed so she could sit down. 'I know he's not a saint,' she said, stretching her legs out beside mine. 'I just don't think it's fair to accuse him of being a midlife crisis guy.'

'You tease him all the time about his age.'

She laughed. 'That's a joke, though. Anyway, if you do end up being free this weekend, I was talking to Alex earlier and he's bought the stuff for us.'

I sat up straighter. Mari had been trying for weeks to get Alex to buy us some acid, but it was a complicated transaction that had to go through his housemate Joss and had seemed unlikely to ever be executed. 'Really?'

'Yeah. We're going to take it at his place on Saturday, if you want to come.'

I ran my tongue over my teeth. Apart from weed, which even my parents and their friends had smoked when I was younger, I had never taken drugs. Mari was much more experienced in that department: the handful of times we'd been to festivals together had always involved her growing looser and looser, pupils like dinner plates, laughing at nothing while I anxiously tried to make her drink water. It wasn't a role I particularly enjoyed. Still, I'd never joined in, even when it was offered to me, because I was too afraid of losing my mind and never getting it back again.

Mari leaned back on my pillows and tucked one arm behind her head. I could see the tendrils of dark hair curling from her armpit. 'I'm not trying to peer pressure you,' she said mildly. 'But it might make you feel better, if you're still a bit down.'

'I'm not down.'

'Okay.'

We fell into silence. I fidgeted with the hem of my doona cover, folding it over and over on itself. I wanted to say more but didn't know how to raise the issue, or which words to use. 'Fuck it,' I said, letting the cover fall back. 'I'll come.'

'Really?'

I shrugged. There was something appealing in the idea of floating off temporarily from my own consciousness, and particularly the idea of doing it without telling Jack. I knew it didn't square with how he thought of me – he was always going on about how capable and intelligent I was, as if I were the one twenty years older than him. Maybe he'd only been trying to convince himself. To Mari I said, 'Yeah, why not. I'll probably never hear from Jack again anyway.'

She rolled her eyes, but not in a way that suggested real irritation. She was never as invested in the complexities of my emotional life as I was in hers. 'I think you should just call him,' she said. 'Can't you do that?'

'It's not really that simple.'

She got up from the bed and slipped her feet into her Birkenstocks. I knew that for her it probably was simple, because she didn't worry so much about things like dignity, but I decided not to say that out loud. 'Well, see you on Saturday then,' she said. 'Thanks for the dress.'

'You're welcome.'

After she left, I went to make a cup of tea. Jack called while the kettle was boiling and I let it ring for six seconds, timing on my watch. Six seconds was a long time. 'Hello,' I said.

'Hi, Elisabeth?' He sounded distracted.

'Yes, it's me.'

'Hi.'

'Hi.' One of my housemates had used all my green tea bags and hadn't replaced them. I looked in the cupboard and found some orange pekoe.

'What are you up to?'

The kettle clicked off and I poured water into my mug. It was one of those Penguin Books mugs, the *Great Gatsby* one. 'Making a cup of tea. What about you?'

'Oh, lecture planning, nothing very interesting. Listen, I thought you were going to come over here tonight.'

I was quiet, pulling the tea bag through the darkening water.

'You usually come over on Wednesdays, right? Or have I been imagining that?'

'No, you haven't been imagining it.' I plopped the tea bag into the compost caddy. 'But I didn't know if you wanted me to come tonight.'

'Why would I not want that?'

'Hold on.' I took the tea back to my room and shut the door. 'Well, I haven't heard from you since Saturday.'

'Darling, that was four days ago.'

'Yes.'

'It's not okay if we don't talk for four days?'

'Well, I usually hear from you every day.'

'Okay.' I heard him take a deep breath. 'Okay, I'm sorry. You know I've got a ridiculous teaching load this semester.'

'I did not know that.'

'Well, academia isn't all fun and games, despite the jokes you and Mari like to make to that effect.' It was mostly Mari who made those jokes, but I didn't point that out. 'I'm actually under quite a lot of pressure at the moment. I was looking forward to seeing you tonight. I'm sorry we haven't spoken in a few days, but you can't expect everything from me, especially not just now.'

'Oh, no. I wouldn't expect anything from you.' I put a slight but deliberate emphasis on the first and last words of this sentence: *I* wouldn't expect anything from *you*.

'What's that supposed to mean?'

'Nothing.'

'Elisabeth? Let's not play stupid games. Say what you mean.'

You think I'm stupid, I thought. I knew he didn't really think that and wasn't even saying it, but it felt good to be offended by it. I took a sip of tea and it burned my tongue.

'Elisabeth?'

'Okay,' I said. 'Here's what I mean. The last time I saw you, I told you – for the second time now – that I felt like you were keeping me secret, like you were ashamed of me. Your response was to not contact me for four days and then accuse me of expecting everything from you.'

'All right, well, what did you expect?' His voice was colder than I'd ever heard it before. 'To be taken out to lunch with every single colleague of mine? Hello, please meet the twenty-five-year-old I'm sleeping with. That would really do wonders for my standing in the department.'

'Right,' I said slowly. 'I didn't realise I was just the twenty-five-year-old you were sleeping with.'

He sighed. 'That wasn't what I meant, I'm sorry. But look, the situation is a bit tricky . . . In my line of work, it'll raise questions. I'm not saying we have to keep this under wraps forever, but for now I just need to be discreet. Can you appreciate that?'

'Sure. No, absolutely. Don't let me get in the way of your – how did you put it? Your standing in the department.'

'Elisabeth.'

'Yeah. It does sound like things are really busy for you right now. You should probably get off the phone, those lectures won't plan themselves.'

There was a long silence. I blew on the tea and sipped it. Finally Jack said, 'Okay. Goodnight, then.'

'Goodnight.'

•

THAT NIGHT I went to bed at the usual time, but my stomach was tight and I couldn't turn my brain off. I kept thinking about the last time Jack had stayed at my house, a few weeks ago after some drinks my housemates had half-organised. Past midnight, in my room, we'd turned off all the lights except the Himalayan salt lamp my mother had given me for Christmas. Jack got a kick out of it for some reason; he called it my hippie lamp. I remembered his quiet voice, fingers running through my hair, and the salt lamp glowing softly orange-pink beside the bed. My face in his neck.

Truthfully, although I'd never told him this, I liked Jack more than anyone I'd ever been involved with before. There was a natural easiness to being with him; he made me laugh, he made me feel like I didn't have to try to be interesting or clever. He was much more tender and solicitous than men my own age. It was painfully embarrassing to know that he was all these things to me, but to him I was a shameful liability. Probably he found something titillating in the shame, and that was the only reason he'd kept seeing me. I had been stupid not to realise it earlier.

When I finally fell asleep, I had lots of complicated and stressful dreams, all running into one another. In one I was driving a car with Mari in the passenger seat, her eyelashes casting fringed shadows on her cheeks. We passed Jack's house on Baynes Street, then rounded the corner and passed it again on the next block. The windows were dark, and I knew something terrible had happened to him and that was why he hadn't called me back. Mari knew what it was, but she wouldn't tell me. 'You're not being fair,' I tried to say, but 'fair' meant something different in the dream, and the words kept coming out mangled. When I woke it was 4.34 am, and I had no missed calls, no messages, no emails. After that I gave up on sleep, because I had to start work at six anyway.

Mari came into the café later that morning. She looked perfectly well-rested, and she greeted me cheerfully. 'Any word from the professor?'

She had never called him that before, and I didn't particularly like it. I shook my head.

'Ah well,' she said, slurping her coffee. 'The course of true love never did run smooth.'

Aisha, who I worked with, looked up from wiping the counter. 'Are you having romantic troubles, Elisabeth?'

'She's fighting with her boyfriend,' Mari said.

'She's got a boyfriend?'

'Oh yeah. A much older boyfriend. Didn't she tell you?'

Aisha was grinning, her eyes huge. She loved gossip. 'No, she didn't! Elisabeth, I can't believe this! You dark horse.'

'He's in his forties,' Mari said. 'A university lecturer. It's a *big* age gap. A real daddy thing, isn't it, Elisabeth?'

'Oh, fuck off, Mari,' I said tiredly.

Aisha made a delighted shape with her mouth and went to clear some tables. I leaned against the counter and looked at the milk fridge, which needed cleaning. I knew Mari hadn't been trying to hurt me, and the two of us had made similar jokes plenty of times, but for some reason I wasn't in the mood for it.

'You all right?' she asked.

'I'm fine. You shouldn't tell people he's my boyfriend, though, I don't think that's true.'

Mari took the lid off her coffee and blew on it. She gave me a look that seemed to imply that I was being unreasonable but that she was magnanimous enough to forgive me, and that later on I would be grateful to her for this. 'Okay,' she said. 'But just give him a call, I'm sure he's dying to hear from you. Shit, there's the bus. See you on Saturday, right?'

'Right,' I said. She was already running towards the bus stop, bag banging against her hip.

I was sure that by Saturday I would have heard from Jack. But the rest of the week rolled predictably past, and then Saturday came and he still hadn't called. By then I had decided this was a perfectly fine way to end our relationship, and in fact it was better for us to split up before I caused him or myself any further humiliation. I was putting a lot of effort into carrying on with my regular routine: eating three meals a day and going to bed early. On Friday Mari messaged to ask if we were having dinner with Jack as usual, but I didn't reply.

On Saturday morning I walked over to Alex's house, going in through the back door to the kitchen. Alex's kitchen looked the way all our kitchens looked then: clusters of bills and cards stuck to the fridge with magnets, dirty dishes piled in the sink and the heart-shaped green leaves of a pothos plant tumbling down from a high shelf. Heidi and Mari and Paul were already there, playing cards at the table.

'Here she is,' Alex said when I walked in. 'Now we can start.'

'No, hang on,' said Heidi. 'I'm about to beat you, Alexei, you can't get away that easy.'

'You are not about to beat me. Here, look.' He laid his cards on the table, and everyone erupted in groans. 'See? It's over for you.'

He got the acid out of the freezer and cut up the little tabs with scissors. 'Just one each for starters,' he said, doling them out. 'You can have another one later if you like. But Joss said this stuff was strong.'

Paul stuck the tab under his tongue. 'Am I going to experience ego death?'

'For you I would say that's impossible,' Mari said, and everyone laughed.

We went out to the garden and lay under the frangipani tree. We lay there for hours, letting everything wash over us: the heady wafting scent of jasmine, the heat coming off the earth in waves. The lawn had been cut recently and the clippings clumped soft and damp under our fingers. The smell of grass in the sunshine swelled up to fill our nostrils, lush and sweet and earthy. It was the smell of summer, the summer that was now almost over, but there was a note there of summers past, something tugging me towards nostalgia for my childhood. I remembered the way the storms would roll through the coast in the late afternoon, and the odd milky light in the sky just before they arrived. This memory seemed significant somehow, and I had the feeling that I was on the brink of some kind of ultimate understanding, a huge meaning that would make sense of everything, but it was always floating just out of reach, and my mind kept circling around, nearly catching it, missing it, circling around again . . .

I sat up and rubbed my eyes. Everything in the garden was burnished with old time and beauty: the wooden table polished with a patina of silver and crumbling into black; the lush deep green of mint and basil in blushing terracotta pots. Heidi watered the garden, tipping sparkling rivulets from a pink tin watering can, and I was in an English village, watering rows of lettuce in garden beds edged with bricks, and turning to see the sun stealing out soft and gentle across fields dotted with wildflowers. I caught sight of a tree wreathed in neon green vines, threads of red running through, and I saw Chinese art, elaborate silk tapestries, the way the trees always seemed horned and slightly menacing. Alex leaned against the garden wall, crumbling red brick fading into orange-pink, and his skin was pink and golden from the sun, and a cluster of pink flowers bloomed above him. He looked like a painting on the cover of a classic novel, the kind of thing Mari would read.

There was Mari. I saw her as a 1920s flapper, all long limbs and sharp angles, wearing a white dress dotted finely with black, and dancing with Heidi on the lawn. She was laughing, her lips dark, and when I moved towards her I saw that she held a cherry between her teeth, biting into its rich bleeding heart. She turned to me, holding out her long-fingered hands, and said, 'Do you want one? They're good.'

I took her hands, and she put her soft lips to mine. I could smell her skin, faintly sweet and powdery, and the harsh note of cigarette smoke. With her tongue she pushed the cherry into my mouth, and I bit the flesh from around the stone. As the liquid sweetness crashed over my tongue, Mari danced away.

I spat the stone onto the grass and went to lie in the green shade of the frangipani tree. Alex was there, and I put my head in his lap. He held a cool hand to my forehead. 'That feels nice,' I said.

'You're a bit warm.' He reached over me and when his hand reappeared, it was holding an ice cube. He slid it over my face, and it dripped cold water into my hair.

I began to laugh. 'Where did you get that?'

'Heidi brought them out earlier. Oh, it's melting. Open up.' He popped the ice cube into my mouth, and I crunched down, melting smooth edges exploding into sharp cold shards. Alex stroked my hair. 'Do you feel good?' he asked.

'I feel good.'

'Good.' His hand was resting on my torso, just below my breasts, and then his thumb was making semicircles across my right breast. It was a little ticklish, and I started to laugh.

'What's funny?'

'Nothing.' I sat up, and then we were kissing. The kiss was sweet, and I pictured our mouths, pink and pulsating like little sea creatures. I don't know how long we kissed, but when we broke apart the shadows on the lawn were longer, and the hot blue air of the afternoon had faded to the warm golden pink of early evening. Across the garden, the others were sitting in chairs, eating bread and cheese and laughing at something.

I leaned back on my hands and watched them, contentment swelling inside me. For the first time, the thought of Jack felt pleasantly neutral, something that would resolve itself in its own time. Everything would resolve itself in its own time. That was the secret of the universe, the only objective fact: the onward march of time, of history. I just had to allow myself to be carried along by it.

Alex stood, offering me his hand. I took it and pulled myself up, and he led me away, not towards the others but up the stairs to the house, down the dim hallway and into his room. Piles of medical textbooks by the bed and a Spanish Civil War poster on the wall. It was strange to think of Alex living out all the intimacies of his daily life here, while I lived out mine in my own bedroom. How many lives were being lived right now, people existing side by side in city houses – neighbours, housemates, strangers – aware of each other's existences but never knowing the full depth and richness, the joys and tragedies being played out only metres away? I thought about this while I examined a pen on Alex's desk in minute detail.

'Come here,' he said, and I lay beside him on the bed. He kissed me again and slid his hand, warm and dry, under my dress. I couldn't see any reason to stop him. It felt good, after all, and the soft blanket we were lying on felt good, and the last of the light coming through the window felt good. A neutral voice in my head pointed out that Jack would certainly not care. If anything, he'd be embarrassed on my behalf at how juvenile the whole thing was. Getting high, fucking because you felt like it – none of that had anything to do with the way he lived his life. No wonder he hadn't wanted any of his friends to meet me. Alex asked if I was okay, and I said I was.

Afterwards, we lay together and watched the sky outside the window slowly drain itself of light. We could still hear the murmur of the others' conversation, the burst of their laughter. And a sweet vibrating hum, plucked out of the air: Heidi playing her guitar. Eventually Alex said, 'Hey.'

'Hey.'

He coughed. 'Sorry, this might be awkward, but I just wanted to ask . . . Jack? I mean, are you still . . .'

'Oh.' The mention of Jack's name made me feel flat and sour inside. 'I don't know. Probably not.'

'I'm sorry. Well, I'm kind of sorry. Not really, actually.'

I folded the sheet over me and smoothed it carefully. 'Why, did you not like him?'

He shrugged. 'He's a nice guy, but he's like twice your age. It was weird, don't you think?'

There wasn't anything to say to this. Possibly it had been weird. I just nodded, and we talked on and off about other things, and later Alex put on some music and brought me a glass of water. I walked back to my house at around midnight. In my room, I pressed my face into the pillow. I didn't cry, but when I was sure that everyone was asleep I got up and took a shower, turning the water on as hot as it would go. Crying in the shower was okay, because the noise and water almost masked it from having happened at all. I sat there for a long time with my head between my knees.

8

ON WEDNESDAY EVENING, Mari's phone rang as she was walking home from work. It was a number she didn't recognise, and she answered brusquely: 'Hello?'

'Hello, Mari? It's Jack.'

Mari stopped. Her arms and legs felt strange, as if they had lost their solidity and might dissolve at any moment. 'Oh,' she said. 'Hi.'

'Hi.' He cleared his throat. 'Sorry to ring you like this. I wanted to wait until you'd left work. You have left work, haven't you?'

'Oh yes, five o'clock on the dot. Four fifty-nine if I'm feeling daring. I'm walking home right now.'

'Good. Good.' He sounded distracted, and she pictured him sitting in an office, surrounded by stacks of papers. 'It's nice to hear your voice.'

Mari found her way to a bench and sat down. The people and buildings around her dissolved into a kind of background blur; the only real thing was the phone pressed against her ear. 'Yours too,' she said. 'I've missed seeing you around.'

'That's kind of you to say. And what have you been up to in my absence?'

'Nothing much. Work, the usual. Oh, last weekend we all took acid together – you know, me, Paul, Heidi, Alex, Elisabeth . . .'

'Ah, Mari. I thought I told you to say no to drugs.'

She laughed. 'Right. Advice you've always followed scrupulously yourself.'

'Yes, indeed. The only drug I need is the heady drug of historical materialism. Ah well. How was it?'

'Very profound and meaningful at the time. I actually had quite a few revelations about my essential character, the nature of time and the universe, the ultimate meaning of life . . . Unfortunately I can't remember any of them now.'

'If you do remember, let me know,' Jack said. 'I wouldn't mind a revelation or two about the ultimate meaning of life. But listen, I didn't ring you just to chat. You probably know that Elisabeth and I have hit a little bump in the road.'

'Oh.' Mari's heart dropped. A bus heaved past her, belching fumes. 'Yeah, I heard.'

'Is she . . . I mean, have you seen her much? Apart from getting together to fry your brains with illegal narcotics.'

Mari bit her lip. In her mind she saw Elisabeth and Alex kissing under the tree, walking into the house together. Lots of their friends slept together casually, and even official relationships often weren't exclusive, but she sensed that Jack had somewhat more traditional ideas. For a second, the thought of telling him danced tantalisingly before her. Then she shook it out of her mind.

'Yeah, I've seen her,' she said. 'She mentioned you haven't been in touch.'

'Right, that's one way of putting it. But, I mean . . . Does she want me to get in touch?'

Mari stared at a dirty wad of gum stuck to the footpath. 'I think so. I think she does want that.'

'Okay. Could you tell her –'

'No.' Mari stood up. 'No, I'm not telling her anything. Tell her yourself, pick up the phone.'

'Look, I don't even know if she'd answer. Last time we spoke on the phone – well, I won't bore you with the details, but I don't think it's the best medium. But, I mean, should I go over to her house? Is that too much?'

Mari began walking fast, letting her heart pump blood around her body. 'Probably too much,' she said. 'She likes her own space.'

'I thought so too. So come on, Mari, put in a good word for me. Or even just an average word. Aren't we friends?'

'Yeah. We're friends.'

'So . . . ?'

She rolled her eyes. The phone call was ridiculous, but a part of her sympathised: it was always difficult to know what Elisabeth was feeling. Even Mari was sometimes afraid to ask, because Elisabeth could be so cold if you said the wrong thing. 'All right,' she said. 'I'm not going to be your envoy, that's not my job. But if you still haven't heard from her by next Saturday and you're desperate enough to risk making a total fool of yourself . . . Heidi and I are having a party, and you could come if you wanted. Elisabeth will be there.'

A brief silence. 'Okay,' he said neutrally. 'Thanks. Hey, by the way, where are you?'

'Where am I? I'm on Boundary Street, just about to go past the bookshop. Why?'

Jack stepped out of the bookshop, his phone pressed to his ear. When he saw her, he smiled and hung up.

Mari went towards him, disbelieving. His appearance satiated a hunger she'd only been half aware of, and she found herself combing her eyes over his face, his body. Here he was. She could reach out and touch him, could close the distance between their bodies if she wanted to. Instead she said, 'Well, hello. This is a coincidence.'

'Isn't it?' He was laughing. 'Come in with me, Mari. Would you like a new book? I'd be happy to buy you a book, to say thank you.'

For a second she didn't know what he meant. When it clicked, she suddenly saw that inviting him to their party had been a stupid, regrettable thing to do. Still, she couldn't change it now. She followed him into the glass and light of the bookshop.

They browsed the fiction shelves together, Mari thumbing through a copy of *My Brilliant Career*. 'You know, I've never read this,' she said. 'And everyone says it's such a classic. I just don't know if I want to read a book called *My Brilliant Career* unless it's ironic.'

'It is, actually. Anyway, you'll have a brilliant career of your own. If you want one.'

'You sound so sure.' She slid the book back onto the shelf. 'Your generation had it easier, you know. What were you doing when you were my age?'

'When I was your age . . . Well, let's see. I think I was in Greece. After I finished my undergrad I went travelling for a year, on my own. Greece was the first stop, and then I went to Italy, Spain, Portugal, France, up through Switzerland and Austria and Germany. There were probably some minor European countries in there that I've forgotten. It was a lot of fun. Nothing booked in advance, you know, I'm not sure it would've been possible even if I'd tried. Once on a Greek island I missed the last boat back, so I just found a house in the village that would let me a room for the night, stayed there, and got the boat the next morning. I don't remember feeling any anxiety at all.'

'And when you got back you did your PhD?'

'More or less. I messed around for a year or so, not sure what I wanted to do with my life, the usual stuff. Then I decided a PhD was better than working, so I applied and got in. Not so different from what someone of your generation might do.'

'Sure, except you got a job at the end of it. Not just a job – a career. Your brilliant career.'

Jack laughed. 'Touché,' he said. 'I had luck. You'll never stop holding that against me, will you?'

'Probably not.'

'Oh well.' He was smiling at her. 'Would you let me take you for a drink, at least? A partial atonement.'

'Oh. Okay, sure.'

'And let me buy you the book. You'll like it, it's got lots of irony in it.'

He paid for the book, and at the bar he told her to find a table while he ordered. She went to the courtyard out the back, where vines crept over the fence and tea lights flickered in glass jars on the tables. When Jack came out he was carrying two glasses of red wine, and Mari was disappointed. Beer took longer to drink, would have meant a longer encounter. But maybe he had something else to do that evening.

'Here you go,' he said, handing her a glass. 'I hope it's okay. Personally, I'm suspicious, but we'll see.'

'You're such an elitist about booze.'

'One of the privileges of middle age.'

'One of the privileges of money, you mean.' Mari sipped the wine. 'See, this is nice! This is perfectly fine!'

Jack took a drink and screwed up his mouth, shaking his head. 'Mari, you've got no taste.'

'Sorry. Not everyone gets to tour through Europe developing their wine-tasting palate at a young age, you know. I come from a long line of cheap booze appreciators. Well, my mother appreciates cheap booze, anyway. Not sure about anyone else.'

'What about your dad?'

Mari flicked the wineglass gently with her fingernail: a high, tinny *ping*. 'I don't know my father. I don't even know who he is.'

'Oh.' He sounded surprised, but not particularly sorry for her. 'That must be frustrating.'

She shrugged. 'It doesn't bother me much anymore. When I was little I used to ask my mum about it – who's my dad, why can't I see my dad, blah blah. She never gave me a straight answer. Later, when I was in high school, I realised she probably wasn't a hundred per cent sure who he was either.'

'Your mum sounds like she's had a tough time.'

'She left home when she was sixteen,' Mari said. It was surprisingly easy to say these things to him, things she'd never said to anyone except Elisabeth. 'I think she was more or less kicked out. She was using drugs pretty heavily, she might have lived on the street . . . I don't know the details, she doesn't like to talk about it. Maybe that's fair enough.'

'Yeah. Hard on you, though.'

'Well, it wasn't easy on her either. Her parents were pretty wealthy, but they never gave us anything. I've only met them once. But I think she kind of cleaned up her act after I was born. Like, she never really *used* heroin, not in a serious way.'

'I didn't know you could use heroin in an unserious way.'

'Oh, she does everything in an unserious way. That's why I'm even here to begin with – she got knocked up, she was only nineteen, anyone else would've had an abortion. But she didn't take it too seriously, so here I am.'

'And you, are you serious? Or unserious?'

Mari smiled at him. Her body felt full of sparkling warmth. 'I don't know. What do you think?'

'Oh, I think you're very serious. Not like me, I'm terribly unserious. My biggest flaw, actually.'

Mari sipped her wine. The glass was almost empty. 'Can I ask you something serious, though? A serious question?'

'Ask away.'

'That was a test, wasn't it?'

'What was a test?'

'When you called. You knew I'd be walking home from work. You knew I'd be near Boundary Street. You were waiting to see if I'd give you what you wanted – if I'd help you out with Elisabeth. And when I did . . .' She pinched her fingertips together and flung them apart, as if to demonstrate magic. 'You appeared.'

He was smiling. 'You've got no faith in me, do you?'

'Not particularly.'

'Ah well. No, as it happens, I was just at the bookshop by coincidence. I wanted to see if they had this new novel; I read a review of it this morning and it sounded good. Then you said you were on your way home and I thought you might be nearby. That's all.'

'I don't believe you.'

'No, you wouldn't. Hey, but you did tell me about this party of yours. You didn't have to tell me, but you did.'

Mari folded a paper napkin into a small square and wedged it underneath the base of her glass. 'Well, I warned you,' she said. 'If you make a total fool of yourself, that's on you.'

'I'll do my best.' He cleared his throat. 'Anyway, I've got a class tomorrow morning, so . . .'

'Yeah, of course.' Standing up, Mari realised she was drunker than she had any right to be after one glass of wine. 'I wouldn't want to get in the way of Dr Bloom's teaching schedule.'

He laughed. 'No one calls me that.'

'The university does.' They left the bar, Mari swinging her hands in her cardigan pockets. 'I remember looking you up online after we met you and all I could find was your staff profile. And it called you Dr Bloom. I thought that was so funny.'

'Why did you think it was funny?'

'Oh, I don't know, it was just weird. You didn't really seem like that kind of person.'

'Did you not see me as the academic type?'

His voice was more serious than Mari had been expecting, and it punctured the balloon floating in her chest. 'No,' she said. 'You're definitely the academic type. But with us, you seemed so . . . Oh, I don't know. Forget I said anything.'

They walked down the street together in silence. In the dim twilight Mari couldn't see Jack beside her, but she felt him there, just beyond the edges of her body. She wanted to embrace him, or scream, or maybe throw herself under a passing car. Her fingers twisted inside her pockets.

After a minute, he said, 'You looked me up online?'

'Sure. Of course.'

'Why did you do that?'

They crossed at the intersection and stopped, facing each other. Mari studied his face for clues, but it was the same as always: his mouth hinting at a wry smile. 'I was interested in you,' she said. 'I mean, I found you interesting. I was pretty disappointed, actually, that you didn't have Facebook or anything like that. The staff profile wasn't much to go on.'

'I'm too old for that kind of thing, Mari.'

She sensed that he wasn't necessarily talking about Facebook. But was it a rebuff or an invitation? Jack could be so inscrutable when it suited him. 'Facebook is actually mostly for old people,' she said lightly. 'You'd fit right in. Anyway, thanks for the book.'

'You're welcome.'

Mari waited – for what, she wasn't sure – but he just stood there looking at her. Feeling that she couldn't leave without doing something, she reached out and took his hand. His fingers were warm, and she registered surprise on his face.

'It's all right,' she said, not knowing quite what she meant. She squeezed his hand – it felt so good to touch him, finally, as if a vault had opened inside her and spilled out its liquid warmth – and turned to walk away, the heels of her shoes clicking neatly on the footpath.

•

SOON AFTER JACK'S last phone call to me – I had begun to think of it that way, with finality – the summer staggered to its end. The air was cool when I walked to work in the mornings and I wanted to feel the brisk snap of productivity that people were supposed to feel in the autumn, but it never came. When I wasn't working, I spent a lot of time lying on my bed and watching the ceiling fan spin. Twice I looked at Jack's staff profile, just to feel the sharp slice of pain in my chest, but after the second time I recognised this as pathetic behaviour, and I cleared my browser history so that I could pretend I hadn't done it at all.

It was around this time that I decided my film project wasn't going to work out. Over the past few weeks I'd been splicing together the footage I'd taken with apocalyptic scenes, either from old sci-fi films or contemporary news reports about natural disasters. Heidi's laugh would cut, abruptly, to a scene of piled grey rubble, a human hand just visible underneath. I'd been trying to say something about climate change – what, I wasn't really sure. The working title of the project was *It's the End of the World, But I Feel Fine*.

Watching it back, I realised that it was a fairly heavy-handed concept, and also that the footage I'd taken was boring. Even conversations I'd found interesting at the time were boring when I watched them again. And even if I finished the project, what would I do with it? No one wanted to buy it, no one even wanted to see it. The Instagram account I'd started for my work had 125 followers. It wasn't just my lack of filmmaking ability that was worrying me: sometimes, late at night when I couldn't sleep, my mind circled uneasily around the fact that a master's degree in philosophy had very few practical uses.

This was not the sort of thing that usually bothered me. I didn't have concrete plans but I'd always thought a lot about the future, and I'd always had confidence that success in my chosen field would arrive without much effort on my part. This thought pattern – which I was now beginning to recognise as magical thinking, exacerbated by possibly overzealous praise from my parents and teachers – had definitely been a factor in my decision to pursue an aggressively useless degree. (Mari, on the other hand, had chosen hers out of something closer to nihilism.) But that autumn the future seemed to be moving up on me, breathing down my neck: I would be twenty-six in November, and in four years' time I would be thirty. What if I got to thirty without doing anything? Suddenly I was thinking about things like that.

Mari and Heidi threw a party in April – to celebrate the new season, they said – and I agreed to go. It was in my nature to agree to go, even though I felt like lying on my bed and staring at the ceiling while the light slowly disappeared. I checked my phone – no missed calls, no messages, no emails – and then I showered and stood naked in front of my clothes rack, feeling bored with myself and everything I owned. Eventually I put on something, I don't remember what, and walked over to Paris Street.

It was still early, and I followed the sound of music and voices down the cracked concrete path to the back garden. Leaf mould frilled the edges of the peeling back steps, vines choked the trees, and the grass on the lawn tickled my ankles. But there was a current of joyful energy thrumming through the whole place, and everywhere I heard the warm babble of talk, occasionally torn through with laughter. Under the banana tree, I found Heidi and Alex sitting on milk crates and arguing about desserts.

'That's why I like baked things with apples in them,' Heidi was saying. 'They make everything nice and soggy.'

'No, that's terrible. You're making me feel sick even talking about this. Like bread and butter pudding, for example –'

'Delicious.'

'Trash! How can you say that?'

'Hello,' I said, laughing. Impulsively I leaned down and gave Heidi a hug, kissed Alex's cheek. After the day we took acid, things between me and Alex had been stilted for a week or so and then had gone back to normal. He was in the process of pursuing his housemate Jen, much to Mari's disgust.

'Elisabeth, what do you think?' asked Heidi. 'You like bread and butter pudding, don't you?'

'Of course she doesn't,' Alex said. 'She's not a monster.'

I held up my hands. 'I'm not getting involved. Do you both want a drink?'

'Yes, please,' said Heidi. 'Get me some punch, would you? It's good, Mari's gone heavy on the rum again.'

Standing in the queue for the punch bowl, I looked around the garden and waved to people I knew. Mari and Heidi had strung up fairy lights, and they winked and glittered gently in the clear evening. My film project didn't seem to matter much in the grand scheme of things. Even Jack didn't seem to matter much. I decided I wasn't going to look at his picture again, or re-read his messages late at night, because he'd never really felt anything for me and it had been stupid to think otherwise. As the queue shuffled forward, I rehearsed in my head how I would tell the story in future: He was a lot older than me, I'd say. It was fun for a while, but it was obviously never going to work out.

On the way back, chipped mugs of punch in both hands, I caught sight of Mari, half-hidden by the crowd. She was wearing my old pink dress, and it looked good on her. She had a cigarette in one hand and a glass of something clear and icy in the other, and she was listening to someone talk, looking up at them and smiling. Her face was lit up with happiness, she seemed to sparkle and fizz with it. When the crowd parted a little, I saw who she was standing with. It was Jack.

Numbly, I put the drinks down and went over to them. Jack was laughing, but when he saw me, he stopped abruptly and said, 'Hi.'

I looked at Mari. Her face was tight, her lips folded together. Finally she said, 'I told him to come.'

'Don't blame her,' Jack said hastily. 'I strongarmed her into it. Actually, I put her in an unfair position, so that's on me. I just wanted to talk to you.'

'As far as I know, my phone still works.'

'I'm sorry, Elisabeth,' he said quietly. Something in my stomach went weak when I heard him say my name. 'I didn't want to get into another argument over the phone. I thought it'd be better in person.'

I glanced at Mari. Her face was still closed up, but there was something flickering underneath, some flame of tenderness; I didn't know if it was for me or for Jack. I thought of the way she'd been smiling up at him. *She's sweet, really.* But then he'd said she was an unstable person, not like me. I felt like I was trying to put together a jigsaw where none of the pieces fit.

She caught my eye and gave a half-apologetic shrug. 'I'll leave you to it,' she said, touching me between the shoulder blades. 'Come and find me later, okay? If you want to.'

After she'd gone, Jack and I stood together awkwardly, not looking at each other. 'Well, here we are,' I said. 'In person, like you wanted.'

'Yeah.' He cleared his throat. 'Listen, I'm sorry about the other night. I reacted badly. I suppose I'm just sensitive about – well, about optics, honestly, but that's hardly your fault.'

'Optics?'

'Well, you know . . . A middle-aged academic and a much younger woman. You're not my student, but it's the next worst thing, isn't it? You know, if word got out about you, people would start watching me very closely when it came to the students. And then if the *students* found out, you can imagine the rumours. I mean, you must have noticed, the current culture isn't particularly friendly towards that sort of thing.'

'I don't care about the current culture.'

'Well, I wish I had your strength of character.' He sighed, his face swimming into a softer expression. 'Anyway, I've missed you.'

'Have you?'

'What do you mean by that?'

I shrugged. What was I going to accuse him of? Holding Mari's attention too well? Making her smile? 'I'm not sure about you and Mari going behind my back like this,' I said. 'You know, she never even told me you spoke to her.'

'No, well, she wouldn't have. Like I said, I made it difficult for her.'

'So you bullied her into deceiving me.'

He looked away, past my shoulder. 'I don't think that's completely fair, no. Look, Elisabeth – don't take this the wrong way, but you know Mari is her own person.'

'What does that mean?'

He opened his mouth and closed it again. In a careful tone, he said, 'I know the two of you are very close, but sometimes you can be a bit possessive of her, don't you think? She's allowed to go for a drink with me, it's not breaking any laws.'

'Oh, you went for a drink together.'

'Well, after we'd run into each other on the street. It's not important. Anyway, I could be completely wrong about all this, and I'm not trying to say you're a bad friend or anything like that, because I know you love Mari very much. I'm not . . . You know, I do understand that, of course.'

I stood very still in the thick grass of the lawn. I didn't move my face at all. My heart was beating fast, and fragments of a conversation happening behind me floated past my ears: someone complaining that the exhibitions at the modern art gallery were 'terrible'. Twenty-five bucks to see some shitty done-to-death postmodernism, he was saying. I'm moving to Melbourne, it's a cultural wasteland up here.

'Elisabeth?'

'Yeah,' I said. 'Look, I don't know why we're talking about Mari. This is between you and me, isn't it?'

'Yes, it is. So what do you think, can you forgive me? I really am sorry, I mean that.'

I looked at him, in his black nylon jacket and grey T-shirt. The jacket was the first piece of cold-weather clothing I'd ever seen him wear, and it looked good on him. I wanted so badly to touch him: the graze of his stubble on my cheek, his clean soapy smell. It seemed possible that these things were more important than my pride, which was beginning to feel sour and withered inside me. 'Okay,' I said. 'I forgive you.'

He put his arms around me, and I leaned my face against his chest. The smell of his skin seemed to unlock something inside me, as though I were wax melting into warm liquid, dissolving under his touch. We held onto each other very tightly, and he pressed his mouth into the top of my head. 'Sorry for being an idiot,' he said, his voice humming through my skin.

'No, I was an idiot too. I should've just called you instead of sulking. Mari tried to tell me that.'

'Oh well.' He kissed the top of my head. 'We're both idiots then. Good thing we've found each other. Do you want to get out of here?'

I said yes. I knew that we would go back to his flat and have sex, very tenderly, and that afterwards he would trace the bones of my face with his finger and say, 'I must have done something very good to deserve you. I wonder what it could have been?'

'Probably something you did in a past life,' I'd say.

Jack took my hand and squeezed it.

'Hey,' I said. 'Before we go.'

'Yeah?'

'There's something I should say. Did Mari tell you about . . . about the other weekend?'

He laughed. 'Oh yes, she did, now you mention it. Better living through chemicals. How did you find it?'

'It was . . .' My mouth felt suddenly stuffed with cotton wool, and I couldn't find anywhere to rest my gaze. 'Well, actually, I did something stupid.'

'Oh, don't worry, we all do stupid things under the influence. I remember once I was convinced the entire universe was a metaphor conceived as a personal joke, and every time my friends tried to convince me otherwise, it just deepened the metaphor . . . Hard to explain but it paralysed me for hours.'

'No, I don't mean, like, a hallucination. I mean – well, you know Alex? My friend?'

'Yes, the medical student. I'm familiar.'

'Yeah. Well, I should tell you, we slept together.'

Jack dropped my hand and stepped back. 'Oh,' he said. 'Right.'

'It was stupid. We were just high, it's not like it meant anything.' The words were jumping and rushing out of my mouth. 'We're just friends, it wasn't . . . But I didn't want to lie to you.'

'Yeah.' He was blank-faced, his mouth tight. 'Thanks for that.'

'I mean, I assumed it was over between us. Obviously I wouldn't have done it if . . .'

'Right.'

He opened his mouth and closed it again. There was a terrifying little silence. 'Jack?' I said.

'Yeah.'

'Can you say something? Just tell me what you're thinking.'

'All right.' He pushed a hand through his hair. 'Since you asked, this is my read on the situation, and forgive me if it's a bit reductive. But basically, it seems like you wanted me to show you some kind of commitment. You didn't want to be kept secret, you wanted to be part of my life. Okay, fair enough. I'll admit that initially I just tried to put you off, but eventually I offered to make a genuine effort, even though it'd be difficult and couldn't happen straight-away. You refused to accept that. Instead, you cut off contact and proceeded to sleep with someone else the first chance you got. What was it, less than a week later?'

I opened my mouth, but he held up his hand. 'Just a second,' he said. 'What I'm trying to say is, I guess it's hard to hear that you want *me* to commit to *you*, but also that you can fuck anyone you like and I'm supposed to believe it doesn't mean anything. That's all.'

'But it really doesn't mean anything.' My throat was blocked up with fear. 'It was stupid, I don't even know why I did it.'

'Yeah. Well, let me know if you figure it out. In the meantime, I should go.'

'What, you're leaving?'

He shrugged. 'I don't want to get in your way. I probably shouldn't have come in the first place – I mean, I'm forty-five, I shouldn't be hanging around people in their twenties. Not exactly normal, is it?'

'No,' I said, and the word felt like a stone sharpening in my mouth. 'That's actually what Alex said.'

I watched him as I said it, but he was good at keeping his face still too. Either that or I had no power to hurt him and was only embarrassing myself further. 'Okay,' he said. 'Well, Alex was right. Have a nice evening.'

He walked away.

I pushed my way through the crowds of idiotically drunken people, went into the house and locked myself in the bathroom. I sat on the floor and thought: I am not going to cry. I am not going to cry. I kept my breathing steady. I bit down on the inside of my arm and didn't cry. Eventually I got up and looked in the mirror, thinking I might look very ugly or else very beautiful, but I looked exactly like myself.

•

EVERYONE DRANK A lot that night, and an exuberant mood ran between them. They told funny stories – Heidi told one about the housemate she'd had before Mari, who liked to watch YouTube documentaries about trains at full volume. She told it well, and everyone laughed. Mari laughed so hard that she found herself with tears in her eyes, the lights in the garden blurring and spilling before her.

She knew it was pathetic, the way Jack's appearance had injected life into the evening. His presence, even on the other side of the garden, made her infuse all her gestures with a certain deliberateness, as though posing for a photograph: Mari pushing her hair behind her ears. Mari laughing. Mari hooking an errant bra strap with her thumb and tucking it under the sleeve of her dress. She refused to let herself look in his direction, and by doing this she felt she was, in some undefinable way, winning a point. If he came to speak to her, the night would be hers. But he didn't come, and when she finally glanced at him, he wasn't looking at her. He had his arms around Elisabeth, and he was saying something into her hair.

Mari noticed that her dress was sticking to her, and her head was beginning to spin. The music seemed too loud. Walking towards the bathroom, she could hear Paul and Aisha trying to identify which historical figures had big dick energy. 'Kurt Cobain?' said Aisha.

'No way,' said Paul. 'Tiny dick energy. Tiny.'

'Che Guevara.'

A howl of delight. 'Yes!'

On her way back from the bathroom, Mari wandered across the garden to the table where Heidi had laid out food. Picking up a knife to cut some cheese, she felt Jack there at her elbow. Something about the quality of the air seemed to shift, announcing his presence. 'Hi, Mari,' he said.

She didn't turn her head. 'Hi.'

'I meant to tell you before, you look really nice tonight. That dress suits you.'

Adrenaline rushed through her. She felt the firm skin of the brie give under the blade of her knife, and she sliced through the softness below. 'Thank you.'

Jack moved closer to her. He lowered his hand to where hers rested, on the edge of the old wooden picnic table, and he touched her pinkie finger with his.

She glanced up. He was looking at her, not smiling, with an intense expression on his face. As if he were listening to her even though she wasn't speaking. 'Jack,' she said, and his name was like a fish slipping out of her mouth.

He opened his mouth to reply, but just then Verity came up behind them, saying something about falafel and hummus, and Mari snatched her hand away. It stung, like she'd burned it. Jack stood back and watched as Mari talked, too fast, with Verity. Yes, there had been falafel earlier but now it was gone. There was still some hummus, and cheese and crackers. When Verity finally left, she turned to find Jack standing calmly, his hands in his pockets. 'Anyway,' he said. 'I'm off.'

'Now? But it's so early. You should try the punch, it's –'

'Mari,' he said. 'I'm leaving. I just came to say goodbye.'

She was still holding the piece of brie she'd cut, and she put it into her mouth and swallowed without tasting it. A slimy lump of fat. 'Okay. Well, goodbye.'

'Goodbye,' he said. And then, quietly, 'Behave yourself, won't you?'

Her breath vibrated in her chest. She had no idea what he meant, but it didn't seem to matter. Without thinking, she said, 'I'm always behaving myself.'

He raised his eyebrows, a half-smile on his face. Then he turned and walked away without hesitating, his back in its black jacket moving through the crowd.

•

I WAS SUPPOSED to work on the Sunday after Mari and Heidi's party, but I texted my boss to say I was sick. I remained sick on Tuesday, when my next shift was rostered, and also on Wednesday. Technically I had no symptoms, but it was also true that I was incapable of leaving my bedroom and making coffee for strangers.

I lay on my bed and looked blankly out the window at the huge blue sky and the tufts of clouds and the gum tree in my garden, its creamy bark rippled with orange and pink, and I thought: Here is beauty. Here it is.

I had given Mari the bare-bones version of the story via message, but we hadn't seen each other or spoken on the phone. On Wednesday night she came over and let herself into my room without knocking, holding two kebabs in paper bags. 'Here you go,' she said, tossing one to me. 'I got them to put eggplant on it, no chilli.'

'Oh, thanks.'

I was slumped on my bed, and she sat cross-legged beside me and unwrapped her kebab. 'Are you sad?' she asked.

'Not really.'

'Not really?'

'Mostly just tired. Thanks for bringing food, that's nice of you.'

To demonstrate emotional equilibrium, I unwrapped the kebab and took a bite. It tasted of sawdust. With her free hand, Mari touched my shoulder. 'You know, it's not, like, bad to have feelings,' she said.

'I do know that. Don't patronise me.'

She gave me a wounded look, one which I privately – in my least charitable moments – thought of as her kicked-puppy look. In the next second I hated myself for being so unkind to her. 'Sorry,' I said. 'I didn't mean that.'

She nodded. For a minute we were quiet, and I listened to one of my housemates clattering out the front door, the tick and whirr of his bike going down the street.

'You know, it's not as if you talk a lot about your feelings either,' I said. 'You just treat everything like a joke.'

'Do I? Like when?'

'Well, like that time you came to dinner, and you kissed me when you went to leave. And you did it again, that time in Alex's garden. Do you remember that?'

She laughed with her mouth full. 'Yeah. So?'

'So, I don't know. I was just curious to know why.'

'No real reason, I just decided to. I was really high.'

'Not the first time.'

She cut me a look. 'Okay, well, that time I was pretty drunk. Look, I don't think I can give you a reason, it just seemed like a fun idea.'

'Right.'

'Plus, you know men like that kind of thing.'

I had no idea how serious she was. The idea that she'd kissed me for Jack's benefit struck me as distasteful, but I could see her doing it as a joke, and even making it into one at his expense. It was impossible to know.

'Anyway, speaking of,' she said. 'Sorry if this is weird, but I wanted to make sure you knew – I didn't tell Jack anything.'

'What?'

'When he asked me how he could patch things up with you, it was right after you and Alex . . .' She gestured vaguely with one hand, and I felt a sick little throb of shame. 'Anyway, I didn't tell him anything at the time. Just in case you were wondering.'

I let my head fall back against the wall. It had never occurred to me that Mari might tell Jack, and hearing her raise it as a possibility – even one she hadn't acted on – made me feel strangely hurt. It was easier to concentrate on this hurt than on the shame, or the guilt snaking through my chest. 'Okay,' I said. 'Well, thanks.'

She broke off a piece of falafel and popped it into her mouth. 'You'll find somebody else.'

'Well, I've been thinking about that. You know, it's probably good that things ended between me and Jack, because it wasn't, we didn't . . .' I rubbed my face. It was the first time I'd said Jack's name since we'd split up, and the shape of it in my mouth still held some residual tenderness, but I didn't want to let Mari see that. 'He should probably be with someone his own age. So I'm not trying to be self-pitying, but I don't actually want to date anybody else. At all. Ever.'

Mari laughed. 'That seems a bit extreme.'

'I'm just struggling to think of, like, a good-news story from the world of relationships. All the couples we know kind of hate each other, or else they just don't fuck anymore, and the alternative is dating and going through stuff like this. I don't see the upside, honestly.'

'So you never want to have sex again?'

'I could have it without any of the other stuff.'

Mari gave me an irritatingly reasonable look. 'I think you'll change your mind,' she said. 'It's definitely possible to meet someone nice.'

I didn't reply. I was thinking that Jack had been nice; he had always been so nice to me, so patient and generous and kind, even when I hadn't deserved it. For a moment I thought of calling him and saying: I've been really stupid, I'm sorry. But he had said he didn't want to hang around people my age anymore.

'Maybe I just shouldn't date men,' I said.

'Oh, not you too. Between you and Heidi I feel like I'm living on a lesbian separatist commune.'

She said it mildly, leaning one foot against her opposite knee. Mari had always said that she 'wasn't opposed' to sleeping with women, but I knew she didn't see it as a real solution; she liked men too much, even when they treated her badly. 'What does Heidi think of all this, anyway?' I asked. 'I'm sure she's pleased.'

'No, no. She feels for you, of course.'

From her diplomatic tone, I could tell that Heidi had expressed some opinions that Mari didn't want to repeat, presumably about Jack but maybe also about me. I'd never forgotten her comment about Jack 'taking advantage' of me. Even though I could see the appeal in choosing to believe it at this juncture, I still felt it to be unfair, and it was strange to realise that a part of me wanted to defend the relationship, to say that we'd loved each other. Except he hadn't loved me.

'Anyway,' I said to Mari. 'I think I'm going to do this filmmaking course at the art college, starting next semester. I looked it up.'

'Oh, cool.'

'It's probably something I should have done ages ago. I think I was only interested in Jack for that reason, really – because I wanted to be a more serious person, and I was too lazy to do it myself.'

'You're not lazy.'

'Well, complacent, then. And I thought being with him was like a short cut to adulthood, so that was stupid. The whole thing was stupid.'

Mari finished her kebab and wiped her mouth with the back of her hand. 'What about him?' she asked.

'What do you mean, what about him?'

'Like, do you still think it was a midlife crisis thing?'

'God, Mari, I don't know. Does it matter?'

She didn't have an answer to that. I finished my food and we talked about other things, and then we watched half a movie before she got too sleepy. It was chilly that night, the first real chill of the year, and she borrowed a jumper of mine for the walk home.

After she'd gone, I lay facedown on the bed. I could still smell Mari there, her shampoo and moisturiser and cigarettes, but for some reason I found myself thinking about Jack. What I'd said to Mari was true, and I'd found it a neat and satisfying argument at the time, but now I was nagged by the sense of another element that I hadn't managed to grasp hold of. Really, I was thinking about the way he'd looked at me when we were alone together. It was a specific look: tender but also searching, as if he saw me as someone with so much depth. No one had ever looked at me that way before. Lying there with my wet face against the sheets, I only wished that I could somehow hold onto the image, find a way to fix it outside of memory, because I knew it would fade from my mind and one day be forgotten.

PART II

9

IT WAS A delicate situation, and Mari felt that to force anything would be to break it. She didn't make plans: she couldn't organise her fluttering thoughts into coherence, and whenever she tried she felt overwhelmed and sick. Too much. But in May, when Verso published a new book about socialist planning systems, she sent Jack a message asking if he had a copy. It was the kind of dull book he usually read, and besides, she really did want to read more non-fiction. It was an important part of her intellectual development.

He said he did have a copy, and she wrote back: *Any chance I could borrow it?* A few hours later, he replied: *Okay. If you want to come and get it on Wednesday night, I'll be here.*

When Wednesday night came, she couldn't eat the dinner Heidi offered her. She lied about having had a big lunch and went to her room to look at herself in the mirror. Elisabeth's face made sense: the features cohered to produce meaning, and the meaning was prettiness. Mari's face didn't mean anything. She put on a pair of thigh-high stockings under her dress, hated herself, took them off. Put them on again. She went out into the cool grey bite of the autumn evening without telling Heidi goodbye.

When she knocked on the door of Jack's flat, he called, 'It's unlocked.'

She went inside, blinking in the dark hallway. 'Jack?'

'Hi. I'm in here.' She followed his voice to the study, where he sat at his desk in the lamplight. A jolt of shock: he was thinner than when she'd seen him last, and his face looked drawn and tired. Without thinking, she said, 'Are you all right?'

He took his glasses off and rubbed the bridge of his nose. 'Hi, Mari. Nice to see you too.'

'Sorry. It's just . . .'

'No, I know. I've been under the weather.'

'Flu?'

'Something like that. Anyway, there's the book.' He gestured at a thick book with a red cover sitting on his desk.

Mari picked it up and realised she'd never been less interested in anything in her life. 'Thanks,' she said. 'So what are you doing?'

'Right now? I'm marking these essays.'

'Any good?'

'Most of them have made an effort. That's all I ask for.' He leaned back in the chair, looking at her. She wondered if he remembered saying: Behave yourself, won't you? She had been running over the memory almost constantly since it happened, so frequently that it no longer succeeded in eliciting much emotion.

She walked around his study, running her finger over the spines of his books and occasionally pulling one out to examine it. She could feel his eyes on her. 'You really have a lot of boring books here,' she said.

'Well, we can't all be scholars of classic literature.'

'You should know better than to call me a scholar.'

He laughed, covering his face with one hand. It was nice to hear him laugh. 'Of course,' he said. 'I apologise.'

She turned from the bookshelf and went over to him. Concentrating on keeping her mind empty, she took his hand and laid it under her coat, under her dress, just where the top of her stocking ended. His face had a blank, abstracted look.

'I see,' he said quietly. 'Is this a good idea?'

She shrugged. With a casualness she didn't feel, she said, 'You can say no if you want.'

'I'm not saying no. I just wonder if you've thought it through.'

'I have.'

'Right.' He brushed his thumb against the stocking's lace edge.

Mari cast her eye over the stack of papers on his desk, her heart pounding. 'Lots of marking.'

'Yeah.'

'It can wait, don't you think?' She leaned towards him and kissed him, and after a second he kissed her back. She felt her knees go weak, which she'd always thought only happened in books, but here it was happening to her. Between that and his tongue in her mouth, his hand under her dress, she didn't know how long she'd be able to stand up. 'Can we go to your bedroom?' she whispered.

'Yeah, okay.' Dark, cold hallway; bedroom. Jack switched on a lamp and she lay on the bed, wrapped in her coat. He propped himself up on an elbow beside her. Something of his old wry expression had returned to his face. 'Mari, far be it from me to tell you what to do, but are you going to take your coat off at any point?'

'I'm cold.'

'Oh, I see. This is where I say something about how I'm going to warm you up, is that right?'

'That's right. You know your lines so well.'

He laughed. 'Actually, it is pretty cold in here. Wait a minute, I'll put the heater on.'

When he turned back from the heater she'd taken off her coat, dress and stockings, and was lying on the bed in her bra and underwear. He laughed again, and she was relieved. 'That was quick,' he said.

'I feel warmer now.'

'Oh, good.' He lay beside her and unbuckled his belt, unbuttoned his shirt. The feeling of his skin against hers sent a thrill coasting through her. This is really happening, she thought. This is really happening and not a dream. Underneath her exhilaration was a thread of relief that things were progressing familiarly – a small part of her had worried that, being so much more experienced, he'd know something about sex that she hadn't yet discovered. But he was pressed against her, the way she'd imagined so many times, and she took his hand and put it between her legs. 'Hey,' she murmured. 'I'm really ready.'

'Yeah, I can see that. Well, feel it.' He stroked his fingers against her. She felt as though there were no solid flesh there, only wetness. 'Let me just . . .' He leaned over to the drawer beside the bed.

Mari put her hand on his arm. 'Don't worry about it.'

'What?'

'Just leave it.' She couldn't stand the idea of the condom, its tight plasticky feel separating their bodies, which were so close now to being together. 'You can pull out, can't you?'

He laughed. 'Mari, that's such an incredibly bad idea.'

'Come on, lots of people do it. People my age, I mean.'

That wasn't strictly true, but she knew it would convince Jack. 'Well, all right,' he said, the drawer coasting shut with a flick of his wrist. 'If that's what you want. You're a terrible influence on me, do you know that?'

She liked that idea. He moved between her legs and pushed into her, and she sucked air into her lungs. 'Fuck,' he said, under his breath.

'Do you still think it's a bad idea?'

'Yes. Very much so.' His breath was shallow and fast. 'Very, very . . . Sorry, what was the question?'

Mari was laughing; she thought she had probably never been so happy in her life. It was easy not to think of Elisabeth, and in fact there was no reason to think of her, so she didn't. Jack moved slowly inside her, and she tried to notice everything: his weight, his scent, the feeling of his cheek against hers. After a while she found it difficult to form complete thoughts about these things, or about anything. Her body was a train rushing along its tracks. Jack said softly, 'Is this okay for you?' and she nodded. His voice so close to her ear. It seemed very possible that she would come like that, just from hearing him speak to her. Don't be so pathetic, she told herself. Don't be desperate. Don't be.

'Just, um,' she said.

'Hmm?'

'Just a second.' She sat up and drank from the glass of water beside the bed, the glass knocking against her teeth. Jack was looking at her curiously. 'Sorry,' she said.

'It's okay. Do you want to stop?'

'No. Really, no.' She lay back down beside him. 'Talk to me for a little bit, would you?'

'Talk to you . . . Okay. Hey, I've always wondered about your name. What's Mari short for?'

'Marielle.' She made a face. 'My mother was going through a Francophile phase. It's silly.'

'No, I like it. Very elegant.'

'Oh.' Mari smiled at him. 'Am I elegant?'

'At this precise moment in time, no. I don't think this is what an elegant girl would be doing with her evening.'

'Oh well.' She reached for him, guided him back inside her. 'I guess I don't want to be elegant, then.'

He began moving in her again, and feeling bloomed through her. Her body arched and pressed against his. 'Is that good, Marielle?' he asked softly.

'Yes.'

'Do you like it?'

'Yes . . .'

'Do you want me to make you come now?'

She could only nod, sucking at the air with shallow breaths. He pushed his hand through her hair, warm against her scalp, and he took a handful and pulled slowly, almost luxuriously. She had no idea how he'd known to do it but all at once she was coming violently, like being pushed off a diving board. Distantly, she was aware of crying out. It was just receding when he began moving faster, and then he said something like: Oh, fuck, and then sudden warm wetness on her stomach. She kept her eyes closed.

'Shit,' he said breathlessly, collapsing beside her. 'Well, no harm done, but that was just in the nick of time. I haven't performed that particular manoeuvre in a while.'

Mari caught her breath, drifting back into herself. Who had she been, only a minute ago? 'You did warn me it was a bad idea.'

'Yeah. Terrible influence, like I said. Hang on.' He went out and came back with a roll of toilet paper, handing it to her without quite meeting her eye. 'Here you go.'

Mari wiped her stomach off, although even as she did it she was aware of a dim urge to rub the milky globs of his come into her skin. Don't be weird, she thought. When she had finished, she turned over towards Jack and said in his ear, 'That was a really good fuck.'

She felt the muscles of his face move into a smile. 'Glad to be of service. I'd make a joke about that not being my usual book-lending practice, but I don't think you really came here for the book, did you?'

'What book?'

He laughed, and she pressed her face against the soft, slightly damp skin of his neck. He smelled so much like himself. In the dark cavern between his neck and shoulder, it was possible to say, 'Actually, I've wanted to do that for a long time.'

'Oh, really?'

'Yeah, I guess you probably knew that. Even in the summer when we, you know, the three of us . . .'

'Yeah.' His voice was like a door swinging closed.

'Sorry.'

'No, it's okay.' He cleared his throat. 'How is she, anyway? Elisabeth?'

'Oh . . . She's fine.' Somehow Mari failed to put the correct emphasis on the syllables of this sentence, and it came out sounding strangled. It was true, though – Elisabeth was fine, almost aggressively fine. Once or twice Mari had tried to bring Jack's name into the conversation, but Elisabeth had always changed the subject, and it was an unspoken but obvious assumption that they would never see him again. It was Elisabeth who decided these things for both of them.

'Good,' Jack said, getting up. 'Mari, I'm going to take a shower, and then do you mind if I go to bed? You're welcome to stay, of course, it's just that I have to teach tomorrow at eight.'

'Oh, sure. Hey, can I smoke in here? Or are you going to make me go outside in the cold?'

He made a humorously resigned expression with his mouth. 'Christ. All right, don't drop ash on the sheets.'

When he'd gone she thought about getting up for her cigarettes, but they were in her bag in the study, which seemed cold and far away. She stretched across the bed, listening to the distant hum of the shower. Her mind was luxuriously blank, but there was a kind of warmth in her chest, going and going, as if someone had lit a candle inside her.

•

WINTER SETTLED IN over the following weeks, and it was always cold when Mari left Jack's flat in the morning. He would be getting dressed or making coffee, and he'd say something like, 'Don't freeze to death out there.' She'd hurry through the narrow streets with her head tucked down. When she got home, Heidi would be drinking tea at the kitchen table, the heater whirring at her feet. She never asked where Mari had been. Nobody else knew about Jack, and Mari was terrified someone would find out, but she also hoped they would, if only to spare her the burden of carrying it all around in her head. Sometimes she arrived at Jack's flat half-convinced that she'd made the whole thing up, expecting him to say, politely but quizzically: 'Mari? What are you doing here?'

She arrived later in the evening – Jack didn't cook for her, the way he had for Elisabeth. He left the front door unlocked, and she let herself in. He'd be in his study, and when she came in he'd say, 'Oh, hello.'

He'd usually be drinking whiskey, just a finger or two in a squarish glass. He'd offer her a drink, and they'd sit there together while he finished what he was doing. Mari sometimes thought he worked deliberately slowly to keep her waiting, glass dripping in her hand, warm and slippery between her legs before he'd even touched her. He rarely looked at her while he worked, just murmured things under his breath and typed in brief spurts. Eventually he'd look up and say, 'Sorry, just had to finish that. Do you want another drink?'

'No.'

His half-smile, flitting across his face in the lamplight. 'All right. What would you like to do?'

'Oh, I thought we could do the crossword together. Maybe watch TV.'

'Mmm. I don't think there's anything good on tonight.' That was her cue to come over to him. He liked her to initiate, and he always put up half a show of surprise, as if he'd thought, up until then, that she really wanted to do the crossword. But when he touched her, she felt her blood thicken, her body shift gears. What he wanted from her, he could have.

Afterwards, they would smoke and talk for a while before Jack got up to shower. That was Mari's favourite part of the evening, because Jack was always in a good mood, his attention warm and focused. Once she told him about seeing a car accident on her way to work, and how she'd been so shocked she felt dizzy, and had to get off her bike and lean against a tree. He made a sympathetic noise and kissed the top of her head. She would happily have witnessed a thousand car accidents to repeat that moment.

One evening she brought him a present: a vinyl copy of *In the Aeroplane Over the Sea*, which she'd silently deliberated over for nearly half an hour in the record store. 'This is for you,' she said, sliding it onto his desk. 'You probably remember when it came out; I think I was six or seven at the time. But it's a good album.'

He picked up the record, looking pleased. 'You got this for me? Mari, that's so lovely. What's the occasion?'

'No occasion, I just saw it and thought you probably liked it. You don't already have it, do you?'

'No. I used to have the CD, years ago, but it got lost. This is great, thank you.'

Something in his voice caught her interest. 'Got lost? How?'

'Oh, it . . . Well, if you must know, it ended up being collateral damage in a rather difficult breakup. Which you won't be hearing any more about, before you ask.'

She smiled. She often asked about his previous relationships, but he was cagey in his answers, citing the need to protect the innocent. He never asked about hers, and part of her was relieved: she didn't particularly want to recount the years spent drifting between celibacy and sex with men who only replied to half her texts, or who tried to choke her without asking first. 'Come on,' she said. 'Tell me. As payback for the gift – you know, reciprocity.'

He laughed. 'I should've known better than to accept a gift from an anthropologist. It's Mauss, isn't it, who goes on about reciprocity?'

'Stop trying to bring Mauss into this. Just tell me.'

'You drive a hard bargain. Well, it was about ten years ago now; I don't even know if I remember all the details. I suppose

the heart of it was that she really wanted to get married, have
children, that kind of thing, and I really didn't. A bit of a zero-sum
game, sadly.' He took his glasses off and began cleaning the lenses
on his shirt.

'What was her name?'

'Alison.'

'Alison.' Mari pronounced it experimentally, rolling it around
her mouth. 'Did you love her?'

'I suppose I did, yeah. At the time.'

'So what happened to her? After you broke up?'

'Oh, nothing too drastic. She met someone else pretty quickly,
and they got married and had a kid. I think they've got a couple of
kids now, actually. I see her at conferences every now and again.'

'Oh! So she's a historian, too?'

'She is. Now that's enough, all right? I think Mauss would be
more than satisfied.'

'All right.' Mari knew she would go home later and look through
the faculty listings of every history department in the country until
she found Alison. 'I wonder if she still listens to the CD.'

He laughed. 'I don't think she even liked it that much to begin
with. Mari, it's really sweet of you, buying this for me. I'm so
touched. Come here.'

She went to him, and he put his arms around her. Don't cry,
she told herself firmly. Do not cry. She must have been clinging
to him too tightly, though, because he said, 'Hey, hey. Everything
all right?'

'Yeah. Just cold.'

'You're always cold.'

He rubbed her back, and she tucked her face against his chest,
breathing him in. There he was, all of him: the soft grey sweatshirt

he wore in the evenings, his familiar smell. There he was with her. Happiness bloomed inside her, like music coming to a pitch. For a moment she imagined explaining to Elisabeth that really it wasn't about sex: the deepest part of her only wanted Jack to protect her, to hold her in his arms as if he loved her. But I love you, Elisabeth would say. You know I do.

10

IN HER MIND, Mari tried to establish boundaries. Outside Jack's flat, she adopted the persona of someone who had never gone to see him in a pair of ridiculous thigh-high stockings, who had never put his hand under her dress, who was certainly not planning on doing it again the next time he had a free evening. It was easier that way. She didn't really believe that anything she did had the capacity to hurt Elisabeth, but she still felt a creeping sense of unease whenever she pictured Elisabeth's reaction to the news, and she tried to put it out of her head as much as possible. When they had dinner together, she put a lot of effort into talking animatedly about other things. But after their food came, Elisabeth looked at her closely and said, 'There's something different about you.'

Mari concentrated on pouring herself a glass of wine. 'Cut my fringe yesterday.'

'No, not that. Is there something on your mind?'

Mari drank her wine. Usually she was glad that she and Elisabeth had known each other so long: it meant that they no longer stood on ceremony with each other, and were free to do things like scroll through their phones in comfortable silence or bitch about people they didn't like. But sometimes she hated the intimacy of being known so well. She was an insect trapped under glass, grabbing fingers coming to tear off her legs. 'Okay,' she said, deciding on a half-truth. 'I actually went to Jack's place the other night. Well, a few weeks ago. I wanted to borrow a book.'

Elisabeth stopped with her chopsticks halfway to her mouth, although Mari suspected she was doing this mainly for dramatic effect. 'What?' she said. 'Why?'

'I thought I should start reading more non-fiction, and there was that Verso book that came out –'

'Oh, come on. You know what I mean.'

Mari put her wineglass down. There was a seed of irritation in her that she now felt determined to nurture. 'Well, we can be mature about this, can't we?' she said. 'I'm not going to pretend to hate him, we're not in high school.'

That blow landed, as she'd known it would. Elisabeth gathered her hair and twisted it into a bun, a carefully neutral expression on her face. 'Okay,' she said. 'But if we were being mature about it, you could have said something before now.'

'Honestly, I didn't even think you'd care.'

'Oh, really.'

'Well, you were pretty abrupt, you know, when you broke up with him. We used to see him all the time, and then one day that was it.' Mari snapped her fingers. The sound was pleasingly crisp. 'Like he was just erased from history. And you didn't care, you said you'd only been interested in him because you'd thought he was a short cut to adulthood, and that was stupid.'

The shadow of some indecipherable expression passed over Elisabeth's face. Mari felt a pinprick of guilt, especially when she remembered – it was strange to realise that in fact she'd briefly forgotten – why she'd really gone to Jack's flat. 'Sorry,' she said.

'No, it's all right.' Elisabeth leaned back tiredly in her chair. 'You can stay friends with him if you like, I don't hate him. But you know it won't be the same as it was.'

'What?'

'Well, we're not going to – I mean, I don't want to see him again, even as friends or whatever. I'm sure he feels the same way about me.'

Mari was relieved – if a little unsettled – by how mistaken this interpretation was. 'No, don't worry,' she said lightly. 'I know Mummy and Daddy don't love each other anymore.'

'Yeah, very funny. Anyway, nobody ever said that word.'

'What?'

'Well, love. We never said we loved each other.'

Mari tried not to hear the brittle note in Elisabeth's voice. She finished her wine and refilled the glass. It was almost gratifying to recognise her own guilt, spreading from her chest into her stomach: it was the correct emotional response, the response of a good person. But could she call herself a good person now? Had she ever been?

When she got home later that evening, she went into the bathroom and forced her fingers down her throat. She hadn't done it in years, but there was a certain muscle memory to the twisting and bucking of her stomach, the food sliding painfully up her throat. The bile and tears came as something of a disgusting relief: infinitely better than sitting in her room with a lump of food in her stomach. When she was finished, she brushed her teeth several times, washed her face, and cycled over to Jack's flat. The cold air whipped her face. It felt good, like breathing in ice, very crisp and clean.

The front door was unlocked, and as she stepped into the hallway, she could hear the mechanical blather of the TV in the living room. 'It's me,' she called.

'Mari? Is that you?'

She went into the bedroom and took off her coat, her tights, her skirt. Jack came and stood in the doorway, watching her. He was wearing jeans and his grey sweatshirt, and his feet were bare. 'Get undressed,' she said.

'What's all this about?'

'What are you standing there for? Just take your clothes off, then you can fuck me. That's what you want, isn't it?'

'What?'

'Sex with a girl twenty years younger than you, no strings attached – you must think you've died and gone to heaven. I don't even make you use a condom. Do you know how fucked up that is, just out of interest?'

'Jesus Christ. Of course I'd use a condom if you wanted, but it was your idea . . .'

'Oh, I know. This whole thing was my idea, so I've got to take responsibility for it, isn't that right? Be a grown-up? You can tell me all about that, can't you?'

Jack ran a hand through his hair. 'Do you mind telling me what's upset you?'

'I don't have to tell you anything.' She pulled her jumper over her head and threw it on the floor. 'What are you waiting for? I don't have all night, you know.'

'I can't do it like this. You're looking at me like you hate me.'

'I do hate you.'

'Why are you here, then?'

'I'm here because I want you to fuck me, was that not clear?'

He looked at her for a minute, his hands in his back pockets. Mari felt her lip trembling, but she held her face together with an effort.

'Okay,' he said eventually, in a neutral voice. 'Have it your own way.'

She lay slackly on the bed and let him touch her the way he wanted to, ran her hands over his body mechanically. Above them, the pendant lightshade swayed minutely. He was hard; that was mildly gratifying, at least. He fumbled in the drawer for a condom, held it up for her to see. 'There. Happy?'

'Not particularly.'

'Mari, for Christ's sake. I can't –'

'Oh, spare me. I want you to do it, okay? I'm a legal adult, I'll sign any fucking consent form, any waiver, anything. Just do it.'

He did. She lay on her back and stared at the ceiling, keeping herself blank. Enduring. She thought about the mess of undigested food in the toilet bowl: brown curls of beef, vermicelli noodles like thin white worms. Elisabeth's face across the table. You know it won't be the same as it was. This is what I need. Treat me like the thing I am.

After a while he said, 'Turn over,' and she got on her hands and knees. Face in the pillow, her mouth open and wet on the clean white linen. She felt him getting close, getting really close. Coming. Good. Do it. Now you have to live with that for the rest of your life.

He got up to throw the condom away, and she turned on her back and studied the ceiling again. When he lay down beside her, he said, 'I feel sick.'

She didn't reply.

'I shouldn't have done that. I'm so sorry, I have no idea why I did that.'

'Probably because I told you to.'

'That's not an excuse.'

'Isn't it?'

'No, it's really not.'

His voice was shaking. She turned to him, so surprised that she forgot to be angry. 'Hey,' she said. 'It's okay. It was my fault, not yours.'

'Don't fucking say that.'

'Sorry. But it's really not a big deal, you know. Just forget it.'

He was silent. It had been overcast when Mari left the house, and now she could hear the quiet tick of rain against the roof. Eventually he said, 'You know what this makes me.'

'What?'

'I'm just as bad as him.'

'Who? What are you talking about?'

'Your teacher, Mari. The one who more or less raped you, and don't tell me you consented, you were sixteen years old. I'm sure he had the same justification too – oh, well, she wants it, so . . .'

'Him?' Mari almost laughed, it was so unexpected. 'You're nothing like him. I never even think about him.'

'He should be in prison. So should I, probably.'

'Well, that's a bit over the top.' Mari stroked his cheek, but he was staring at the ceiling, his face hard. 'Jack,' she said gently. 'It isn't your fault. Really.'

He shook his head. 'I don't know,' he said. 'That story's always bothered me. It's fucked up to begin with, but when you told me how things were for you at school . . . I mean, you sounded like a lonely kid, really. You would've been vulnerable to that kind of thing.'

'Well, everyone's vulnerable to something.'

Jack put his hands over his face. 'Are you defending him?'

'No.'

His hands dropped to his sides. 'Sorry,' he said. 'It's up to you how to feel about it, of course. But if I ever ran into him I would probably have to cut his balls off.'

Mari pressed her face into his shoulder. She couldn't speak. Jack took her chin in his hand and tilted her face up. 'Hey, what's the matter?' he asked. 'Are you crying?'

She was; there was no point trying to hide it. 'I'm sorry,' she said unsteadily. 'For making you do those things. I get in moods like that sometimes, I don't know why.'

'You get in moods to force men to have sex with you while you lie there completely disinterested and make them feel like shit?' But he was smiling as he said it, and she knew she was safe. 'That's weird, Mari.'

'I know. I'm sorry.'

'All right, well, we're both sorry.' He put his arm around her. 'Have you got your cigarettes handy? I could do with one.'

'Aren't you supposed to smoke cigarettes after good sex?'

He laughed. 'Brutal. Look, that wasn't within my control and I'll be putting in a formal request to have it expunged from my record. But in the meantime, cigarettes, please.'

She fetched them from her bag. They smoked in bed all the time, the two of them, even though Jack said it was a disgusting habit. Later he found her a T-shirt to sleep in, and she curled up against him. His body felt warm and solid beside hers. Lately she'd been having trouble falling asleep, but maybe in his bed it would be easier.

He turned out the light, and she listened to his breathing deepen and slow. He would sleep soundly all night, she knew, and in the morning he'd roll over towards her and slide his hand under her T-shirt. He would go back to playing the role he'd played forever – the role of a man who was good in bed – and she'd be his audience. Sometimes she suspected the role was what he really cared about: not her pleasure, not even her happiness, but the idea of himself generously bestowing all that upon her. A man who cared about women. Surely she had no right to resent him for that. She would have liked to discuss the matter with Elisabeth, and as she lay awake in the darkness she found herself imagining how intently Elisabeth would listen, the way she'd nod and say: Yes, I know exactly what you mean.

•

I WAS BUSY that winter – I enrolled in the film course that I'd told Mari about, and that took up a lot of my time. I had the idea that my eventual success as a filmmaker would cancel out the residual humiliation of my breakup with Jack – or that at least if we ever saw each other again I would be more mature and intellectually able, and he'd regret ever saying that I was possessive of Mari. I enjoyed the course too; it was nice to have things to think about and do on a schedule. I had always been good at being a student. The winter days were beautiful, crisp and blue and clear, and the cool weather seemed to bring with it a clarity and resolve that I'd been lacking in the thick heat of summer.

The only dark thread running underneath my days was the fact that Mari and I weren't seeing much of each other. She didn't go out often, and when she did, she sat on the edge of conversations and checked her phone a lot. The replies she sent to my messages were brief and impersonal. One Saturday in July, at a dinner party organised by Heidi, I cornered her in the kitchen and asked how she was.

'Fine,' she said. She was leaning against the counter, staring into the middle distance. She could do this when she wanted, close herself off to me like slamming a door. Sometimes she did it deliberately to punish me, although I didn't always know what for. 'I'm just tired, not sleeping well. It'll pass.'

I put my arm around her, and she didn't hug me back, but she didn't move away either. Her shoulders felt sharp and bony. 'Are you eating enough?' I asked.

'Yes.'

'Okay. And is everything all right? At work and . . . everything?'

She chewed her lip. 'Work's fine. I mean, terrible, but fine. How's your film thing going, though? The course?'

I told her about it, making her laugh by describing all the bad short film ideas my fellow students came up with. When she laughed her face came alive, and it seemed possible that I'd been imagining the distance between us. 'Hey,' I said. 'Do you want to get dinner somewhere, just us? Or we could go back to my place and watch something, I think there's a new season of that tiny-house show you hate.'

She wanted to say yes; I could see it in her face. For a second I let myself imagine that she would, and we'd spend the evening watching TV in my bed and making fun of the tiny-house people. Maybe she'd sleep over, and in the morning we'd get banh mi. I'd order tofu because of slaughterhouses, and she'd order pork because there was no ethical consumption under capitalism, and we'd have a leisurely argument about it, her letting me win, while we browsed through the op shops. But then she was shaking her head. 'I can't,' she said.

'Oh. Okay.'

She leaned down to put a bottle of wine in the fridge, and I looked at the narrow shape of her back in its black turtleneck. I could see one of my hairs clinging to her shoulder. When she straightened up, she said, 'So why are you doing this course, anyway? I mean, do you think you're going to be a filmmaker or whatever?'

The question was cruel, she'd meant it to be, and for a second I was winded. Keeping my voice light, I said, 'Or whatever. It's just a preliminary thing, to see what it's like. Later on I might enrol in the degree.'

'You're going to get another degree? You know there's a limit to how much you can borrow on HECS.'

I paused. The truth was that my parents would gladly lend me the extra money, and I knew that Mari knew this. 'We'll see,' I said carefully. 'I might not do it.'

'It seems kind of like a waste of time and money. But I guess that's not a concern for you.'

'Well, I'm not that invested in it. I just thought it would be interesting.'

'Yeah. I thought a degree in anthropology would be interesting, but look where it's got me.'

I leaned back against the counter. Mari never usually expressed this kind of anxiety, and I wasn't completely sure how to respond. 'Okay,' I said. 'I'll keep it in mind. But listen, are you sure you're all right? You seem so down these days.'

'Look, enough, okay? Can't you just leave me alone?'

My voice froze in my throat. I stood very still with my heart pounding, a metallic taste in my mouth. Of course, a part of me had always feared this: that she wanted me to leave her alone, that I was too involved in her life. She was looking at the floor, and when she spoke again, her voice was reedy and strangled.

'I'm sorry,' she said.

'Mari?'

'Sorry, I'm really sorry. Don't listen to me. I'll see you later.' She went into her room and I stayed where I was, staring at the corner of the fridge. There was a scattering of crumbs underneath it, and a dark sticky stain spreading over the floorboards. I was biting my lip very hard.

Heidi came in then and asked me to help her bring the food out, and without thinking I said yes. I still remember that dinner party, how we sat on the living room floor and ate lots of different Middle Eastern salads, and how I drank wine out of a mug because there weren't enough wineglasses. We talked about our friends who had recently become high-school teachers, how strange it was to think of people our age commanding a classroom. We talked about funding for state schools and private schools. We talked about religion. Mari didn't come out, and nobody mentioned her absence.

While we were washing up, I asked Heidi if Mari was all right. She took a long time to answer, carefully drying a plate.

'She's okay,' she said eventually. 'You know Mari.'

'What does that mean?'

'Well, it doesn't take much to upset her. Like, if she has to talk to her mum on the phone, they always end up arguing, and then she cries . . . And I mean, I do sympathise, but everyone has problems with their parents. My mum still wants to believe I'm straight, I've probably come out to her like twelve times by now.'

'She won't talk to me,' I said. My voice caught stupidly on the words. 'She was a bit hostile, actually.'

'Yeah, well.'

I glanced at her, polishing a wineglass with a tea towel. She and Mari had always got along well, even though Heidi pretended to be annoyed by Mari's untidiness. But I sensed that something had shifted: that Heidi knew or suspected something, and it was testing her patience. I knew her primary allegiance was still to Mari, and she wouldn't tell me anything if I pressed her, so I just said, 'Well, if you don't know . . .'

'She'll be okay. Just give her some time.'

I walked home that night trying to convince myself that Heidi was right: that Mari was just going through some minor private difficulty – something with her mother maybe – which would soon get better. It didn't really work. When I got home I scrolled around the internet for a while, and then I opened the folder where I'd stored the footage from my film project. For reasons that weren't fully clear, I'd put the footage of Mari in a separate subfolder.

I turned off the light and watched it for a while, sitting in bed with my laptop on my thighs. There she was on the screen, telling Alex that if she were to become religious, she'd be Jewish or Catholic or Muslim – 'You know, a serious religion.' There she was laughing, smoking, telling me to put the fucking phone away. Her long body, pale legs and knobbly knees. It had always been unbelievable to me that she couldn't see how beautiful she was.

That night I dreamed that her palm was peppered with small black nails, the points protruding from under the skin, and I was meticulously picking them out. There was satisfaction in this task, and Mari didn't seem to be in any pain. We sat together in contented silence while I worked the nails out from under her skin. When I felt myself waking, I kept my eyes closed and tried to feel my way along the rope of the dream. I wanted to go back there, back to the place where we sat quietly together, but it didn't work. I was awake, and the room was cold.

11

MARI COULDN'T SLEEP in Jack's bed. She couldn't sleep in her
own bed. Her eyes burned with fatigue, and at her desk during
the day she often felt right on the verge of falling asleep. She'd lost
her appetite and was surviving mainly on cereal and milk, the
occasional slice of toast with peanut butter. She needed comfortable
blandness; everything else was too harsh against her tongue. In
the office lunch room, the dressing on her salad made her gag.

'Are you sick?' Frank from payroll asked, getting ready to
back away.

'No. Well, maybe. I don't know.'

He gave her a puzzled look. Mari smiled at him beatifically.
She no longer cared what anyone at work thought. She no longer
cared what Heidi thought, hearing her leave at night. Her world
had been reduced to a single point of focus, which was Jack's
bedroom. Every time he ushered her inside, she tipped her head
back and smiled up at him dizzily. She never felt tired when she
was with him. She would have stayed up talking to him all night
if she could have.

One night she got up the courage to ask him – in a studiously
casual tone – whether he was seeing anyone else. (This was

language she had rehearsed exhaustively beforehand – 'seeing someone' seemed to hit the right note for describing their own arrangement, a comfortable middle ground between 'sleeping with' and 'dating'.) 'It's okay if you are, of course,' she said.

'Oh, well, thanks. Why do you ask?'

'No real reason. But some nights you don't want me to come over, so I thought . . .'

She'd been worried that the question would irritate him, but he was grinning. 'You're very quick to jump to conclusions,' he said.

'So I'm wrong?'

He traced his finger down her forehead and across her left eyebrow. 'I think we can both sleep with whoever we want. Doesn't that seem fair to you?'

'I guess so.' He trailed the finger over her left breast, down her ribcage. She squirmed away.

'What's the matter?'

'Nothing. I'm so – I just hate the way my ribs stick out.'

'Oh no. You've got a very nice body.'

Mari let the words throb through her. It was really happening – she was really here with him, in his bed, hearing him say the words: You've got a very nice body. 'You don't have to say that,' she said.

'I know I don't have to, but it's true. I do find you reasonably attractive, I thought you'd have realised that by now.'

She let a smile spread over her face. 'Should I send you a picture sometime?'

'A picture?'

'You know.' She gestured at herself, making a sweeping motion up and down. 'Of me.'

'Oh, I've heard about this. People your age love sending each other compromising pictures, don't they? I'll pass, thanks.'

'I don't mind. I know you wouldn't show anyone.'

'I certainly wouldn't. Actually, it's me I'm worried about, not you. I'd rather not possess that kind of incriminating material.'

Mari rolled onto her back. She hadn't known that refusing nude pictures was a thing that men did. 'Okay,' she said. 'Suit yourself.'

'Hey, it's not that I don't appreciate the offer.' He ran a hand lightly over her stomach, and she felt her muscles tense pleasurably. Sometimes she hated the way her body responded to him. 'I actually think you'd photograph very well. All long lines, black and white. You're an Aubrey Beardsley sort of girl – did Elisabeth ever tell you that? She'd know who Aubrey Beardsley is, even if you don't.'

'I know who Aubrey Beardsley is.'

'All right, good. And listen, about the other thing . . . You're so young. How young are you exactly?'

'Twenty-six.' It had been her birthday the week before, although she hadn't told him, wanting him to find out on his own. Later she realised how stupid that was, but by then it was too late.

'Twenty-six. Honestly, Mari, you should be free while you can. You've got time to make plenty of mistakes, it won't matter. Lucky you.'

'Am I making a mistake now?'

'You know that better than me, I'm just passing through. In five years' time I'll be a funny story to tell your husband.'

Mari felt that as a blow to the chest, but she took care not to show it. 'Do you wish you were twenty-six again?' she asked.

He did, she knew that. She liked to play up how young she was compared to him: if he mentioned some memory of his, she'd say, 'I was two when that happened.' Or six, nine, fifteen, not yet born. He didn't really like those comments, but at the same time she could tell that the age gap between them turned him on. She could also tell that he preferred not to admit this, or think about it.

Now he just smiled. 'I wouldn't be twenty-six again if you paid me.'

'But you drink and smoke like a twenty-six-year-old.'

'You're one to talk.'

'It's okay for me, though. Like you said, I'm free to make mistakes. Lucky me, right?'

He didn't reply. Mari felt a surge of aggression. 'Because, I mean, some people might find it a bit weird,' she continued, keeping her voice bright. 'How old are *you*? Forty-four? Forty-five? Why haven't you got a partner and kids like everyone else your age?'

'Maybe I don't want that.'

'Oh yeah, you prefer fucking young girls.'

It was thrilling to say it, like hurling a dagger across the room, but it didn't hit its target. Jack just looked at her calmly, as though he knew she'd apologise eventually and was prepared to wait until she did.

She rolled away from him. 'I'm really tired.'

'Oh, okay.'

'From staying up late all the time.' She was addressing the wall now, angrily. 'You know, why do I always come over here? Why don't you ever come to my house?'

He was silent.

'Well?'

'I don't think it would be a good idea.'

'Because of Heidi, you mean? Are you that terrified of Elisabeth finding out? Is it really the worst thing that could happen to you?'

'No, it's not the worst thing that could happen to me. To you, though, I don't know.'

'I'm not –' Mari took a deep breath. She knew she had lost control of the conversation, lost it badly. 'I'm not *speaking literally*. I just want to know why things between us are so unequal, that's all. You get to have everything the way you want and I'm just there, ready to service your every need. I'm the one who comes over late and leaves early and fits my entire life around you. How is that fair?'

'You don't have to,' Jack said mildly. 'If you feel that way, I mean. You can stop coming over, I'm not forcing you.'

'Right.'

'Actually, I'm kind of surprised you've kept it up. Seeing as Elisabeth is supposed to be your friend.'

A tidal wave of humiliation coursed through Mari, and everything inside her gave way under its force. So you do know, she thought. You know what kind of person I am. No wonder you just want to use me for sex. The thought arrived unbidden: Elisabeth would never let anyone treat her like this. But then, Elisabeth would never do what Mari had done. She couldn't quite get the thought to make sense, but she got out of bed anyway and started pulling her jeans on.

Jack's face stayed passive as she stuffed her feet into her boots, tugged her jumper over her head. 'You'll probably want to get to sleep soon,' she said. 'Work tomorrow.' He nodded. She knew she shouldn't slam the door behind her as she left, but she did it anyway. It felt good.

•

FOR DAYS AFTERWARDS she waited to hear from him, checking her phone compulsively. If she had to put it away during a meeting at work she would return to it feverishly, certain there would be a message from him. Sometimes the message icon did appear, and everything inside her pitched to a crescendo, but it was never from him. Then she was left feeling worse than before, her heart thudding unpleasantly hard in her chest. She hated herself for behaving this way, even more because she couldn't help it.

Heidi knew something was wrong, and she probably connected it to the fact that Mari was no longer staying out at night, but she didn't ask. Mari wanted desperately to be asked. She wished she were a different person, the kind who could knock on Heidi's door and say something like: Do you have time to talk? If she were that person, she'd sit on Heidi's bed and tell the whole story in a way that was scrupulously fair and sensitive to everyone involved. Her retelling would unwrap layer upon layer, bringing to light complex and previously unexplored emotional realities that nonetheless seemed, upon naming, indisputably true. Her recounting – and Heidi's listening – would make the whole thing into something quite beautiful: painful and messy, yes, but shot through with beauty and something resembling personal growth. But Mari wasn't that person. She was trapped with her anger and sadness like a bullfighter in a ring.

On Monday night, Heidi tried to convince her to attend Paul's birthday drinks that weekend. By then it had been over a week since Mari had last seen Jack. 'I don't feel like it,' she said.

'I know,' said Heidi. She was wiping down the countertops while Mari sat at the table. 'But it'll do you good.'

'I'm tired of things that do me good.' She laid her head on the table, as if to demonstrate how tired she was.

Heidi wrung the dishcloth out and went to sit beside Mari. With damp fingers, she touched Mari's head gently, and Mari felt tears flood her eyes. She stood up and put the kettle on, clearing her throat wetly. She wasn't really eating anymore, but she was drinking a lot of tea, because it was liquid and hot and flowed easily around the stone in her throat. The stone wasn't real, of course – she had checked in the mirror – but sometimes it felt so real that she couldn't swallow food, could hardly breathe. In her few uneasy hours of sleep, she had recurring dreams about stones falling from her mouth, a whole riverbed of them, black and glossy. Below her, the kettle rushed and burbled its way to a boil.

'Look,' said Heidi, 'I'm not asking for details, but is this about a man?'

Mari nodded weakly. From behind her, she heard Heidi tsk her tongue. 'Time to pivot to women,' she said. 'I'm telling you.'

Mari gave a shaky laugh. 'You and Verity are hardly a walking advertisement for that.'

'No, things are completely different between us now. Total honesty, we agreed.'

'Right.'

'Anyway, like I said, you don't have to tell me anything. But don't beat yourself up. Whatever happened, you don't deserve to be miserable.'

The tears swelled past Mari's eyes and dripped down her cheeks. 'I wouldn't be so sure about that.'

'That bad, hey?'

'I . . . Yeah. Never mind.'

'Just come on Saturday, you'll feel better. Take your mind off it.'

It was the kind of blandly comforting thing that people always said to friends with relationship problems. Mari herself had said the same thing to Heidi many times. But she found herself crying so hard that she couldn't respond, so she just nodded. Her cheeks were wet with tears and with the steam of the kettle. Heidi came over and put an arm around her shoulders.

The week stumbled on. Mari went to work, sitting limply under the fluorescent office lights. Her phone stayed silent. One evening she went to a seedy pub near her office and pretended to read a book while she drank bourbon until she couldn't even make out the words on the page. She did it deliberately, to turn herself into a girl who'd go home with anyone who asked, who'd even go out the back of the pub, pull her skirt up and let a stranger fuck her against the wall. She'd done it before. She would do it again. But no one approached her, and eventually she went home on the bus. Later that night, she plucked her eyebrows – previously thick arches, ragged at the ends – into short plump dashes. They seemed like new punctuation marks on her face, signifying brevity, staccato.

She agreed to go with Heidi to Paul's birthday drinks, but when they arrived, she felt it had been a mistake to come. All of it – the familiar faces and voices, the familiar bar, the familiar music – felt overwhelmingly wearisome, as though she had been to this party a thousand times before and was doomed to go to it a thousand times again, every weekend until she died or just spontaneously combusted from boredom. Paul asked if she'd had her hair cut, and she said no.

'Oh,' he said, studying her over his beer glass. 'There's something different about you . . .'

They all turned to look at her. Mari thought she might scream, but instead she said, 'I plucked my eyebrows.'

A murmur of understanding moved through the group. 'It's great!' Verity said. 'It makes you look so different.'

Mari smoothed her fingers over her eyebrows. 'What do you mean? What did you think of them before?' They all laughed: it was a Mari joke, the kind of thing she always said to make them laugh.

She hadn't seen Elisabeth since the night of Heidi's dinner party, nearly two months ago now, and the memory still made her feel sick. She knew she should message Elisabeth to apologise but she couldn't make herself do it, and that made her feel even worse, trapped in a shame loop of having said those awful things and not even being able to apologise for them. But when Elisabeth arrived and moved around the table hugging everyone, she didn't hesitate to hug Mari too. She looked the same, she smelled the same, and Mari clung to her in an embrace that was too tight and went on for too long.

'Hey,' Elisabeth said softly. Her sweet voice; the foreign tickle of her curls against Mari's cheek. 'Are you okay? What did you do to your eyebrows?'

'I plucked them.'

'Oh.' Elisabeth stepped back and studied her, frowning a little. 'I liked the way they were before. Kind of fierce, like a vengeful Greek goddess.'

'I thought the gods were the ones with fierce brows. Or are you thinking of Homer? You know – deep-brow'd Homer.'

Elisabeth smiled. 'Was Keats talking about his eyebrows? Anyway, you should grow them back. You look so manicured now, like a Young Liberal.'

Mari laughed. The sensation was pleasurable but unfamiliar, an old muscle brought suddenly to life, and she realised it was the first time she'd laughed in weeks. 'Does it earn me some kind of special dispensation?' she asked. 'So you won't film me, I mean.'

'Oh. No, I'm not doing that anymore, it was stupid.'

Mari couldn't remember, now, why she had objected so strongly to Elisabeth filming her. The fuss she'd made seemed incredibly childish. 'I probably ruined it for you,' she said. 'Sorry.'

'No, you didn't ruin it, it was just a bad idea.' Elisabeth perched on the stool beside Mari and poured herself a beer from the jug on the table. 'Why did you hate it so much, anyway?'

'I don't know. Sorry.'

'I mean, it wasn't worth much from an artistic viewpoint, but from a sentimental viewpoint . . . I don't know, could've been kind of interesting. Like a time capsule.'

Mari smiled. Elisabeth always worried so much about things like that: preserving, cataloguing, remembering. 'Was that what you were going for?' she asked.

'I wasn't really going for anything, I guess that was the problem.' Elisabeth tugged her hair free of its bun, and Mari caught the scent of her synthetic-apple shampoo. 'Actually, maybe I should've done it on that kind of meta level. I'm sure there's some historiographical theory about it – you know, like self-consciously creating historical documents. Jack could probably explain it to us.'

'You always hated it when he explained things to us.'

'That's true.'

Mari opened her mouth. She was going to tell Elisabeth everything, spill all her hoarded secrets out before her. Elisabeth could take the things she wanted, discard what she didn't. Mari could already feel a hint of the relief confession would bring. 'Hey, so,' she said.

'Hmm?'

Mari took a deep breath and glanced out the window. Across the street, people were sitting in the bright white light of the Vietnamese restaurant; they were getting off the bus and smoking in groups on the corner. All these people, living their happy everyday lives. It occurred to Mari that some of them, too, must have made mistakes, done things to hurt themselves and other people. She took another breath. That was when she saw Jack, walking down the street beside a woman with a shiny black bob.

It must have shown on her face. Elisabeth followed her gaze out the window to where Jack and the woman now stood at the pedestrian crossing. Jack was wearing his second-favourite blue shirt and gesturing with one hand as he talked, and the woman was nodding, about to smile. She was in her thirties, wearing black ankle boots and a plum-coloured coat. Elisabeth gave a terse little laugh. 'Well, speaking of explaining things,' she said. 'Didn't take him long to find a new student, did it?'

It was inconvenient that Mari's eyes should choose that moment, of all possible moments, to fill with tears. She dropped her gaze, thinking she'd pretend to look for something in her bag, but it was too late: the tears were making hot tracks down her cheeks, splashing onto the table. Her shoulders were shaking. She was crying, really crying, right there in the bar.

'Oh,' Elisabeth said gently, reaching over to touch Mari's wrist. Seconds passed. And then Elisabeth said again, with more understanding, 'Oh.'

Mari stared at the wood grain of the table. Distantly, through the music and laughter, she heard the electronic judder of the walk signal outside: Jack and the dark-haired woman would be crossing the road, probably going back to his flat. She stayed completely still, Elisabeth's warm fingers on her wrist. Quietly, hardly moving her mouth, she said, 'I'm sorry.'

Elisabeth withdrew her hand. For a long moment she didn't say anything, but when she spoke, her voice was slow and considered. 'Right,' she said. 'Well, I get it now. Why you've been so weird.'

'Yeah. Look, it wasn't while you – it was after . . .' Mari cleared her throat. 'It started when I went over to borrow that book.'

'Okay.' Elisabeth's voice was mild. Mari kept her eyes on the table. 'And how's it been?'

'What?'

'Is it good? Do you like it?'

The strange coincidence of her wording – so similar to what Jack said to her, in bed – threw Mari off. She shook her head weakly.

'You don't like it? Well, you probably shouldn't be doing it, then.'

'I do like it.' This was also, clearly, the wrong thing to say. 'I'm sorry.'

'Why are you sorry? You're an adult, you can sleep with whoever you want.'

'Well.' Mari tried to think carefully about what the correct answer might be. 'I'm sorry I didn't tell you.'

Elisabeth shrugged, her face perfectly blank. 'I should've guessed,' she said. 'I knew you had chemistry with him – I asked him about it, actually. Why he gave me his card at the graduation thing and not you.'

'What did he say?'

Elisabeth smiled faintly. 'Oh, nothing really. I can't remember.'

Mari knew this wasn't true, but she also knew she wasn't in a position to push it. 'Right,' she said.

'Anyway, lots of people have chemistry, I'm not uptight about that. And it was fun, in a way, when it was the three of us. You brought a kind of charge to things.'

Mari swallowed. She had the familiar feeling of being completely overwhelmed by Elisabeth's mind, which operated in dimensions she wasn't even aware of. 'I don't know why you're trying to justify this for me,' she said.

'I'm not.'

'You are, though.' Mari knew she had no right to be angry, that being angry was the worst possible reaction, but there it was: she was angry. 'You're always trying to justify everything for me, always being so fucking reasonable. Is there anything I could do that would upset you? Or are you going to keep taking shit from me your entire life?'

'You want me to be angry with you?'

'Okay, maybe you shouldn't be. Maybe I did you a favour.' Mari was dimly aware that her face was very hot, and that she was not speaking so much as hissing. 'Is that why you kept me around, because you liked the *charge* I brought? I'm not just there to do whatever you want, you know. Neither is Jack, actually, although I guess you found that out the hard way.'

She stopped, blood pounding in her limbs. Somehow their arguments always ended up like this, with Mari being the unreasonable one, the one making a scene. She had promised herself countless times that she wouldn't let it happen again, but it always did.

In a gentler tone, she said, 'Look, I know it's a complicated situation, but –'

'Sure. Hey, maybe we can have dinner again sometime, the three of us. I've missed Jack's cooking.'

Mari had no idea whether she was serious. It was definitely plausible that Elisabeth would force Mari and Jack to host a mutually torturous dinner party, just because she could. But maybe she wouldn't find it torturous. Maybe her ethical code and sexual politics had advanced to the stage where she no longer experienced jealousy, and she would be genuinely pleased to revive the friendship between the three of them. There was no way of knowing. Cautiously, Mari said, 'If you want.'

Elisabeth smiled absently, as if she were already thinking about something else. 'So tell me,' she said. 'How's it going with Jack?'

'What? Fine, I guess. Good.'

'What do you guys do together? Does he take you out to dinner?'

'Well . . . No, we sort of decided not to go out together in public. For now, anyway.'

'Oh, so he cooks for you.'

Mari wanted to lie. She wanted very badly to lie and say yes, but instead what she said was, 'No.'

'No?'

'Well, I usually go over after dinner.'

'Ah, I see. And then what, do you watch TV together? Does he ask you about your day?'

'We talk, yeah.'

Elisabeth gave a bright, humourless laugh. 'Oh, well, I'm glad he talks to you. He's such a good guy, isn't he?'

Mari gripped the edge of her stool. 'You don't know anything about it,' she said tightly. 'You think you do, but you don't.'

'Okay, I don't know anything about it. Just seems like he's really having his cake and eating it too.' Elisabeth stood, holding up her empty glass. 'I'm going to get another drink. But anyway, I'm glad you like it.'

'You're glad I like what?'

Elisabeth was walking towards the bar, and she turned back briefly. 'Fucking him,' she said, loudly enough that all the people around her turned to look. 'I'm glad you like fucking him. I hope that makes up for the rest of it.' She gave a little shrug and turned away, leaning over the bar to say something Mari couldn't hear.

•

MARI RODE HER bike to Jack's flat, fast, not stopping at the cross-streets. When she arrived, she locked the bike against the fence and went up the front steps, making a lot of noise and hoping to wake him up. The front door was locked, and she hammered at it until she saw the light in his bedroom go on.

He opened the door wearing just his boxers, his face blurred with sleep. 'Mari? What are you doing here?'

'I have to talk to you. Let me in, will you?'

He frowned. 'Look, it's late. Can I give you a call tomorrow?'

'Yeah, I'm sorry to wake you, but it's important. We can stand out here and discuss it, or you can let me in. Your choice.'

'Discuss what exactly?' Jack said, but he stood aside for her to enter.

As she went down the hallway, Mari glanced into the bedroom. The sheets were rumpled on Jack's side of the bed, and the room was empty.

Jack saw her looking. 'What is this?' he said irritably. 'Did you come over to try and catch me in the act? Sorry to disappoint you, but I was actually just sleeping. Alone.'

'So it didn't work out tonight?'

'What?'

Mari sat on the couch and crossed her legs. The flat was tidy, as always: the cushions plumped, the kitchen surfaces gleaming. A copy of the *London Review of Books* was folded neatly on the coffee table. It was like Jack himself, she thought – you could go in anytime and it would all look nice, but you wouldn't necessarily find much. She watched, saying nothing, as he sat opposite her and massaged his temples.

'I'm not in the mood for riddles, Mari,' he said. 'Spit it out.'

'All right. Well, I saw you.'

'You saw me?'

'On the street, just now. I saw you with . . .' As she began to say it, she grasped how ridiculous she sounded, the mistake she'd made in coming at all. She was drunk, she realised too late. 'With whoever she was,' she finished lamely.

Jack stared at her. 'You're serious? You saw me with a woman on the *street* and you thought you'd come over and give me a hard time about it?'

'Well, I –'

'That was a colleague of mine – Rosina. She and I have been friends for years. She's *married*, for God's sake. We had dinner together, she suggested a drink but I was tired, so I walked her to the bus stop and then I came home. And I'd just got to sleep when you started pounding on the door –' He stopped, shaking his head. 'I can't believe I'm explaining myself to you. You know, don't you, that none of this is remotely your business?'

'All right, fine.' The words coming out of Mari's mouth felt hot and somehow animated, as though they had a momentum of their own and couldn't be stopped even if she tried. 'Well, just so you know, I was out tonight too. I saw Elisabeth. And I told her about – about everything.'

Silence thickened the air. Mari's mouth was dry and sour; she wanted a glass of water. She wanted to be in her own bed. She wanted Jack to kiss the top of her head, she wanted to press her face into Elisabeth's soft shoulder and breathe in her familiar scent. Jack closed his eyes and opened them again. 'Right,' he said tonelessly. 'Well, what did she say?'

'She . . .' There was no possible way, Mari realised, to describe Elisabeth's reaction in terms that Jack would understand. 'She suggested we have dinner again sometime, the three of us. She's missed your cooking.'

He didn't reply. Mari hunched miserably on the couch, hoping he'd come and put his arm around her, but when she looked at him, he was staring into the middle distance. Eventually he said, 'Mari, I don't actually know why you're here.'

Mari recognised the quicksilver flash of cruelty. It seemed impossible that this was the same man who had once put his arms around her in the study, who had said to her: I'm so touched. A weak current of fear travelled through her stomach, and also something like anticipation.

'Quite frankly,' he said, 'it seems like this is an issue between you and Elisabeth, not you and me. Obviously I've played a role here, but I haven't deceived anyone, I haven't betrayed anyone. Things ended between me and Elisabeth, and then a short while later, things started between you and me. Maybe not the best arrangement, given your relationship with Elisabeth, but once again – that's your relationship, not mine.'

'Oh,' Mari said, almost laughing. 'Well, that's neat and tidy. You always like to keep your hands clean, don't you?'

He made an exasperated noise in the back of his throat. 'Look, whatever's going on between you girls, you need to sort it out yourselves, not come over to my house in the middle of the night having hysterics –'

'Are you serious?' Mari was raising her voice now, and there was a certain dark pleasure in pushing the conversation into the raised-voices stage. 'You have eyes, don't you? You have a brain? You can see how hard it's been for me, keeping . . .' She gestured vaguely at the air between them. 'Keeping everything a secret? I had to go behind everyone's backs, I never knew what you were thinking, I couldn't talk to anyone about it, and then I just stopped hearing from you . . .' She broke off, her throat tight.

Jack sighed, rubbing his temples again. 'Well, look. I'm sorry to hear that, of course, but I can't see it as altogether my fault.'

'Oh no, God forbid anything should be your fault.'

He ran a hand over his face. 'Mari,' he said, 'be honest now. You know I never told you to keep it a secret, that was your decision. And I'm sorry if this sounds harsh, but I can't take responsibility for the complicated politics of your social circle. If you had a falling-out with Elisabeth, well, I'm sorry to hear that, but I don't want to be woken up and called into a crisis talk about it. Much less blamed for it.'

Mari was filled, in that moment, with the urge to break something. She suddenly understood why people hurled glasses at each other, why plates ended up smashed against the wall. 'You think you can have it every which way, don't you?' she said, her voice shaking. 'Walk in when you want to, walk out when you want to. Have your cake and eat it too. Elisabeth told me that tonight, you know, and she was right.'

'Oh, Mari, just stop it.'

'Don't tell me to fucking stop it. *You* stop it. Trying to pretend you were never involved – it's laughable, you're laughable. You liked being involved, when it suited you. You liked sleeping with us, you liked being invited to our parties, you liked having us over for dinner and flirting with both of us at once. But as soon as we asked you for anything more, you backed off and said you were never really there. *Oh, that's your problem, not mine.* You think you're so much smarter than us, don't you?'

Jack got up and went into the kitchen. He poured a glass of water and stood at the sink drinking it, his back to her. When he turned around, he said, 'Look. If you want my opinion, it's been clear to me for some time that I'm just a convenient stage for you and Elisabeth to play out whatever complex psychodrama exists between the two of you. It's actually quite dangerous to be caught in the middle there. I don't want to be caught in the middle. Why should I have to suffer the destructive effects of a relationship I'm not even part of?'

'What are you talking about? What complex psychodrama? What destructive effects? You always talk like such a fucking academic, I'm so tired of it.'

He sighed, leaning his hands on the kitchen counter. 'Okay. Well, if you're going to push me, I might say, for example, that Elisabeth exercises an awful lot of control over you.'

'What? But she –'

'Oh, I know, she dresses it up as concern. As love even, but –'

'She does love me,' Mari said. She was beginning to feel sick. 'You don't know how much she's helped me, you really have no idea. She taught me to *drive*, did she ever tell you that? She's done everything for me, and I –'

'You repay her like this, yes, I get it. A little Oedipal drama with the parents you never had . . . It's all quite predictable, if you don't mind my saying so.'

'Oh, is it? I'm sorry, next time I'll try to come up with something more original. Maybe you'll give me a better mark.'

He shook his head. 'You can be clever about it if you like. The point stands, though.'

'What point? That Elisabeth controls my every move? Do you think I'd be here if that were true? Do you think you and I ever would have slept together?'

'But you told her, didn't you. You didn't have to tell her, actually it would've been much easier on everyone if you'd just kept your mouth shut, but you couldn't. It's like a compulsion with you. I mean, come on, Mari. You know she's never been able to leave you alone, even when she and I . . . It was her I gave my card to, not you, and certainly not both of you. But she wouldn't let you go. What does Mari want, what does Mari think, let's have Mari over for dinner, let's get Mari on film. Of course, like I said, it's easy to see that as love. And it is love, in a way. But it's love that wants to pin you down.'

'You know all about us, don't you?' Mari said hollowly. 'You've done a nice little psychological study.'

'Well, you asked.' He walked around the counter and sat down again. 'Anyway, you're aware of all this yourself – how could you not be? Sleeping with me is just your latest and most brazen attempt to break Elisabeth's hold on you. Or maybe not to break the hold, but just to test its limits. Tell me, did she get angry with you when you told her? Did she shout at you?'

Mari was silent.

'No,' he said, 'thought not. She never will shout at you, not really. That's a failing of hers, perhaps, because sometimes you really do deserve it.'

Mari looked at him. 'Do I?'

A few seconds' silence. He held her gaze, and then he stood up and walked over to where she sat. 'Yes,' he said. 'Sometimes you really need someone to put you in your place.'

Her breath was hot and shallow. 'Are you going to put me in my place?'

He looked down at her, his lips parted. She moved her legs slightly apart and he leaned over her, pressed one hand against the back of the couch and slid the other between her thighs. Mari's mind blinked out, disappeared, as if it had never existed. Mechanically, she tugged her dress over her head and wriggled out of her underwear, parted her legs further, and he pushed into her. She cried out, and he pushed himself deeper.

'Be quiet,' he said, and his voice was hard. 'Keep your mouth shut for once in your life.'

She made a sound, and he clamped a hand over her mouth and thrust into her again. Mari felt crushed under his weight: punished, brittle, small. She wanted him to grind her under the heel of his boot. He thrust into her again. Again. Her body was full of a dark hot trembling. Again. Her stomach muscles clenched and spasmed. Again. 'I'm going to come,' she said, her voice muffled and vibrating in the skin of his hand, and he said, 'Not yet.' Her breath caught in her chest and she was hanging by her toes on a trapeze wire, swinging violently back and forth, back and forth, each time sure she couldn't hold on any longer, and then he said, 'Okay,' and she let go and fell, somersaulting wildly through the air. And he was coming too, tightening his hand over her mouth and pushing her body deep into the couch. Later she would find a small splay of purple bruises on her thigh, from where his other hand had gripped her.

Then it was over and he lifted his weight off her. 'Shit,' he said blankly. 'Fuck, I'm so sorry. I didn't mean to do that.'

'I know. It's okay.' Words: empty noises in the air. She went blindly to the bathroom and sat on the toilet, staring at the dark cracks between the tiles, her whole body stuttering. Okay. Deep breaths. Thick and slippery between her thighs. Just wipe it away. Out, damned spot. Don't make a fucking literary reference now, who are you trying to impress? Okay. Teeth chattering. I didn't mean to do that, he'd said. She thought it was quite possible that he had. There was malice in him after all, but it was in her too. They brought it out in each other.

When she came out, he'd put on his boxers and was boiling the kettle, not looking at her. Her nakedness seemed incongruous, silly. She found her dress and put it on, stepped into her underwear.

'Do you want a cup of tea?' Jack asked. His voice sounded tired and far away.

'No.' All at once she felt sick with herself, boiling over with poisonous shame. 'I'd better go home.'

'Okay.' He was bobbing a tea bag in a mug, still not looking at her.

'I think,' Mari said carefully, 'it would be better if we didn't see each other anymore.'

He looked up, surprise on his face, and she fought the animal urge to put her arms around him. 'It's just messy,' she said, keeping her voice cool and hard, like marble. 'Too messy. Like you said, you don't want to be caught in the middle.'

He nodded. 'You're probably right.'

'So.' A wall of tears was building up in Mari's throat. 'See you around. Maybe.'

'Maybe.' He turned to the fridge. Mari looked at the pale curve of his back leaning down, lit from below by the fridge light's cold fluorescent glow, and she thought of him stroking her hair. The rough prickle of his morning chin against her neck. Mari, that's so lovely. Then she thought about how whenever he told a joke, he'd look at Elisabeth to check if she was laughing. You always liked her more, she thought, and the thought felt clear-edged and solid, like something she could run her hands over.

'Bye,' she said, stepping into her shoes. If Jack said anything as she left, she didn't hear it.

12

IN THE FIRST hot week of spring we went to Stradbroke Island, the four of us: me, Heidi, Paul and Alex. We took two cars on the ferry across the bay, and then we drove to the rented holiday house at Point Lookout on the winding road that cut through thick green bush on either side. I went in one car with Paul, and Alex and Heidi went in the other. Paul and I played the Avalanches song about Frank Sinatra, singing along with the chorus, and I thought: This is like being in a movie about happy, carefree young people. This is the kind of thing I'll remember when I'm old. Or would I? Part of me wished – for the first time since Jack and I split up – that I was still working on my film project, so I could have recorded the moment and always kept it with me.

In the early evening, we went for a swim. The water was baby blue, tinted pale pink with the setting sun, and the waves spread their lacy foam across the surface. We were all a little drunk and we swam for an hour, laughing and tossing a tennis ball between us. I dived under the water and opened my eyes to the sting of salt, stayed under until my breath burned in my lungs, and then I burst back up, my hair heavy and matted on my shoulders. Mari had stayed at home, apparently sick with a cold, but I thought she was probably spending the week with Jack. It would suit her nicely to have us all out of the way.

I was still playing with the idea of the three of us having dinner together; I hadn't decided if I wanted to go ahead with it. There was an appealingly sophisticated aspect to it, as if we were part of a bohemian milieu where trivial bourgeois emotions like jealousy had no currency. And part of me did believe that sexual jealousy was a capitalist construct, that monogamy relied on the concepts and language of private property. I had read long articles about this online. Jealousy also seemed, ultimately, too small a concept to describe how I felt about Mari and Jack. What I'd said to Mari was true: the chemistry between them had always brought a charge to my relationship with Jack. Even now, the idea of them kissing and touching each other wasn't altogether unpleasant to me. Physically, they were so well suited: I could imagine their long, lean bodies twining around each other like vines.

I hadn't asked Mari how things had started between them, but over the past few weeks I'd spent some time trying to imagine different scenarios. Had she got drunk and made a spontaneous proposition? Had she planned it out beforehand? Tested the waters via text message? In any case, I was certain she'd been the one to initiate; Jack was too passive. But maybe I wasn't certain after all, because I'd been blind to everything all along, believing like a child that nothing was happening if I couldn't see it. I thought of Mari saying in the bar: You don't know anything about it.

I dived back under the water. It was probably a good thing Mari hadn't come with us, because actually she was afraid of the ocean. She hadn't grown up swimming in it like I had – she'd been a cramped city kid, pale and unathletic, trapped inside her own head. I felt sorry for her, really. She'd never admitted to her fear, and she went into the ocean if she couldn't avoid it, but her face was always tense and she was visibly relieved when it was time to get out. I could've held her under the water if I'd wanted to. I was stronger than she was. She never would have stood a chance.

•

ALONE IN THE house, at first Mari was relieved at being able to cry as much and as loudly as she wanted to. Upon waking she felt neutral, but after lying in bed for a while and staring at the ceiling, tears would begin to leak out of her eyes. This seemed to happen naturally, regardless of what she did or thought. Sometimes, to distract herself, she'd slide her hand under the waistband of her underwear and think about Jack saying: Do you like that, Marielle? The way his voice tickled and hummed in her ear. When she came it felt hollow and mechanical. She always ended up disgusted with herself.

Eventually she'd get up and drink coffee at the kitchen table, chain-smoking because Heidi wasn't there to tell her to go outside. Smoking felt okay, a rote comfort, but eating was a problem. She seemed to have forgotten how to swallow: when she put food into her mouth, her throat closed up. Eventually she'd force down some toast or a piece of fruit, telling herself that most girls went through their dumb anorexic phases in high school, and what did it say about her that she still couldn't eat like a normal person? Not that eating or starving made any difference to the way her body felt: heavy and dead, a model made of clay. Something she just had to drag around.

She still couldn't sleep at night. Often she lay awake until four or five in the morning, listening to the dark quiet hours edge themselves slowly along. She fell asleep as the birds started chirping outside, dozed a few hours, and woke feeling worn thin, like an old dishrag. But that was all right because she didn't have to go to work. She had quit her job the week before, with the vague idea of living off her savings for a while. Quitting was easy, after all – once she'd done it, she wondered why she had waited so long.

Now the days stretched out before her, full of empty time to bob around in. She read, nothing too sentimental: Graham Greene, Nancy Mitford. She stared at the wall. Crying jags came on without warning: pouring water into the coffee plunger, she suddenly lost her strength and had to lean over the counter, her mouth a silent square of pain. Later on she smoked a joint in the bath, watching the alien white shape of her body move under the water and feeling nothing at all. It was spring, and the air was thick with the sweetness of frangipani and jasmine.

After a few days, she abruptly lost interest in tears. A gnawing emptiness took their place: a feeling of high, ringing grief. It wasn't like before, when she'd waited and hoped for him – she knew he wouldn't call, wouldn't come to the house. This was what she had purported to want, so now she had to live with it. You're probably right, he'd said. She turned the phrase over and over in her mind: You're probably right. You're probably right.

The worst part was knowing exactly how pathetic she was. Elisabeth was right – Jack had used her, and she'd let him do it. A part of her had probably sought it out. She was a sack of numb, polluting meat, and she would only ever hurt the people she loved, Elisabeth most of all. She tried to write Elisabeth a letter to that effect, but reading back over it left her feeling frustrated, as if there was something else under the surface that she'd failed to bring up. She screwed up the paper and aimed it at the bin.

Leaden tiredness was beginning to settle into her limbs, as it did every afternoon. She lay down and closed her eyes, and when she opened them it was dark. A fragment of dream still floated in her mind: the view of a glass on a table, from above. She'd expected it to be filled with water but it was filled instead with a murky brown liquid, which had sparked in her a feeling of foreboding.

She lay still and listened to the sounds of evening: tree frogs, TV news, the clatter of pots and pans. People going home to their families, who loved them. She let herself imagine that Jack was lying beside her, and that if she turned on her side she'd see him: his slack-mouthed sleep face, softer without his glasses. She would watch his chest rise and fall, his face flicker in a dream. But when she turned the bed was empty; she'd known it would be, of course.

•

ON SUNDAY PAUL drove me back to the ferry and, after we docked at Cleveland, back home. I watched the sun-bleached sprawl of the outer suburbs give way to the riverside mansions of Norman Park, and then the weathered old Queenslanders of East Brisbane. The river gleamed behind the whisper and rustle of Moreton Bay figs. It was a hot day, the light coming down thick and golden like honey, and the sky was achingly blue. We drove west down Vulture Street towards the setting sun.

As we approached the Boundary Street intersection I said, 'You can drop me here, Paulie.'

'Are you sure? I can drive you home, I don't mind.'

'No, I need to get some fruit. Just drop me here.'

'Okay.' He pulled over outside the church. 'Hey, will you make sure Mari's alive?'

'What? Oh, I'm sure she's fine. You should ask Heidi about that.'

'I'm asking you.' He switched off the ignition and looked at me. 'Listen, I know everything's a bit weird at the moment, but you know Mari. She can take things pretty hard.'

'That's not my fault.'

'Oh, come on, Elisabeth.'

'What? I mean, I hope she's okay, but it isn't my job to look after her.'

Paul said nothing. I hauled my bag out of the back seat and thanked him for the lift.

In the fruit shop, I stood under fluorescent light and ran my eyes over the fuzzy brown kiwifruit, the oranges in their tight dimpled skins. Soon there would be mangoes and pineapples in the shops again, and after that, cherries and peaches and apricots. I thought of Mari biting into the rich dark heart of a cherry that afternoon in Alex's garden, and how she'd beckoned me over and put her lips to mine. The sweet flesh of the cherry pushed into my mouth. Someone behind me said, 'Elisabeth?' and when I turned, Jack was standing there.

A bolt of hard-edged feeling went through me, as sudden and violent as touching an electric fence. I straightened my back and looked right at him. He was wearing a grey linen shirt with the sleeves rolled up and holding a filmy plastic bag with what looked like mandarins inside. 'Hi,' I said.

'Hi.' He cleared his throat. 'Long time no see.'

'Yeah. I hear you've been seeing quite a bit of Mari, though, so maybe that makes up for it.'

He looked at me tiredly. 'Yeah, okay. That's . . . Well, I don't know if she told you, but actually we're not seeing each other anymore. If that matters to you at all.'

'Oh.' My images of them spending the week together slid suddenly out of focus. 'Right.'

'So she hasn't said anything?'

'Not to me. We aren't . . .'

'I see.' He rubbed a hand over his face. 'Well, look. I've always had a lot of time for Mari, I like her, but it wasn't . . . It wasn't like it was between you and me. I just want to make that clear.'

'Oh, so you were only using her for sex. Great, Jack, that's so much better.'

'Well, no, I . . . Look, she's an adult, she can make up her own mind about these things. I certainly wasn't trying to use her for anything. In fact, she was the one who broke it off with me.'

'Oh.'

'Yeah.' He rubbed his face again. 'And to be completely honest, I think she did it – in a roundabout way – for you. I think she was trying to choose you. At the point where such a choice became necessary.'

I picked up a kiwifruit and ran my thumb over its rough surface. 'She hasn't said anything to me about this.'

'No. Well, you know Mari, she doesn't necessarily move in a straight line. But I think that was more or less her logic.' He paused. 'She does love you, Elisabeth, you must know that.'

I turned away, towards the trays of shiny apples. Granny Smith, Pink Lady. Behind me, Jack said, 'Listen, I know I've behaved badly, and maybe you don't want to hear this, but I do still feel a lot of affection towards you. I've missed you, actually. Very much.'

I kept staring at the apples, lined up so neatly in their rows. 'Okay.'

'Yeah, okay.' I could hear him cracking his knuckles. 'Well, all I'm saying is – it doesn't have to be an operatic drama, does it? We can still see each other, be friends, that sort of thing?'

I turned to face him but found I couldn't meet his eye, so I looked at the corner of his shirt collar. 'Fuck you,' I said quietly.

There was a small silence, during which I didn't feel much of anything – not triumph, not regret. 'Yeah,' he said. 'I – okay. Fair enough.'

'Hey, one other thing – don't call me. Don't email me. Don't send me any messages, don't talk to my friends, don't come around to my house. I really never want to hear from you again. I can't be clear enough on that point.'

He nodded wearily. He looked like he hadn't shaved in a few days, and light was catching on the fine needles of grey stippling his chin. He had grey in his hair too, only when we were together I had decided not to notice it. 'Right,' he said. 'Well, I'm actually going on a research trip to Italy in a couple of weeks, so I'll be out of your way. Yours and Mari's.'

'Good. Have fun.'

I saw him nod again. He went up to the cash register, and I turned away and pretended to examine some bananas. After a few minutes I left without buying anything. I was crying, that was true, but it was getting dark and most of the people I passed seemed not to notice. I walked quickly, each step firm and strong in front of the other. I meant to go home, but I found myself walking towards Paris Street instead.

I went in through the back door. The house was dark, but I could see a light on in Heidi's room and hear the low hum of the radio: You're listening to four – triple – zed. I walked quietly down the hallway and opened the door to Mari's room.

At first I thought she wasn't there. The room was dark and smelled strongly of cigarettes, and the floor was covered in an amorphous clutter that I couldn't make out in the dark. I was about to close the door and go ask Heidi where Mari was, but then there was a movement on the bed and I saw the pale shape of her face peering at me. 'Elisabeth?'

I took my shoes off and picked my way across the room. Mari's sheets were all twisted up, the bottom sheet pulled half off the mattress. She was huddled under a grubby pink blanket, and when I lay down beside her, she tucked it over me. I caught the tang of sweat on her skin. 'What's going on?' I asked.

She shook her head gently, almost sweetly. I wondered if she might be drunk, but I couldn't see any empty bottles, or smell alcohol on her breath. Eventually she said, 'Nothing much.'

My eyes were adjusting to the darkness, and I could see that her face looked drained, her lips pale and flaking. Her hair clumped dark and greasy on the pillow. 'Mari,' I said softly.

'Mmm.'

'Are you all right? You don't look well, to be honest.'

'Yeah. I mean, no. I haven't been well.'

I took her hand; it was warm and clammy. 'I ran into Jack just now, in the fruit shop. He told me you'd split up.'

'In the fruit shop,' she said reflectively. 'That's funny.'

'Why is it funny?'

'I don't know.' She stretched her legs under the blanket. 'It's funny to think of him buying fruit just like anyone else. I guess I always thought he was somehow above that, like he didn't need to cook and clean and shop the way everyone else did.' She paused. 'That was really the problem, wasn't it? My thinking of him that way.'

I brushed the hair off her face. 'Well, there were a lot of problems.'

The brief white flash of her teeth. 'You can say that again.'

I kept stroking her hair, letting the strands run through my fingers. 'It's stupid, isn't it?' she said. Her voice sounded thick, a little sleepy. 'Fighting over a man. Such a cliché.'

'We never fought over him, not really. It was more complicated than that.'

'Yeah. He said that, actually – that he was just a "convenient stage" for us.' Her long fingers sketched quotation marks in the air. 'So we could play out our – what did he call it? Our complex psychodrama.'

I laughed. 'Complex psychodrama. He never drops the academic language, does he?'

'That's what I said.'

I kissed her on the mouth then, I don't know why I did it. She didn't seem surprised – she kissed me back, sweetly and docilely, like she would have gone along with anything I suggested. I slid my hand under her T-shirt and cupped her breast, flicked my thumb over the firm nub of her nipple. Her body felt soft, like a small animal. After a few minutes I moved the sheet back and kissed the soft milky flesh on the inside of her thighs, I could almost taste her, but then she sat up and said, 'Oh, I can't.'

'It's fine, Mari. It's okay.'

'No, I just . . .' She lay back down beside me. 'It's not a good idea. For lots of reasons.'

'Like what?'

She was quiet for a long time, and when I looked at her I could see the shiny tracks of tears glinting on her face. 'Well,' she said in a tiny voice. 'For one thing, I'm pregnant.'

I might have made a sound then, I don't remember. All the air seemed to have been sucked out of the room, and I had the hurtling, teeth-juddering feeling of being on a rollercoaster, only I was lying completely still. It was strange, but I kept thinking about the fact that we weren't alone, there was a third party in the bed with us: a tadpole, a clump of cells dividing and subdividing, an outsider, an observer, unseen. I heaved in a mouthful of air. Another one. I worked on keeping still. Finally I said, 'Are you sure?'

She nodded miserably. 'Four tests.'

'And – it's Jack's?'

'Couldn't be anyone else's.' She gave a wet sniff and wiped her nose with the back of her hand. 'It happened, um . . . Right at the end.'

'Does he know? Have you told him?'

'No. You're the only one who knows.'

My brain was still buzzing with shock, and my lungs felt hard and shrivelled. I looked up at the ceiling and took three deep breaths: in and out. In and out. In and out. Beside me, I could hear Mari's shaky little sob-breaths. I thought about Jack, the night Mari first came to dinner, saying: She's a bit of an unstable person, isn't she?

'Elisabeth?'

I breathed out and put my arms around her. Into her hair, I said, 'You are such an idiot.'

'I know.' Her face was wet against my neck. 'Trust me, I know.'

'How did this even happen? Did the condom break?'

'Oh . . . Hard to explain. It was just stupid. I wasn't what you'd call careful.'

'Obviously not.' Gently, I wiped the tears on her face with my thumb. 'But it's Jack's fault, really. He should've known better.' It seemed obscene, in that moment, that we had ever trusted Jack.

I thought of him telling me that I was beautiful, that I was an interesting person, that he'd been nervous in the restaurant because he'd thought I wouldn't turn up. And I'd smiled and believed him, drunk on his expensive wine. My face felt hot.

'Yeah,' said Mari. 'Anyway, it's such a weight off my mind, now I've told you.' She tucked her head against my shoulder, her breath tickling my skin.

'Well, don't worry,' I said. 'You can't be more than – what, five or six weeks? We'll call the clinic tomorrow and see when they can fit you in . . . Hey, we could get Jack to pay, if you don't mind telling him. He'll go completely out of his mind with guilt, so that's a bonus.'

I felt her go still. 'Oh,' she said.

I waited for her to say the next thing, but she stayed quiet. Something cold and slithering gripped my stomach. 'Mari?'

'Yeah?'

'You're not – I mean, you're going to have an abortion. Obviously.'

'I, um.' She shook her head faintly. 'Yeah. I don't know.'

I sat up. 'No, come on, you do know. Don't be ridiculous.'

'Well, I –'

'Oh, grow up, Mari, be serious. You can't have a kid – I mean, look at you, you can't even keep your room clean. And what about Jack, do you think he's going to be happy about this? What's the plan there?'

'Look, I don't know. I don't know, okay? I just want to think about it for a while.'

I got to my feet. In the darkness, the pale oval of Mari's face ticked downward, faded, reappeared and ticked downward again. My stomach was heaving. 'Okay,' I said thickly. 'I have to go.'

She sat up. 'Don't.' Her face wet with tears; the dirty blanket, the half-stripped bed. The tiny wriggling tadpole in her womb. I turned away, bile rising heavy and acidic in my throat.

'Elisabeth?'

Blindly, I shoved my feet into my sandals and slung my bag over my shoulder. I stumbled towards the door, my mouth flooding with saliva.

'Don't,' Mari said again. 'Please don't go.'

'I have to.'

'Can I call you? Later, when I've had the chance —'

'No.' My hand grasped the knob and I opened the door. In her room, Heidi was still playing the radio. I turned back to Mari, but the light from the grate above Heidi's door had ruined my night vision, and I couldn't make her out. Just a cluster of mounds, dark huddled shapes, and the smell of stale cigarette smoke in the air. I ran down the front steps and vomited neatly into the gutter. When I got home my housemates were watching a movie, and I sat down and watched with them as if nothing had happened.

13

IT TOOK ME a few weeks to organise everything. I gave my notice at the café and packed up my things, putting half the boxes into my car and leaving half under Paul's house. Aisha agreed to take over my room. I didn't tell many people that I was leaving, and when Mari called me, I pressed ignore all ten times. In the middle of November, just before my twenty-sixth birthday, I drove to my parents' house.

It was a hot day and I drove with my windows down, the wind tearing at my hair. The Glass House Mountains rose in their familiar jagged humps on the horizon. I'd last made that drive the day after staying at Jack's house for the first time; I remembered that my mouth had been tender and sore from kissing, and that I'd looked at my phone in every traffic jam to see whether he might have messaged me. I felt a lot older than the person I'd been back then.

My parents were standing in the driveway when I pulled up, concern on their faces. I hadn't told them much on the phone, only that I was coming home and didn't know how long I'd stay. They helped me carry my things inside, into the house that was just the same: the books, the woven wall hangings, the piano with its neat row of shining keys. The single bed in my room was made up with floral-sprigged sheets, familiar to me since childhood. My parents never threw anything away.

As I was unpacking, my father came in with a cup of tea. 'Here you go,' he said. 'Thought you might like this, after the long drive.'

'Thanks.'

I sat on the bed, and he sat beside me and put his arm around me. 'Sweetheart,' he said gently. 'It's not that your mum and I aren't happy to see you. We're thrilled, and of course you can stay as long as you like. But we're a bit worried about you.'

'Don't worry about me.'

'But we have to, that's our job. Come on, love, what's the matter? You seemed so happy in Brisbane, with all your friends.'

I stared at the tea: too milky, he always made it that way. 'Things got a bit complicated.'

'Complicated how?'

He was gazing at me anxiously. His face looked older than I remembered, but it always did, every time I came home. All at once, I realised that my parents would never understand the situation between me and Mari and Jack; that in some sense I was more adult than they were, and my life contained complexities they couldn't grasp. 'I'm fine,' I said. 'I don't want to go into it, but I'm fine. Can we leave it there?'

'But you –'

'Dad, I'm not pregnant, I'm not addicted to drugs, I don't owe anybody money. I just want to stay here for a while and not be asked any questions. Is that okay with you?'

His face tightened; I'd never spoken to him that way before. 'All right,' he said, standing up. 'If that's how you feel.'

I kept staring at the tea, and he went off to feed Benji, the terrier my parents had adopted after my sister Charlotte left home. I heard the dog yapping, my father speaking to him in a bright voice. It was a hot day and I could feel sweat starting to trickle from my armpits, bead at my hairline.

I withdrew from the filmmaking course. My father called to explain, and if there were fees involved, I was sure that he paid them. Officially my status as a student was suspended, but it seemed unlikely that I would ever go back. I was glad, actually, to have it off my plate. The whole idea seemed stupid and mildly embarrassing. Mari had been right: a waste of time and money.

In any case, work now seemed impossible. Living at my parents' house made me feel sleepy and thick-headed, my limbs slack and muscles gone soft. I slept ten hours every night and woke still tired. I developed a coarse rash on one side of my face. I tried to read but the words swam in front of my eyes, so mostly I lay around with heavy eyelids, not thinking or feeling very much. My parents said it was good that I was resting up.

A few weeks into the new year, Paul called to tell me about Mari's pregnancy. I told him that I already knew, but I appreciated him reaching out.

'I thought you probably did,' he said. 'But I didn't want you to find out by seeing it on Instagram. Really Mari should be the one calling you, but she's being bloody miserable about it. Seems to think you wouldn't pick up even if she did call.'

I looked out of the window, where my mother was weeding a flowerbed in her old green gardening hat. 'Mmm.'

He paused. 'You know, she and Jack are sort of back together now. Like, they're going to move into a place of their own before the baby comes.'

'That seems sensible.'

'Yeah . . . Well, honestly, I'm not sure how it's going to work out. I saw Jack the other day and he had a kind of hunted look in his eyes. I wouldn't be jealous if I were you.'

'I'm not.'

He sighed. 'Anyway. You're coming home soon, aren't you? We could find you somewhere to live and . . . Actually, Jen's moving to Melbourne in a few weeks and Alex says they haven't filled her room, so that's –'

'Is she showing?'

'What?'

'Mari. Is her pregnancy showing?'

Paul was silent. I pictured him rubbing his forehead with the heel of his hand, the way he did when he was nervous. 'Um – a little bit, I guess. I don't know, Elisabeth. Why are you asking me this?'

'Forget it.' I turned away from the window. 'I was just curious. Send her my best, won't you?'

'Send it to her yourself! Elisabeth –'

I hung up. I had never hung up on Paul before, nor anyone else for that matter. I sat on my bed with my knees drawn up to my chest and tried to imagine Mari's long, graceful body swelling with the round bud of pregnancy. I couldn't. It seemed entirely plausible that she wasn't actually pregnant, would never have a baby – much more likely, in fact, than the alternative possibility that she would. In spite of everything, a part of me believed that if I drove back to Brisbane I'd find everything the way it had been before – Mari waiting for me in her room on Paris Street, and Jack safely back in his old life, the life he'd had before he met us.

I'd told Paul that I wasn't jealous and it was true, mostly. Jealousy was irrelevant because all this seemed to be happening very far away from me, like something in a movie or a book. Maybe it was even a little bit funny, the way things had turned out. Could I laugh about it? I found that I was biting my thumbnail. I remembered what Jack had said to me, the day I came back after Christmas: You seem like the kind of person who always gets what she wants. Well, he'd misjudged me. He'd misjudged Mari too; we both had. A flash of pain told me I'd bitten the nail down to the quick. I kept chewing, and soon the hot iron tang of blood filled my mouth.

•

WHEN MARI WAS six months pregnant, she and Jack went to inspect a three-bedroom cottage near the river. It was the beginning of autumn, and the heat of summer had died away quickly, leaving the air mild and clear. Jack was late, and Mari made stilted conversation with the real estate agent while they waited: Yes, due in June. Yes, a girl. No, no name yet.

When Jack finally arrived, he said, 'Sorry, sorry, I got held up after class. It's the exam next week and suddenly they're all very interested in what I have to say.'

Mari glanced over to see the real estate agent's face go slack with shock. She gave him a little smile and he looked down, embarrassed.

The cottage was large and airy, with polished timber floors and high ceilings. The agent pointed out the reverse-cycle air conditioner, and the jacaranda tree in the garden. 'Just outside the window there. Beautiful when it's in bloom in the spring.'

He smiled at Mari. 'You'll be getting the hang of things by then. With the baby, I mean.'

'Right,' said Mari. The remark made her feel strangely panicked, knowing it was too late for anything else – this year's jacaranda season with a baby, and every jacaranda season after that.

'How much were you thinking of in terms of rent?' Jack asked. The agent named a price and Jack nodded calmly. Mari pretended to inspect the backsplash in the kitchen. She had no idea whether the price was reasonable – she had no idea, she realised, with a hot rush of embarrassment, what they could really afford. Her role in the inspection suddenly seemed false and childish. She saw herself and Jack the way the agent would see them: younger woman, older man. Weird, he would think. Daddy issues.

The agent shook hands with Jack and then with Mari, meeting her eye and gripping her hand firmly. Jack said they would be in touch soon. Mari took this to mean they could afford the house, although it wasn't necessarily clear – Jack often conducted transactions with total confidence, uttering smooth promises which he later assured Mari he had no intention of keeping. But after they had said goodbye to the agent and were walking down the block, he said, 'So you liked it?'

'It's beautiful.'

'Nice to have a deck out the back. And I can turn the third bedroom into my study.' He shook his head. 'I never thought I'd live in a place like that, you know. Lead glass in the front door, that claw-foot bathtub . . . All the bourgeois horrors.'

'Well, adulthood comes for everyone,' Mari said. 'Even you.'

He gave a half-laugh. 'You're right,' he said. 'No, you're right. Suppose I'd better meet it halfway.'

Until then, Mari had kept her room on Paris Street – as Jack had pointed out, there was no reason to move her things into his flat only to move everything out again a few months later. But once they signed the lease on the cottage, she and Heidi packed everything up over the course of a weekend, Alex borrowed his brother's ute, and Paul came over to load the boxes onto the tray. Mari tried to help, but they wouldn't let her lift anything.

'Jesus,' said Heidi, watching the ute rattle off down the narrow street. 'This is weird.'

'I'm not going far, Heids. I'll be ten minutes down the road.'

'I know. That makes it weirder, actually.' She stepped back and looked at Mari, whose belly had reached the proportions that made strangers offer her a seat on the bus. There was a worried tilt to her mouth. 'He's going to look after you, isn't he? Jack?'

'Of course he's going to look after me. What else would he do?'

He did look after her. As her pregnancy progressed, Jack was unfailingly considerate and even tender: rubbing her feet, cooking her meals, telling her not to get up. And yet they lived together a little awkwardly, two supporting actors awaiting the arrival of the star. Up close, Jack turned out to have some alarmingly grown-up habits: he cooked a proper dinner every single night, using groceries he bought on a Sunday. He never stayed up late wasting time on the internet, but went to bed at ten and read for half an hour before turning out the light. Settling down beside him with her own book, Mari sometimes felt as though she were play-acting the part of an adult, and her first thought was of how much she and Elisabeth would laugh about it, if Elisabeth were there.

It quickly became apparent that they had very different standards of cleanliness. Jack never nagged her about housework, but she saw his mouth tighten when he came home to find the bed unmade, breakfast dishes still in the sink. Mari tried to be tidier, but he seemed to see messes she couldn't. And everything took so much effort: she was uncomfortable all the time, her body heavy and packed too tight. She thought about all the years she'd taken her slimness for granted, when she'd sat cross-legged on the floor and rolled over in bed without thinking. Then her body had just been a convenient vehicle, practically invisible. Now it was everything.

Jack came with her to the scans and together they stared at the grainy image on the screen, the heartbeat filling the room with sound. 'There she is,' said the ultrasound technician, smiling. 'Good strong heartbeat, that's what we like to see. Beautiful baby girl.' No matter how much Mari looked at it, she could not make herself believe that the image on the screen had anything to do with the inside of her body. It seemed much too far-fetched, like science fiction. At home, she shoved the envelope of printed-out images into the back of a drawer and didn't look at them again.

As the weeks went on, the reality of the baby became harder to deny. Mari began to feel kicks all the time, and sometimes Jack put his hand on her belly to feel them too. One night, as he was resting his hand there, she said, 'Hey, do you remember when you told me about losing your Neutral Milk Hotel album? The first one?'

'That formidable memory of yours. I'd forgotten I told you that.'

'Yeah. Well, you said the breakup was because you didn't want to get married or have children.'

'Mmm.'

'Do you still feel that way?'

He smiled absently. 'Bit late for that, isn't it? I'm pretty sure that's a foot. Although if you're asking me to marry you, I do draw the line there.'

'I'm not asking that. But you – I mean, you'll love her, won't you? When she comes?'

Gently, he traced the linea nigra on her belly: a faded fault line. 'Hey, don't worry about that,' he said. 'I'm not the absentee-father type.'

'No, I know.' She leaned her head on his shoulder. 'I think you'll be a good dad. Not that I know much about it. Honestly, I can't even picture myself as a mother.'

'Ah well. All these mysteries will be solved in roughly five weeks' time. Let's just try to be better than our own parents, I think that's a good place to start.'

Mari lifted her head. 'I thought you were the golden boy in your family. Spoiled rotten, you said.'

'Oh, with my sisters, yeah, but my parents were never all that enthusiastic. They didn't really mean to have me, you know, and it was clear they didn't like me much.'

Mari struggled to accommodate the idea of anyone not liking Jack. 'But you would've been a lovely little boy,' she said. 'I can picture you being so gentle.'

'Well, that was the problem, actually. Insofar as I wasn't interested in sports, and that made my parents, shall we say, anxious.' He tilted his glasses up to rub the bridge of his nose. 'There were certain whispers about my sexuality from very early on, which was confusing because I knew I liked girls, but I sort of had the impression that I wasn't supposed to . . . But I shouldn't be too hard on them, they were only doing their best. I just didn't live up to their idea of a son.'

'What idea was that?'

'Some kind of emotionally repressed cattle farmer, I suppose. Not a bloody pinko intellectual. My father was always borderline hostile towards me; my mother went in for polite mystification. Anyway. That's all over now, thankfully.'

'Well, you never know,' Mari said. 'We might have an emotionally repressed cattle farmer in here. Maybe these things skip a generation.'

He laughed at that – really laughed, the way she hadn't heard him laugh in a while. 'Jesus,' he said. 'I hope not. For all our sakes.'

When labour began, Mari was in the bath, and she looked down to see blood threading the water. Cramps, mild at first, then bad. Then gradually worse. Then a black wrenching agony, all the doors in her mind closing off to trap her in an endless corridor of pain. The bright antiseptic hospital, footsteps squeaking on the shiny white floor. Near her, a constellation of shapes that occasionally cohered into Jack's face, looking white and panicked. A woman's voice telling her it was too late for an epidural, it was almost over now, just a little bit longer. Not usually so quick, with a first baby, but you'll be all right. Sobbing: I can't. Yes, you can. You are. Her fingers clawing at the pillow, at the sheet. Elisabeth. Where's Elisabeth? Won't she come back to look after me? She could hear a woman screaming. It's all right, Mari, you're nearly there. You're doing really well. Elisabeth? Occasionally a brief wink of respite from the pain, and she would find herself kneeling on all fours or standing with her hands braced against the wall, with no memory of how she had got there. A rope twisted and tugged violently inside her, it would rip her from the inside out, it would kill her, but she was the rope. She was the pain. There was no escape. The thought filled her mind: I want to die.

You're nearly there, just a few more pushes. Kill me. One more big push now. I'm dying. Oh look, look: here she is.

It was over, an empty lightness where the pain had been, and they put a bundle into her arms. Mari saw a small face crusted in waxy white, a black winking eye, the tiny wrinkled starfish of a hand. It seemed to have nothing to do with her, this collection of miniature human body parts in a blanket. She passed the bundle to Jack and collapsed back on the bed. Someone in the room said, 'Mum's tired.'

Jack, when she turned to him wearily, was looking down at the bundle and crying. Really crying: tears were streaming down his face, and his shoulders were shaking. The sight pierced through her numb exhaustion, and suddenly she was crying too, crying with shock and relief and love, reaching out her hands to him. She had never wanted so desperately to touch him. He leaned over to kiss her, his face wet with tears. 'You did so well,' he murmured, kissing her again and again. Mari cried harder, feeling she was too small a vessel for the joy that coursed through her, wild and huge and sweet.

A midwife tucked the baby into Mari's arms and helped to latch her mouth onto the nipple, her head a small dark globe against the huge white swollen breast. She was peered at, pronounced to have 'a good strong suck'. They delivered the placenta, helped Mari into a clean hospital gown, and wheeled her into another room. She found she could bear all this with equanimity: her body was a piece of machinery to be worked on.

When they asked the baby's name, Jack glanced at Mari and said, 'She looks like a Tessa, don't you think?' This was one of the names they had been considering.

'Yes,' she said. The baby didn't look like anything to her, but it seemed as good a name as any.

The first day floated by in a haze of exhausted happiness. Jack took endless photos of Tessa and sent them to everyone he knew. He gazed at the baby with adoration, no matter what she was doing. To Mari, her repertoire seemed fairly limited – eat, sleep, cry, shit – but Jack was enchanted. 'She's so beautiful,' he said. 'I never thought she'd be beautiful. Aren't newborns usually ugly?' Mari laughed at him.

He spent most of his time cradling the tightly rolled bundle in one arm while Mari hung on his other arm, leaning her cheek against his sleeve. When she fed the baby, he'd sit beside the bed and look at them with wonder, and she'd meet his eye and feel so exposed, almost afraid of the intimacy that seemed to blossom between them and fill the room. She was so full of tenderness, so full of wanting, it was painful. Her heart was a bruise that she was desperate for him to press on.

On their first night at home, he helped her settle in bed, propped up on pillows – 'Is that okay? Do you need another one?' – and lay beside her, holding the baby in the crook of his arm. The room glowed softly with yellow lamplight. Mari took his hand and said quietly, 'Hey.'

'Hey.'

'I love you. Did you know that?'

He smiled, looking down at Tessa's sleeping face. 'I didn't know that, no.'

A creeping dread began in Mari's stomach. 'Oh,' she said. 'Okay.'

She waited. Jack was still looking at Tessa. 'She makes such funny expressions in her sleep,' he said. 'Do you think she dreams?'

'Jack?'

He looked at her. 'Mari . . . Oh no, don't cry. Please don't cry.'

She shook her head, turning away from him. 'I'm sorry,' she said into the pillow, her voice thick with tears. 'It's hormones. Just forget I said anything.'

'Oh, Mari, don't . . .'

She cried harder. The force of her sobs shook her body, and it hurt, but the pain felt good. She wanted to be in pain for the rest of her life.

'I'm sorry,' Jack said wearily. 'But I don't want to be dishonest here. I think we both know that if it weren't for Tessa, we would've parted ways some time ago. We did, actually. And that was your choice, remember?'

'But I . . .'

'No, I know, it's not that simple. Anyway, no point dealing in hypotheticals. We do have Tessa, I wouldn't trade her for the world, and she's here because of you, so that's . . . You're an incredibly special person to me.'

Mari lifted her head from the pillow. 'I'm a special person to you. That is worse than if you hadn't said anything.'

'Oh, sweetheart, I wish you wouldn't . . . Look, what I'm trying to say is, no one can ever take your place with me, and obviously we're together for the foreseeable future, so maybe in time . . . Mari, I'm doing my best here. I really am.'

After that she felt vaguely embarrassed around him, and had trouble meeting his eye. His behaviour towards her was affectionate but depressingly fraternal – he kissed her forehead sometimes, or put his arm around her, but he never showed any sign of real desire. She tried to forget the incident, but it cropped up in her mind regularly: a little stab of pain, like a shard of glass buried in her foot.

It took them a few weeks to settle into a routine, which the midwives said was the most important thing. Tessa's routine involved feeding every three hours, which meant that Mari never got more than three hours' sleep at a time. Exhaustion set in like the flu, her mind thick and slow. When the baby cried, her body clenched with dread: sometimes Tessa would stop crying when she was offered the breast, but sometimes she wouldn't. Hours of crying, for no reason, like a car alarm that went off randomly and couldn't be silenced. 'Poor little baby,' Jack said, and Mari tried to mimic his tenderness, even as she longed to put Tessa down and walk out the door and keep walking until she reached her house on Paris Street with her old bedroom, and all her old things, and Heidi cooking dinner and complaining that Mari never took the compost out. This other life, surely, was a bad dream. It seemed unbelievable that she was expected to actually live like this – that other women lived like this, presumably, and didn't throw themselves off bridges or simply get in their cars and drive away. Well, some did, of course. Mari tried not to let herself think about them.

At odd points in the never-ending loop of day and night, in the space between wakefulness and snatched sleep, a disquieting wish sometimes floated through Mari's mind: to put Tessa back where she came from, to let her be reabsorbed into the strange, unreal world of Mari's body. Even when Mari was awake she would occasionally forget – for a blank, frightening moment – that the baby existed. 'Tessa's hungry,' Jack would say, or, 'I think Tessa needs changing,' and she'd just manage to stop herself from answering, 'Who?'

Jack went back to work when Tessa was four weeks old, citing the deadline for a book he'd been contracted to write. By then,

Mari could do most of the tasks the baby required, but always in the back of her mind was the thought that Tessa's mother must be coming to get her soon, that Mari was nothing more than an overworked babysitter. Sometimes when she stood with Tessa's solid weight in her arms, her knees went weak and fuzzy, something rose in her throat, and she had to sit down abruptly. There was only so long, she knew, that she could blame this on her recovering body.

With Jack back at work, her friends started coming over almost every day. This was partly because of the baby, but partly, Mari suspected, because of the warm house. 'Wow,' they all said, stumbling through the door in their coats. 'It's cold out there!' They said this with amazing uniformity, like a line they had rehearsed together. Mari took their word for it – she preferred to stay inside and close the blinds against the harsh winter sunlight. They sat with her in the dim living room while she fed the baby – she was always feeding the baby, it seemed never-ending; her nipples were cracked and raw but still Tessa cried and clung, wanting more and more and more – and told her about the things they were doing out in the world. She watched their mouths move and tried to nod at appropriate intervals.

Every morning, after Jack left for work, she decided that day would be different. It would be the day she'd go out with Tessa, sit at a café with the baby in a wrap on her chest, the way mothers did. 'I'm sorry,' she'd say to the small pink baby who slept, fists balled beside her head, in the Moses basket. 'Let's start again, okay?' And Tessa would sometimes move a little in her sleep, or grunt, which Mari took as a sign. But always, by mid-morning – when Tessa had cried for a long time, or thrown up after a feed, or Mari had considered the sheer amount of stuff she needed to take with her to leave the house – the ambition crumbled.

So she stayed home and stuck to the routine. It was difficult to believe she'd once had whole days to herself, vistas of empty time rolling out before her. Now Tessa demanded everything from her, although nothing seemed to give her noticeable pleasure. She cried if she was put down, but in Mari's arms she flailed and jerked awkwardly, making jagged noises that threatened to become cries. Mari knew she was too young to smile, but she couldn't shake the sense that Tessa wouldn't smile even if she could, that she'd never smile, never be content. She mentioned some of this to Heidi, attempting a casual tone.

'She's only six weeks old,' Heidi said gently. 'It's really normal, honestly it is.'

Mari made a noncommittal noise, but secretly she was relieved that the situation was being mistaken for something in the realm of normalcy. Maybe if she could continue doing things for Tessa, no one would notice that something was wrong deep inside her; some key had broken and would not play a note. Of course, Elisabeth would have seen it straightaway. Maybe it was for the best that she wasn't there.

Heidi turned her attention back to Tessa, who was propped up on her lap. The baby was her usual bundle of wriggling discontent, but this didn't seem to bother Heidi. 'Hello, baby girl,' she said, with the affectionate crooning tone that Mari could never rouse up in herself. 'Are you the most beautiful baby in the world? Are you? Yes, you are!'

Tessa began to fuss in earnest, and Heidi rocked her rhythmically, patting her back. Watching her, Mari was struck by how good Heidi was with the baby, how confident and tender. A thought rushed in: Tessa should have been born to Heidi. Why hadn't it happened that way?

'A little Gemini,' Heidi said, stroking Tessa's cheek. (The skin on the baby's face seemed to Mari too soft to be exposed, almost raw in its tenderness.) 'I could do her chart if you wanted.'

'God, no.'

'I was only joking.' She paused. 'You know, Geminis don't dwell on the past. They don't spend too much time thinking about what might have been.'

They both looked down at the baby's precise little face. Her tiny round nub of a nose; the ghosts of eyebrows like fine pencil-drawn arches. She was so small. The familiar thought darted through Mari's mind: Tessa had been born prematurely, although no one realised it, and soon some terrible symptom would arise and it would be too late to save her.

That was ridiculous, Mari knew. Tessa had been more than a week overdue; they were on the verge of inducing her when labour finally began. Mari had felt nothing, then, except terror – not at the prospect of labour but at the knowledge that at the end there would be a baby, and the baby would be hers. And Jack's.

Jack was working so hard on his book now that she barely saw him. When he was home he spent most of his time at his desk, often typing with one hand while he jiggled Tessa in his other arm. 'Don't do that,' Mari said. 'If you're going to hold her, pay attention to her.'

'Mari, she's not even two months old.' He never called her Marielle anymore, just Mari, in that patient tone of his. 'She doesn't know if I'm paying attention or not.'

'She *does* know.' Mari had the inescapable sense that everything they did with Tessa mattered greatly, and would almost certainly arise in some future therapist's office. The baby began to whimper, and Mari held out her arms. 'She's hungry. Give her here.'

He made a pantomime expression of dismay at the baby. 'Hungry? Are you hungry? Oh no! Poor little girl!'

'Jack, just give her here. She'll be screaming in a second.'

'Jesus, okay.' He passed the baby to her and turned back to his computer. 'First I don't pay her enough attention. Now I'm paying her too much attention. Maybe you could draw up a schedule, let me know in advance exactly what I should be doing at any given moment?'

'Oh, don't play the martyr. It's all right for you – you can get some peace and quiet at work, but I'm stuck here by myself all day.' They looked at each other bitterly across Tessa's small head, clasped blindly to Mari's breast.

'Right,' he said. 'I forgot you were here by yourself all day. Only you're not really by yourself, are you? All your mates come over while I'm not here. Funny how we never saw much of them when Tess was first born and I was at home, but now I'm back at work they can't get enough.'

'Oh, so on top of everything else I'm not allowed to see my friends anymore?'

He didn't answer.

'Okay,' Mari said. 'I see what you're saying, but it's not that they're avoiding you. It's just a weird situation, and with Elisabeth . . . They've got loyalty to her too, you know.'

'Yeah, it's real Shakespearean stuff. Well, you can sort that out between yourselves, but the reality is that I've got a deadline. It's a bad time.'

'Oh, it's a bad time? I'm so sorry, how inconvenient for you.'

'Mari, I can't change it.' He looked up from his computer, the screen bathing his face in cold light. 'Might have been something to think about before we decided to have a baby. Well, you decided, really.'

'Oh, right. I artificially inseminated myself, did I?'

He didn't respond.

'Hey! Are you listening? You came inside me, or do you not remember that part?'

'Yeah. Look, that was my mistake and I'm sorry, but I assumed a woman of twenty-six would be capable of going to the pharmacy the next day and sorting it out. Or failing that, you know, there are clinics.'

Mari froze up. She was a statue, a cold, still thing. At her breast, Tessa sucked eagerly. 'Oh,' she said weakly. 'Right. The clinics.'

He sighed. 'That came out wrong. Look, of course I don't regret Tess –'

'Don't you? It really sounds like you might.'

'Sorry. No, obviously I love her. But sometimes it feels like I've been swept along on this wave and I've had no fucking say in any of it. I mean, you just presented it as a fait accompli! I came back from Italy and you asked me to meet you for coffee and you said: I'm having a baby. That was it. The circumstances could hardly have been worse but that didn't seem to bother you. I couldn't say anything, I couldn't ask you any questions, that was just it. I still don't really understand your logic, if I'm being honest. You never seemed like a baby person.'

Mari looked down at Tessa's small face, mashed against the breast. 'I don't know,' she said miserably. 'Elisabeth was gone, you were gone, I was really lonely, and I just felt . . .'

'You just felt. Okay. Well, it's your decision and you made it, but I didn't get any input and I won't have you lecturing me now about how much time I spend working. I'm doing my best here, under the circumstances.'

He turned back to his computer, and Mari lifted Tessa to her shoulder. The abandoned breast flopped onto her stomach, creamy and blue-veined. She felt disgusting, like a sow. All her new swells and contours were alien to her, as if she'd been transported into someone else's body overnight and expected to believe it was hers. She remembered Jack calling her an Aubrey Beardsley girl, a long time ago now.

She settled Tessa in her basket and crawled into bed without bothering to shower or brush her teeth. She could hear the rhythmic clicking of Jack's computer keys from the study. He was right about one thing: Mari wasn't a baby person. She knew there was no real explanation for what she'd done in having Tessa, and it was quite possible that it had been a terrible mistake. Still, as she lay there listening to the small noises Tessa made in her sleep, Mari felt a startling sense of – what would she call it? – solidarity, perhaps, with the baby. For the first time, she felt like Tessa's real mother, someone who stood up for her. It was an odd feeling that she held carefully within herself, bringing it out often to examine over the next few days. 'Hello, baby,' she said to Tessa, as she changed her nappy. 'I'm your mother.' The word felt rubbery and strange in her mouth.

14

WINTER ON THE Sunshine Coast was comforting in its familiarity, in the things I'd known as a child: clear blue days, everything sharp-edged in the sun, and the deep cold wafting from the bush when I walked down the driveway to get the mail. I helped my parents in the garden and cooked dinner twice a week. Most afternoons I drove the dog to the beach and walked for an hour or so along the sand, letting the wind whip my hair and not thinking about anything. Intellectually, I knew that things had changed: that the game the three of us had been playing, half-winking at each other, had shifted gears and become real. But whenever I tried to muster up an emotional reaction to this – tears, for example – I just came up blank. There seemed to be a huge reservoir of numbness inside me, which didn't exactly feel good, but I thought it was preferable to feeling bad.

I knew, of course, that Mari's due date was approaching. My friends in Brisbane stayed in touch, and they all carefully avoided mentioning it, but I'd done my own calculations a long time ago. Actually, their attempts to skirt the topic mostly struck me as endearing. Only once, towards the end, I ran out of patience and messaged Aisha: *Mari must be nearly there now?*

Aisha: *Nearly where?*

Me: . . .

Me: *You know what I mean*

Me: *She must be nearly ready to have her baby*

There was a long pause while Aisha typed. I watched the ellipsis bouncing on the screen, my mouth oddly dry. Eventually a message appeared, but all it said was: *Yeah, she's pretty big these days.*

Not long afterwards, I came back from the beach to find my mother slicing tomatoes for a quiche, my phone on the kitchen countertop beside her. 'Heidi rang for you,' she said. 'While you were out.'

'Oh, did you speak to her?'

My mother was the kind of mother who answered her children's phones and spoke at length to whoever was calling. She knew all the details of my friends' lives, and Charlotte's friends too. 'Yes,' she said. 'We had a nice chat. She'll call back for you, she said.'

'Okay, thanks.'

She looked at me, her knife poised above a tomato. 'What's this about Mari?'

I opened the fridge and scanned its contents: cheese, eggs, olives, last night's leftovers. Half an avocado wrapped in cling wrap. 'What about her?'

'Well, it sounds like she might be about to have a baby.'

I took the avocado out and closed the fridge. 'I believe that's the prevailing medical opinion, yes.'

'But that's – why didn't you say anything? Heidi assumed I knew, it was a bit embarrassing.'

I got out a chopping board and some bread. 'I don't have much to do with it. It sounds like she's doing fine, so. That's good.'

My mother put the knife down and looked at me. I concentrated on slicing a thick, even slice of bread. 'Elisabeth, love.'

'Yes.'

'What's going on there? With Mari, I mean.'

'Nothing's going on, Mum. I'm sure you know how pregnancy happens, I don't need to explain it to you.' I spread the avocado on the bread. 'Can I have some of those tomatoes?'

She passed me the chopping board, and I picked out a couple of tomatoes and laid them on the bread. Their wet red flesh, slimy pockets of seeds. 'But there's a father involved,' she said. 'Isn't there?'

I almost laughed; it was so absurd to think of Jack that way. 'Yeah, I guess so.'

'Heidi clammed up when I asked about that too.' She paused. 'Tell me if I'm barking up the wrong tree here, but does he have anything to do with the whole situation? You and Mari falling out, and you coming up here at such short notice. I mean, the timing seems –'

'Mum, stop. Can you just stop? It's really none of your business.'

She folded her lips together, and I could see she was hurt. After a minute she said, 'Well, anyway. I thought I'd send Mari a parcel, just a few bits and pieces for the baby. Poor thing, you don't know what to expect when it's your first, and her own mother probably isn't –'

'Oh my God,' I said. 'Do not do that.'

'Elisabeth –'

'Sorry. But I'm asking you, don't send her anything. Please don't.'

She sighed. 'If you say so.'

I said I did say so. She didn't bring it up again.

About a week later there was an email from Heidi with the subject line: baby. Seeing it in my inbox was a relief, the same relief I imagined a condemned prisoner felt when he was finally led away to be executed. Okay, I thought. It's about to be over. I opened the email to find a picture of a pink-faced baby with downy dark hair, tightly closed eyes, and a tiny pursed-up mouth. She was wrapped in a white blanket and she was being held in someone's arms, but you couldn't tell who from the picture. Looking at her felt like having an arrow shoved through my heart. It was interesting, actually: I hadn't expected it to hurt so much.

Heidi didn't include many details, just that it was a girl, they'd named her Tessa, she was doing well and so was Mari. 'I didn't know if you wanted to be told,' she wrote. 'I hope I did the right thing.'

I didn't reply to the email but I looked at the picture of the baby for a long time, sitting cross-legged on my bed, until the pain faded and my whole body came alive with longing. I could imagine the solid weight of her in my arms, the sweet milky smell of her skin, the way I'd press my lips to the top of her warm head and ruffle the wisps of her hair with my breath. I could imagine the way she'd kick and stir in her blanket, eyes fluttering under their blue-veined lids.

For a few minutes I switched back and forth between tabs mindlessly, reading nothing. The screen was jumbled with meaningless text and images. The only thing that made sense was the picture of the baby: her little rosebud mouth, the way her dark hair sat on her forehead. She had come from Mari's body. I got up and walked out of my bedroom, past my mother who was sitting in the living room with a book. I heard her say something to me but I didn't answer. I went out the back door without stopping to put my shoes on.

I drove to the beach, or I must have, because then I was in the carpark, getting out of the car, walking onto the sand and going straight into the sea, fully dressed. I kept walking through the freezing waves until my feet slipped out from under me, and I was bobbing in the cold salty water, gasping, slipping under, bobbing to the surface and gasping again. The waves crashed and pounded, and my dress billowed in a circle around me. The current was strong. After a minute I noticed that my mouth felt loose and my cheeks were warm, and that in fact I was crying, huge ragged sobs tearing their way out of my chest. I dived under the water and stretched my eyes open, staying suspended there. My ears began to throb. I forced myself to stay under longer. My lungs burned. Longer. Was this what it was like to drown? Longer. Blood pounded in my face, in the tips of my fingers. Longer. A roaring filled my ears. Longer. If I weren't here, the world would go on existing just the same without me, and that would be all right. Peaceful, even.

I surfaced, swam back to shore, and drove home. That evening I went online and bought a ticket to Mexico, one way.

15

Six months later

From Mexico I went to Cuba, back to Mexico, then to Guatemala and down to Bolivia. In La Paz I stayed with an old couple, Franz and Maria, who had a boarding house on the top level of their home. They were a bit confused by me – all the other foreigners who boarded with them were volunteering for charities, and they couldn't work out what I was doing there. Nothing, I wanted to tell them. I'm doing nothing. After travelling for almost six months, my days seemed to add up to a kind of blank. I spent most of my time doing what needed to be done: buying food, washing my clothes, finding wi-fi, booking my tickets to the next place. Every few days I went to an art gallery or a museum and spent an hour or so looking at the things they had there.

La Paz was different from Mexico, different from Central America. A dusty city in a scooped-out bowl of a valley with a snow-capped mountain looming over it. The air was clear and thin, and the sun burned hot during the day. The cold nights brought their own loneliness: the loneliness of my room with its single bed, its striped woollen blankets, its lamp with the blown-out bulb. I would get a new bulb for it. I would have to. These were the kinds of things my life had narrowed down to.

When I'd been in La Paz for two weeks, I got an email from Mari. Seeing it in my inbox was strange, and at first I thought I might be hallucinating, but I got up and went to the bathroom and when I came back it was still there. It had been sent about twenty minutes prior, which was – I checked – 4.19 am, Brisbane time. No subject line. I opened it.

hey

so i guess by now you would've heard about the baby. here are the relevant facts: a girl, tessa, 3.5 kg, born at 11.02 pm on 19 june. i don't know if that's of interest to you, but it's what people tend to ask about.

to be totally fucking honest, i have no idea how the human race has managed to sustain itself via childbirth. or why anyone, having gone through it once, would ever do it again. i won't go into detail here but suffice to say i'm thinking seriously about getting my tubes tied. (i'm not joking, i googled it last week.) anyway, the important thing (as everyone likes to remind you whenever you complain about having been through the worst pain of your life and ruining your vagina in the process) is that i'm alive. and the baby is alive. and jack is alive too, even though he said it was 'really scary' to witness. so i guess we should all feel grateful.

there wasn't a lot of fanfare around her birth, so you didn't miss much. jack's parents are dead, as you know, and his sisters weren't too thrilled to hear that he was having a baby with a random 26-year-old. i called my mother and she said congratulations, but who knows what that means.

i know this is weird but when i was pregnant, i never thought much about what it would be like to look after a baby. (i usually skipped straight to the part where she was a precocious and interesting teen, identifying with some wave of feminism that hasn't been invented yet.) anyway, turns out it's extremely fucking tedious. my only purpose in life these days is to feed the baby, and change the baby, and play with the baby, or at least make sure she doesn't stick her fingers into a plug socket. this is much more labour-intensive than it sounds. most days i truly have no idea how i ended up in this situation, except maybe it's the kind of situation i was always going to end up in.

i hope it's ok to send you this. i don't know where you are but i miss you all the time.

m

ps: heidi said she was going to send you a picture of tessa. let me know if you want to see another one – there are approx. 400,000 on jack's phone.

This last proposition was interesting. Mari hadn't put any pictures online, so the only image I had of Tessa was that first one: little rosebud mouth and a head of dark hair. I had it saved on my phone, and whenever I looked at it I felt like a gaping hole had opened up inside me. I decided I didn't want to see any others. In a strange way it would have ruined the mystique for me, to see that she was a real baby and not the image on my phone. I began typing a reply.

Dear Mari,

I did hear that you gave birth. I'm sorry you didn't get enough attention over it.

Dear Mari,

Babies are a lot of work. I think that's a fairly standard piece of conventional wisdom. As for how you ended up in this situation,

I deleted both these drafts. The next day I walked up and down the steep streets feeling strangely agitated, combing the email over in my mind. Little fragments of it popped out at me, seeming significant: *It's what people tend to ask about. This is much more labour-intensive than it sounds. I won't go into detail here. I miss you all the time.* I had the persistent feeling that it was an email written in code, a puzzle I was supposed to solve. A nice little tease. All in lower case, of course. Mari always typed that way, as if nothing she had to say to you was important enough to warrant capitalisation.

I thought again of forcing her head under the ocean. The thought was familiar by now, like a friend. Then the image shifted: an empty room, a bucket on the floor, her kneeling before it. Her pale knobs of vertebrae, long white feet on the dirty floor. I'd put my hand to the back of her neck and push her head into the bucket. Would she cry out, the sound muffled by water, bubbles streaming frantically to the surface? How long would it take for her limbs to start jerking around? I breathed in deeply, the air catching like cold splinters in the back of my throat. I'd let her up to gasp a breath, two breaths, three, and push her down again, the splash of her head going under the water. I kept thinking about it until I got back to the boarding house. That night I slept very soundly and didn't have any dreams.

•

IN JANUARY, MARI and Jack took Tessa to Lismore for a visit with Mari's mother. On the car journey, she tried to prepare Jack for the reality of the situation. 'She's not like most people's parents, you know,' she said.

'Thank God. Most people's parents bore me to death.'

'No, but my mother . . . Well, okay, she drinks. Like, a lot. You should be prepared for that. She'll probably make snide comments, jokes, but it's not about you. She's doing it to get at me, just remember that.' Mari's hands were slippery with sweat. She wiped them on her dress.

Jack stopped the car at a red light and glanced over at her. 'Are you sure you want to go? We can turn around if you want. Just say the word.'

'No, I promised her. She wants to meet Tess. Let's get this out of the way.'

'All right, if you say so. Look, I'm sure she's not that bad.'

Mari's mother was waiting for them outside her unit block, and when she saw the car approaching, she waved her hands over her head. She was as skinny as ever, and the skin on her upper arms sagged and flapped. Mari winced. Beside her, Jack was smiling as he pulled the car over. 'See, she's come out to greet us! That's nice of her, isn't it?'

Mari made a face and got out of the car. Her mother gave her a hug, smelling of cigarettes and the spicy perfume she'd been wearing ever since Mari could remember. 'Hello, mother,' she said.

'Hello, daughter. Nice to see you. And this must be Jack! The famous Jack.'

'Please don't call him that.'

They both ignored her. Jack held out his hand for her mother to shake but she looked down at it and laughed, throwing her arms around him. Jack was caught by surprise, but he managed to make his surprise into a joke that they all laughed at together. Even Mari laughed.

Jack leaned into the back seat of the car and lifted Tessa out triumphantly – as if showing off a prize-winning pedigree dog, Mari thought. At seven months, the baby was chubby and pink-cheeked, with a cap of silky dark hair. Mari supposed she was cute; certainly people said so.

'This is Tessa,' Jack said. 'Tessa, say hello to Nanna.'

'Oh no,' Mari said. Jack shot her a warning glance. Her mother didn't seem to notice – she was cooing over Tessa, who stared at her warily.

Jack jiggled her in his arms – 'Do you want to say hello? Give Nanna a smile?' – and she put her thumb into her mouth. 'She's tired,' he said, even though Tessa had slept for most of the car journey.

'Mari was just the same,' her mother said, giving Mari a sly look. 'A bit of a cold fish. Well, not much has changed, has it?'

'She's seven months old, Mum,' Mari said. 'Don't take it personally.'

'I'm not taking anything personally. All right, shall we go inside? Do you want some lunch?'

For lunch they had a loaf of fresh sourdough bread with sharp crumbly cheese and braids of small truss tomatoes. There was a log of peppery salami that her mother unwrapped from its wax paper – 'I don't eat meat, but I know Mari does, and I thought you might too,' she explained to Jack – and a dish of small bead-like olives floating in murky oil. Tessa sat on Jack's lap and gnawed on an arrowroot biscuit from the box he'd packed for her.

Jack ate a lot and said how good everything was. Mari picked at her food. It was by far the nicest meal she'd ever eaten at her mother's house, but she was embarrassed by the knowledge that this was her mother trying to put together a nice meal, carefully selecting exactly one meal's worth of things she wouldn't otherwise have bought. For her and Jack it would have been an ordinary lunch, probably thrown together from things they already had. They wouldn't think about it. They certainly wouldn't neurotically wrap the tiny remaining square of cheese in cling wrap, as Mari's mother did at the end of the meal – they'd eat it or throw it away, secure in the knowledge that they could buy more whenever they wanted to.

After lunch Jack changed Tessa's nappy, laying out the changing mat on the living room floor and talking softly to her. She usually struggled and cried when Mari changed her, but of course with Jack she was all smiles and sweetly kicking legs. 'That was the last one in the bag,' he said, standing up and handing her to Mari. 'I'll just go and get some more.'

'I don't mind going,' Mari said. 'You drove all the way down here, you must be tired.'

'It's fine, it'll take ten minutes. Anyway, Tess will probably want a feed soon, won't she?'

Mari sat down, resigned to her defeat. It was another thing no one had bothered to tell her about before she had Tessa: the way that breastfeeding chained her to the baby, made her body a slave to the rhythms of someone else's. Actually she thought Tessa was getting old enough to wean, but the only time she'd mentioned this to Jack he'd looked at her like she'd suggested piercing Tessa's nose. 'Fine,' she said. 'See you later.'

When he'd left, Mari looked up to see her mother standing in the doorway, an oddly sympathetic expression on her face. 'Nappies,' she said. 'I don't miss those days.'

'Really? What's not to miss about being up to your elbows in someone else's shit?'

Her mother sat down beside her on the couch – a little tentatively, Mari thought – and Mari handed her the baby. 'Here,' she said. 'Your granddaughter.'

'She looks like you.'

'Well, I look like you. Or that's what people always said, but I guess there wasn't anyone else for me to look like.'

Her mother ignored this, meeting Tessa's solemn stare. 'Hello, baby,' she said softly. 'Hello, little one.' With a small dimpled hand, Tessa made a grab at the beads around her neck.

'She's not so little anymore,' Mari said. 'She'll be one this year.' As soon as she said it, she felt a twinge of disbelief and confused sorrow. It was impossible that Tessa could turn one, but it was true: she would keep growing up all her life, and Mari would never get the chance to start again with her. It was too late. It was always too late.

'You forget how little they are,' her mother said, as if Mari hadn't spoken. 'Not to mention how much work. I hope he's doing his share?'

'Well, he's busy with work. So he does what he can.'

'It's the summer holidays, isn't it? I thought academics got the summer holidays off.'

'Not really. Anyway, he's got this book project . . . It's complicated, Mum. He's doing his best.'

Her mother raised her eyebrows. 'If you say so.'

Mari fidgeted with the hem of her dress. In her mind's eye she saw Jack's delighted smile as he came home from work and lay down on the floor to play with Tessa, while Mari slumped, grainy-eyed with exhaustion, among the toys and unfolded laundry.

The casualness with which he asked if she'd had the chance to pick up his dry-cleaning that day. 'Jack isn't the problem,' she said. 'He works full-time, you know, to make money. So we can have things like food and a roof over our heads.'

'Oh, come on, Mari. Don't try to pretend you ever went hungry.'

Mari breathed in deeply. 'I'm not trying to pretend anything.'

'I always made sure you had food on your plate.'

'Yes. Okay.'

'I mean, it was different for me,' her mother said, gathering steam. 'I didn't have money like you, but I was living in a share house, so at least I wasn't on my own. You grew up with three or four extra parents around the place. More than most people get.'

'Three or four extra parents who liked to shoot up in the living room while I was at home.'

Her mother laughed. 'Oh, that only happened once. Maybe twice. Anyway, you're well beyond that now. Three bedrooms, did you say on the phone?' She bounced Tessa on her knee. 'Nice, if you like that sort of thing.'

Mari flopped back against the couch and said nothing. By the time Jack returned, a packet of nappies under his arm, Tessa was beginning to grizzle and mouth at the air. Mari went into the bedroom to feed her – she did not, for some reason, feel capable of doing it in front of her mother – and after a few minutes Jack wandered in and sat beside her. 'Okay?' he asked.

Mari made a face. 'Can we go? Let's just get in the car and go home.'

'It's fine. She's fine. I don't know what you're so worried about.'

He propped himself against the pillows and opened his computer to his book manuscript. Watching him, Mari felt nothing but a fierce, gnawing envy of this other life of his, the one he could slip into whenever he wanted. She had nothing like that. Now that the baby novelty had worn off for her friends, Mari hardly saw them at all anymore. The idea of joining a mothers' group made her want to tear her own skin off, and she doubted whether she could have found another job even if she'd wanted one. But she often thought that the thing she missed most about her old life – more than sleep, sex, or bodily autonomy – was the chance to lose herself in a novel, to spend hours floating in a world inside her head. Now she was forced to live full-time in the world of base materiality. Breastmilk, nappies, laundry, dishes. Chapped hands and pureed apples.

When Tessa had finished feeding, Mari sat her on the bed and gave her a rattle, which she played with for about a minute before squawking with boredom. 'I wish you'd go to sleep, Tess,' Mari said.

'She won't,' Jack said absently, his eyes on the screen. 'She slept for too long in the car, she'll be awake for hours now.' He often made authoritative statements like this on the subject of Tessa, and irritatingly enough he was usually right. In comparison, Mari felt hopelessly ignorant and blundering. Tessa gave another squawk, holding her hands to her cheeks the way she did when she was getting ready to cry.

'I'll take her,' Jack said, closing his computer. 'I can't get any work done here anyway, this bed is like a slab of rock. We can go for a walk, can't we, Tess? Can't we?' He lifted Tessa high into the air, and the dark cavern of her mouth opened into a brilliant smile.

Mari watched him buckle the baby into the carrier on his chest. 'Do you want to come?' he asked, and she shook her head wordlessly. 'Okay. Say goodbye to Mummy, Tess.' He held up the baby's small hand and waved it back and forth.

'Jesus,' Mari said. 'Don't call me that.'

She was lying on her back, but from the corner of her eye she could tell that he was standing with his shoulders slumped, looking at her tiredly. 'I'm making an effort here, Mari,' he said. 'Can't you make an effort?'

'I make an effort all day, every day.' Mari's throat was tight. 'You come in at evenings and weekends and play with her and take her for walks, but you have *no idea* what it's like –'

'Okay,' he said abruptly. 'We've been through this. Never mind, I'm sorry I said anything. See you in a bit.'

He went out and Mari stayed on her back, looking at the faint brown edges of a water stain on the ceiling. The bleakness of the room – its thin walls, rough brown carpet, lingering smell of cigarette smoke – pressed down on her. She heard Jack clicking the front door behind him and going down the stairs. After he'd left there was silence, except for the sounds of her mother moving around in the next room.

•

THE SPAGHETTI THEY had for dinner was overcooked, the tomato sauce too sweet. Her mother had opened a bottle of red wine, and Mari thought she'd probably drunk another bottle over the course of the afternoon. That had been her habit, even when Mari was a child, and she had never shown any sign of wanting to change it. Still, she didn't seem agitated, and Mari thought that maybe Jack's charm would be enough to keep the peace. She had seen it before: people became the best versions of themselves around him, courting his approval.

Jack and her mother were discussing whether Tessa, who had just started eating solid foods, should be given some of the pasta.

'Do you think it's too spicy for her?' Jack asked. 'She's only had bland food before – you know, biscuits, bananas, that kind of thing.'

'Oh, she'll be fine. Mari used to eat everything, even before she had teeth, and she never came to any harm.'

Mari poured herself a little of the red wine. One glass a day was fine, according to the internet. 'It won't surprise you,' she said to Jack, 'to learn that I had a laissez-faire upbringing.'

His smile was a little nervous. 'Oh well, there's something to be said for that.'

'Do you think so?'

'Well, parents worry too much, I know I do. Tess will probably resent me for it later – over-protective father and all that.'

'I wouldn't know what that's like,' Mari said.

Silence, except for the chink of cutlery against plates. Her mother put her wineglass down, perhaps a little harder than necessary. 'Of course,' she said. 'In case any of us were in danger of forgetting about your terribly deprived childhood.'

'I didn't say anything about terrible deprivation.'

'Don't test me, Mari.'

'Well, don't put words in my mouth.'

Her mother took a deep breath in through her nose. 'Okay,' she said. 'Okay. Anyway, what do you want to do tomorrow? We could drive to the beach if you like?'

'We'll have to leave earlyish,' Mari said. 'Jack has to work on his manuscript.' It was a weak excuse – Jack could work on the manuscript anywhere, and she was sure her mother knew that. Across the table, he shot her a quick glance and then went back to helping Tessa with her sippy cup.

'Of course,' her mother said drily. 'One wouldn't want to stand in the way of the manuscript. Well, I'm so glad you could spare the time, darling.'

'Okay, Mum.'

'From your busy schedule.'

Irritatingly, Mari felt herself flush. 'All right,' she said. 'You've made your point.'

'Even though you don't work yourself, of course.' She turned to Jack. 'Mari's always considered herself too good for work.'

Jack laughed uneasily. 'I'd say most of us are too good for work, when it comes down to it.'

For a few seconds Mari thought the conversation might end there, and she was ready to be grateful for the reprieve. She would even make the effort to be friendly to her mother if they could just talk about something else. Please, she thought, please. But another part of her thought: Go on then.

'Anyway,' her mother was saying, still addressing Jack, 'I'm surprised you're defending her. Given her history with you.'

Mari felt the cold hook of dread in her stomach. Here it was. She stared down at her plate of spaghetti: the spatter of the sauce made a pattern of tiny red dots across the thick green ceramic. As a child, she had often had cause to study the minute aesthetic details of her meals in just this way.

'Yes, I did manage to get to the bottom of that story.' Her mother refilled her wineglass. 'Very complicated, but I suppose love triangles usually are.'

Jack cleared his throat. 'I don't think —'

'She set a nice little trap for you, didn't she? Babies make such good traps.'

'This is none of your business, Mum,' Mari said. She put a forkful of spaghetti into her mouth. It tasted of nothing.

'None of my business, none of my business. I just want to give you some advice. Is that so terrible, for a mother to give her daughter some advice?'

'I'm not actually interested in your advice.'

'Oh, you're not interested. Well, Elisabeth was a good person, a good friend to you. I have to say, though, you didn't repay her very well.'

Mari was silent.

'No, but you never had much time for good people, did you. You're too much like me, sad to say.'

'Oh, go fuck yourself,' Mari said. She stood up, and her mother was on her feet too, screaming at her. Something about how ungrateful she was, swearing at her own mother who had cooked for her and given up her bed for Mari to sleep on. Mari's heart was pumping very fast, and she was aware of a feeling of triumph, she was high on it, it was the most satisfying thing in the world to make her mother scream like this. At the same time she knew that very soon she would be crying desperately, unable to stop. Then a plate was arcing through the air, crashing and splattering behind her head. Mari turned to stare at the thin red stain left by the sauce, the slimy strands of spaghetti inching wetly down the wall.

In the next second she became aware that Tessa was screaming, and that Jack was holding her in one arm and using the other to steer Mari across the room. They went down the narrow cement stairs, and Jack unlocked the car and buckled the baby into the back, murmuring soothingly to her. Mari got into the passenger seat.

She was shaking so hard that it took her three attempts to buckle the seatbelt. 'Our stuff,' she said. 'All our stuff is still inside.'

'We'll come back. Let's just go for a drive, give everyone a chance to calm down.'

They drove through the empty streets. In the back, Tessa fell silent, sucking her thumb. Mari looked out of the window at the neat little houses, bordered by wide strips of grass. The grass was green and lush; they must have had some rain recently. 'She's always been like this,' she said, her voice trembling. 'I tried to warn you.'

He nodded. 'Not fair on you.'

'No.'

'She's had a tough life, though. Didn't you say her parents kicked her out when she was a teenager?'

'Can't say I blame them. Are you making excuses for her?'

'No, not excuses. I wouldn't ever want to be yelled at like that, I hate that she did it to you. But on the other hand . . . You know, she brought you up, she kept you with her even when it was really difficult. I just think that has to count for something.'

Mari let her breath out in a huff. 'Yeah, she's a hero. Single mothers are all heroes, I know.'

'Not a hero. But not necessarily a villain either. Just a person, like the rest of us.'

Mari leaned her head against the window. She was thinking of a haircut her mother had given her when she was six, dragging a kitchen chair out to the garden, and how she'd cried when she was finished, saying Mari looked so grown-up. Mari had sat in the chair and felt her mother's attention like the sun shining on her, and she'd been so happy she couldn't move. There were other times like that, too: times when Mari had been sick and her mother had read to her, had taken her temperature and brought her orange juice. Times when they didn't have money for a bus fare, and her mother had told her long stories as they walked hand in hand, stories always starring a girl called Marielle who was special and beautiful and had powers no one else could see.

They drove in silence. Mari pictured her mother alone under the fluorescent kitchen light, surrounded by dirty plates, the broken one in jagged pieces on the floor. She steadied her breathing. 'That thing she said,' she ventured. 'About Elisabeth, and everything. She's right, actually, I didn't behave very well there. Neither of us did.'

Jack turned a corner. His face, in profile, was hard to read.

'We're not bad people,' Mari said. 'Are we?'

He was quiet for a minute. Finally he said, 'Are you ready to go back?'

When they returned, her mother had cleaned up the kitchen and put the food away. She was apologetic, and Mari was too. In the morning they all walked down to the farmers' market together, Tessa in the carrier on Jack's chest, and Jack bought her mother a bunch of daisies from a stall selling fresh flowers. 'To say thank you for having us,' he said.

Driving back to Brisbane, Mari and Jack didn't talk much. They listened to the radio instead: there was a report on working conditions in mobile-phone factories in China, and another on sexual abuse in aged care. Tessa slept soundly in the back. Mari had the feeling of having shown Jack the deepest and most awful part of herself, and it made her so violently ashamed that it was almost a relief. Her body was very warm and heavy. When they got home she checked her email, but there was nothing from Elisabeth.

•

IN LA PAZ I lived on almost nothing: food was cheap, and I didn't buy any souvenirs or clothes. This was unusual for me – I'd always enjoyed buying things, and my windowsill at Spring Street had been cluttered with bits and pieces that had appealed to me for one reason or another. A long-necked pink ceramic vase; a tiny sage-green porcelain cup; a cut-glass saucer that Mari had once used as an ashtray. I'd snapped at her then, and she'd been taken aback. 'Okay, okay,' she'd said, tipping the ash out the window and wiping the saucer clean with the bottom of her T-shirt. 'It's just a plate, don't get your knickers in a knot.' And I'd felt stupid, because it was just a plate.

But now I found myself no longer interested in objects, and at some point I stopped going to museums and art galleries and started going to churches. I went almost every day and sat there in the dim quiet, sometimes for hours. The churches were different from the rest of the city: they were built from gently crumbling old stone, and the light was soft, coming in from high dirty windows. People streamed in and out, praying in the pews or at the altars nestled around the sides. Sometimes I saw them going into the booth to make their confessions.

In the evenings, I'd walk until I came across a restaurant that felt right, and I'd order something from the menu at random. I'd eat the whole thing, even when I didn't really know what it was, and it always tasted delicious. This was usually my only full meal of the day. I wasn't often hungry, but my clothes were baggy on me, and sometimes people stared at me in the street. They looked away quickly when I met their gaze.

After dinner I'd walk home through the dark steep streets. Walking, I let myself think about Mari: the ocean, the bucket. I alternated these with another fantasy about holding a pillow over her face while she slept. It was important to cover the whole face – I didn't want to look at her while it was happening. I didn't even want to think about her. Mostly I focused on the visceral details: the splash, the streaming bubbles, the pillow wet with saliva and tears. Her pale feet on the dirty floor.

One night, there was another email from her.

hi again

i hope you're doing well and enjoying mexico. (are you still in mexico? paul said that's where you went but i don't know. you should put something on insta one of these days.) last weekend we holidayed in the equally exotic setting of lismore, where we went to visit my mother. it went pretty much as you might expect, i.e. she got drunk and accused me of all sorts of things. according to her, 'love triangles' (?!) are 'always complicated', and i set jack 'a trap' by falling pregnant. it would've been funny if it weren't so terrible.

maybe you don't think it's funny. maybe you agree with her. did i 'steal' jack from you? it never felt like that, but maybe i'm not qualified to make that assessment. i really am sorry that i let it go on for so long without telling you, i know that was a shitty thing to do. i was afraid you'd hate me, i guess. but now i think that if i'd asked you beforehand you would have said yes. it was always the three of us anyway, we were just playing musical chairs regarding who slept with whom. or maybe that's a delusional and self-serving interpretation, i don't know.

anyway, lest you think i 'won' somehow: tessa is seven months old and doesn't feel like anything to do with me. i don't remember what it was like to experience sexual desire. i'm tired all the time, every second of every day, and when jack comes home i go into the bedroom and lie there with my face in the pillow. he's given up asking me what's wrong because i just say i don't know. and feel sad for not knowing, and stupid for feeling sad. sometimes i feel so sad i can't move, but mostly i just feel nothing. and on the way home from lismore i was thinking about how i've failed at all my significant relationships: with my mum, with tessa and with you. i'm not a net benefit to anyone, least of all myself. jack's still here, trap notwithstanding – although in the interest of fairness i should say that his feelings towards tessa have always been 100% correct. primal protectiveness, deep love like he's never known, et fucking cetera. full marks to him, as always. but he didn't have to give birth to her, he doesn't have to stay at home with her, and he had a whole life before she was born. mine was just beginning, and now it's gone.

m

•

THE DAY AFTER I got Mari's second email, I left La Paz and crossed into Peru, staying overnight in a small town near the border. I got the bus into Cusco early the next morning. When I arrived the city was waking up, shops opening for the day, and the air smelled clean and fresh after the dusty haze of La Paz. At the top of the mountain overlooking the city I could see Cristo Blanco, and above him the sky was a deep blue bowl.

In the cathedral, mass was underway. Standing room only. I stood in the aisle and looked out at the congregation, their lips moving in prayer. *Padre nuestro que estás en los cielos, santificado sea tu nombre* . . . The cathedral rang with the sound of it. *Perdona nuestras ofensas, como también nosotros perdonamos a los que nos ofenden* . . .

Incense wafted. The voice of the priest droned on: *Señor, Señor, Señor.* We turned to each other and clasped hands: '*La paz. La paz.*' I felt tears spring to my eyes. I didn't wipe them away, I let them sit there and eventually they rolled down my cheeks. It's possible that after a few minutes I was crying quite openly. No one stared at me. The priest offered communion, but I didn't take it. You were supposed to be in a state of grace. I walked down the cathedral steps and into the plaza and felt light and tender and very, very tired. My skin felt much too exposed, like it would burn from the sun; like it was the skin of a newborn baby, the skin of Tessa.

Later that day, sitting in an internet café crowded with backpackers, I described the scene in an email to Mari.

> It was the first time I've cried in months. Not that I've ever been religious as such, but the communion was so beautiful. At the same time, it made me feel so small and alone – I wished I could have been like the others, taking the body of Christ on my tongue.
>
> I'm sorry I haven't responded until now. Your emails were hard to read. Of course you didn't 'steal' Jack – he's a grown man, even though he doesn't always act like one. If anything, he was the one who stole you away from me. (Musical chairs, like you said.) But I've had a lot of time by myself recently to ponder things like human nature, and I've come to the conclusion that people only do things because they want to. We all end up in the bed we've made, the bed we want to lie in. You, Jack, your mother, everyone. It might help you to look at things that way.
>
> I hope things get easier for you, but please don't send me any more emails. You're not the only one who sometimes feels too sad to move. When we were friends, you seemed to take everything between us so lightly – you could kiss me as though it meant nothing. I always thought there were parts of your inner life that

you didn't let me see. (I was right, as it turned out.) And I think you did it partly because you enjoyed the fact that I cared enough to probe you: if you hid, I sought. It was a game we played together. Now I read your emails and I get the same sense: you want me to read between the lines, bring you an offering. But I don't want to play that game anymore, Mari. It makes me feel too tired.

Since you asked where I am, I'll tell you – I'm in Cusco and the sky is very blue. Bluer than the winter sky in Brisbane, and once I thought no sky could be bluer than that. After I send this email, I'm going to walk up to Cristo Blanco, the big white Jesus on top of the mountain. Months or years from now I'll look back on today and think, that was it, the day things ended between me and Mari. But I hope what I'll remember is the feeling of being perched up there, high above the city, as if I were really God on the hillside looking down on it all.

Amen,
Elisabeth

I wrote this email quickly. When I had finished, I pressed send without reading over what I'd written, and walked out of the café.

PART III

PART III

16

Five years later

Tessa came out of the school gates looking flustered. She was holding a piece of red paper with the remnants of leaves glued to it, and when she reached Mari she shoved the paper into her hand and launched into a long explanation of that day's art project. 'And then we had to sit on the mat and pass them around, and Chloe ruined mine, Mum, she pulled most of the leaves off!'

'I'm sure she didn't mean to,' Mari said soothingly. She tucked the paper into her bag and took Tessa's small chubby hand in hers.

'She should have been more careful,' Tessa said, but the note of outrage had gone from her voice. 'Mum? Our house is that way.'

'We're going to the supermarket, sweets. Tell me, did you do any reading today? What did you read?' Tessa was one of the few children in her Year 1 class who could read, a fact that Mari and Jack were privately smug about. They agreed that Tessa was different from other children her age: smarter, clearly, but also funnier and more delightful. Sometimes Mari would be reading to Tessa, or lying with her in bed (she demanded an intricate bedtime

251

ritual including songs, stories and what was beginning to amount to a guided meditation practice) and the thought would stab her without warning: You're the same person as that baby I couldn't love. Then she'd stop, swallowing hard, and Tessa would turn to her with round brown eyes and say, 'Mum?'

'Sorry, darling,' Mari would say. She'd press her face against Tessa's warm neck and kiss her over and over, until Tessa laughed and squirmed away.

Pushing the cart through the supermarket aisles, Mari devoted about twenty per cent of her attention to Tessa's chatter and the other eighty per cent to her grocery list. She bought the name-brand version of everything. This was a habit she'd picked up since Jack became an associate professor, and it wasn't only groceries; she bought herself designer clothes, expensive homewares from the upper levels of department stores. At first she'd felt guilty about the spending, but the guilt had quickly faded as she discovered the rich veins of pleasure that money could tap. These days, buying something new and expensive gave her a feeling not unlike the one she used to get when she had her first drink of the day: the unspooling of tension, the release in the chest.

Actually, she and Jack hardly drank at all anymore, or not in the way they used to. Most nights they had one glass of wine each, with dinner. They would have two or perhaps three glasses if they went to a party (never a real party – a barbecue or afternoon drinks) on the weekend. Most of the people at these gatherings were much older than Mari, and she found herself spending a lot of time with Tessa, giving her attention she didn't strictly need. She'd once overheard one of Jack's friends – a man called Geoff from the political science department – refer to her and Tessa as Jack's 'girls'. As in: Better go and collect your girls, Jack, it's time to go home. Mari had been wounded by the remark, although she knew it hadn't been made in the spirit of insult. She was sure that Geoff would have said it to her face without a second thought.

Her own friends had mostly left town. Heidi worked for an NGO in Melbourne, Paul for a TV production company in Sydney. Aisha and Verity both lived in London, although they rarely saw each other, and Alex was practising at a clinic an hour outside of Mackay. Mari kept up with their lives online and saw them occasionally when they came back to Brisbane. They always brought presents for Tessa, who was pleased but obviously didn't remember who they were. 'You know Heidi! She came to hold you in the hospital when you were born!' Mari had said to Tessa on the last of these visits, as if she expected Tessa to remember the occasion. Tessa had glanced shyly at Heidi, clutching the new doll she'd been given.

Arguably the thing to do, for someone in Mari's situation, was to make friends with the other mothers at Tessa's school. Dropping Tessa off in the mornings, she was confronted by a crowd of them, mostly with babies in prams. The uniformity was absurd, as though they'd all received a memo to breed at the same time. But what really surprised her was how old they were: she guessed the average age to be around forty. Mari could sense their surprise, too, when they looked at her and Tessa. The surprise was even greater when they saw Jack.

Eventually one of them asked her about it, while the others gathered around pretending not to listen. 'So, your husband . . .'

'He's not my husband.'

'Oh, sorry. Your partner. Remind me of his name?'

'Jack.' Mari watched Tessa run into the classroom with another little girl, their hands clasped together.

'That's right, Jack. What does he do?'

'He's a university professor. History.'

'Oh! And did the two of you –'

Mari turned towards the bank of curious faces. 'Yes, he's twenty years older than me. No, I was never a student of his. No, I didn't break up his marriage to someone else. Any other questions?'

The other mothers laughed weakly. Mari was not invited for coffee once the bell rang.

She walked home telling herself that she didn't care. They weren't her kind of people anyway, although these days she rarely met anyone who was. She knew it was irrational, but in her secret heart she believed that no one could really know her if they hadn't known Elisabeth. It was ridiculous, after so long, but Mari still felt Elisabeth's presence like a phantom limb: the itch that wasn't there. Over the years Elisabeth had visited her parents on the Sunshine Coast twice, but she'd never come back to Brisbane, and at one point Heidi had mentioned that she was living in Argentina. This situation was so alien that Mari didn't even bother trying to imagine it. South America had taken on the quality of a black hole in her mind, an unknowable blankness that had swallowed Elisabeth up. Arguably, that was what Elisabeth wanted.

Every year on Elisabeth's birthday, Mari toyed with the idea of sending her an email, and every year she re-read the last email Elisabeth had sent her and decided against it. *People only do things because they want to.* Sure. *It was a game we played together.* Okay. That's fine, reasonable. *It makes me feel too tired.* Mari never got through it without crying, but the crying was a release, and afterwards she felt better. It was a small, shameful ritual that she had to undertake each November. She never told anyone about it.

•

SOON AFTER TESSA started school, Mari got a job. It happened almost without her trying – at a barbecue on the weekend, she fell into conversation with David, the husband of one of Jack's colleagues, who was high up in the Department of Housing. He mentioned that his team was looking for someone to do some part-time policy work, and he encouraged Mari to apply. ('You've got a degree, haven't you?' he asked.) When she went in for the interview her palms were sweating, and afterwards she felt stupid for having wasted their time, but they called two days later to tell her that the job was hers.

It was her first real achievement in years. She wasn't excited by the work itself, but Jack was pleased – Mari had long suspected that he was vaguely ashamed of her not working, as though it reflected badly on him among the overachieving professional couples in whose circles they moved. Or maybe her not having a job made her seem even younger than she was, a child bride. ('Better go and collect your girls, Jack.') In any case, it seemed to make him happy to watch her get ready for work every Tuesday, Wednesday and Thursday morning. They took turns picking Tessa up from school. But in the evenings they were both tired, and the weekends seemed to be taken up with all the chores and errands they didn't have time for during the week. Sometimes Mari felt as though they were housemates who happened to have a child together.

One afternoon she arrived unannounced at his office, thinking they could have lunch, but the room was empty, the computer screen black. She looked around the small office, which gave the impression of bursting at the seams with books. A wooden picture frame on Jack's desk caught her eye, and when she picked it up she saw that it contained a photograph of herself, wearing a white sundress and holding two-year-old Tessa on her hip. Tessa was peering suspiciously at the camera, but Mari was smiling. She remembered Jack taking the photo on holiday in Byron Bay, but she hadn't known he'd framed it and put it on his desk. Seeing it there gave her a rush of love, but also the feeling – familiar by now – that she had no real understanding of her relationship with Jack; that she would never know who the woman in the photo was to him.

She put it down and turned to leave, a little embarrassed at having come at all. But then Ellen, who worked in the office next to Jack's, put her head around the door. 'Mari! Hello! I thought I saw you going past.'

'Hi, Ellen.'

'If you're after Jack, he's teaching at the moment. He won't be back for a couple of hours. But the class is just over in the Chalmers Building, if you wanted to pop in and see him in action.'

The idea first struck Mari as ridiculous. But walking back across campus, she saw the sign for the Chalmers Building and hesitated. Would she? Before she could think about it too much, she slipped into the main lecture hall. It was a large class and Jack didn't look up as she found a seat at the back.

'So that again raises a lot of serious questions,' he was saying. 'And the people who dealt with those questions – the twentieth-century thinkers who had to grapple with Marx's harsh critiques of the state and the way the state functions – they had to try to adapt Marx's theory, try to explain why things hadn't gone to plan in the twentieth century. In particular – why, in places like Italy and England, where the working class was very powerful – why weren't they able to confront the state and replace it? Why were they defeated, beaten back?'

He looked handsome, standing in front of the crowded lecture hall in his crisp white shirt. Mari saw him as his students must see him: attractive, relaxed, confident. She wondered whether he ever mentioned Tessa, just as a passing remark in his lectures. When she was a student, she'd had lecturers who did that – always men – and she'd envied them their cosy family lives, the love that lit up their faces when they said their daughters' names.

After a few minutes she slipped out, catching the bus to pick Tessa up from school. She didn't tell Jack she'd been to his class. But that night, after she'd put Tessa to bed, she came into his study and announced that she thought they should both be allowed to sleep with other people.

He looked up from the computer and leaned back in his chair. 'Right,' he said. 'Do you mind telling me what brought this on?'

'Nothing brought it on. It just makes sense, this being a marriage of convenience. Without the marriage part.'

'Come on, Mari. Have you got your eye on someone? Who is it, someone at work? A dad on the school run?' He sounded amused.

'No.' Mari sat down on the couch Jack kept in his study and tucked her legs underneath her. 'Why? Would you care if I did?'

'I'm just trying to work out where this is coming from. Don't you think I've got a right to know that?'

'Well, you made it clear a long time ago that you don't . . . that we're together basically for Tessa's sake. So why not? Besides, I'll be thirty-three this year and I suppose I'd like to get laid at least one more time before I die.'

He gave her a wry look. 'That might be a bit dramatic, don't you think?'

'I don't know. We don't have sex very often these days, do we? But I guess you're just not attracted to me anymore.'

'Oh, come on. Of course I am.'

'Okay, so let's do it.' Impulsively, she unbuttoned her blouse and tossed it aside. 'Let's fuck.'

He made a sound halfway between a sigh and a laugh. 'Not just now. I was in meetings all day today, I'm exhausted.'

'Are you sure? I can get on my hands and knees so you won't have to see my face. You can pretend I'm someone else.'

'Mari.'

'I'm so tired of hearing you say my name like that. *Mari Mari Mari*, like I'm Tessa's age. Why don't you call me Marielle anymore? God, you know, that used to turn me on.'

Jack shook his head and turned back to his computer. Mari began to feel silly, sitting on the couch in her skirt and bra. 'You're going to sleep with one of your students sooner or later, aren't you?' she said.

He made an exasperated noise. 'How on earth would I find time to do that?'

'Oh, that's fantastic. What a great response. No, that really makes me feel better, thank you.'

'Sorry.' He closed the computer. 'Obviously I'm not going to do that. But listen, Mari, you have to understand – work's busy at the moment, like really ridiculously busy. If I don't have boundless time and energy anymore, that's just the circumstances. Nothing to do with you.'

'You like young girls,' Mari said sadly. 'I used to be young.'

'I don't – Jesus, you make it sound like I'm in the habit of searching for barely legal porn. Anyway, you're still young. Thirty-two is young, trust me.'

Mari studied the polished timber floorboards, dark veins twisting through the rich wood. 'Maybe it's not my age that's the problem,' she said carefully. 'You're fifty-two, you know. Getting old.'

He gave another half-laugh. 'That's a bit harsh, don't you think?'

'You tell me.'

She said it casually, but when she glanced back at him, his face was serious. 'All right,' he said. 'I'll tell you.'

He got up from his chair. Hardly breathing, she watched him come over to the couch. He stood above her and let his hand wander gently over her head, stroking her hair, her cheek. Taking hold of her chin, he tilted it up towards him. 'I'm not going to let you fuck anyone else, Marielle,' he said quietly. 'Understood?'

'Yes.'

'All right. Lie down now.'

As if in a trance, she lay back on the couch and pulled her skirt up. She could hear him unbuckling his belt. He's going to use me, she thought, and she wanted to be used like that: to be a thing, a possession. She told him that, looking at the ceiling, and he said, 'I know.'

She waited for him to kneel over her, but when she looked at him, he was rubbing the back of his neck, his belt unbuckled and hanging loose. 'Sorry,' he said, not meeting her eye. 'Sorry. I'm just . . .'

'Oh.' She wriggled upright, tugging at her skirt. 'That's okay.'

He sat down heavily beside her and looked at his hands. 'Getting old, I suppose. Like you said.'

'I didn't mean that.'

'Well, whether you meant it or not, it's objectively true.' He sighed. 'And listen . . . Honestly, sometimes I don't know how far to go with that stuff.'

'What stuff?'

'Well, you know. The things you say, during sex – I mean, obviously I don't really want to use you, or anything like that.'

Mari felt her limbs go cold and still. 'Oh,' she said. 'Right.'

'You don't really want that, do you?'

'I don't know.'

'All right.' He took her hand, and she let it lie limply in his palm. Her body felt drained of everything. It seemed clear that she could only ever humiliate and disgust him, no matter what she did; no matter what kind of person she tried to be.

'Anyway, maybe you're right,' he said tiredly. 'About seeing other people. You're still young, even if I'm not. Seems only fair.'

'No, just forget it. It was a stupid idea.'

'Are you sure? You were the one who suggested it.'

'I know. Now I'm un-suggesting it.' She stood and straightened her clothes. 'I made my bed, so I'll lie in it.'

'Mari . . .'

'No, it's fine, really. Forget about it.' She went to the bathroom and stood under the shower for a long time, leaning blankly against the wall. When she got out of the shower, she checked her phone and saw that Elisabeth had posted a new picture: a shot of Brisbane at night, from the window of a plane.

17

IN MY DREAM, I was back in Mexico City: dusty streets, sunlight filtered weak through smog. I was in the back seat of a taxi, bartering a price before setting off. The driver wanted five hundred pesos, and I tried to tell him it was very expensive. *Muy* . . . My mind faltered. What was the word for 'expensive' in Spanish? *Muy* . . .

I woke to the sound of the phone ringing. When I got out of bed to answer it, my breath made puffs of steam: it was cold all the time in my little flat on Sussex Street. One bedroom, one bathroom, combined kitchen/living. Neat and tidy, the real estate agent had said.

On the phone was a woman called Jeanette who owned a clothing boutique in New Farm where I'd applied for a job. She invited me to come in for an interview, and I took the bus out that afternoon, arriving early. The boutique was on the corner of a quiet street lined with huge whispering trees, ending in the silent glint of the river. The door rang a discreet, melodious bell as I opened it, and the clothes on their heavy wooden hangers rippled slightly in the quiet breath of the air conditioner.

Jeanette was in her mid-fifties with short, artificially red hair and round glasses. She greeted me enthusiastically and showed me into the back office, where we sat across from each other at her desk. 'If someone comes in, I'll just have to pop out again,' she told me. 'Would you like some green tea? Mineral water?'

'I'm fine, thanks.'

'Good, good. Well, thank you so much for coming in, Elisabeth.'

'No, it's my pleasure. The place is beautiful.' I could feel the muscles of my face stretching into a smile, my head tilting downward to meet Jeanette's eyes. These were the things I did to charm people, to make them like me.

She asked if I'd ever worked in a boutique before. I said I hadn't but that I had been a barista and worked in bars and cafés all over Central and South America, as well as teaching English and doing other odd jobs.

'How fascinating,' said Jeanette. 'You've really lived, haven't you? And why did you come back to Brisbane?'

'Well, my parents are getting older, so I didn't want to be too far away. And I'm thirty-two, you know, I thought it was time to settle down a bit.'

She nodded enthusiastically, her eyes searching my face. It was only when she started talking in definitive terms about what my duties would be, when she wanted me to start and for how many hours per week, that I realised I'd been hired. Just like that, I could see the pieces of my life falling into place: the job, the flat, the bus rides back and forth. It was satisfying to remake myself this way, but underneath my satisfaction was something else, a trace of mild disappointment, as though I'd had to give something up. *Caro* – the word popped into my head as I got on the bus home. *Muy caro*, very expensive.

I got a call from Jack about a month after I started working at the boutique. It was easy for him to get in touch, he explained – I still had the same phone number. He did too. 'I thought about emailing you,' he said, a little apologetically, 'but then I remembered you prefer talking on the phone.'

'I'm not fanatical about it. An email would have been fine.'

'Oh, well, sorry. Maybe I should have emailed.' He cleared his throat. 'It's really nice to hear your voice, Elisabeth.'

I walked over to my bedroom window, looking out at the street without seeing it. 'That's flattering. What's this phone call about?'

'Right.' He cleared his throat again. 'Okay, I'll cut to the chase. I'm calling to ask if you'd consider coming to see us – Mari and me. Understandable if you don't want to, of course, but we just thought, with all the time that's gone by . . .'

'Oh, I see. Let's make up, play happy families, is that it?'

He paused. 'Look, it's totally up to you. You'd be well within your rights to say no and we'd both understand that. But we're making the offer, it's there if you want it.'

'What's the offer, exactly?'

'Well, it really depends what you want, we're happy to work around your schedule. But we thought maybe you could come for dinner this Friday, if you're free. Mari would love that.'

'Would she?'

'Of course she would. She's really keen to see you, she's just sending me to be the diplomatic envoy.' He hesitated. 'Just one thing – you know, of course, that we've got a little girl.'

I stretched my mouth open and let all the air out of my lungs quietly. 'Yes.'

'Right. Tessa. She's a lovely kid, you'll like her. Okay, I just . . . Sorry, Elisabeth. It's been so long, and you were away at your parents' place when she was born. I wasn't sure how much you knew.'

I took this to mean that he didn't know about the emails Mari had sent me when Tessa was a baby. 'You know, they get internet and phone coverage on the Sunshine Coast too,' I said. 'Of course I heard about it.'

'Yeah, of course. Sorry. I should have called you myself at the time, I know. No real excuse for that.'

I let the silence grow between us for a minute, and then I said, 'What's your address?'

•

THE ADDRESS HE gave me turned out to be a weatherboard cottage on a quiet street near the river, with an overgrown garden out the front. Everything seemed overgrown in Brisbane, and I couldn't tell whether I was just used to the sun-bleached parts of South America or whether the city had really let itself go in my absence. Everywhere plants burst from cracks in the concrete, vines engulfed trees and power poles, and the humid air was cut with a hint of rot. I didn't know if I liked it.

I knocked on the door, which had a panel of red and green leaded glass in it. After a few seconds I heard footsteps thudding towards me, and then Jack opened the door.

He was fifty-two by that point, and he looked it. His hair was definitely more grey than otherwise, and age was beginning to creep into his face, the features thickening and blurring. But he was still tall – I had forgotten how tall – he still carried himself well, and he still wore those black-framed glasses.

'Elisabeth!' he said, holding out one arm to give me an awkward hug. 'So good to see you.'

'You too.' His body was warm, and he smelled the same to me.

I found that my heart was beating a little faster than I would have liked.

'Come in, come in.' He stepped aside and closed the door behind me in a proprietary way. 'Mari's in the kitchen. I don't let her cook but she is allowed to supervise.'

I followed him down the hallway – walls hung with photos of a smiling dark-haired baby – and into a large kitchen and living area, with French doors opening onto a deck. I recognised Jack's framed poster from Hanoi on the far wall, but everything else was unfamiliar to me. A black leather sectional couch. A big wooden coffee table with magazines and art books stacked on its lower shelf. On the large patterned rug, a small girl was sprawled on her stomach, drawing on a sheet of paper. And standing stiffly at the wide granite-topped kitchen counter, wearing a cream cashmere sweater and an unreadable expression, was Mari.

I stepped forward; she did too, and we embraced. Her body pressed soft against mine, hair tickling my nose. Our heads knocked together awkwardly, and she gave a brittle laugh. 'You've cut your hair,' she said.

'Yeah. It got to be too much work.'

'Those beautiful curls of yours.' She looked at me hungrily. Her own haircut was just the same, but she looked older: there were lines on her face that hadn't been there before, and her skin had lost some of its dewy plumpness. Her body had changed too – she wasn't much bigger, but she seemed more solid, grounded, with none of the nervy racehorse thinness she'd had before. She looked like a mother. She was one.

'Can I get you a drink, Elisabeth?' Jack asked, manoeuvring around us to open the big double-doored fridge. 'We've got white wine, red wine . . . gin and tonic . . . or I could make you a cock-tail. You know, I never drank negronis before, but Mari made me one the other night and it was bloody good.'

'White wine is fine. Thanks.' I sat on a stool at the counter and watched as he poured the wine. Mari stood awkwardly in the middle of the kitchen, tugging the sleeves of her sweater over her hands. When I looked at her, she turned to the stovetop and lifted the lid off a heavy red stoneware pot with spatters and burn marks up its sides.

Jack handed me the wine and looked over my shoulder to the living room. 'Tess!' he called. 'Come and say hello.'

I heard small footsteps pattering up behind me, and before I could think about it too much, I turned around.

I hadn't seen a picture of Tessa since the newborn photo Heidi sent me. Then she had looked like a fragile porcelain doll, but now she was a real child, round-bellied and solid in her pink pyjamas. She had long dark hair, cut in a blunt fringe across her forehead, and inquisitive dark eyes. 'Hello there,' I said, working to keep my voice even. 'Don't you look just like your mum.'

'Everyone says that,' Mari said. 'I think she looks like Jack. She makes these amazing expressions with her mouth, just like he does.'

Tessa ignored this and gazed at me steadily. 'This is Elisabeth,' Jack said gently, crouching down beside her. 'A friend of ours. What do you say?'

Tessa smiled bashfully at him, then at the floor, then at me. 'It's nice to meet you,' I said, trying to smile back. 'How old are you?'

'Nearly six,' she said, in a sudden burst of confidence. 'My birthday's June the nineteenth. How old are you?'

'I'm thirty-two, the same age as your mum. Did you know your mum and I were friends before you were born?'

Tessa looked at Mari, seeking confirmation, and a smile darted across Mari's face. I had forgotten the way her teeth looked: small and neat, like seed pearls. 'That's right,' she said. 'Before you were even thought of. A very long time ago.'

Tessa turned back to me. 'I'm doing a drawing of cats in a house,' she said, in a confidential tone. 'You can see it later if you like. Daddy got me some new coloured pencils but I'm only using the pink and purple ones.'

Jack stood up, masking a smile. 'All right, sweetheart. Go and finish the drawing, and then it's bedtime soon.' She trotted off.

'She's lovely,' I said. There was something in my stomach that felt like a heavy and exceptionally hard rock. 'You came up with a good genetic combination.'

I saw their eyes meet briefly. 'Yeah,' said Mari. 'Well, she's got Jack's charm. She's got my temper, unfortunately, but that might be because she's five.'

Jack laughed. 'Suppose we'll wait and see, hey. Elisabeth, tell us, what are you doing with yourself these days? Since you got back, I mean.'

I told them about the shop. By then I'd collected a few funny stories about Jeanette and the customers, which made them laugh. Jack moved around the kitchen chopping things and stirring them into the pot, and Mari leaned against the counter. I noticed that she never came to sit with me on the other side. After a while Jack said, 'Okay, that just needs to cook down for a bit, so shall we go outside?'

We took our drinks out to the deck, where there was a long timber table and chairs. Mari lit a candle in the middle of the table and the flame cast its soft flickering light onto her face.

Jack brought out a platter of cheese and olives and vine leaves. 'From the Greek market,' he told me. 'It survives, unbelievably.'

'I know, it's amazing. I expected a café to be there by now.'

'Have you been past Mari and Heidi's old place? On Paris Street?' I said I hadn't, and a grimace flickered briefly across his face. 'Knocked down and redeveloped.'

That gave me a pang of sadness, but I didn't want to let them see it. 'Oh well,' I said. 'Everything gets knocked down eventually, doesn't it?' Mari stood up abruptly and said she was going to check on the food.

After she'd gone the conversation seemed to fizzle, even though she hadn't been saying much. Jack cleared his throat as if he were about to speak, but then Tessa came out through the French doors and climbed into his lap.

She looked at me shyly and buried her face in his chest. He shot me a glance above her head – apologetically, I thought. 'Here's a girl who should be in bed,' he said.

'Mum said I could stay up.'

'That seems unlikely. Come on, I'll read you a book and then it's lights out, all right?' He put his glass down and stood up, hoisting her onto his hip. 'Say goodnight to Elisabeth, and then we'll go and give your mum a kiss.'

'Goodnight,' I said. Tessa peeped at me and didn't reply. Over her head, Jack mouthed the words 'back soon' at me and carried her into the house. After a minute I heard her voice raised in protest, then Jack's soft voice, and Mari's. Laughter, and a shriek.

Mari came back out, holding a bottle of wine. 'Sorry about that,' she said. 'Tess isn't a huge fan of bedtime.'

'No, that's okay. She's really sweet.'

She smiled, fidgeting with a topaz ring on the third finger of her right hand. (Her hands hadn't changed – those long knobbly fingers.) 'It's weird seeing Jack like that,' I said. 'Such a dad.'

'Oh, he adores her. I think it's the only thing I've ever done to make him happy.' She said it lightly, and I wasn't sure if she was joking. 'Do you want some more wine?'

'Sure.' I let her refill my glass. 'You've turned into a good little hostess. You're living the bourgeois dream out here, aren't you?'

She looked a little shocked when I said that, but then she pulled her face together. 'Oh, yes. Three bedrooms, entertaining on the deck . . .'

'All your wildest dreams come true.'

She gave a half-smile. 'Yeah. Sometimes I do think about the kitchen at Paris Street – remember that asbestos panel in the wall? Everyone thought Heidi and I were going to die of mesothelioma.'

'But now you're rich.'

She leaned back in her chair. 'It's not my money.'

'Maybe it should be. Wages for housework and all that. Are you working these days? I mean, in a real job, quote unquote?'

She made a face. 'Just three days a week. I'm doing policy work in the Department of Housing – the state government, you know. Seems like I can't escape the state bloody government, I'm destined to work there until I die.'

'But do you like it?'

'It's okay. You know, it's wage labour, what can I say? But I'd been a hausfrau long enough, isn't that right, Jack?' He had come back out, carrying a stack of plates.

'Right,' he said. 'It's not on, these days, for a mum not to work. I think Tessa's teachers were going to stage an intervention if you went on for much longer without a job.' They shared a humorous look across the table. Despite Mari's comment about not making Jack happy, there was a funny kind of affection between them. I thought of him saying: We'll go and give your mum a kiss. I wondered if they would have another baby.

Dinner was slow-cooked lamb, with potatoes in a creamy sauce. (I'd given up vegetarianism soon after arriving in Mexico.) The conversation was friendly and neutral – we talked about how fast the inner city was gentrifying, how terrible it was to see so many new apartment buildings along the peninsula. 'We should move out to Darra,' Jack said. 'Lots of space out there, Tess could go to school with kids who aren't white, and we might be able to actually buy a house. You know, we're still renting here, even on two salaries.'

'That's outrageous,' I said. They appeared to take this remark seriously.

After dinner, Jack cleared away the plates and topped up our drinks. The white wine was very good, dry and crisp, like all the expensive wine he used to buy. Mari had a gin and tonic, but I noticed that she was drinking it very slowly.

'So,' I said, when Jack came back from putting the wine in the fridge. 'I brought something to show you.'

They turned towards me. Jack looked curious, anticipatory. Mari looked wary. 'What is it?' she asked.

I took my laptop out of my bag. 'The other day I was looking on my hard drive, and I found some footage from that film project I was working on, back when we . . . you know. The one you hated, Mari.'

She opened her mouth to say something, but Jack got in first. 'That's right!' he said. 'Jesus, I'd forgotten all about that. Archival footage. Can you play it for us?'

'Yeah, if you want.' I pushed the computer down the table so we could all see the screen. 'I cut all these scenes together. Most of them I don't even remember.'

We watched the footage for a while. It was – predictably, I guess – very stupid: a lot of it seemed to involve us sitting around and drinking. We weren't as funny as we thought we were. But there were small moments when the essence of something seemed to cut through: the angle of Paul's neck as he tipped his head back in laughter, or Heidi tucking her hair behind her ears as she began to speak. There was Mari, too, smoking a cigarette and giving the camera the finger. 'Stop it,' she said, her skin so smooth and milky on the screen, her dark hair glossy. 'I told you to put that fucking thing away.'

'Oh no,' Mari said. 'I look so young there, I can't believe it. I wish you hadn't shown us this.'

'Are you kidding?' Jack said. 'It's great. My God, I remember that kitchen. Hey, wasn't that Heidi's girlfriend? The one she was always breaking up with?'

Then Jack appeared on the screen. He looked more well defined somehow, more muscular, and his hair was darker. He and Mari were sitting at Paul's table, surrounded by people going in and out. They were next to each other on one side of the table, and I – or the camera – was on the other side. They were both watching something happening behind me. On the screen, Mari had a glass of wine halfway to her lips when she paused and leaned over to say something to Jack, sotto voce. His face moved into a laugh.

'There you are, Mari,' said Jack. He was trying to be jovial, but I could hear the strain in his voice. 'Drinking like a fish, as usual.'

I glanced at Mari: she had a strange, stricken expression on her face. I looked back at the screen.

'Do you ever appear in this, Elisabeth?' Jack asked. 'Or is that the privilege of the filmmaker – to be invisible?'

'Here and there,' I said. 'Mostly it's me filming the two of you, though. I'd forgotten how much time we used to spend together.'

Neither of them had anything to say to that. We watched a few minutes of Heidi and Paul demonstrating a dance they'd made up, finally collapsing in laughter on the floor. The footage cut to Mari and Heidi's kitchen, the images on the screen jumbling and somersaulting as the phone was passed over from me to Mari. I could be heard saying, 'Here, you film for a bit,' and then the camera focused on Jack, sitting across the table. There was a small slice of me in the frame – my shoulder, my bare arm, and a few wisping tendrils of hair. I'd got rid of the red linen dress when I went to Mexico.

On the screen, Jack was giving the camera his conspiratorial little smile. The smile that made you feel like it was just you and him, in on a joke that no one else understood. My stomach curled. We heard him say, 'Hello.'

'Hey.' Mari. The grubby kitchen wall behind him, the bottle of gin on the table. Outside, a shout from the party.

'My cinematic debut. What should I say?'

'Doesn't matter.' Mari's voice was young and sweet, with the slightest edge of knowing flirtation. I could see why he'd been so attracted to her. 'Say anything that comes to mind.'

He surveyed the camera for a beat, on the edge of a smile. Then I heard my own voice: 'You should educate us. Teach us –'

'Turn it off, Elisabeth,' Mari said harshly. 'Please.'

I closed the laptop and looked at her, but she wouldn't meet my eye. She was twisting the ring around her finger again.

'Sorry,' she said eventually. 'Sorry to snap. I just – it's hard to watch, I'm sure you understand that.'

I shrugged. 'It's just what happened. Nothing more, nothing less.'

'Oh, Elisabeth, you know that isn't true.'

Jack cleared his throat. 'Look, let's forget about it. It was a long time ago anyway. Water under the bridge.' He stood, touching Mari's shoulder briefly. 'Would you both like tea? Or coffee, Elisabeth? We have that too if you'd prefer.'

I slid the laptop into my bag. I never drank coffee after midday; he used to know that about me. 'Tea's fine,' I said. 'Thank you.'

He brought out a pot of tea and three mugs, and an apple cake with salted caramel. While we ate, Jack and I talked about a literary magazine we both read and whether it was going downhill under its new editor. Mari picked at her cake silently, not looking at me. The candle on the table was guttering now, giving off unsteady bursts of flame.

When I'd finished my tea, I pushed my chair back and said, 'Well, thanks for dinner. I'm working tomorrow, so I'd better go.'

'I'll drive you home,' Jack said, standing up.

Mari shot him a look. 'Are you okay to drive?'

'I'm fine.'

'Are you sure? It's Friday, the cops will be out looking to catch people.'

'I can get the bus,' I said.

'Don't be silly. It's past ten, you'll be waiting ages. Mari, I'm fine, honestly.' She shrugged. We went into the house and Jack started looking for his keys.

When he'd found them and we were moving towards the door, Mari stepped forward and gave me a sudden hug, holding me stiffly. 'Sorry if I was rude,' she said. 'It was just strange to see that footage after so long.'

'That's okay.' Her sweater was soft and warm against my cheek, and her hair smelled exactly the same as I remembered. 'Maybe it was my fault. Should I not have brought it?'

She gave a funny little shrug. 'Water under the bridge, like Jack said.' That didn't seem to answer my question.

'In any case,' Jack said, 'come again, Elisabeth, won't you? It was so good to see you.'

'Yes,' Mari chimed in. 'Really, we're not just saying that. Come for dinner again, or maybe we could have coffee, some day when I'm not working.'

'Okay,' I said. 'Or you could come out to the shop. I could get you a linen shift with my staff discount, it would suit your new lifestyle.'

She gave me a tight little smile. We said goodnight, and Jack and I went out to the silver Skoda in the driveway. Inside, the car smelled clean and expensive. We didn't talk except for me giving him directions. When he pulled up outside my building, he said, 'I hope that wasn't too hard on you.'

'It wasn't hard on me. Was it hard on you?'

A motorbike cracked and rumbled down the street. Jack waited for it to pass before he said, 'A bit, yeah.'

'Well, do you really want to see me again? If it's going to be hard?'

'It'll get easier.' In the dark, I couldn't read his expression. 'You know, I feel a lot of responsibility for how things went wrong. At the time, I tried to convince myself that I wasn't really involved, but now . . . Anyway, I feel some responsibility for putting things right, too. If I can. So yeah, I do want to see you again. Mari does too.'

'Okay.' I opened the door. 'You know where to find me.'

I didn't look back at the car, but I heard him drive away as I was unlocking my front door. Inside, I turned on the overhead light and flopped down on the grubby two-seater couch, feeling blank with exhaustion. On the bookshelf across the room I could see the novel Jack had given me all those years ago; I'd carried it with me everywhere, even though I knew he had only meant it as a loan. *Vogliamo Tutto*, the spine announced. We want everything.

18

WHEN A WEEK passed and I didn't hear from either of them, I began to think that they had changed their minds. I knew that whatever happened next had to be initiated by them, so I kept doing the things I always did: going to work, buying food, going home. I checked my phone and email, but no more than usual. The weather was getting colder and I enjoyed that; it made me feel like things around me were changing.

Working at the boutique was so dull that I sometimes thought I could feel my brain liquefying as I clipped tags onto dresses, or refolded T-shirts (white, grey, bone) for the eighth time that day. Next time I look at the clock, I'd tell myself, it'll be past ten. Past twelve thirty. Past three. I won't look until then. But when I looked, it was always much earlier than I'd hoped.

The customers (the 'clientele', as Jeanette called them) were mostly, as far as I could tell, friends of hers. In any case, she seemed to know them all by name, although they were indistinguishable to me: polished rich women, shiny-haired and loose-limbed, smelling of expensive perfume. I couldn't imagine ever looking like they did. My instructions from Jeanette were to be 'friendly' and 'welcoming', but never 'aggressive' or 'pushy'. I gathered that the real objective was to avoid any acknowledgment of the fact that we were selling, and they were buying. When she'd been training me, Jeanette had always seemed practically anguished over the act of ringing up a purchase, and sometimes I thought she'd hired me mainly to avoid ever having to do it again.

When I wasn't working, I sat around the flat and did little drawings, watered my plants, read long essays online about politics and culture. Once I read a piece that I thought Jack would like, and I drafted an email to him with the link, but I deleted the draft almost as soon as I'd written it.

Later I came across a short film about Egyptian funerary art at the end of the Roman Empire, and I lay on the couch and watched it for a while. The women in the paintings all looked like Mari, with their dark liquid eyes. I thought of her twisting the topaz ring around her finger. The voiceover was saying something about death when there was a knock at the door, and I paused the film.

When I opened the door, Jack was standing on the little concrete step. 'Hi,' he said. 'I was hoping you'd be home.'

He was wearing dark blue chinos and a grey crew-neck sweater, and he had a leather messenger bag slung over one shoulder. 'Shouldn't you be at work?' I asked.

'Thursday is a research day. No teaching, so I don't have to be on campus.'

'Does this count as research?'

'Well, that depends. Are you going to let me in?'

I stood aside, and he stepped past me into the kitchen. It was a small room, with fake-wood linoleum and cheap plywood cabinets. 'Pretty basic,' I said. 'Not like your place.'

'Well, thank God for that.' He sat down at the table I'd found on the street and dragged home by myself. 'I've had enough of my place.'

'Bullshit,' I said mildly. 'Don't tell me about the quiet desperation of having an ensuite.'

He smiled. 'I don't actually have an ensuite.'

'Well, you know what I mean. Or we could always swap, you're welcome to the mould in my bathtub. *La vie bohème.*'

'Okay, okay.' He held up his hands. 'Point taken. Any chance of a cup of tea?'

I boiled the kettle, standing by the window in the bright sunlight. He was quiet, looking around the room. When I brought him a mug of tea he said, 'Thank you.'

I got the milk out of the fridge and put it on the table. 'You can add your own. I don't know how much you want.'

He poured a little into the mug and stirred it, the spoon clinking loudly against the ceramic. 'I should have brought you something,' he said. 'A cake, or something like that. Isn't that what people do when they come over for afternoon tea?'

I stirred my own tea, watching the milk bloom pale through the brown. 'Why are you here, Jack? Is this another diplomatic mission?'

'No, no. Mari doesn't know I'm here, actually.'

'Oh.'

'I guess I felt . . . I don't know. It was nice, seeing you the other night, but we didn't really get to talk. The two of us, I mean.'

'Well, your partner and daughter were there. It wasn't exactly an intimate dinner, was it?'

'No. And I thought that would be best – to leave all that in the past, you know, and try to start fresh. But then after I dropped you off, I realised there were still some things I wanted to say to you.'

'What things?'

'Well, okay.' He sipped his tea. 'First of all, I just want you to know that when I ran into you that evening in the fruit shop and I told you that Mari and I had split up, I was telling the truth.'

'I never thought you were lying.'

'She got pregnant at the very end, and I didn't find out until later. I went to Italy, you know, on that research trip, and when I got back she was nearly four months along and she'd decided to go ahead with it. Not much I could do.'

'Why are you telling me this? Do you want me to absolve you?'

'No, that's not . . .' He rubbed the back of his neck. 'Look, obviously Tess is great, but before she was born, I was . . . Well, I was a bit freaked out. I thought there was a fairly high chance it was going to ruin my life.' He glanced at me. 'Sorry. Maybe you don't want to hear this.'

I shrugged, sitting down opposite him at the table. I didn't actually know whether I wanted to hear it, but at least it would fill in some gaps.

'It's just that I've never really told anyone before. Anyway, when Mari first told me she was pregnant, I was completely devastated. I just sat in the flat for days, drinking too much, smoking too much – you would've been pretty disgusted. I was too, but I sort of couldn't move, it kept going around and around in my head. Eventually Heidi rang – I can't remember much of the conversation, I wasn't absolutely sober, but I know she told me that Mari was very unwell. I remember those words, 'very unwell', and something about them rang true. And she said you'd gone to stay with your parents, and that was a shock, it sort of recalibrated the situation in my mind. The whole time I'd been half-thinking that at least you'd be looking after Mari, but when I realised you'd gone, I kind of grasped how bad things must be for her.'

I got up to put the milk back in the fridge, taking possibly a little longer than I needed to. When I turned around, Jack was looking at me. 'Carry on,' I said.

'Right. Well, Heidi made a few choice observations on my character, none of which I could really disagree with, and the upshot was that I had to do something to fix the mess I'd made. So, I thought I'd do the right thing for once in my life – couldn't do much about you, you'd made your wishes clear on that front, but I patched things up with Mari. We moved in together, all the rest of it. I wasn't thrilled with the situation, but I just kept telling myself, well, there's nothing you can do about it, and now you've got to reap what you sowed.'

'So to speak.'

'Yeah. Actually, it felt like just punishment, in a way.'

'What for?'

'Well, I shouldn't have been messing around with women half my age, it was never going to end well. Not so much with you, you can look after yourself, but Mari . . . Anyway, I wasn't feeling great about any of it. And on top of that there was a baby on the way. But when Tess was born, it was just . . .' He smiled to himself, a soft little smile. 'Look, there are so many clichés about having children, but I have to admit they're mostly true. As soon as I held her . . . It sounds silly, but I just fell in love. Caught me completely by surprise, but there it was. I remember saying to my sister on the phone, I don't know why I was always so afraid of being a father. I would've done it years ago if I'd known it would be like this.'

He paused and glanced at me, as if he expected me to make some response. I cupped my mug of tea in both hands and blew on it.

'Anyway,' he said, 'I can't say I regret everything with Mari, because I've never regretted Tess. Not even close. But Mari and me . . . Well, we make the best of it, but it's not really a love thing. Not for me, anyway. I can't speak for her.'

I stayed quiet. Outside, a crow sent its harsh croak through the chilly blue air of the autumn afternoon.

'I don't know,' he said. 'It's not as though we fight all the time, but we do seem to disappoint each other. Maybe we should have stayed separated. It might have saved a lot of misery.'

'Well, you did what you could. You wanted to give Tessa a proper family.'

'That was the thinking at the time, yeah. Now I wonder about the merits of a proper family.' He drained his mug of tea. 'Maybe I'm being unfair to Mari. It hasn't been easy for her either.'

My mug had left a damp ring on the table. I pushed my finger through it. 'Do you still sleep together?' I asked.

'Sometimes. Not that often, to tell you the truth.' He was looking at the ceiling. 'But since you asked, I suppose it's only fair to tell you that we did the other night, after you came to dinner.'

'Right.' In my mind, I saw them entwined on the leather couch, the dishwasher humming in the kitchen. Or had they gone into their bedroom? I pictured a king-size bed with linen bedcovers, the walls painted some avant-garde colour like eggplant. 'Bit of a role reversal there, hey. Well, I guess your own particular role stayed the same.'

He sighed. 'I don't feel good about any of this, Elisabeth.'

'But you'll take what you can get.'

'I don't know. What else am I supposed to do? I've spent countless fucking hours lying awake, turning this over in my mind, so if you have any insights to share, please go ahead.'

I turned my face away. After a minute he said, 'I'm sorry.'

'It's okay.'

'No, it's not. None of this is your fault. Oh God, I don't know.' He put his head in his hands. 'I don't even know why I came here, it was selfish of me. I should probably just go away and leave you alone, shouldn't I?'

I stared down at the table: grubby white formica flecked with grey. Moving my mouth carefully, I said, 'I don't want you to leave me alone.'

I heard him push his chair back, and I thought he was about to come over to me, or else leave, but instead he went to the window and looked out into the bleak concrete courtyard. 'Do you remember the first time we went for a drink together?' he asked. 'After that terrible seminar, the one about the 1944 referendum or whatever it was.'

'Yeah, I remember.'

'You were the one who kissed me. Then afterwards you said something about how you weren't actually interested in that referendum. And I remember thinking, my God, this girl is so fucking cool. I was so intimidated by you.'

'You were intimidated by me?'

'Oh, incredibly. You didn't realise that? I thought you realised.'

'No,' I said. 'I just wanted you to take me home, I kept waiting for you to ask. It seemed so old-fashioned that you asked me out for dinner instead.'

I saw his shoulders move in a laugh. 'Yeah. Well, I didn't know what people your age usually did, I didn't want to overstep the mark.

And I thought if you wanted to go home with me, you'd probably just suggest it yourself. You seemed like that kind of person.'

'Well, I'd already practically stalked you at the seminar, instructed you to take me out for a drink and then kissed you. I thought it was your turn to take the lead.'

'No, you're right, it was. I liked it, though. How confident you were. I would have done anything you told me to do.' He leaned his head against the glass. 'Honestly, I'd probably still do anything you told me to do.'

I went over to him. He stayed still, looking out the window, and I leaned my cheek against his arm. We stood like that for some time. Then I said quietly, 'Turn around.'

His mouth when he kissed me was warm; it still tasted the same, and I found myself remembering the day in my room at Spring Street, after I'd come back from visiting my parents. Me on the bed in my towel and him in the desk chair, and the way we'd looked at each other. How young I'd felt. How young I'd been. In the end, it was the humiliation I minded more than the pain. But here I was again, perched on the edge of the table with my legs wrapped around him, and he was kissing me, deeper and deeper, and I flung my head back and he said, 'Jesus, Elisabeth.'

'Do you want to stop?' I tried to say it casually.

'No.' He was unbuttoning my dress urgently. 'No, fuck no, I don't want to stop.'

We went into the bedroom. Somehow my dress was off, my tights were off, and he was kissing my neck, he was pushing my knees apart and putting his mouth between my legs. I arched my back against the mattress. I had the feeling of standing on a cliff edge, being buffeted by strong winds. After a minute he stopped and said, 'Elisabeth?'

'Mmm?'

'Sorry, this is . . . I don't have a condom. Do you?'

I was glad to hear him say that. If he'd come to my flat with a condom in his wallet, I couldn't have slept with him. But maybe he knew that. 'It's okay,' I said. 'I'm on the pill.'

His face relaxed. 'Okay. Just checking.' We kissed again. I was pushing myself against him, I wanted to feel his touch everywhere. I knelt over him, and he held onto my hips as if to steady himself. It felt different without a condom: deeper and closer than I remembered. Longing gathered in my chest, in my stomach. I looked at him and looked at him, and he held my gaze, and then I closed my eyes and I heard him somewhere saying my name.

Afterwards, I stared peacefully at the wall. The afternoon light was coming through the west-facing window, and I thought of the churches I'd been to in La Paz, the way the light came down soft through the dirty windows. The holy silence. 'Are you okay?' Jack asked.

'Yeah. Are you?'

'Never better.'

'Never?'

'Literally never.' He stroked my hair. 'I'm a bit sad about your hair, though. I always pictured you with your curls – I mean, after you went away.'

'You pictured me.'

'Of course I pictured you. You've been like a ghost in my life for years. It's hard to believe you're here, actually. I keep wanting to pinch myself.'

'And Mari? Did she ever think about me?'

He paused. 'Well, we've never discussed it much. But you know, when she was having Tess, she did ask for you . . . She was in a lot of pain and they wouldn't give her anything for it, they said it was too late. It was quite scary, actually. Anyway, she kept calling for you. I don't know if she remembers that.'

I didn't reply.

'Sorry,' he said. 'That must've been strange to hear.'

'I hated her,' I said, half into the pillow. 'When I was away, the first year or so, I used to have these fantasies about hurting her. Holding her head underwater, suffocating her with a pillow . . . I couldn't stop thinking about it.'

'Yeah. Maybe that's understandable, given the circumstances.'

'I just –' I stopped, shaking my head.

He touched my cheek. 'It'll be okay,' he said.

'How do you know?'

'I just think you're the kind of person who'll always be okay.' He moved his head back a little, as if to get a better look at me. 'You're different since you came back. Well, we're all different. But you seem . . . I don't know how to put it. There's a kind of directness to you.'

'I wasn't direct before?'

'Well, I don't know.' He sighed. 'Honestly, you've always been a bit of a mystery to me. Even when we were together, I usually had no idea what you were thinking. It used to bother me a bit.'

'Really? Like when?'

He paused. 'Well, I guess like when you stayed at my house for the first time, and in the morning you just casually announced that you were off to the Sunshine Coast for two weeks. And I tried to say something about how much I'd enjoyed spending time with you, and you just gave me this indulgent little smile, like, okay. So I thought maybe you just saw it as a casual thing.'

'No, I didn't see it that way. I liked you.'

'Well, that wasn't exactly clear. Honestly, I found it a bit exhausting trying to keep up with you – every time I tried to talk to you about how I felt, or anything like that, you'd always be so ironic about it. And I didn't know whether that was just the way everyone your age talked, or whether you really saw me as a bit of a joke . . . Anyway, I used to worry about it. And then you told me you'd slept with – what's-his-name. Your friend, the medical student.'

'Alex.'

'Yeah, him. You just brushed it off, like – these things happen, what's the big deal? But it really hurt me, it still hurts me to think about it. Maybe that's pathetic of me.'

'It's not pathetic of you. Not at all.' I took his hand, and he stroked my thumb with his. My chest felt tight and blocked up, like there were bricks stacked inside it.

'Well, I overreacted, I did eventually realise that. It was too late by then, though.'

'Too late in that you were already sleeping with Mari.'

'Yeah.' He rubbed his face. 'Look, I don't pretend to have behaved very well in any of this. But at the time I kind of thought that whatever I did or didn't do, I'd probably never see you again, you were off with medical students or whoever. You'd made it clear you didn't care about me, or not the same way I cared about you. And – look, I'm not courting the sympathy vote here, but after we split up, I was really depressed. I mean, terribly. For about a month I couldn't eat, couldn't sleep, just felt blank and miserable all the time. So when Mari came along . . . You know,

I liked her, she made me laugh. I wanted to feel better. It wasn't the best idea, but I've never exactly proven myself to be a man of good ideas.'

I swallowed. 'You thought I didn't care about you?'

'Like I said, I overreacted. But yeah, that's what I thought at the time.'

I leaned my head back so that I was looking right up at the ceiling. 'But I only did it because I thought you were ashamed of me.' My voice was small. 'And because I felt so powerless. It was the wrong thing to do but it didn't mean anything, not about you and me.'

He was quiet for a long time, holding my hand. Eventually he said, 'I didn't realise you felt powerless. You never said anything about that.'

I let my breath out. 'You were so much older than me,' I said. 'Well, you still are, but it was a bigger deal back then. You had a real job, you made real money, you had this whole adult life that we weren't part of – Mari and me, I mean. Obviously we had our own power too, I'm not trying to say you were manipulating us.'

'No. Actually, I always felt like the two of you treated me with a bit of contempt, if anything.'

'Did we?'

'I'm not saying I didn't deserve it. You both knew the score – a middle-aged man, two beautiful young women. A bit pathetic, isn't it? I certainly felt an enormous amount of contempt towards myself over it.'

'But you make it sound so . . . It wasn't like that. You know it wasn't like that.'

He shook his head. 'Is it for any of us to say definitively what it was like? Anyway, sorry. You were saying.'

'Well, on the face of it, in the outside world, you had more status. And I kept asking you not to keep me a secret, I don't know why I cared so much about it, but –'

'No, that was my fault. Look, it was stupid, but I was worried I'd be seen as some kind of creep. I guess, deep down, I was worried that I *was* some kind of creep. And it's very dicey these days, with the students – there's a lot of paranoia, maybe justifiably so. But that's not really an excuse, I was just being cowardly. As usual.'

'I guess it wasn't much fun for you to introduce Mari to your friends, then. Not only is she twenty-six but she's pregnant.'

He laughed. 'Oh yeah. You know, it was a bit awkward – my sisters weren't happy, and I think one friend's wife stopped speaking to me for a while – but they got over it soon enough. Seems obvious in retrospect, but no one actually cared that much about my sex life.'

'I tried to tell you that.'

'I know.' He kissed the palm of my hand. 'You were right, of course you were right. I'm sorry I didn't listen to you.'

'I'm sorry too,' I said miserably. 'But this is all coming years too late, isn't it?'

He pressed my hand to his cheek and held it there. 'Oh well, better late than never. Honestly, you have no idea how happy you're making me now.'

I didn't say anything because I didn't want to cry in front of him. His cheek felt warm under my hand. After a minute he said, 'Hey.'

'Hey.'

'Listen, I'm really sorry to do this, but I've got to pick Tess up from school. Mari's working today, so it's my turn.'

'Right, right.' I swallowed. 'Of course.'

He kissed me, a long and tender kiss. I felt my body warming up to him again, I couldn't help it, and he moved towards me and said, 'Shit. I want to, but I've really got to go.' He pulled away. 'I'm sorry.'

I watched as he got dressed, in a rush, and shoved his feet into his shoes. His shirt was crumpled, and when he pulled his sweater over it, the cuffs stuck out awkwardly. He came over to the bed and cupped my face in his hands. 'I'm very glad I came to see you.'

'I'm glad too.' Inside I felt unbearably tender, like I'd been scrubbed clean. My eyelids were heavy.

'Can I come again?'

'Yes.'

'When?'

'Any time you like.' That made him smile.

'Okay. I'll see you very soon, then.' He kissed me and went out. After he left I fell asleep, and I slept for a long time. Nearly twelve hours, I think.

19

AFTER THAT, JACK started coming to my flat once or twice a week. I gave him a key, and usually when he arrived I'd already be in bed, which was the warmest place in the flat. We'd have sex, quickly and without saying much, and then lie in bed talking. The sex was very good, and I felt a rush of intense guilt whenever I thought about it, which I thought must also increase the pleasure at an unconscious level.

I assumed Jack was also feeling guilty, but it was difficult to know. He only ever mentioned Mari in an offhand, logistical sense – Mari's working tomorrow, or, I told Mari I'd take Tess to her swimming lesson this afternoon. One Saturday morning I saw the three of them at the markets, where the crowds made it easy for me to stand back and watch them. Jack was wearing a blue T-shirt and had canvas bags slung over each shoulder. Mari was holding Tessa's hand, and Tessa was saying something to her with a plaintive expression. I saw Mari glance at Jack, as if to ask his opinion, and he smiled and opened his mouth to reply. As he was speaking, they turned the corner and disappeared.

I walked home without finishing my shopping. I'd always thought that Mari had a tendency to adopt the role of the victim – a role that, as I'm sure she knew, had its own particular power – but it was difficult to deny that she really was the victim in this situation. For a while I tried to come up with a theory about her, or about our relationship, that would make it okay for me to sleep with Jack. Most of these had to do with her earlier behaviour towards me: I remembered her kissing me that summer, first in Jack's hallway and again in Alex's garden, and how both times she'd laughed and flitted away, leaving me behind. I remembered her lying very still beside me and saying: I don't know, I just want to think about it for a while. For some reason these things figured more prominently in my mind than the fact that she'd slept with my ex-boyfriend and repeatedly lied to my face about it. But really I knew the situation was different now, and anyway there was something petty and demeaning about that level of score-keeping. It seemed beneath all of us.

The following Monday, I told Jack that I'd seen them at the markets. I was expecting him to look pained, but he only raised his eyebrows.

'You should have said hello,' he said.

'Would you really want that?'

'Well, it's not about what I want. You know, you shouldn't feel as though you can't talk to Mari, or . . . Oh, I don't know. I'm probably being naïve here but I don't like to think of the two of you being on bad terms. I do wish things were different.'

'You're talking like you had no hand in making things the way they are now.'

He gave me a funny look. It was true that I was being a little aggressive. 'I told you about the way things shook out between me and Mari,' he said. 'It was out of my hands, I just had to go along with it. Not the best situation in the world.'

'Well, that's one way of looking at it.'

'What's the other way?'

I looked past him, out the window, where the tree branches were sharp and black against the pale sky. 'Well,' I said. 'You were in your mid-forties, you'd kind of been drifting in and out of these short-lived encounters, and then the universe just gifted you a beautiful twenty-six-year-old girlfriend and a child you adored. Most men would be pretty pleased about that. And I don't know what your contraception arrangements were, but obviously they weren't very comprehensive. I mean, surely you knew you were tempting fate there.'

He rubbed the back of his neck, colour rising in his cheeks. 'Well, look, I don't want to get into the technical details, but –'

'Jack, you can't make excuses now. What's that saying? The proof is in the pudding.'

'All right, all right. Sorry, I didn't realise I was going to be prosecuted over this.'

'You're the one who brought it up.'

There was an unfriendly little silence. 'Okay,' he said. 'I'm sorry. Let's not talk about this, it doesn't matter anyway. What's done is done.'

'Yeah. That's the point, actually.'

He shook his head. 'If you're going to make this unpleasant, I may as well leave. I've got a lot of work to catch up on anyway.'

'Oh, I'm sorry, I forgot it was my job to make things pleasant for you.'

I knew he wasn't really going to leave, and he didn't. Instead he sighed and kissed my forehead, my eyelids, my mouth. 'I'm sorry,' he said. 'I'm sorry, I'm sorry, I'm sorry. I shouldn't take my frustration out on you, it's not fair.'

'It's okay.' It felt good to forgive him, and to know I had the power to forgive him, to show him mercy. 'I'm sorry too. Forget it.'

'You just –' He shook his head. 'You don't know how much I look forward to coming here. Most of the time I feel like shit, frankly. I know I'm treating Mari badly and I hate myself for it, I really do, and on top of that I've got Tess to think about. Her childhood. And then there's you, it's not fair on you either, and . . . Jesus Christ.' He stopped, short of breath. 'Sorry.'

'It's okay.'

'No, I shouldn't put all that on you. My fault.' He rolled his head into the hollow of my shoulder and pressed his face against my neck, breathing deeply. I stroked his hair. After a minute he said, 'You smell so good to me.'

'Do I?'

'Yeah. Can't describe it. But you always have.'

I wondered vaguely if Mari could smell me on him when he came home, but it didn't seem like the right question to ask. We moved slowly into having sex again. Was this how he did it with her? I let myself imagine that it was her neck he kissed, her ear he breathed into. I asked him to tell me how good it felt, the way he used to in the beginning, and he did. Of course he did. He told me everything I wanted to hear.

•

ON A FRIDAY afternoon in June, Mari went to the boutique where Elisabeth worked. On the bus, she refused to let herself think about any specificities of the situation beyond the immediate: I'm putting my headphones in, I'm looking out the window, I'm pressing the stop button and getting off the bus. When she went into the shop,

Elisabeth was behind the counter filling out a form, and without looking up she said, 'Hi there. Let me know if you need anything.'

Being in Elisabeth's presence without her realising it made Mari feel vaguely powerful, but without any real sense of what she might do with that power. It was the same feeling she'd had when she spotted Elisabeth watching them at the farmers' market, thinking Mari couldn't see her. Eventually she said, 'Hi.'

Elisabeth glanced up. For a second she looked shocked – and, Mari noted with interest, a little afraid – but she ironed her face out and said, 'Oh, hi. What are you doing here? Did you want to buy something?'

'Actually, I was wondering if you wanted to have lunch with me.' Mari straightened her back. 'I'm paying.'

Elisabeth clicked her pen. It was warm in the shop, and a square of bright sunlight fell on the floor between them. 'Okay,' she said. 'Give me ten minutes.'

Mari waited while Elisabeth finished filling out the form, tidied a display of scarves, and conferred with her boss about a delivery arriving the next day. 'Are you sure you don't want anything?' she asked, coming out from behind the counter with a cotton tote bag over her shoulder. 'I've got a twenty per cent staff discount.'

In fact, Mari could see a few things she wouldn't have minded trying on, but she wasn't prepared to give Elisabeth that particular satisfaction. 'No, thanks,' she said lightly. 'Let's go.'

They went to a café around the corner. Mari had assumed Elisabeth would order the most expensive dish on the menu as a pointed gesture, but instead she waited for Mari to order a chicken salad and then said she'd have the same thing. It was useless, Mari realised, to try to pre-empt what Elisabeth would do.

As the waiter began to walk away, Mari called him back and asked for a glass of white wine.

She asked Elisabeth a perfunctory question about her job and studied her as she answered. Elisabeth's new cropped haircut emphasised the delicate bones of her face and made her eyes and mouth look larger. She was wearing a long, shapeless blue dress. Blue tended to wash Mari out, but it was Elisabeth's best colour: it brought out her eyes and the pink undertones of her skin. Mari assumed she knew this, because when she'd come to dinner she'd been wearing a little blue sweater.

On the street outside, a green sedan with learner plates began to jerk its way into a reverse parallel park. Through the windscreen, Mari could see a red-faced teenager and her mother. The mother's mouth was moving rapidly, and the teenager was shaking her head, her lip trembling. 'Remember when you taught me to drive?' she asked.

'How could I forget,' Elisabeth said. 'That was one of the top ten most stressful experiences of my life. No, wait, I forgot the time you tried to turn the wrong way down Vulture Street. Top five.'

'What about the time I drove halfway to the reservoir with the handbrake on?'

'That's right. Top three. But you passed your test on the first go, so it all worked out.'

'I still don't drive much,' Mari said. 'You know, when we get in the car, Jack automatically gets in the driver's seat, and I automatically get in the passenger seat. Sometimes I think we should do it differently, for Tessa's sake. Or for the sake of, I don't know, feminism. But then I think, what a stupid fucking thing to worry about. Why not worry about global sex trafficking, or Black deaths in custody? Climate change?'

'Well, I don't know if lack of worry is really the problem in any of those cases.'

The waiter brought Mari's wine, and she swallowed a mouthful gratefully. 'You're right,' she said. 'Even feeling conflicted about this stuff is so middle-class, isn't it.'

'It's not a crime to be middle-class,' Elisabeth said. 'Jack told me that once, actually. And I'm sure Tessa doesn't care one way or another about your driving arrangements.'

'I know. I just wonder sometimes if she'll grow up thinking I'm kind of useless. I mean, I've never travelled, I don't really have a career . . . The only big thing that's ever happened in my life was having a baby, and even that was an accident.' Mari hadn't planned to say any of this, but the words came out anyway. All at once she remembered Jack saying: It's like a compulsion with you. Another mouthful of wine slipped down her throat.

Elisabeth tilted her head to one side. 'I didn't think you worried about things like that,' she said.

'Things like what?'

'You know, like the future, how your life was going to turn out. You were always so blasé about it. I used to envy you that.'

Mari laughed shortly. The idea that Elisabeth had ever envied her anything struck her as amusingly misguided. 'Well, we're past that point now, don't you think?' she said. 'I'm not worried about how my life's going to turn out, I'm worried about how it has turned out.'

'Well, I wouldn't say it's necessarily turned out just yet. You're still young.'

It was the same thing Jack had said. As if it were that easy. In truth, after Elisabeth had left, Mari's life had assumed exactly the kind of formlessness she'd always imagined, as though without their familiar dynamic she hardly knew how to exist. But obviously Elisabeth hadn't felt the same way: she'd gone to Mexico and never looked back, she'd reshaped her life without Mari in it. *We all end up in the bed we've made, the bed we want to lie in.* 'Well,' Mari said. 'We'll see, I guess.'

'Yeah.' Elisabeth pressed her lips together briefly. 'But anyway, what you were saying before, about Tessa – there's no way she'll think you're useless.'

'How do you know?'

'Well, obviously you're a cool mum. You're young and hot, you used to take drugs, you know about music . . . All her friends will be so jealous.'

Mari laughed. It was nice to hear Elisabeth say those things, even though she was clearly just trying to make Mari feel better. 'I don't know about music anymore,' she said. 'Everything on the radio sounds the same to me. I used to make fun of Jack for being middle-aged – you remember – but now I feel so middle-aged myself. I always pass young people on the street and think, oh, do I know them? And then I realise they're like ten years younger than me. It's pretty pathetic.'

'No, I do that too. It's weird now everyone's moved away, I keep expecting to run into them.'

There was a little silence. Elisabeth reached for the carafe of water on the table, filling first Mari's glass and then her own. Mari had been well into her twenties before she'd learned it was polite to do it that way – she thought, in fact, that Elisabeth had probably been the one to teach her. Before then, she'd always filled her own glass and left the others empty.

Elisabeth cleared her throat. 'Anyway,' she said, 'I wanted to ask – what are you going to tell Tessa? About me, I mean.'

This hadn't occurred to Mari. 'I don't know. Do I need to tell her anything?'

'Oh, not necessarily. I just thought we should probably get our story straight, the three of us.'

Without thinking, Mari gave a short, humourless laugh. 'Sorry,' she said, as Elisabeth looked up in surprise. 'But it hasn't been the three of us for years, has it?'

'Oh,' Elisabeth said carefully. 'No, I guess not.'

'I think all that ended when you went away, actually. And the last time I saw you, if I remember right, you were saying I couldn't have a kid, I couldn't even keep my room clean. Do you think we should tell Tess about that?'

'Okay. Okay.'

They lapsed back into silence, and Mari stared at the curved shining edge of her wineglass. She had the sense that a mature, rational person would say one thing, and a petty person would say another thing, and there might be a third course of action open to someone who was tired of being manipulated, and a fourth to someone who wanted to love Elisabeth and be loved by her, the way she used to. Finally she said, 'Forget it.'

'No,' said Elisabeth. 'Actually, you're right to be upset. I behaved badly there, I'm sorry.'

Mari kept staring at the wineglass. Elisabeth had hardly ever apologised to her before, for anything.

'I was worried about you, obviously, but it was your decision. I shouldn't have been so pushy. Really I was angry with Jack, for doing that to you.'

'He didn't *do* it to me. Well, he did, but . . .'

'But what?'

Mari looked at the table. She could feel her face getting warm. 'Well, I never made him use a condom,' she said quietly. 'Actually, I told him not to. It was stupid, I knew it was stupid even at the time, but I didn't . . . Anyway, one time we just got carried away.'

Elisabeth was looking at her from across the table; Mari could sense it, even as she kept her eyes steadfastly on the corner of her napkin. 'You mean he didn't pull out,' she said. 'Even though you'd asked him to.'

'Yeah. I mean, no. That's right.'

'But that must have been really upsetting.'

Tears pricked Mari's eyes. She was remembering, against her will, what it had been like to sit on the toilet in Jack's bathroom and shake so badly that she couldn't even tear a square of toilet paper off the roll. And then, weeks later, sitting on the toilet in her own bathroom and watching the second line form in the window of the pregnancy test. She'd been shaking and crying then, too, but deep down she hadn't been surprised. A part of her had always known that things like this happened to people like her, that her body would betray her in some sordid and humiliating way. But to Elisabeth, she just said, 'Yeah, it was.'

'I wish you'd told me.'

'I should have. Only it was so embarrassing – you know, it's literally what every single sex-ed class tells you not to do. And you think, of course not, who'd be dumb enough to do that?' Mari gave a shaky laugh. 'The whole thing just seemed so sordid. Not the kind of situation you'd ever get yourself into.'

'Oh, I don't know about that.'

Before Mari could ask what she meant, their food came. The whole business of thanking the waiter and organising cutlery seemed to indicate a change of subject, and while they ate they talked disparagingly about the NGO that Heidi worked for in Melbourne. 'It's kind of awkward,' Mari said. 'Whenever I see her, I have to pretend not to think it's a morally bankrupt organisation. Jack doesn't bother pretending, I think he even asked her last time what it was like to compromise your values for the sake of a job. But you know, he did it in such a charming way that I think she almost felt complimented.'

'Jack's never compromised any of his values for the sake of a job, of course.'

'Oh no, of course not.'

'You know, the first time we went for a drink together, he said something about how he wished he'd been a factory worker or packed boxes in an Amazon warehouse. Can you believe that? I said your average Amazon worker would kill to be a tenured academic and he was like, yeah, yeah, I know.'

She did an impression of Jack's hangdog face, and Mari laughed. Laughing this way felt slightly disloyal, but attempting to trace the validity of this feeling was so complicated that she abandoned it. 'I think he prefers it that way, though,' Mari said. 'He sold out early, he knows it, everyone knows it, and he can talk about how bad it makes him feel while he collects a big salary and spends his life writing about Gramsci. Not a bad deal.'

'Oh, Gramsci, there's a name I haven't heard in a while. He would've been happier with Gramsci than with either of us, don't you think? His first love.'

Mari laughed. 'Poor Jack. We really used to bully him, you know.'

'Did we?'

'Oh yeah. Remember when we made him drive us to Surfers Paradise and take us to that flashy restaurant, the one with the ice sculptures? And we kept ordering expensive drinks and threatening to go to the casino? It was the absolute pinnacle of everything he hates. I think he was in physical pain.'

Elisabeth gave a funny little smile. 'He did pretty well in the end,' she said. 'Don't feel too sorry for him, ice sculptures or no ice sculptures.'

The waiter came with the bill then, and Mari felt a pulse of disappointment, although there was a certain satisfaction in sliding her credit card into the soft leather booklet. Elisabeth looked absently out the window while Mari signed the slip. When they walked out onto the street, she said, 'Thanks for lunch.'

'That's okay.' Mari felt a little high, fizzing with energy and possibility. It had been years, she realised, since she'd had lunch with a friend and enjoyed it. 'What are you doing now? Do you want to come with me to pick up Tess?'

'Oh, I would, but I'm working till six.' Elisabeth glanced at Mari with a little smile, her hands in her coat pockets. 'Was that a date? I won't tell Jack. Or will he find out when he looks at your credit card statement?'

Mari laughed. 'Jack's never looked at a credit card statement in his life. He just pays it when it comes due.'

'As he should.' Elisabeth's skin in the sharp winter sunlight looked very fair, and her cheeks were pink. Mari thought about saying: All those years without you felt like being held underwater, but instead she said, 'Let's do it again. He doesn't have to know.'

'All right.' Elisabeth moved towards Mari and hugged her, resting her head on Mari's shoulder in a gesture that seemed

302 | Joanna Horton

to convey weariness and a certain element of surrender. Mari heard her draw in her breath slightly, as if she were about to say something, but instead she stepped back with a half-sad smile and said, 'See you soon.'

20

MARI AND I did go out for lunch again; we went several times. If I didn't have to work I would go with her afterwards to pick Tessa up from school, or we'd walk along the river and have long, enjoyable conversations. Once I actually cancelled on Jack so that I could see Mari. I had no idea how to feel about this, and I suspected he didn't either. On the phone, there was a brief pause and then he said, 'Right, okay. Have fun.'

'Are you jealous?'

'Mmm, I don't know. Should I be?'

'Well, let's both agree not to be. Should I tell her you said hello?'

'No, please don't.' He was laughing. I was too, although really it wasn't very funny.

Around this time I started to help Mari and Jack with Tessa, picking her up from school if they both needed to work late. I don't remember how this arrangement started, but soon it became regular, and Tessa would run over to me with a smile when she saw me at the school gate. Sometimes I took her to the park, or we'd go back to the house and play together. If she was tired, we'd watch YouTube videos or children's TV shows. She was surprisingly good company.

Once I took her to the art gallery to see a visiting Van Gogh exhibition, and we wandered around looking at the paintings. 'Why did he put blue and green on his face?' she asked, staring at one of Van Gogh's self-portraits.

'Well, our skin might seem like it's pink, but if you look closely, we have bits of blue and green in the pinkness too.'

'Not me,' Tessa said confidently. 'I'm just pink.' She squinted up at me. 'You are, too.'

We left the gallery and walked to the bus station, Tessa swinging my hand and chattering about her upcoming birthday party. It was late afternoon, cold and brilliantly sunny, and the people we passed on the street smiled at us. When we got on the bus it was crowded, and I sat with Tessa on my lap. She lolled against me, her ponytail spilling down my chest.

I usually stayed for dinner with Mari and Jack after they got home. It was too cold to sit on the deck, so we ate at the smaller table in the dining area, after Tessa had gone to bed. We had warm, rich meals: pork and white bean stew, pasta with meatballs, a crisp green salad alongside. There was always a bottle of good wine on the table, and one of them would refill my glass if it ever got below halfway empty. But Jack and I never touched during these dinners; we never even made much eye contact. He was actually pretty affectionate with Mari, and I didn't mind that. I thought they were more attached to each other than they realised. Sometimes they made obscure inside jokes and smiled at each other significantly, and part of me enjoyed seeing that, knowing they thought I didn't notice.

Mostly our conversations were easy and happy, but occasionally I'd glance at Jack doing something ordinary – chopping onions, or clearing Tessa's toys off the couch – and in his face I'd see the shadow of our afternoons in my flat, when he was a different person and did different things. Then I'd have to go to the bathroom and do deep breathing exercises. It helped to focus my attention on one thing in the room – the bright yellow bottle of children's shampoo, or the faux-pharmaceutical label on one of Mari's skincare products – and try to commit it to memory. When I came out, they'd be carrying on the conversation. Sometimes Mari would have her feet propped in Jack's lap, and he'd be holding one of them absent-mindedly while he talked or listened.

In a way, I appreciated these sudden episodes of guilt as reminders of what was actually happening. Most of the time, it was disconcertingly easy to forget that Jack and I were having an affair. (Even the word 'affair' sounded silly and overdramatic in my head, as though it couldn't possibly have anything to do with our lives.) Between the three of us, our old dynamic darted in and out of the conversation like a fish among reeds, showing itself and then disappearing again. Jack cooked for us, and he seemed very concerned that we enjoyed the food. We teased him a lot, the way we always had, and he pretended to be victimised by it, the way he always had. Once, after dinner, Mari and I spent a long time telling him that if he really believed in feminism, he'd clean up the kitchen despite having already cooked the meal. It began as a joke, but he did eventually clean up the kitchen, even though he said he couldn't believe he was doing it.

'Oh, you can absolutely believe it,' Mari said. 'You've always loved doing whatever Elisabeth tells you to do.'

When she said this I had the panicked, freefall feeling of missing a step on a staircase. I glanced at her quickly, but she just looked a little drunk and was smoking a cigarette contentedly. (She and Jack had both started smoking after dinner, although they spent a lot of time telling each other how bad it was and that they'd have to stop soon.)

Lightly, Jack said, 'You know I live to serve the women in my life.' He touched her shoulder as he went past, and she reached up and squeezed his fingers.

I poured myself some more wine, hoping Mari didn't notice my trembling hand. It seemed insane, and slightly sinister, that Jack could affect such calm. He was loading the dishwasher, humming to himself. The light in the dining area seemed very bright. From far away, Mari was saying, 'Elisabeth?'

I forced myself to look at her. 'Yeah?'

'Do you want to stay here tonight? I don't think Jack can drive you home, he's had too much to drink. We could put you on the couch in the study if you like.'

'Oh.' I played with a fork on the table, pushing the tines down so that the handle lifted up, and then letting it fall back. 'No, that's okay. I'll walk.'

'I'm actually fine to drive,' Jack said.

'You actually are not,' Mari said.

'I am. Look, I've just cleaned up this whole kitchen, that's a mark of sobriety, surely.' He took the cigarette out of her hand and inhaled briefly, then put it out in the sink. 'You've got to stop this.'

She smiled up at him. 'I'll stop when you do.' They were flirting with each other, I could see that.

'I have stopped,' Jack said. 'That cigarette I had earlier was actually my last. Okay, Elisabeth, are you ready?'

In the car, I concentrated on breathing normally and keeping my fists unclenched. The streets were dark and empty, and the radio was playing softly: *The Book Show*. When Jack stopped the car outside my building, I didn't move.

'You okay?' he asked.

I kept staring straight ahead. 'How can you do it to her?'

He was quiet for a long time, a minute at least. 'Yeah,' he said eventually. 'I know.'

'I hate it.'

'I do too.' He hesitated. 'But I think you should know, she's really changed since you came back. She's cheerful, she takes an interest in things, she makes jokes . . . And, okay, you might not want to hear this, but things between the two of us are actually much better.'

I didn't reply.

'Sorry,' he said. 'I shouldn't have said that. I'm sorry.'

'No, it's good,' I said tonelessly. 'I'm glad you're fucking your wife again.' I referred to Mari as his wife sometimes, and it always made him flinch. The funny thing was that I actually was glad – I wanted them to be happy. I wanted them both to be happy.

Jack sighed. 'It's not just that. You know, things weren't very good for Mari, after Tess was born. I don't think I was particularly helpful either, but . . . Anyway, you've made her much happier. Me too, although I know that's not the point.'

I nodded. If anything, that made it worse, but I was too tired to explain that to him.

We sat in silence for a while. On the radio, they were talking about a novel I hadn't heard of and wasn't interested in. Finally Jack said woodenly, 'Should we stop seeing each other? Obviously I don't want to, but I'd understand if you did.'

Miserably, I shook my head. We kissed then, but without much conviction. He put his forehead against mine, hard and warm, and I breathed in the cigarette smoke on his skin. After a while I told him he should go, and he agreed. I wished I were like Mari, who cried easily, but instead I just got out of the car and watched him check his mirrors, indicate and drive away. He had always been such a careful driver.

•

THINGS WENT ON like this through the winter. Mari was going through a busy period at work, so I looked after Tessa at least once a week, and sometimes I picked up groceries or ran other small errands. Mari called me her wife, in a joking way. She made a lot of jokes, and I could see that Jack was right about her – she carried herself with more confidence, she had colour in her cheeks. She was happy.

Usually she came home before Jack, and we'd sit at the table together and drink tea. On those afternoons, she talked to me with surprising openness about things she'd never mentioned before. She told me about the six months she and her mother had spent sleeping on friends' couches when she was seven. ('We were homeless,' she said, her face oddly blank. 'I only realised that a couple of years ago.') She told me about watching our friends move away, one by one, while she stayed put. One afternoon she said, 'You know, I had a hard time when Tess was born.'

'Was the birth really bad?'

She gave an ironic little laugh. 'That too. I mean, it was fine by their standards, apparently, but not by mine. No, emotionally, I meant. I struggled. Maybe you could tell from my emails at the time.'

This was the first time she'd mentioned the emails. 'Yeah,' I said carefully. 'I mean, it seemed like something was up, but it was hard to tell just from an email. And I didn't know anyone else who'd had a baby, I didn't know what was normal . . .' It was embarrassing how pathetic these excuses sounded when I said them out loud.

She glanced over to the couch, where Tessa was watching something on her iPad. 'I couldn't love her, to tell you the truth,' she said quietly. 'I wanted to, but I couldn't. I'd look at her and think, I've thrown my life away, and for what? For you? I don't love you, I don't even like you! And she was always there, always crying, clinging, wanting something; it never seemed to end. When I got away from her even for half an hour, just to go to the supermarket or something like that, it was the most amazing feeling. Like I'd been swimming with a weight strapped to me and suddenly the weight was cut off and I was floating free.'

I took a long time to drink a mouthful of tea. It was good tea: loose-leaf Earl Grey, brewed in a heavy glass teapot. Finally I said, 'But you seem to love her so much now.'

'Yeah. Did I tell you, I'm actually planning to get a necklace with her name on it.'

I laughed. People who wore jewellery engraved with their children's names had been an object of our shared derision, although I'd forgotten this until she mentioned it. 'A nice rose gold?'

'Mmm, I was thinking something with diamonds. Anyway, the whole thing got a lot easier around her first birthday. She weaned herself, actually, and I finally told Jack that we had to put her in child care two days a week or I was going to lose my mind. And then it was like . . . I don't know, it was like the fog started clearing in my brain. I started to feel like she was a real person, and I was really her mother, not just playing the part. One day I went to pick her up from child care, and when I came into the room she looked up and smiled, and I just felt my heart fill up with love, I couldn't believe it.' She laughed. 'Cue the swelling violins.'

'Did Jack know about all this?'

She grimaced. It was the same grimace Jack made when an uncomfortable topic came up, but I don't think Mari was aping him consciously. She'd rubbed off on him, too: occasionally I glimpsed one of her expressions on his face, like a mask that slipped on and then off again. 'Not officially,' she said. 'We never talked about it – I don't think he really wanted to know. But I was so lonely, and I blamed the baby, which was pretty fucked up, but I couldn't help it . . . I used to listen to her cry and think, why can't you be quiet? What do you want from me? And then I'd hate myself even more for having those thoughts. I was so jealous of you, travelling by yourself on the other side of the world.'

'That was lonely too. I was really lonely for a long time.'

'Well, at least that's a normal reaction. It's normal to be lonely if you're by yourself in a foreign country. But if you have a partner, a baby, you're supposed to be happy.'

'But you're happy now.' I left the statement a little bit open, trailing the string to see if she would pick it up.

She looked into her mug of tea. The parting in her hair was a thin white line. 'In a way,' she said. 'Things with Tess came good in the end. Things with Jack – oh well, I don't know. If we weren't ever happy, that would be one thing, but sometimes we are happy . . . Lately we've been really happy. Which is weird, actually. It kind of feels like cheating.'

'Cheating? In what sense?'

She shook her head. 'Hard to explain. I guess I always assumed – and this started long before Tess, before Jack, even before I met you – that there was something wrong with me. Something that meant I'd never be happy or normal, the way other people were. Sort of like a condition. I know that doesn't make very much sense.'

'Oh.' I sipped my tea, breathing in its deep fruity scent. 'Well, obviously you don't have a condition.' It seemed important that I tell her how much she deserved happiness, how much she deserved love and indeed how much I loved her, but I couldn't make myself say the words. Instead I said, 'I'm glad things are good now. Between you and Jack.'

'Oh yeah. Well.'

'What?'

'No, things are good. It's just –' She darted a glance at Tessa, who was still engrossed in the iPad. 'I don't know. It's stupid.'

'What is?'

'Well, what's the time now? Six thirty?' She shook her sleeve back and looked at her watch, its narrow black strap around her thin wrist. 'Quarter to seven. Jack used to get home by five thirty, six, but he's always late these days. Then when he is here . . . Oh, I don't know. It's nothing concrete, but I just feel like he's got something on his mind. You know, I always thought one day he might sleep with one of his students.'

I swallowed a mouthful of tea too fast and coughed. 'That's his worst nightmare,' I said. 'When we were together, he always dreaded people thinking I was his student. It was kind of an obsession of his.'

'Well, exactly. I'm not saying he wouldn't feel bad about it – he'd feel terrible, actually – but that wouldn't stop him. So maybe that's it, or maybe it's a colleague, or just some woman he met. Doesn't really matter, does it?'

There was a little silence, during which I found I couldn't meet her eye, or breathe very steadily. 'I'm sure he's not,' I said lamely.

'Yeah. Like I said, there's nothing concrete. Just, he keeps calling me sweetheart – you know, hi sweetheart, bye sweetheart,

sweetheart did you remember the olive oil, or whatever. He only calls me that when he's feeling guilty about something.'

'Well,' I said. There was a horrible taste in my mouth. 'It seems pretty unlikely. But I don't know.'

'No, you're right, I'm being paranoid. Tessa –' she called into the living room, 'I'm going to run a bath and you're going to get in it, all right?'

'No,' Tessa called back, without moving her eyes from the screen.

Mari rolled her eyes at me. 'It's Jack's fault, you know, he never disciplines her. Anyway, what do you feel like for dinner? I'll have to cook it myself if he doesn't turn up soon.'

I drained the last lukewarm mouthful of tea. 'Sorry, I forgot to say. My sister's in town, I'm supposed to be having dinner with her.' This didn't happen to be true, but it seemed crucial that I leave before Jack arrived.

We said goodbye, and as I went down the hallway I could hear Mari's firm voice, followed by Tessa's whining cry. I opened the front door, clicked it shut behind me and took a deep breath in. I couldn't think directly about what had happened so I just stood there breathing for a while. It was a very cold night and the brackish smell of the river was clear and sharp in the air.

•

WHEN JACK CAME to my flat the following week, I told him what Mari had said. He grimaced. 'I wondered if she'd suspect something. You know, say what you like about Mari, but she's sharp.'

I didn't like the sound of that – *say what you like about Mari*, as if he expected me to insult her in front of him. 'Well,' I said. 'Maybe you should start spending more time at home.'

'I should. I would, but you see, I've got to catch up on work in the evenings because so many of my afternoons are taken up with this beautiful woman.' We were in bed, the blankets pulled up to our chins.

'You never told me you were seeing a beautiful woman. You really must be busy.'

He frowned at me. 'Not like you to make self-deprecating jokes.'

I looked away. Truthfully, I didn't like it when he complimented my looks: it made me feel petted and indulged, like a child, or like his much younger mistress. (The fact that technically I was his much younger mistress was something I tried to avoid thinking about.) Really I wanted him to be awed by my great intellect. But where was that these days? I was thirty-two years old and I worked in a shop.

'Elisabeth?'

'Sorry,' I said. 'No more self-deprecating jokes. I'll try to have more confidence, if that's what you find attractive.'

He shook his head, smiling, and kissed my forehead. His chin was rough. 'You're right about the other thing, though,' he said. 'I'll start taking some work home in the evenings so Mari can keep an eye on me. That might calm things down for a while.'

I didn't really like that either – *calm things down for a while*, as if Mari were a fractious toddler. But all I said was, 'Mmm.'

He had his arm around me, and he stroked my shoulder gently with his thumb. 'Hey,' he said. 'This is a weird question, but are you okay for money?'

'What?'

'Sorry, it's probably none of my business. But it's always really cold in here, and I wondered if you were avoiding getting a heater because of the power bills. And you never seem to have much food around, and I know retail work doesn't pay that well . . . Anyway, I could help out a bit if you like. That's all.'

'Oh.'

'Actually, you've been helping so much with Tess, it's only fair. I mean, we wouldn't expect anyone else to look after our child for free.'

It was the first time I'd heard him say that: *our child*. 'Right,' I said coldly. 'I take it you discussed this with your wife, then. Did you both agree to compensate me adequately for my time?'

'No, no, I didn't even mention it to Mari. Look, I'm just trying to do the right thing by you, but maybe it's not appropriate. I'm sorry.'

'I don't want to be paid off.' I wasn't quite sure what I meant by this, but it felt true to say it.

'No, fair enough. I'm sorry I offered, really.'

I didn't reply.

'I know things are a bit hard at the moment,' he said. 'With Mari and everything. It'll get better soon, I promise.'

'Are you going to leave her?'

'Is that what you want?'

'I don't know.' It was oddly painful for me to imagine Jack and Mari splitting up. In a strange way, I enjoyed the space I occupied in their domestic life: a confidant to them both, but just enough of an outsider that I still felt the thrill of desire, a gap I could never quite cross. Mundane things in their house – the magnets on the fridge, or the jumble of shoes in the hallway – fascinated me for reasons I couldn't explain, like seeing pictures of a celebrity buying groceries. And I liked what Jack had said about me making them happy – I liked the idea of myself as a saint, conferring the blessing of happiness upon them. I knew, of course, that this was laughable and poisonously dishonest.

He was quiet, stroking the back of my neck. Finally he said, 'I fucked things up between you and Mari once, didn't I? It hardly seems fair to do it again.'

'Well, if you really felt that way, you wouldn't be here.'

'No, you're right.' He sighed. 'I'm making excuses for myself, I'm terrible like that. It's got to the point where I don't know whether anything I think is real or if I'm just trying to excuse my latest bit of inexcusable behaviour.'

I lifted my head to look at him, and he held my gaze. He was right, of course: he'd behaved badly. Even acknowledging his own bad behaviour was really a way of deflecting from the more serious problem of his chronic passivity and indecisiveness, his wish to have it both ways forever. But I couldn't hate him for any of it. I kissed him, opening his mouth with mine, and when he moved into me he had such a sad look on his face. I felt tears beginning in my eyes. They spilled onto my cheeks and he kissed them gently, gently. 'It's okay,' he said, and for some reason I thought this was the tone he must use to console Tessa when she was upset, and that made me cry harder. 'It's okay, it's okay.' He moved his hips in a circular motion and I came in a shuddering rush. After it was over he held me in his arms. 'I love you,' he said quietly, into my hair.

I didn't reply. Actually I thought I was incapable of saying anything. I was thinking about Mari, the way she'd appeared to me when we'd taken acid all those years ago: tall and willowy, a 1920s flapper in her black and white dress. Dancing on the lawn, cherry juice dripping purple down her chin. Saying: Do you want one? They're good. I wanted to bite the cherry out of her mouth. I wanted to go to her when she called for me. I wanted to hold her head under the water. I was so tired of her, and so tired of myself. Jack held me gently and didn't ask any questions.

21

IN AUGUST, MARI turned thirty-three. They had a party for
her, a drinks thing on a Sunday, beginning in the late afternoon.
When I arrived the light had almost faded from the sky, and the
air was cold and clear. The other people who came were their
friends, mostly academics around Jack's age. They wore dark wool
coats and brought bottles of expensive wine for Mari, bouquets
of native flowers wrapped in brown paper. I didn't know any of
them, and I didn't introduce myself.

Jack seemed very happy to see them. When I arrived he smiled,
kissed my cheek, said, 'Thanks for coming,' and then he went off
to talk to someone else. Paul happened to be there, on a work
trip from Sydney, and we sat together in a corner and made catty
comments about everyone else at the party. Mari came to sit
with us once or twice, but we couldn't really be catty in front of
her, and other people kept calling her away. Neither she nor Jack
seemed to notice Tessa's bedtime approaching, so I took her into
her room and lay down with her. Paul had left by then. Tessa and
I read books together, and I made up a long story for her about
a pony called Magenta, towards the end of which she fell asleep.

I turned off the lamp and lay in the soft glow of the night-light, listening to Tessa's breathing going gently in and out. When I was out in public with her and she was being difficult, mothers with small children would shoot me sympathetic glances, thinking I was one of them. And in a strange way, I felt as though I was: as though Tessa was somehow my daughter too, a child the three of us had had together. After all, if it weren't for me, she never would have been born. I heard footsteps outside, and then Mari put her head around the door and gave me a little smile.

She came in and sat cross-legged on the floor, leaning against the bed, and I moved down to sit beside her. 'Doesn't she look angelic when she's asleep,' she said softly. 'Thanks for looking after her.'

'It's okay. I like hanging out with her.'

'Oh, the feeling is definitely mutual. She talks about you all the time, you know. Elisabeth said this, Elisabeth and I did that. Her face always falls when she sees it's me picking her up from school and not you.'

It was nice to hear that. 'Sorry for being so antisocial,' I said. 'Your friends probably think I'm rude.'

'No, it's fine. They're really Jack's friends, not mine.' We could hear the faint sound of Jack's voice, saying something in a declarative tone. He was getting deliberately drunk, something I'd never seen him do before.

'By the way,' I said. 'I didn't wish you happy birthday. Thirty-three, hey?'

'So I'm supposed to believe.' She smiled, her teeth flashing white in the semi-dark. 'Remember how much I used to tease Jack about his age when we first met him? I feel a bit bad about it now.'

Tessa turned, kicking the blanket off in her sleep, and Mari got up to tuck her in. Sitting down again, she drew her knees into her chest and rested her head on her kneecaps. She looked a bit like a child herself in the dim half-light. I remembered finding her asleep on Jack's couch in the early morning, and how for a brief dizzying second I'd thought I was seeing her real self, the person she kept secret from me. 'Mari?' I said.

'Yeah?'

'A little while ago – after we first had dinner together – Jack came over to see me.'

'Oh, I thought he might. We both had to talk to you separately, didn't we? Like you were a therapist. Or a priest.'

'We, um.' I glanced quickly at Tessa, who was snoring softly with her mouth open. 'We slept together, actually. We didn't plan to but that's how it ended up.'

Mari's head stayed still on her knees. She took a long time to say, 'Okay. I see.'

'Yeah.' My heart was pounding miserably. 'So, anyway. I wanted to tell you.'

She stood up. 'Let's go somewhere else.'

I followed her down the hall to their bedroom. It was a room I had only glimpsed in passing, but as Mari switched on a lamp, I saw that my hunch about the decor had been almost entirely right. The walls weren't eggplant, but they were close enough, and the bedcovers were a stylishly crumpled grey linen. The vanity table was covered in a feminine clutter of tubes and bottles, and a pair of black tights snaked from a drawer. There wasn't much evidence of Jack, except for a couple of impenetrable-looking books about Marxism on a bedside table. I sat on that side of the bed, propped against the pillows, and Mari sat on the other.

'So,' she said. 'You were saying.'

'Yeah. Look, I don't know how much you want to hear . . . Like I said, it wasn't planned. Or not the first time, anyway.'

'Oh, not the first time.'

'Yeah. No. We just . . . He comes to my flat once or twice a week, usually in the afternoon. I'm sorry.'

'Are you?'

'I'm sorry if it hurts you, I guess. I don't want to hurt you.'

'I think you probably do,' she said mildly. 'Okay, so you and Jack slept together again. Not only that – you've been carrying on an affair, I guess you'd call it, and you lied about it, and waited until my birthday to tell me the truth. I wouldn't have chosen that to happen – it does hurt me, but maybe it's not the worst thing in the world.'

'What do you mean?'

'Well, maybe it evens things up a bit between us. Between all of us.'

I squeezed my eyes closed and opened them again. 'Fuck,' I said. 'God, Mari. Is that how things are between us? Just tit for tat, evening up the score?'

She glanced at me, surprised. 'I thought it was quite a mature way of looking at things.'

'But I don't want to know how you *look* at things. I don't want to know what you think the fairest response is on paper. I want to know how you actually feel.'

'How I actually feel.' She blew a sigh upwards, ruffling her fringe. 'Well, that's not an easy question to answer.'

'But I'm asking it. Come on, you owe me this much.'

'I thought you said it wasn't about owing.'

I gave her a look.

'Fine,' she said. 'Well, I guess I was angry with you. I am angry with you, for all sorts of reasons.'

'What are the reasons?'

'Okay.' Another sigh. 'For starters, since you really want to know, you left me alone when I was pregnant. And it was so awful, I didn't know what to do. I made an appointment, you know, and I cancelled it, and then I made another appointment and cancelled that one too. I was so sick all the time, Jack was in Italy and I couldn't get in touch with him, and you'd made it clear you didn't care what happened to me.'

'It wasn't that I didn't care. I probably cared too much, if anything.'

'Well, you had a funny way of showing it. I mean, I know it was a shock, but you made it all about you and your hurt feelings. You weren't there for me, you didn't even try to be there for me. You just left.'

I made a sound that could have been interpreted as a laugh. 'Right. So I was supposed to hang around and let myself be humiliated.'

She frowned. 'Humiliated?'

'Jesus, Mari, do I need to spell it out for you? You were having a baby. You and Jack, the two of you together. The entire thing happened behind my back, and you thought – what? That I'd be happy for you? Did you want me to come to your baby shower, congratulate you on the mammoth achievement of having fucked without a condom? I'd rather die.' I realised I was bunching the doona in my fist, and I smoothed it down and cleared my throat. 'That was how I felt at the time, anyway.'

'We didn't have a baby shower,' Mari said quietly.

'Of course. Too bourgeois.'

'No. Actually it was because nobody cared enough to throw us one. After you left I had no one, you know. I couldn't talk to Heidi or the others, they didn't understand. Jack did his best, kind of, but I knew he found the whole thing really embarrassing. And when I told my mum I was pregnant, she just said if I wanted to ruin my life, that was my business. You were the only person I wanted, and you'd gone to the other side of the world.'

I laughed. 'I was the only person you wanted. Good one.'

'It's true.'

'It's never been true. You've always seen me as a consolation prize.'

'What? How can you say that?'

'Because it's obvious, Mari. Are you having memory loss for once? Do you want me to give you a history lesson? Because as I remember it, you started sleeping with Jack and you basically cut me out of your life. I barely saw you that whole winter, do you remember that? Obviously you just wanted to get into bed with him and once you did, you had no use for me anymore.'

'That wasn't it.' Her voice cracked. 'It was terrible, keeping it from you, I couldn't bear it. Things were really falling apart for me. I don't think you realised that.'

'Yeah, okay. You were making suffering into an art form, as always. Well, maybe you shouldn't have slept with him, did you ever consider that? You could've chosen me. That option was always open to you.'

'So you can have both of us, but I have to choose? Is that how it works?'

That was unexpected. 'The circumstances were different,' I said after a few seconds. 'You know that. But anyway, why don't you keep telling me why you're so angry with me.'

She looked at me, but I kept my eyes on the framed Cézanne print hanging on the wall opposite us. Soft light on oranges. The abstract red and blue painting that used to hang in Jack's bedroom was nowhere in the house; maybe he'd thrown it away. 'Fine,' she said. 'Well, you left, and then Tess was born and I had to go through all that by myself too. And I hated myself so much, I felt like I was rotting on the inside, and I was so fucking lonely. You never responded to the emails I sent you, except that last one, and that wasn't very nice for me to read. And then you appeared back on the scene after years and years and came to dinner with that terrible footage. You knew it would be hurtful, but that was the point, wasn't it? You wanted to hurt us, you wanted to throw a grenade into our lives.'

'Well, I –'

'And even before that, you always wanted so much from me, you wanted to know everything I was thinking, you wanted to film me, you even wanted me to be part of your relationship with Jack. And when I wanted my own relationship with him, you hated me for it. Everything had to be on your terms, didn't it? Actually, everything still has to be on your terms.'

'It wasn't like that,' I said weakly. 'I didn't mean it like that.'

She shook her head. For a few minutes we sat in silence, listening to the noise of the party. Someone came down the hallway, loudly wondering where the bathroom was, but neither of us moved. Eventually Mari said, 'We seem to keep going in circles, don't we? Maybe we should get it over with and just fuck. It's the only combination that hasn't been tried.'

I glanced at her sharply, but she was looking straight ahead, chewing on her lip. She was wearing a short black skirt, black stockings and a soft pink sweater. A delicate silver bangle on her left wrist. The idea of sleeping with her was still very appealing to me, but I didn't know how I'd behave. What if I got one of my flashes of blank hatred and suddenly hit her, or stuffed her face into a pillow?

She turned to look at me. She had put on some makeup – something she never used to do – and her skin had a pearly sheen to it. Her face was very close to mine, and she was smiling, a knowing little smile. When she kissed me, her lips tasted of a mild refined sweetness, the kind you get with expensive lipstick. My mind thickened and blurred, but I could feel her against me, a soft warm thing among the pillows. Then she moved her hand between my thighs.

I was wearing woollen tights, I remember that, and I remember wriggling them down quickly, with the sense that she might change her mind if I was too slow. I had on plain black cotton underwear, not particularly sexy, and that was the kind of thing I thought about with Jack, but not with her. Nothing like that mattered with her. When she stroked her fingers against me, I felt my whole body pulse around her hand. I must have made a sound, because she said something in her sweet, low voice, something about being quiet. I buried my face in her neck and breathed in the scent of her skin. She moved her fingers rhythmically. It didn't take very long.

For a minute or so afterwards I just lay on my back and tried to get my vision steady. Gradually I became aware of the sound of my breath, and of my tights and underwear bunched around my knees. I tugged them up and straightened my dress. Then I leaned back against the pillows and said, 'Fuck.'

She laughed. She didn't seem fazed at all.

My mouth ached with how much I wanted to kiss her, but instead I said, 'You know I love you.'

'I know.'

'I was only so terrible to you because of how much I love you.'

She stroked my hair. 'I know.'

I took her hand and traced circles on her thumbnail with the pad of my thumb. There seemed nothing more to say. We heard people go clattering down the hallway, calling goodbyes. Mari stood up. 'They'll be wondering where I am.'

'They'll think you're with Tessa. Come on, stay.'

'I can't. Apart from anything else, they'll keep drinking till the early hours of the morning if I don't get out there and start pointedly clearing things away.' She smoothed down her skirt. 'You can stay here, though, if you like. You don't have to go back out.'

I nodded. She left, padding across the floor in her stockinged feet, and I switched off the lamp and lay back on the bed. The sheets smelled clean. I lay there for a while, I even drifted off to sleep briefly, and I woke with the brassy light of a streetlamp coming in through the window. My watch said 8.18. I slipped out the front door and caught the bus home.

•

AFTER THE LAST guests had left, Mari finished stacking the dishwasher and went out to the deck, where Jack sat with a glass of whiskey. His face was blurred with alcohol, and he was squinting a little. You look old, she thought, and for a moment she almost felt sorry for him.

'Hello,' he said. 'The woman of the hour. Happy birthday.'

'Thank you.'

'Did you have a good time?'

'Oh, you know.' She sat down opposite him. 'Nice to see everyone. I had an interesting talk with Elisabeth, actually.'

He shot her a cautious look.

'Yeah,' she said neutrally. 'She did tell me. I suppose I should have guessed.'

Jack closed his eyes. Mari wrapped her arms around herself, against the cold night. 'So,' she said. 'Happy birthday to me.'

'Oh, Marielle.'

Pain clawed at Mari's insides, and she caught her breath in a gasp. 'Don't start that now.'

'I'm not starting anything. Listen, sweetheart, I'm sorry. I really am.'

'Oh, well, that changes everything. You've been fucking my oldest friend for months, but as long as you're sorry about it.'

'Mari, you know that's oversimplifying things. But, yeah, okay, what can I say? When you get down to it, I fucked things up. Again. Maybe you shouldn't be surprised by this point.'

'Oh, don't be so self-pitying. Take responsibility, can't you? You're fifty-two years old and I don't think you've ever taken responsibility for anything in your life.'

Jack exhaled sharply through his nose. 'I took responsibility for Tessa, in case you've forgotten.'

'Oh, yes. Very good of you.'

'Well, it also meant taking responsibility for you. And I didn't exactly get a lot of say in the matter, but –'

'Oh, here we go. I suppose you wish you'd left me living with Heidi, working some dead-end job, raising Tess by myself. You could've just paid child support and got out of there. Hands clean, that's your motto, isn't it? Hands always so fucking clean.'

He shook his head. 'We've been through this, haven't we? I'm sick of going through this.'

'Well, if you're sick of it, let's change the subject. Did you ever fuck Elisabeth in our bed?'

'No. Of course not. Jesus Christ, what do you think of me?'

'I'm not sure if you really want to know what I think of you.'

Jack got up and leaned on the railing of the deck, looking out into the dark garden below. 'Okay,' he said. 'Fair enough. But just leave that for a minute, there's something else I want to talk to you about. Last month, Ross rang me about a vacancy at Melbourne Uni. A professorship in their history department. He said my CV fitted what they were after and he promised to put in a good word for me, so I sent in an application. I didn't mention it at the time because it seemed so unlikely, but they got in touch last week and they want to interview me for it. I've booked a flight down there for Thursday.'

Mari went hot, then cold. Her hands felt clammy. 'Oh,' she said weakly. 'Well. Congratulations.'

'Mari, listen.' He turned to her. 'I've been thinking about this. It might be good, don't you think? We could move there, you and me and Tess, and make a kind of fresh start. People down there don't know us, they don't know Elisabeth, it'd be kind of like it never happened. Maybe that's wishful thinking, but . . .' He looked at her with a hollow face. 'Listen, I know I've treated you badly, but I want to make things right. I really do.'

Mari stood up, numbly, and felt above the rafters for the pack of cigarettes she kept there. She didn't look at Jack while she lit one. 'I see,' she said.

'At least think about it. You could find another job, easy – the Victorian state government is basically a full-employment program for people with arts degrees. On my new salary we might be able to buy a house down there. We could have another baby, if you wanted. I think I'd really like that.'

She shook her head. 'Buy a house? Have another baby? What are you saying?'

'Well, I guess I'm saying, why not? Why not? You know, I always thought I was doing the right thing by you, being honest about – about how I felt. Or didn't feel. I thought it was better to tell you the truth from the start. But now I think maybe I was just trying to punish you, or maybe I was holding back, trying to protect myself. Maybe I was being cowardly, and you were brave. Certainly wouldn't be the first time.'

The cigarette was making Mari feel breathless and lightheaded. 'So – are you saying your feelings have changed?'

'I don't even know what my feelings are.' He took his glasses off and rubbed the bridge of his nose. 'Like, okay – remember earlier this year, before all this stuff with Elisabeth, when you said you wanted to sleep with other people?'

'Yeah.'

'Well, hearing that – it made me feel sick, I hated the idea so much. I know it's incredibly hypocritical to say that now, but it's true. After you left the study I just sat there for about an hour, staring into space, thinking, well, that's it, she doesn't love you anymore, and sooner or later she's going to leave. It was one of the worst feelings I've ever had in my life.'

Something clutched at Mari's heart. She looked at him, blinking fast. 'But you – it seemed like you weren't that interested anymore. Sexually, I mean. And that night in the study . . . The things you said, it sounded like you thought I was abnormal. Like I disgusted you.'

'You don't disgust me. Far from it.'

'Oh.'

'If anything it's the opposite. I just felt like I couldn't . . . I don't know.'

'What? Couldn't what?'

He sat down beside her. 'Well, I felt like I couldn't give you what you wanted. In bed, I mean, or anywhere else for that matter. And you'd just told me you wanted to sleep with other people, and part of me thought, yeah, why wouldn't she? She's young and beautiful, and you're a boring old man. It seemed ridiculous to think you could want me.'

Mari drew on her cigarette. Her hands were shaking. 'I've always wanted you,' she said quietly. 'Always.'

He kissed her shoulder. Then he took the cigarette from her hand and put it out in his empty glass. 'Bad habit,' he said. 'Mind you, I've always found it incredibly sexy, watching you smoke. Even when we first met.'

'I didn't know that.'

'Oh yeah, it caused all kinds of problems for me. You were always at it, too, it was pretty fucking distracting.'

She laughed. He kissed her then and put his hand on her thigh. His mouth had the faint sour tang of whiskey. Idly Mari thought: There was a time when I would have done anything for this. Anything at all. She pulled away.

Jack looked at her quizzically. 'What's the matter?'

She shook her head. 'I can't stop thinking about it.'

'About what, sweetheart?'

She lit another cigarette, keeping her hands steady. In a small voice, she said, 'You know what.'

Jack took his hand off her thigh. 'Okay. Yeah. Fair enough.'

Mari concentrated on letting the smoke out of her lungs slowly. 'You know, you say all these nice things to me, but you've been fucking her. And lying about it. For months. How am I supposed to feel?'

'I know.' He sighed. 'There's probably nothing I can do to make it up to you. But what I said before – I meant it. I want to make things right.'

'Okay, well, that's very noble of you. But where does she fit into this? Elisabeth?'

He gave a little grimace. 'Well, that's – I mean, it's not easy. Obviously she and I won't see each other anymore. That's kind of why I thought Melbourne was a good opportunity, coming at this time. Clean break.'

Mari glanced at him. He was looking at her intently, his face pink with alcohol and with the cold. 'Do you love her?' she asked.

'Do I what? Do I love her?'

'Well, do you?'

He looked at the tabletop. 'I don't know what you want me to say.'

'Well, ideally you'd say no, but I'm sensing that might not be a hundred per cent true.' She paused. 'All right. For old times' sake I won't make you say it.'

'Fine. Fine. Like I said, it'll be difficult. But I'm trying to do the right thing here, can you appreciate that?'

'Do you think she loves you?'

'What? I don't know, Mari, do we really need to get into this?'

'You do know, though. You can tell these things, you're not an idiot.' Mari ground her cigarette out on the table, which was Victorian ash and had been expensive. 'You always knew I was in love with you, for example. You took full advantage of that.'

'I don't think –'

'Yes, you did. You let me have that doomed little affair with you, even though you could see how much it was hurting me. You let me say: Oh, don't worry about the condom, just pull out.' Mari's heart was thudding. 'Obviously it was stupid of me, but I was twenty-six, I did all kinds of stupid things. You should've known better. Elisabeth said that, actually, when I told her I was pregnant, and she was right.'

Jack frowned. 'When you told her you were pregnant? When was that?'

'We talked about it. Before she went away. You don't know everything that's happened between us.'

'Yeah, that's a pretty huge understatement.' He sighed. 'All right. There's probably a bit of truth in what you were saying – although you were twenty-six, Mari, not sixteen. Old enough to make your own decisions, and I think we both remember it was you who took my hand and put it up your skirt, not the other way around. But I take your broader point, and I'm really trying to make things better now. If you'll give me the chance.'

'If I'll give you the chance. You've had every chance, every fucking chance.' Mari's voice was shaking. 'Well, maybe Elisabeth does love you, it wouldn't surprise me. But maybe she just wanted to find a way of destroying our life together. And why shouldn't she? Our life together isn't worth all that much.'

'So you think she has destroyed it.'

'Maybe. I don't know.'

There was a long silence. Jack got up and looked out over the garden, and Mari stared at his back in its navy wool sweater. Finally he said, 'What does that mean?'

'It means . . .' Mari looked through the French doors at the kitchen, the dining table and chairs: all of it seemed unreal, dissolving. Her heart skipped miserably. 'It means I don't know. I can't give you an answer now, I'd have to think about it.'

'Okay.' His voice sounded mechanical.

'It's just a big thing you're asking, obviously.'

Somewhere deep in the garden, a tawny frogmouth hooted softly. Jack leaned his hands on the railing. Without turning around, he said, 'Do you mean going to Melbourne? Or staying together?'

'Both, I guess.'

'Right.'

She felt too tired to say anything else. They went inside, and Jack closed the door and locked it carefully.

'Do you want me to sleep on the couch tonight?' he asked.

He said it tonelessly, his face drained of colour. Still, Mari sensed that a small part of him was relishing this ritual, the ritual of confession and punishment. 'No,' she said. 'You can sleep in the bed.'

'Are you sure?'

'Yes.'

They undressed and got into bed without speaking. Lying on her back, Mari asked, 'What's her flat like?'

'Whose flat?'

'You know who, don't play dumb.' Mari lifted her head and punched her pillow into shape. 'I was just thinking about that – all these months she's been coming here, but I've never even seen where she lives.'

'Yeah, okay. Well, I don't know – it's small, pretty basic. A bit cold.'

Mari said nothing. She was thinking of Elisabeth lying alone in a small, cold flat. The image brought a rush of sympathy, and all at once she remembered the look that sometimes crossed Elisabeth's face when Mari showed her something new she'd bought: a skirt, a book, a bottle of good wine or a loaf of good bread. It was a look of carefully concealed envy, and Mari knew it well. Having money had plastered over those particular cracks in herself, but she knew they'd gape open again if the money ever went away. It wasn't just the things it bought but the kind of life it gave you – a life where everything was comfortable, everything was easy, and the things you'd always thought of as belonging to other people could belong to you too. You were normal after all.

But it was obviously ridiculous to excuse Elisabeth's behaviour just because she didn't have much money. After all, she had two degrees; she could have found a decent job and a house, but she liked flitting back and forth between lives. It gave her more control, not less. Still, Mari remembered Elisabeth's reticence around Jack's friends, her tight face at the edge of the party. She remembered finding her in Tessa's room, lying still in the melancholy glow of the night-light. And she remembered Elisabeth pushing her tights down around her knees, her cheeks flushed and her lips swollen, looking at Mari as if she would have let her do anything at all. Mari didn't know how to interpret that look. She suspected that even Jack had never seen it, and she knew – as she listened to the echo of his slow sleep breaths beside her – that she would never tell him about it. It didn't seem like anything he needed to know.

22

AROUND MIDDAY, MARI sent me a message asking me to meet her at the park that afternoon. I was at work, and just as I saw the message a customer came in, so I shoved the phone back into my pocket and didn't reply until later. When I went to meet her she was sitting on a bench in her black wool coat, watching Tessa on the playground. The late afternoon sunlight was glinting off the slow-moving river, and the park echoed with the sounds of children's voices. Mari was holding two cups of takeaway coffee. When I sat down, she handed one to me and said, 'Thanks for coming.'

I had no idea where things stood between us. Humorously I said, 'Are you breaking up with me?'

She smiled vaguely. 'Well, after you left last night, Jack and I had a talk.'

'Oh.'

'Yeah, it's all out in the open now. So I guess that's a relief.'

I sipped my coffee; it tasted burned. 'I don't feel too relieved.'

'No, me neither, really.' She was looking straight ahead. 'Anyway, incidental to that, he's applied for a new job – a professorship, in Melbourne. He suggested we move down there, have another baby, make a go of it. Clean break, I think those were his words.'

'Oh.' My voice was very small. I watched Tessa swing to the end of the monkey bars and drop heavily to the ground, grinning triumphantly at us. My stomach curled in on itself. I thought about Jack telling me he loved me, the way he'd said it quietly, into my hair: I love you. And Mari, sitting back against the grey linen pillows with her lashes cast down on her pearly cheeks.

Mari huddled into her coat, watching Tessa run over to the swings. 'Anyway, I didn't know what to tell him. I said I needed time to think it through.'

I sucked a breath in. Across the playground, a red-haired toddler on the slide was screaming with fear or joy, I couldn't tell which. I let the breath out slowly, in small, quiet bursts. 'Okay.'

'I mean, if I say no, he won't go down there by himself. He won't leave Tess. So I suppose . . .' She turned to me with a funny smile, not quite humorous. 'I suppose he'll be yours then. To do with what you will.'

I cracked the plastic coffee cup lid with my teeth. I knew that Jack had probably said lots of complimentary things to Mari, things she wouldn't repeat to me because she was a good person and didn't want to hurt me. 'Well, he's not a stray dog,' I said. 'He likes to pretend he was so powerless in all this, everything just happened to him, but it's not really true. He's an adult, he knew what he was doing with you.'

Mari twisted a button on her coat. 'Sort of,' she said. 'I mean, about a million years ago he wanted to fuck me, but he never wanted to settle down with me, that part really was an accident. I'm sure he's told you as much . . . But he's not a bad person, you know. Just a bit of a coward.'

'Do you think he's being a coward now?'

'Well, that's what I keep asking myself. Like, does he actually want us to commit to each other properly, or is he just trying to find a version of himself he can live with? I don't even think he knows the answer to that.'

I leaned back against the bench. I was thinking of Jack kissing my face, stroking my hair, telling me it was going to be okay. *You've been like a ghost in my life for years.* Had he been planning even then to apply for a job in Melbourne? 'Okay,' I said to Mari. 'But what do you want?'

'What do I want?'

'I mean, do you want to . . .' My voice was brittle, I couldn't say the words. 'Do you want to say yes? To what he's offering?'

She sipped her coffee and took a while to answer. 'It's tempting,' she said. 'You know, having a home, a real family, getting married or whatever – I always wanted that, deep down. I just never told you because I knew you thought it was all so conventional.'

'Oh.'

'And then there's the other stuff – living somewhere else, finding a new job, maybe doing something different with my life. So yeah, it's tempting. But I don't know, I just wish . . .'

She let the sentence trail off. For a while we sat quietly together, the sun sinking down behind the river. I looked at Mari's face: mouth set in a straight line, small spray of wrinkles at the corners of her eyes. I knew that if I told her to stay, she'd stay. Otherwise she'd slip away from me, a fish wriggling out of my grasp: she would go to Melbourne and find new friends, stop returning my phone calls. She would never again dance on the lawn, or hold out her long-fingered hands to me.

'Mari,' I said.

'Yeah?'

I took her hand. Her fingers were cold, and I wrapped them in mine. Looking not at her but at the river, I said, 'You should go.'

She turned to look at me. Her lips were parted, and her brow was a little creased. I thought she looked so beautiful, I wanted to hold onto her hand forever. I made myself let go of it. I thought of Jack all those years ago, saying: You know Mari is her own person.

'Do you think so?' she asked.

'Yeah. It's a good opportunity for you, and Jack, and . . .' Saying his name felt like biting down on glass. 'I don't want you to go, obviously. But maybe it's better this way. We can't keep playing musical chairs forever.'

I saw her throat move in a swallow. 'Yeah,' she said quietly.

'It's not really sustainable in the long term, is it? We always knew that.'

She nodded, and for a few minutes we were silent. She began gathering her hair into a ponytail, let it fall back. 'I'll miss you,' she said. 'If we go.'

'I'll miss you too.'

'This is going to sound weird, but sometimes I feel like I don't really know who I am without you. That was part of why it hurt so much to watch that old footage – it was like seeing how well you always knew me, how much of a handle you had on me. Sort of like you knew me better than I knew myself.'

'I never felt like that.'

She gave a choked laugh. My cheeks were very cold, and the tips of my fingers were beginning to turn numb. The way she'd said *if we go* made it clear to me that they would go; they would go and leave me, the way I'd once left them. There was nothing I could do it about it now.

'Anyway,' I said, trying to keep my voice even. 'Speaking of the film thing – I brought you something.'

'What?'

I put my hand into my coat pocket and felt the USB stick there, nestled into the corner. 'Here,' I said, pressing it into her hand. 'It's you.'

'It's me?'

'It's all the footage I have of you. I put everything on there, and I deleted it from my hard drive. It's the only copy.'

'Oh.' She looked down at the USB stick and spun its plastic casing around. Its square metal tooth exposed, covered, exposed again. 'Okay.'

'I've been meaning to give it to you, I just never actually . . . Anyway, you can do what you want with it. Get rid of it if you like. It didn't seem fair for me to keep it.'

She looked at me for a long moment, and I couldn't read her face at all. My throat felt full of broken glass. Then she leaned down and kissed my cheek. 'Thank you,' she said quietly. 'And for the other thing, too. I know it's not easy.'

It was the first time she'd ever spoken to me that way: with gentle consolation, as though I was a child and she was my mother. I couldn't reply, so I just nodded. The spot on my cheek was still warm where she'd kissed me. She slipped the USB stick into her coat pocket and walked away, and I heard her call Tessa from the playground.

•

MARI DROVE SOUTH on a Saturday, only one small bag in the boot of the car. Tessa cried when she left, but by the time Mari checked her phone in a traffic jam outside Logan, Jack had messaged to say that she'd recovered and gone off to a birthday party. Mari was relieved. It was beginning to seem possible that Tessa was basically okay; that whatever Mari's deficiencies, she'd survived and would grow up to talk about her mother with no more than the usual degree of resentment. In the end, it was as Jack said: they'd been better than their own parents, and that had been a good place to start.

Mari was going to stay with her mother in Lismore for a few nights, and after that she was planning to drive further down the coast, without any real itinerary. She'd taken two weeks off work, and she had the vague idea of looking for a different job on her return. In any case, she and Jack had agreed that when she got back, they'd break the news of their separation to Tessa and he would move out. While Mari was away, he was going to find a flat and get his things together. He was concerned, of course, with the logistics of their separation: timelines and distances. He was concerned with keeping things as normal as possible for Tessa. It occurred to Mari that he had the perfect disposition for an amicable separation, and she was grateful for that. She was grateful for him, really very grateful, now that she no longer had to be with him. But when she pointed out that Elisabeth had a perfectly good flat on Sussex Street, he tightened his mouth and said, 'Yeah, well.'

'It doesn't bother me, you know. Actually, I thought she might help you with Tess, while I'm away.'

'No, I know. Look, I rang her yesterday and we agreed to give each other some space for a while. Think it over. And I don't want to confuse things for Tess . . . Once you're back, I'll take her out to dinner and we'll see where we are.'

Mari shrugged. She knew Jack's pretence of caution was meaningless, because ultimately he'd do whatever Elisabeth wanted.

But it was still unclear what Elisabeth did want, and Mari had realised – after they'd got home from the park that day, after she'd put Tessa in the bath and sat on the back deck thinking for a long time – that it hadn't featured in their conversation at all. She didn't know how to interpret this. It had always been Elisabeth's wants – so clear and well defined – that determined the shape of their lives, and without that familiar structure, Mari felt adrift. Sprung free, maybe. When Jack came home that evening, she told him that she'd made her decision.

The traffic crawled forward, stopped, crawled forward and stopped again. Mari reached over to the passenger seat and fumbled in her bag for her cigarettes, enjoying the thought of how horrified Jack would be if he could see her smoking in the car. She'd have to buy a car of her own soon. She'd never owned one before.

Instead of the cigarettes, her fingers found the hard plastic casing of the USB stick Elisabeth had given her. Mari had been carrying it with her everywhere over the past week, and often her fingers would return to it unconsciously, caressing it like a worry bead. She hadn't heard from Elisabeth since their conversation in the park, but when she held the USB stick in her hand she sometimes thought she could feel Elisabeth's energy radiating through it – an intense psychic force that was love, or something close to it.

Now she took it out and considered it. Five centimetres of metal and plastic, but it seemed to Mari to contain everything. She hadn't looked at the footage on it, but in some corner of her mind she believed it would show not only herself at twenty-five but also herself as she was now, and the years in between. All her tenderness and hunger; the pain and joy of her life with others. And everything before then, too: the long, airless years of loneliness, her mother's rage-strangled love. As though Elisabeth had seen everything there was to see. But she'd given it back now, she'd said it wasn't fair for her to keep it. Mari had run over those words so many times in her mind. Were they decisive, did they signify some change on which a relationship might be remade? Or had Elisabeth just been telling her what she wanted to hear?

Mari held the USB stick out of the open window, feeling the heat pulsate from the road. How easy it would be to let it fall from her fingers, let it be crushed into hot metal on hot tarmac. How easy, too, to put it back in her bag and keep it for later. Ahead of her, the line of cars began to move.

ACKNOWLEDGEMENTS

MANY PEOPLE WERE instrumental in bringing this book into the world. I'm very grateful to my agent, Sally Bird, for her early belief in the novel and her work on its behalf. Thank you to everyone at Ultimo Press for supporting and shaping *Between You and Me* in many different ways, and especially to Brigid Mullane and Sophie Mayfield for their work in guiding the book through to publication. My gratitude also to Simone Ford and Alan Vaarwerk for their close attention and thoughtful comments on the manuscript, and to Alissa Dinallo for designing such a beautiful cover. In particular, I am grateful to Alex Craig for lending the novel her wisdom and insight, and for understanding it so well from the beginning.

Thanks to all my friends, whose support, humour and love enrich my life beyond words. Special gratitude to those who read early drafts of *Between You and Me* and offered words of encouragement: Ned Chandler-Mather, Madeleine Nargar, Elena Quirk, Eva Tolo, Rosie Katunar, Alice Given, Jackson Lapsley Scott, Rosie Cuppaidge, Ryan Layden, Amy MacMahon, John Ballot, Camille Freeman, and Matt Halton. Thanks also to Ruby Ludski for answering my questions about pregnancy and childbirth.

Sincere thanks to Brendan McMahon, whose help allowed me to write this book.

I'm grateful to my parents – Robin Law and Stephen Horton – for lots of things, but especially for making reading and writing such a big part of my life.

Finally, Max Chandler-Mather believed in this novel long before anyone else did. He was a constant source of calm encouragement, and his feedback and insight were invaluable. Without him, the book would certainly not exist. Thank you.

Joanna Horton is a writer living in Brisbane. She has an MA in anthropology from the University of Chicago, and is currently a doctoral candidate in sociology. Her work has appeared in *Overland*, *Jacobin*, *StylusLit*, and *The Millions*.